The Bookminder

M. K. Wiseman

© 2016 by M. K. Wiseman
All rights reserved.
No part of this publication may be reproduced, stored in a retrieval system or transmitted in any form or by any means, electronic or mechanical, including photocopying, recording, or otherwise, without written permission from the publisher. For information visit www.xchylerpublishing.com

This is a work of fiction. Names, descriptions, entities, and incidents included in this story are products of the author's imagination. Any resemblance to actual persons, events, and entities is entirely coincidental.

Xchyler Publishing,
an imprint of Hamilton Springs Press, LLC
Penny Freeman, Editor-in-chief
www.xchylerpublishing.com
1st Edition: January 2016
Cover Illustration Egle Zioma
Titles by Sarah Hyatt
Interior Design: M Borgnaes of The Electric Scroll
Edited by Penny Freeman, Danielle E. Shipley and Jessica Fassler
Published in the United States of America
Xchyler Publishing

Chapter One

Liara was out in the garden when Old Woman Babić marched purposefully up the steps of St. Sophia's, face alight with a mix of fury and condemnation.

"Oh, Father Phenlick is not in, Zarije," Liara offered, rushing to the fence. When the hard-faced matron did not return Liara's half-smile and greeting, she wasn't surprised—she was used to that. The familiar epithets hung unspoken in the air: *fey child. Orphan waif.* But the look of smug victory in Zarije's eyes as she strode past alarmed Liara.

The book! Dropping a bundle of weeds next to discarded tools, Liara ran in through the back door of St. Sophia's, intent on her monk's cell—one of her hiding places for all manner of stolen trinkets. Not that she considered her treasures stolen, exactly. No, things such as Zarije's precious prayer book were Liara's way of having a life independent of charity. People ought to care more for their things if they wanted them back. And now here was Zarije, wanting her book, and Liara with no good lie ready on her lips.

Maybe I can pass it off as having just picked it up. Liara sweated through her rapid journey through the stone halls of the church building. She thought quickly. Her story needed details. At sixteen years of age, she'd found ample opportunities to discover exactly what it

The Bookminder

took to pass a lie as gospel truth. *That's it. I found it when I cleaned the pews this morning. On the floor, right by the—*

Gone! Zarije Babić's prayer book wasn't where Liara had left it, this fact ascertained by the bleak reality of an empty room. It was not as if she wasn't used to emptiness. The Father demanded simplicity of all under his roof. Rather, someone had raided Liara's cache, her collection of castoffs, trinkets, and ill-gotten gains. Even the secret place she'd hewn from under a loose flagstone lay exposed, the slab knocked askew as if to say, 'Yes, even here.'

Was she ever going to catch it now. Old Woman Babić had never liked Liara—*but who did, in this crummy little town?* And family prayer books were worth a fortune. Not that Liara could have done anything with it, but such books were precious. Only half a dozen existed in all of Dvigrad, all owned by the Church and wealthiest of families.

Like Zarije's, who'll likely have my hide for her next book. Liara gave vent to the colorful and wicked image, smiling darkly. It was sort of a fun challenge, this getting out of trouble. And Liara was an adept, having had sixteen years to practice—ten of them as a ward of the Church.

Father Phenlick wouldn't hurt her. Liara wasn't even sure he could. For all his gruffness, he was a gentle sort. The man had to be a hundred years old. No, the real danger was further angering Zarije, a woman who could have her revenge in the form of slights and whispers, who could set the children of Dvigrad after her with a word.

~*~

The clattering, disorganized sound of booted feet reverberating on stone floors caught Liara's ears too late. Even the clamorous heralding of a half-dozen of the Venetian guard wasn't enough to prevent her from running smack into the lead soldier as she rounded the corner.

Before rough hands could detain her, Liara sprang backwards, long black hair whipping around her startled face as she sought to regain her composure. The words bubbling up on her lips died under the withering gaze of Father Phenlick, standing in the midst of the armed men.

Liara could practically hear the good Father's lecture, one she'd heard so many times before. *See, my girl, this is what comes of running in the halls.* Casting her eyes to the side, Liara carefully sloped her shoulders, projecting just enough humility to spare her the familiar words, while her brain tried to register what exactly was going on.

Had Old Babić called the guards on her? Unlikely. Even though the woman had the biggest mouth and largest portion of trade in Dvigrad, she couldn't possibly hold sway over even a fraction of the guardsmen. No, they had to be there on Church business.

A prickle of fear shot down Liara's spine—fear mingled with excitement. Mayhap there was an invasion coming.

"Come, Liara." Father Phenlick's words shook the girl out of her tumble of thoughts. He sounded gruffer than usual—more than ever before, in fact. Though his face was stern, Father Phenlick's guiding hand was gentle, his touch at Liara's back almost nonexistent as he escorted her down the hall, as if he recoiled from contact. A look at the armored guard confirmed it: they were afraid of her. At this revelation, Liara completely forgot that she was supposed to have let the Father know Zarije was looking for him.

Their short walk concluded, the priest invited, "Into the vestry, if you please. We must speak privately."

'Privately' apparently involved half-a-dozen of Doge Contarini's finest.

And Zarije.

Seeing the woman's smirk as they entered, Liara instantly regretted having taken that detour to her room. It would have been nice to have the edge on things, to have gotten first into Father Phenlick's good graces before this rather public interrogation.

No matter, she had her answer ready. Couldn't Liara be just as surprised at the turn of events? There was no proof that she'd stolen the items in question. Perhaps, she'd only had them hidden for safe-keeping. And wasn't the incursion into her rooms equally unjust?

One of the soldiers shut the door, moving to stand in front of it. Inwardly, Liara rolled her eyes.

Though it doubled as the place where Father Phenlick met with parishioners, the vestry was barren, a small cell not unlike Liara's own. Where some men might preach austerity, Father Phenlick lived it.

Even so, Liara startled at the hollow, empty look in the good Father's face as he turned to question his ward. "Let me first warn you, my girl: there are serious charges being laid against you." The priest nodded his head, indicating the guard's and Zarije's, presence. As if Liara needed a reminder.

"How many times have we had this conversation, Liara?"

In answer, Liara shuffled her feet, fixing her eyes downward. Phenlick valued humility. And while it wasn't her first choice for self-defense, the tack he was taking demanded it. Liara rehearsed her story, waiting for the priest to continue.

"I thought that what we had here was a mere proclivity for not returning what others had . . . lost." She looked up sharply, noting that Father Phenlick's lips twitched with a small bit of the humor she had come to rely upon. Her heart lifted and she fought the impulse to cast Zarije a triumphant glance.

Liara and her reluctant master had made her shortcomings a game between them, after a fashion. Then again, between the circumstances of her birth and her preference for solitude, Liara liked to think she fit Phenlick's expectations. She was, in many ways, the priest's most rewarding challenge, whether he realized it or not.

Phenlick's near-smile collapsed into a stern frown, drawing Liara's thoughts back to the present. His next words carried no hint of humor. "But it would seem that your light-fingered ways are not an occasional lapse in judgment—in morality—but a *modus vivendi* for you. And that is a serious problem for someone who wishes to remain a ward of the Church."

Liara flicked her accusatory gaze to Zarije. If that woman undid everything for her . . .

"Liara." The barked word drew her attention back on Dvigrad's priest. "Have you an explanation for yourself?"

"Now, see here. The Republic's laws against thieving—" One of the guards stepped forward, a lanky fellow with drooping mustaches. Liara frowned, disliking him immediately.

Phenlick's eyes flashed and he pointed a bony finger at the guardsman, restraining him with a look. "Hsst. Our agreement was to let the girl speak."

His bright gaze turned back to her, where she stood trembling in the center of the room. "Liara?"

"I took it. But only because it was so very pretty and I've never *had* anything pretty," Liara blurted out, her eyes on Zarije. She felt the rush of heat before the blush hit her. Guilt, though she tried to pass it off as anger. Liara's least desire was to apologize to that woman and her words amazed even her. But they had everything—*almost everything*—and this was a game Liara was unused to playing. The rules had changed.

Father Phenlick, too, looked surprised. "The book?"

Liara nodded, gulping air. *Lie. Lie your way out of it. There's still time.*

Slowly, Father Phenlick shook his head, as if reluctant to continue. Father Phenlick, man of God, and surest man she knew. Liara felt for him, felt bad that she'd caused him such apparent anguish.

It's just a book. A book that you already recovered. She tried to telegraph her thoughts with a look. *It won't happen again. I promise.* Like a hundred such promises that had preceded it.

But Father Phenlick stared at the wood of his desk, unable to meet her gaze. "Liara. You know that it's not just the one—"

A knock on the door made everyone jump. Two more soldiers stood just outside the vestry.

"If you please, Father, we've . . . we've found the rest of it. In a hollowed-out tree."

Around her, Liara could feel the tension grow in the room. Hands tightened on hilts and armored legs tensed, ready in case the girl should run.

"I—" Liara found herself tongue-tied, unable to defend her actions or lie her way out of her predicament. She felt exposed, violated. The rules had changed, indeed. The tree was her nest—her staking a claim on a little corner of the world and filling it with things that delighted her. It was just like the cache in her cell, but multiplied tenfold. She had whiled away many an hour in the hollow of the old tree. The thought of these men rifling through it, judging her, hating her . . . the guilt Liara felt quickly melted away under the heat of newly ignited anger.

She wanted to ask how they'd discovered it, but found she couldn't, rage robbing her of her voice. However, in the second it took her to find it again, Phenlick had risen from his chair, exiting the room to hold hushed conversation in the hallway. Zarije moved to follow, stopped short by one of the soldiers barring her path with a quiet but nonnegotiable frown.

From where she stood, Liara couldn't quite make out the angry exchange. But from the strain on her face, it appeared Babić could not hear either. Liara indulged a satisfied smirk, feeling her pulse retreat from its frantic rush. Again she ran her argument in her head: Father Phenlick would help. He always did.

As if in agreement with her thoughts, Father Phenlick reentered the room, leaving the two soldiers out in the hallway. Liara felt the fledgling sense of triumph

The Bookminder

leak out of her. There was something new in Father Phenlick's eyes.

Pain. That's what she saw. Pain, compassion, and disappointment. Guilt returned in full, redoubling its attack on Liara's conscience.

"It would appear that even I was greatly mistaken as to the scope of things. Liara, if you please—" Again the hovering, apprehensive guiding hand of Phenlick followed her out the door. Plus, the eight Venetian soldiers. Plus, Zarije, whom no one dared stop now that things had gotten interesting.

Interesting, yes. Buoyant again, Liara yet refused to see the discovery of her secret haven as complete disaster. Perhaps now Phenlick would see how desperate she was to have anything to call her own. Maybe now he'd see that she needed something to grab hold of in her empty little life.

The two soldiers who'd discovered Liara's nest took the lead, Father Phenlick hurrying his steps to catch up with them and engage in another agitated conversation, the harsh whispers of his words drifting back unintelligibly. This left Liara surrounded by the remaining six soldiers. And Zarije.

Even so, she refused to let it scare her. Phenlick's words had turned to wild gesticulation. It appeared that he was not of a mind that they should all be dragged out into the forest for a mere repeat of the discussion they'd just had in the vestry. Liara agreed. Most of the items secured in the trunk of her tree were private—embarrassing, even.

Liara performed a quick inventory in her head and decided to make her move. Jolting forward as their little party exited Dvigrad's front gate, she spoke up, "Father, may I—?"

A soldier's gloved hand pulled her back, harshly cutting off her words.

At her side, Zarije huffed, "Silence, you ungrateful, pernicious, living and breathing curse of a—"

The brief scuffle brought Phenlick's attention back on them, stopping Babić from continuing. The woman fixed the priest a simpering smile, earning his disinterest. But the poisoned words, accompanied by the soldier's quick restraint, had begun their work. Liara hiked the rest of the short distance in sullen silence, fear warring with anger and bringing a flush to her cheeks.

They passed the woodman's cottage, Liara ducking her head, hiding amongst the soldiers in case her friend should be home. She did not desire any further witness to her disgrace, much less *his*. Oh, to be found out—and in such a manner. Mortifying!

Her thoughts circling back, she wondered at how they'd discovered her tree at all. She'd been going there for over eight years with nary a disturbance. And why nosy old Babić was being allowed to come along . . .

But then, in asking the question, Liara had her answer: Phenlick's strange disquiet and careful but distant treatment of Zarije in the face of the Venetian guard. That woman had gone above the priest's head and he was none too happy with her, Liara was sure of it.

And she could bet Babić hadn't just today noticed her book gone missing. Her gossip's tongue had likely gone 'round town taking note of every complaint of missing trinkets and treasures, biding her time until she had built a case against Liara, one big enough to reach the

The Bookminder

ears of the guard and set them searching the woods for the place Dvigrad's outcast had spirited herself away to for hours on end.

I'll have to start anew. Liara stumbled blindly over a rock in her path, her mind already leaping ahead. *Perhaps a spot near the river, one with a better roof and softer floor. Somewhere I can stay whole days, if needed.* The hollow of a tree offered no comfort, even with her improvements—years of effort and luck.

The small company came to a slow halt, their escort craning their necks to espy their mark. This provided Liara with the answer to her first question, that of the manner of the guards' discovery.

Curse the sunlight, wind, and greedy birds of the woods. Liara glared at the damning evidence before her. Tangled in the lower branches of her tree winked the bright gleam of metal. A coin on a chain. Liara remembered the one—it had some sort of foreign markings. She'd been delivered up by one of her own trinkets, likely dragged out of its hiding place and then abandoned by any one of the little trespassers who called the woods home.

She had nothing. Couldn't they just leave well enough alone?

The color was back in Phenlick's cheeks. It gladdened Liara to see it. More so, he seemed a touch amused by the entire proceedings. Rome's representative dragged out into the forest in search of a cache of lost ribbons, coins, feathers, and chips of precious stones? Preposterous.

Still, Babić loomed up at Liara's elbow, forbidding as ever and quite sobering. "That's it. That necklace there

I heard about last week. Went missing under mysterious circumstances, it did. I only heard about it when I—"

"Thank you, madam. As I said, we'd found the rest of the items the girl's been taking. Along with a lot of other . . . things." This from the captain of their military escort and said with a curl of the lip. Liara wanted to kick him. Things, indeed. She'd been collecting her treasures since she was eight. What did they expect?

"Show me." Phenlick's command came tired, renewing Liara's confidence. If he was sick of this whole affair, then perhaps it was already half-forgotten.

Moving to the side, the guard afforded Phenlick—and consequently Liara and Zarije—a closer look within the bole of the tree. Feeling her chest tighten in horror and indignation, Liara gasped. These men had cut away at all her careful concealment of the entrance, such as it was. Hacking with their swords and sticks, the military men had not just discovered Liara's hideaway, they'd defiled it. Tears stung her eyes and, shamefaced, she blinked them back.

Her tree had weathered much. A lightning strike had opened its center to her, creating the very space she'd developed into a cozy sanctuary. Wind and rain had shaped and grown the old wood, knitting the split trunk back together until the hollow below was just the right size for Liara and her cache of shabby riches.

But now these mistrustful, reckless men had torn it open with their cruel hatchets, splintering and scoring the bark, trampling the soil. Even now, one of them leaned his head in, laughing scornfully. The laugh turned to a shriek, igniting quivering sparks along Liara's spine as the soldier leapt backwards, his face white.

The Bookminder

"What is it, man?" Phenlick was impatient.

"Careful, sir. There's something . . . unnatural . . . at work here."

"I knew it. The girl is a witch!" Babić was quick to get a word in, pointing an accusatory finger at Liara. "I've had nothing but aches and pains these two years since my gold chain went missing. Cursing us, she is."

Far from causing their intended distress, Babić's words drew a smile from the priest as he shook his head, unbelieving. Liara was with him in that regard. Superstitious nonsense.

Believe me, if I had magick, I'd have used it on all of you fools long before now.

She let the long-threatening smile creep back into her face, her fingers itching at her sides. Animal bones and pressed flowers. Oddly shaped rocks. So easily frightened, these brave soldiers-at-arms. From the corner of her eye, Liara could see an anxious edge seep into Babić's glower, and she was glad that, for once, the woman seemed to have regretted her hasty words.

Phenlick's back filled the opening of the tree for one long moment. He then turned to face them once more. "Liara, child. The sin of envy is a human weakness. As you know, to take unlawfully from another requires reparation." He paused, looking to the dark-faced guards that flanked his ward, as if asking to be spared his next words. "But the crime of witchcraft—a sin of demons—is something beyond forgiveness."

Witchcraft. Fear ripped through Liara, leaving her gasping. The next moment found her pressed against the hard metal of a soldier's breastplate, the man having moved forward to block her unconscious step backwards.

No retreat, then. No hiding from Father Phenlick's cold, terrifying, impossible words. She felt her flushed cheeks drain to bone white and her fingers prickled, a malady she'd noted whenever she thought of magick or needed desperately to lie her way out of trouble.

She opened her mouth to speak and found that, again, she hadn't any words. The impulse to simply apologize, to beg for mercy, crossed her mind. Mercy. She could be stoned, hanged, burned for such a crime. A quick glance at the soldiers confirmed that they thought as much, too. She tensed, wondering if she could run, if there was anywhere to run.

He who is without sin among you, let him be the first to throw a stone at her. The words the good Father taught her came easily to Liara's mind. *But Father Phenlick doesn't sin . . . does he?* Fear turning to terror, Liara found her tongue, the words tumbling out. "But I didn't—I don't know how. Even wanting to, trying to. Because of my father—"

"See? She admits it. She's tried to do magick." Babić crowed her victory, the words coming shrill, shaken. It was as though she'd seen a ghost, Dvigrad's past come back to haunt them.

Father Phenlick strode forward, throwing his words at Liara and silencing Zarije. "Because of your father, the entire valley of Limska Draga lives in fear. I thank God every day that the attack that brought you into being was the last. You cannot imagine the burning, the killing, when the Uskoks came rampaging through, over and over."

The last of Liara's self-possession crumpled under the priest's tirade. Shrinking from words that fell like

13

blows, she hardly knew she'd again begun to back away, stopped by the imposing bulk of one of the doge's men. Sagging, the iron grip on her arm seemed to sap her strength. The trap was closing around her. All was lost. Taking a deep breath, she closed her face to the onslaught, rigid and unyielding.

Phenlick continued to pelt her with accusations. "Look at that tree, girl. Magick wove together the branches of your little lair. Magick made its mossy floor softer. And magick made it damned near impossible to find. Look inside and see the shelves made of living wood, lined with your ill-gotten gains. Unnatural. Wicked. Don't you dare tell me you didn't know what you were about here."

"I didn't!" Liara choked on the words, wiping her runny nose and eyes with a much-abused sleeve. Two words. And they might have been the most genuine thing she'd ever said.

"Cut it down," the captain of the guard barked. "Burn it and salt the earth of its ashes. Cleanse our wood of that conjurer's curse and then bring her to the square for the meting of punishment, that of death—"

"No!" Liara surged forward. "I didn't do anything wrong. I don't have magick. I don't have anything. It's a mistake. It's like the book, just a big mistake."

"A mistake. Or another lie?"

Hostile hands detained her, in spite of Phenlick's questing words. The sensation of imprisonment reignited Liara's anger and she struggled against them. It was all over. She'd told the truth and been condemned. "Then you lied to me, as well," she accused. "You've always told me I had no magick."

"Indeed. I did." Father Phenlick looked at her hard, saying nothing further for one long moment.

Dvigrad's priest then shook his head at the guards. "Liara tells the truth—finally. I did say she had—has—no magick. Unhand her."

Zarije spoke up, "But she—"

The captain spoke over her. "What's this? Another exception to your rules, then?"

"Enough. We were mistaken. There is no magick in this girl, only deception." Father Phenlick's words were unyielding. "That tree? She's friends with the woodworker's boy. Surely, she has picked up a trick or two over the years."

"But—"

"I am the law here. Delegate, by the Holy See, to the Republic of Venice. Official representative of the doge's supreme authority. Must I remind you of that?" Phenlick's decision brooked no argument.

"You do not. Sir." Furious, the captain directed a curt nod of his head. "Release the girl. Burn the tree."

The men took their discontent out on Liara, the command prompting a none-to-gentle release. She fell hard, her hands and knees pricked on twigs and rocks. For a moment she did not move, not wanting to give them the satisfaction of watching her pick the moss and soil from her hands. Phenlick was still on her side. That realization alone nearly brought her to a shuddering relief.

The violent crack of splintering wood shook the air and Liara scrambled to her feet. Chips of wood swarmed like angry bees, as no less than three of the Venetian guards hacked at the old wood of the tree's narrow doorway, tinder to be added to the combustible treasures and comforts within.

"Please." Liara's word was less a plea, so much as a command.

Even Zarije seemed alarmed by the turn of events, the older woman stomping forward, her head wagging. "Don't you torch that tree just yet, young man. I need my necklace first."

"Sorry, mum. Orders."

Babić wheeled on the captain of the guard. "I was promised restitution," she protested. "Is this how Venice dispenses justice?"

"It would appear that is how some representatives would have it." The animosity in his response came thinly veiled; a quick, rancorous flick of his eyes towards the priest and then the imperturbable military mask was back in place. "But I will do my duty as thoroughly as possible. To quash this sorcery, everything must go. Not a trace of her taint can remain."

With that, the ringing of steel on flint sounded in the disquieted forest, giving way to the soft snap of newly birthed fire. Within moments, the bole of the tree was filled with orange flame, smoke wreathing out of the ancient tree's center and rising upward into the new spring leaves.

A gentle hand on Liara's shoulder made her jump. Father Phenlick.

"Come, child. There is no need to witness this." His words, kind for Liara, contrasted with the wrathful glance he shot the captain of the guard.

"She should be made to watch," Babić was quick to interject.

Liara shook Father Phenlick off, perversely responding to Zarije's urging. She wanted to witness the destruction. After the morning's events, she reveled in the pain, anger hot as the searing inferno in front of them. Distantly, Liara could hear Zarije say something else. But, eyes still on her tree—the last of anything she had to call her own—Liara paid her enemy no heed. Grave danger narrowly avoided, she already channeled her fervor towards a new aspiration. Revenge.

Chapter Two

The march back to Dvigrad had given Liara time to build her ire anew and she bristled at the reproof. Phenlick looked tired again, the starch taken out of him. Good. Let him feel her wrath, her impotent rejection of this town and their silly ideals. Her anger was all that had been left her.

Only when the two of them were safely within Phenlick's vestry with the door firmly shut did the priest address Liara again. "You haven't the faintest idea of how lucky you are to have gotten off today."

"I know, Father, and if I had really thought there was magick in me, I—"

"Magick? And we are back to that already? In spite of all that just happened."

So this was to be it then. The questions that had haunted her for as long as she could remember never to be answered. Reviled for powers she did not have. Ordinary. Was that why her father, the wizard—the man whose demons had raped her mother—had never come back? Perhaps he'd known of her all along, his non-magickal flotsam of war.

The priest seemed to sense Liara's careful inattention for he waited, hands folded patiently. His eyes blazed, not with a fury to equal her own, but with a fierce supplication. And she knew him well enough to understand and she hastily hid her scowl, curiosity over what he had to say stronger than her stubborn ire. Eyes flicking to the door and then back to her, Phenlick continued, his voice low and urgent, "And if all along you'd have known yourself to have such powers, how would that have shaped you? What would you have done? Revenge? Retaliation? We—I—would have you raised better than that.

"Liara, I have watched you grow into a strong, capable young woman. Even with the slights and knocks; even under the hailstone of buffets and spitting. Even with the Zarije's of the world. You've your mother's endurance and your . . . your father's iron will."

Liara could tell from the falter at the end of Phenlick's words that he'd meant to say something else. But she did not stop to question it, her own rejoinder already on her lips. "Endurance," she sputtered bitterly. "The spells that made me drove my mother mad. Dying was her escape—from the madness and 'the Zarije's of the world.' Then, you just hid her—her and the memory of everything that happened to her. And buried me in a monk's cell to keep me out of sight."

"Liara!"

"Stop blaming me for what happened. I wasn't there when the raiders came. I wasn't there to stop the wizard from attacking. Me with magick? You should be so lucky. Dvigrad is helpless against it. Magick makes me better, Father. It makes me greater than, than . . ." She gestured to the bleak gray of stone and mortar.

"Don't you dare. Don't you dare insult the walls that have kept you safe. After all I—" He stopped short and Liara couldn't tell if he had checked his words or merely lost his way. In that instant, Liara felt the little girl inside of her return in a rush.

Beyond the lectures, the reprimands and impromptu homilies, this man had dried her tears, treated her hurts. *In the face of the Zarije's of the world.* And though she often resented the priest's interference with the rest of her life, she was well aware that, when pressed, reminding her assailants that she was under Church protection had gone a long way in saving her from anything worse than a split lip or bruised cheek.

. . . Like earlier today.

But that was the problem, wasn't it? Hiding behind the priest's skirts. Always beholden. Never powerful, self-sustaining. Did he not see that she couldn't stay his ward forever? She needed more. And they kept taking that from her.

". . . always about you," his words bled into her thoughts. "And I know that you know better, Liara. Your life was not over at conception; nor did it end with the Uskok's cry fading into the woods."

Phenlick's words washed over Liara, as if from far away. Or perhaps the distance was self-imposed, some instinct screaming at her that something was coming, something worse than a tree set afire, or idle threats by pompous men with swords and false power. Something terrible was about to happen and Phenlick was trying to warn her.

"You are not a lesser person for the superstition and enmity that follows you. You are stronger for it. I know, for I have seen your littlest moments and greatest pains. But you limit yourself when you only see what everyone else says of you. And when you look only at yourself, you discount the pain of others. You are correct, you were not here for the troubles that Dvigrad saw. For that I thank God daily."

The words were familiar, said a hundred—nay, a thousand—times to her in this very same room. But the tone was different. Again, the foreboding from before rose within her and Liara felt her arms and legs tingle, her throat clench.

"Liara, if you remember one thing, remember this: do not throw kindling onto the blaze. Give that other cheek, endure the snubs, the rejection and give them nothing more to embolden such littleness of heart. Can you not stop and think before you act? Before you give us reasons to dislike you on top of the multitude of imagined reasons? Commit this one thing to your memory, if nothing else, and I will have done right by you, in spite of all."

Recoiling from the priest's impassioned speech, Liara's building apprehension gained control over her voice and she used it now to outstrip the fears that pressed at her heart. "Fine words from someone who is loved and respected by all. But I'm a castoff. I can't afford to think that way. I can't control the rumors, but the soldiers would have hanged me for them. Nobody would lift a finger to defend me if the Uskoks came back. They would feed me to the mage that made me."

Father Phenlick flinched as if struck. "Yes, you stubborn girl. Yes, you have magick running through your veins. I thought to save you from it; to give you a real life. Love, belonging, in spite of all. You say that we have done nothing. And yet it is precisely because of you that Dvigrad cut itself off from the world, lest rumor of the mage's offspring reach the wrong ears. In protecting you—and us from the threat of a similar attack—we have tolerated the presence of a half-fey whip of a girl who couldn't care less about any of us."

"That's not true!" Liara spoke through her tears, though to which part she most objected—the accusation of magick or that she didn't care—remained unclear. She suspected the last, but would never have owned to it.

Phenlick's comfort reached out to her, even as he kept his careful distance, the same adrift pain of earlier lining his careworn face. "You've questioned me about your parentage for as long as you've been able to speak. And I've seen all of you as you've grown. You've a heart divided, Liara. Wanting so desperately to be normal, to be accepted despite your origins, and yet hungry for the particulars and how they might be of use to you even now."

"So you did know who my father was." Liara leapt on the priest's comment, making room for a glimmer of hope. The guards had long gone, the charges dropped. Phenlick was speaking to her more openly than she could ever recall, back from wherever his distant meanderings of thought that had taken him moments before. She was safe. It was time to get a little of her own back.

Father Phenlick shook his head. "Had any of us known more than what I've told you, when your mother died you'd likely not have been shoved off on a dusty old priest like me."

Liara tried to gift the 'dusty old priest' a smile, but it came out broken. He really had tried with her. And in her own way, she'd tried her best for him. She did care. Surely her personal failings were not larger than the singular

The Bookminder

regard that had grown between them.

"But now we've a problem, Liara. The law demands . . ." Father Phenlick closed his eyes.

Left with the half-sentence hanging in the air, Liara waited anxiously for the priest to continue. He did this to her a lot, praying in the middle of a sentence. Preferring action, Liara found it annoying. Considering the priest's next words, though, Liara would have for once preferred the silence to continue indefinitely:

"I'm sorry, Liara, but you can no longer stay in St. Sophia's."

~*~

Funny thing about being an orphan-turned-ward-of-the-Church: it came with little to no possessions. *Especially as they've burnt the only things I ever owned.* Liara packed in a matter of seconds. Which was lucky, for it gave her scarce time to dwell on what had just become of her life.

But the second she stepped out into the spring sunshine, it all became painfully real. Familiar faces, everywhere. Silent, cold, judgmental. Liara was pretty sure that most of the gathered crowd hadn't the faintest idea of why Phenlick's orphan ward was leaving, and yet they'd come to watch her go and guess at it.

Let them wonder. Feeling the hot prick of anger rise to her cheeks, Liara closed her face to the villagers, shifting her meager pack as if eager for the journey ahead. *The journey to God-knows-where.*

It was laughable, really—this silent gathering of onlookers, their blank, stupid faces. But the looming gate at the end of the street . . . the gate that she must exit, should nobody come forward to claim her. Not that she particularly cherished that idea, but neither did she have anywhere to turn.

Liara risked a furtive glance around the multitude of faces. Maybe somebody yet wanted her. Half the people there practiced some form of witchcraft in the privacy of their homes: housewife cures, symbolic offerings and prayers to gods not recognized by those of Father Phenlick's cloth—not that any of it necessarily worked. Perhaps Liara would even learn something, a way to harness and make use of her inborn skill.

Surely she must have *some* magick in her for the tree to grow as it had. The fear on the soldiers' faces was confirmation enough, was it not? Or maybe her tree was just a natural—if convenient—occurrence, as Phenlick had said. But then, he was protecting her. But from which? The hard justice of the Venetian guard? Or the crushing disappointment of being nothing more than a common orphan, and a bastard at that? Sixteen years of jeers and insults would have come to naught.

And then there was Krešimir. *Where are you?*

Krešimir, her one friend. His regard seemed a bitter lie now, though the woodsman's son had made her no promises. How could he have? He was a somebody—a *handsome* somebody—and she was less than nothing.

Liara ceased her nervous searching, seeing nothing but unfriendly faces. Zarije Babić was there, frowning as always, even in her triumph. *Yes, this worked out better than you could ever have dreamed.* Liara returned the sour frown.

Her long walk from St. Sophia's continued, leading

The Bookminder

her to where Father Phenlick stood waiting in the center of town. Looking upon his face, one wouldn't know the turmoil that had recently lived there. Stoic and calm, the priest watched as Liara approached, not offering her even the barest hint of a smile. Only his whispered apology when she reached his side offered comfort, the quiet words speaking volumes to his former ward who had nobody else to turn to.

Father Phenlick turned to the crowd, raising his voice to echo in the quiet streets. "My heart is saddened by recent events. As ward of the Church, certain expectations were required . . . and not met. The delicate circumstances surrounding the birth of Ana's daughter have not served either side well, I fear. And so, per the laws of the Republic of Venice which I serve, and in view of the witnesses gathered here, I release you, Ana's daughter, and ban you from dwelling within the walls of our fair city, *Anno Domini Nostri Iesu* 1679."

The words washed over Liara, drowning her with each wave. *Ana's daughter. Ward of the Church.* Father Phenlick's words were carefully impersonal. Stripped of feeling, ten years of a relationship, and the closest thing Liara had to family, the words were a sentence, a condemnation. Standing in the glinting sunlight, she felt a hot pressure building between her ears as the color bled from her vision. For a moment, she worried she might faint.

"I'll take her in, if nobody objects."

A chill shivered up Liara's spine, snaking its way down her arms and legs, as the crowd parted to reveal a tall, dark figure who stood under the eaves of a nearby cottage. The man lingered there for a long moment, as if savoring the stunned reaction from the crowd, then strode forward.

"You're—you're the wizard Nagarath." Liara's words emerged as a whisper. As if the dark cloak of power and ornate staff weren't indication enough, his was a face that every child in Dvigrad knew from description alone. From ice-gray-blue eyes, to the tip of his craggy nose, to the speckled-gray hair gathered and bound at the nape of his neck, the wizard's reputation had long preceded him. For, though magick was forbidden, children would be children, and many a long hour had been whiled away playing at wands and spells, pretending they were the wizard in the wood, the Mage of Parentino who lived on the other end of the Limska Draga valley.

The mage's eyes flicked to Liara for an instant, then fixed themselves on a point somewhere over and behind her shoulder. With a jolt, Liara turned to watch as Phenlick locked eyes with the newcomer. Liara could only guess at whatever conversation passed in that silent exchange, but at the resultant nod from the priest, she let out the breath she'd held.

The mage turned to her. "If you come with me, you must understand that I am not apprenticing you in my Art. Not ever. Understood?"

Liara was still stuck on his first words. "If I come with . . . ?"

Nagarath blinked in surprise. "Yes. It is your choice, Liara."

A choice. Liara couldn't remember having ever been given a choice. But how could there be any other option when a wizard offered to take her into his castle, offered her a home and a place away from the dark memories of

Dvigrad? Of course she was going with him. And she said as much.

It was only when they had left the town, the southern gate swinging closed, that Liara wondered: *How did he know my name?*

~*~

Even within Father Phenlick's hallowed soil of Church, diligence and duty, the wild black bird that was magick had flown over Dvigrad, dropping the seed that would one day be Ana's fey girl. In spite of the good Father's best efforts, Liara had grown untamed and unchecked, a weed in the midst of Dvigrad's crop of good folk. It was only right that one such as she should be plucked up and cast outside the town's safe and sturdy walls.

Or, as was the case this day, given to one of her own.

The wizard looked down on his new ward as the massive gates of Dvigrad swung shut behind them. The girl didn't even flinch. In fact, she looked impassive.

Nagarath wondered at the non-reaction. *What a coldhearted little thing.*

A solitary wizard, living alone for ten years in the ruins of Dvigrad's twin fortification, Nagarath had expected chatter, girlish excitement from the child. From his sporadic correspondence with the priest, he assumed Liara was nothing but an endless string of impertinent questions, noise and teenage babble. And here she was, walking alongside him, face cold and resolute.

Likely sulking because I won't teach her magick. Nagarath frowned, their brief exchange in Dvigrad rising again to his mind. The priest had caught his eye, appearing almost amused. The question 'What have I done?' redoubled its presence in Nagarath's mind, speaking to disappointment, in addition to the academic puzzlement he had already entertained.

He didn't know what to do with a sixteen-year-old waif. *She's not my problem, after all.*

But even this argument with himself fell flat. The girl was, in many ways, exactly his problem. And it was high time he owned to it.

Besides, Father Phenlick hadn't quite known what to do with a six-year-old orphan, but he'd managed. Had managed for ten years. Picturing Liara as a sullen six-year-old, dumped unceremoniously into Phenlick's care, Nagarath found himself fighting a smile. Surely he'd fare much better than Dvigrad's stern priest.

If only the girl wasn't so quiet, though. It was like traveling alongside a conjuring.

Of course, immediately following these thoughts, Liara chose to speak. *Perceptive.* Nagarath eyed the slip of a girl walking stolidly at his side. *I'll have to watch this one, then.*

"You didn't mean that, right? Now that we're on our own, you'll be teaching me magick." Liara was direct now that they'd entered the wood, leaving the little township behind. Her eyes flicked to his carved staff meaningfully, then darted away.

Eyebrows raised, Nagarath revised his assessment of her yet again. He'd not have to watch Liara so much as be wary of her. She didn't know how to let a thing drop. 'Spritely,' Phenlick had called her in one of his letters. The description was apt.

The Bookminder

Nagarath struggled to find the words, afraid that he had no satisfactory answer prepared, and annoyed that she hadn't taken him at his word back in Dvigrad.

Liara continued, clearly misinterpreting the pause—though whether this, too, was willful or merely through force of personality, Nagarath couldn't tell. "It makes sense that you would. And that you'd hide it from the priest. After all, I am the most magickal person living in—who's lived in—Dvigrad. And Phenlick obviously let you keep on your magick all these years, so—"

"I will not teach you magick, Liara. I thought I had made that clear." The urge to smile intensified, but he wrestled it into submission. He continued, his voice stern. "I promised Father Phenlick and have my own good reasons for doing so, never mind that it is banned in the valley. And besides, what magickal tendencies have you shown thus far in your short, untutored life?"

Remembering the catch in Liara's voice as she'd spoken of Dvigrad, and seeing the black look that crossed her face, he softened his words. "We all wish you safe, Liara. Not wandering the world, prey for who-knows-what. That is the extent of it. No apprenticeship. No magick." He paused, adding almost as an afterthought, his face cracking into a playful smile, "You'll also find that I am much harder to steal from than our mutual friend, Father Phenlick."

For a moment, Nagarath feared the girl would cut and run. She had that look about her.

Instead, Liara appeared to consider his words, again falling into her strange, sullen silence with a, "Yes, Master Nagarath."

Satisfied, Nagarath led the way once more. Clearly

he did not know Liara, in spite of the details given him from Father Phenlick over the years.

"So. Where are we going?" Her query came bright, almost cheerful.

Now I'm getting to her. Nagarath smiled down at his new ward. "Parentino. My home on the south—"

"The old ruins?" Liara interrupted, excited at long last. "I didn't think you actually lived in them, you know. The whole place is on the verge of collapse. I know—I saw it once."

"They're not 'ruins,' Liara. Least not anymore," Nagarath sniffed, pride temporarily overriding his urge to chide the girl for the interruption. Thoughtfully running a finger along his jawline, his smile deepened. "So, you saw Parentino and thought it naught but a heap of old stones . . . You know that I've been living there for over—"

"Since the last magickal attack, I know." Liara again ran slipshod over Nagarath's words. "You're our Wizard of the Wood, you know. Krešimir and I used to play at being you . . ." The girl trailed off, blushing.

"Ha!"

Nagarath's short laugh split the air, loud, booming, as if the humor building up inside had found the quickest vent possible, his head thrown back and eyes sparkling. *Played at magick in the woods? Pretending to be me?* The picture he conjured was as ludicrous as it was flattering.

Perhaps, for once, he could finally drop the dark wizardly demeanor and stop running from his past. It felt good to laugh again. To speak freely with another might feel even better. It had been so long since either had occurred that he was more than willing to overlook the girl's small oddities.

Perhaps this won't be all that big a challenge. Nagarath turned back down the path, eager now to impress Liara and perhaps provoke another bout of merriment.

~*~

Though her resentment toward her situation had doubled the moment Nagarath reaffirmed that he wouldn't be teaching her magick, Liara couldn't help but feel a small spark of warmth for the man as his laughter rang out in the darkening wood. The wizard was nothing like Phenlick, who'd have likely scolded her for her impudence. She liked the difference.

Encouraged by the mage's response, she pressed him for details, feigning interest in answers magickal and nonmagickal alike, teasing out in the exchange what bits of information she might find useful later on. She would again build her nest, this time with knowledge rather than mere trinkets. After all, she was about to enter the home of a wizard. There would be time to press the issue of her magickal education later. With Liara, a tactical retreat was never surrender.

And, she was curious. Superstitious accounts of a wizard were one thing. It was another thing entirely to come face to face with said rumors, finding that the fabled wizard of the wood actually existed.

Clearly Father Phenlick knew him. She'd seen their silent conference, noting that the men recognized one another. The priest had outlawed magick in the Limska Draga valley some twenty years ago, and here was Nagarath, wizard of Parentino, come to claim Dvigrad's magicked orphan girl. Why hadn't Phenlick banished him?

It occurred to Liara that perhaps this wizard was a sham, a fake. He certainly didn't look the part of wizard: eyes alight with laughter and good humor, face open and honest.

"So you're a real wizard?" Liara approached the matter directly.

"I'm not sure what you mean by 'real,' but yes, I am a mage who performs magick." Nagarath's reply came with a sly smile. Liara suspected the wizard might be playing her own game against her.

"Even though Father Phenlick said you shouldn't."

"He and I have an understanding, if that's what you are getting at." Nagarath seemed more cautious, prompting Liara to switch tactics.

"I just wanted to know how you're able to live in the wreck of a castle, that's all."

The last of the late evening sunshine had ceased to illuminate the small footpath before them. In the deepening gloom, Liara imagined she could see Nagarath's answering smile. But no words followed to answer her query. Quiet alarm reentered her mind. She remembered the journey across the valley to Parentino's ruins from her excursions with her friend, Krešimir. It was not long, nor difficult, and though the fading daylight rendered the landscape foreign, she knew they should be close . . . if, in fact, that was their destination.

Lost in new worries, her footsteps lagging, she nearly ran into the wizard from behind. Nagarath turned, gently ushering Liara ahead of him on the path.

The Bookminder

"Behold, Liara. My humble home."

Rising darkly amidst the towering wood, Parentino looked just as Liara remembered it. Stone thrown from stone, crawling vines crisscrossed over broken walls, the ruins were every bit as forbidding as she feared. And while the tops of the nearby trees still wore their crown of late-evening gold from the sun's fading rays, the ruins stood in hulking darkness.

Facing the wreck of the old castle, Liara almost wished that the wizard had been spiriting her off to somewhere unknown.

Deep and gravelly, Nagarath's voice sounded behind her, the foreign words delivered in a near whisper, strange and sharp. Liara felt her skin prickle, first from apprehension, then from the mage's touch as his hands rested gently upon her shoulders.

Liara had little time to ponder the spell—for spell it must be, of this she had little doubt. The sight before her demanded all of her attention: Parentino was growing. Twisting upward, the stones shook off their leafy cover, piling neatly upon one another as walls and sagging battlements righted themselves. In the space of a breath, the castle ruins became a wonder, restored to their former glory by the mage's power.

Reluctant to look away from the fortress, lest it somehow change back to tumbled stone, Liara stared at the castle with hungry eyes until Nagarath dropped his hands, calling her back to herself.

"And that is how I manage to live in a 'wreck of a castle,' Liara." The mage was smug. He had every right to be.

Liara let out a slow breath, her mind still trying to

process what she had just seen. "How did you—?" She reached up to her shoulder thoughtfully. Had Parentino just changed, or had she?

"The illusion that Parentino has stayed untouched but for the ravages of time is something to which everyone, save I and I alone, is subject. Until now, of course. You'll find that I have all manner of . . . defenses . . . built into my home. Defenses that I need to alter to allow for you, now."

Liara tried to follow the rush of words. Did this mean that he'd magicked her just now? Or did it mean that all who lived in Limska Draga lived under Nagarath's spells without their knowing it? At this thought, a prickle of fear returned. She longed to ask, but did not wish to expose her ignorance. *Perhaps if I pay closer attention?*

Nagarath strode forward eagerly, gesticulating at things and babbling magickal theories that were far beyond what Liara could ever hope to understand. The mage seemed quite lost in his showmanship, content to allow his new ward to follow meekly in his wake.

You will teach me magick, Liara thought hard at the mage, making sure her face conveyed nothing save a common sort of bright interest. *I will learn the magick I was always accused of having, the magick I was meant to have from he who made me.* Tactical retreat.

DVIGRAD

"What have I done? Dear Father in Heaven, what have I done?"

Alone on his knees in the early evening twilight, St. Sophia's priest gave vent to the fears that cleaved to his mind. He'd abandoned his post. He'd given up the girl.

Would you do it again? Faced down by the guards sent here at your behest? Father Phenlick had no doubt he would. He had little choice in the matter. It was send Liara away, cover up her clumsy and accidental use of magick, or be forced to sentence the young woman to the proper punishment dealt witches—punishment demanded by a law he himself had decreed.

Briefly, he wondered what he had done to deserve this. The lament was ungrateful and he knew it, though it wasn't the first time he'd bemoaned his situation. Ten years as the fey child's guardian, and Phenlick had never quite faced it with the openhearted charity he preached.

The longstanding guilt blossomed in his chest, helped further by the fact that the girl was now gone, just as he'd often secretly wished. Gone and lost to the wild wood and the wizard within its depths. And even though Nagarath had long proven to Phenlick that he was a man worthy of respect, of trust, the fact remained: wizards were wizards, even if they were on your side.

The Bookminder

The ban on magick had gone a long way in protecting the Limska Draga valley, but it had also left them defenseless against outside magickal attack. The soldiers sent from Venice could only do so much—as evidenced by Liara's very existence. Nagarath's silent support these ten-odd years had done far more than anyone other than Dvigrad's priest would likely ever know. Phenlick owed the mage Liara. And besides, the handoff had been terribly convenient.

After all, what was I going to do with her? Phenlick reasoned with himself, his staunch conscience keeping him honest before God. The magick was growing. The girl used it unconsciously—her 'nest' was proof enough of that—and Phenlick was far out of his depth when it came to keeping her from it. No, better that Nagarath deal with it. Let him ensure that the girl was saved from herself, from her past.

But now for damage control. The afternoon had been rough, the villagers coming in turn to argue with Phenlick over his lack of foresight. Not that he could blame them. They, like Liara, had been through a lot. Also like Liara, they never wanted to see how their checkered past had embittered them.

He was only glad that Old Woman Babić had kept her distance, frowning her disapproval from afar. The woman had long made her dislike of the girl clear. The sour-faced Zarije would likely have cheered and served cakes at Liara's hanging.

That was uncharitable. Phenlick crossed himself, feeling guiltier than ever. Yes, it was best that Dvigrad was rid of Liara. *The girl will be happier apart from . . .*

A shuffle of feet in the doorway behind him called

the priest to his right mind, and he rose to greet his visitor.

Zarije Babić. Lovely. Clearly, he was not to get away from the day without at least one more argument. Father Phenlick made sure that he had a kind, attentive smile fixed on his face before he approached.

"Father. I must speak with you about this wizard business."

"Yes, yes. Please . . ." Phenlick cut off the brash woman, indicating that their conversation would be best held out of the sacred place of worship. That Zarije held her tongue as far as the sacristy was a credit to her reverence.

But the moment they were clear of the church proper, her tongue lashed out as sharp as ever. "It's high time we had a demonstration of what the Venetian soldiers were called here to do! You saw firsthand what that girl was doing in the woods. And then to turn her over to that man? Everyone says he's a wizard himself."

"Rumors, nothing more." Phenlick was doubly glad they'd left the church, now that he'd given a lie. But his protection of the girl was complete. He wasn't about to have it all undone by some gossipy old woman.

"Rumors or not, there would have been no love lost on anyone here if we'd have made an example of Liara. Mother dead. Father some demon from hell. Who would have missed her? Or does Venice not care anymore what happens to us lowly Dvigrad peasants?" Babić clicked her tongue.

Phenlick felt his face go purple with anger. "Enough. You hear me? Liara is not some kitten to be drowned."

"No, Father. No she is not. She is a wolf to be

smoked out." Zarije's response was oily, her face as calm as Phenlick's was irate. "Letting that child go build an alliance with that wild man—that wizard who took our Parentino and made it into some tower of untold evil!"

"You know as well as I that Parentino is not fit for habitation. Every traveler these ten years past has told us as much. Your own children, your children's children have played amongst its ruins. No, rumors and superstitions. Your supposed 'wizard' is not a threat. You want to believe in something, believe in God."

Phenlick spun on his heel, turning his back on Zarije's stunned face. In moments such as these, George Phenlick knew exactly how Liara had felt when she dwelt in Dvigrad. Perhaps that was why he missed her already.

Chapter Three

Liara did not like being tired.
Sleep kept one from doing more exciting, more important things. Not that she had much experience with things important or exciting. Still, it galled her to be tired, even at the end of such a day.

This is your first night in a wizard's castle. You should be out exploring, Liara argued with her sleepy self. Her brain finally settled on a compromise: she could wait until Nagarath was abed. Snooping was best done on the sly, and it would do no good to get in trouble on the first day.

Liara also had to be mindful that she'd likely be called to wakefulness early. So far, there had been no mention of her duties, but she could guess at them. The mage was slovenly. In the brief and careless tour he'd provided of the first and second floors, she had seen all manner of bachelor-like mess.

It made sense, really. Her duties had been much the same at St. Sophia's. Cooking. Cleaning. That was all someone like her was good for, what with magick apparently not in her future. *Though I'll change that,* Liara reassured herself.

Phenlick had been absentminded, too. *Perhaps all men are. They need women to keep after them,* she concluded. She wondered if Krešimir was like that and she

The Bookminder

simply hadn't noticed. Nagarath certainly was. Parchment, dust, and inkpots lay scattered about tables, chairs, and even the windowsills. It took the edge off of the awe and terror Liara had initially felt to realize that Nagarath was just an average man. Even so, when he'd bespelled her—or was it un-bespelled?—Liara had felt lightning in her veins. It was delicious, and she wondered: did all magick feel that way, or just his?

Her cold feet made contact with the wooden floor of her room. She simply had to know.

Padding quietly to the door, Liara listened for a moment before entering the darkened hallway. She wasn't entirely sure where the wizard's room was, so she practiced a variety of excuses as she crept along. It would never do to be caught without a good lie ready on her lips.

The need to relieve herself crossed her mind. Too obvious, though. It lacked imagination, and in the short time in which she'd been acquainted with Nagarath, it seemed as though imagination went far with him. She considered her other options for a nocturnal excursion to far-off parts of the castle. A noise? A sudden fright? Liara rejected both—she was no coward and did not wish to paint herself as one. Again, she figured she had a pretty good read on the wizard. That man had little respect or interest in fainting maidens.

A slash of light crossed the floor of the hallway, moonlight from an open window casing. The dynamic contrast to the dark stone and wood drew Liara's eyes. She crept softly to the window, savoring the damp night air that tickled her nose and brought her to even greater wakefulness.

The moon had risen over the nearby hills, cresting the trees and dotting the landscape with ghostly brilliance. Swollen and yellowed, it did not wear the fresh white of spring that Liara would have expected. In some ways, it looked more like a moon of autumn, indicative of endings rather than beginnings. Even so, she decided that her angle was no good. Clearly, she must find another window for the proper vantage . . . one perhaps facing a different direction and on another floor.

Her excuse now set, Liara scurried off down the hall, intent on the stairwell that would bring her up and into what she hoped were the more magickal parts of Parentino. Already her hands were tingling. *I knew it. This is where our mage keeps his sorcery.*

Each step upward into the deeper darkness of the third story confirmed Liara's suspicions and played to her hopes. The ground floor was nothing save kitchen, privy, and other mundane living spaces: a series of rooms with tumbledown bookshelves and comfortable, lived-in furniture. However, the second floor had held promise during Nagarath's brief tour. Even unused storage closets and long-vacant state rooms could well be exciting. Nagarath seemed the sort of mage that put dangerous and enchanted items away in cabinets and left them forgotten for later discovery.

Liara had inspected her own room and found no accidentally forgotten spells or artifacts. The hallway that led to the stairs had borne a similar lack of fruit. And although she'd poked her head in half a dozen doorways and gently rattled a handful of doorknobs, Liara had discovered nothing more exciting than mouse droppings and old furniture draped in white sheeting.

The Bookminder

It was only her excuse should she be caught nosing about, but Liara did feel as though the moon called to her. Pale and bright, the rays of the sun's nocturnal brother called her up the stairs, filling her with a galvanizing mixture of excitement and foreboding.

The future was but a few yards away. Here she would discover the means by which she would learn magick, Nagarath or no. Already she could feel her fey blood singing in her veins, in answer to the power calling from behind the rows of locked doors lining the hallway of Parentino's third floor.

I will be able to find my father on my own. The new thought struck Liara, adding to her tingles of excitement. No longer would she be a charity case. With magick, she could have every question answered, including the one nearest to her heart. No boundaries. No rules. Just Liara with the world at her feet and everything her heart desired.

Breath held, Liara crossed the pale line of the moon's path upon the upper landing . . .

With a gush of breath, Liara sat upright in bed.

How did I—? Liara interrupted her own question, frowning her disappointment and shaking off the sleep still clouding her head. *I must have dozed off and dreamed the whole thing.*

The moon shone brightly from its lofty perch. A sliver of its white light crossed the room from where the door stood slightly ajar, the luminescence beaming across pillows and covers. Liara followed its path with her gaze, calculating the moon's position in the sky and grateful that it had been so insolent as to interrupt her slumber. Stifling a yawn, she judged her waking was a lucky break—or perhaps fate calling her to greater things. With the late hour, she was now even less likely to be discovered snooping.

Liara swung her feet out from under the covers. Her bare toes came into contact with the cold floor, waking her more thoroughly.

A haunting sense of familiarity itched at the back of her mind as she strode to the door, swiveling her head left and right before entering the darkened hallway. The coast was clear. All was quiet within the castle. The wizard was abed. She tiptoed forward, ignoring the doorways she passed on her brief crossing to the stairs.

If Nagarath's tight grip on his staff and subtle glances into the un-introduced rooms and unexplored stairwells weren't indication enough, experience had taught Liara that the giving of free rein in one's home came only from people who were certain that their valuables were ensconced elsewhere. The mage had shown Liara the first and second story, even giving her a room in the latter. Clearly his secrets were best kept in other quarters, behind lock and key.

Heart pounding, for here was where the memory of her dream stopped, Liara looked up toward the third floor landing, palms tingling and breath tight with the thrill of her daring. Boldly climbing into the moonlit recesses of the stairwell, Liara smirked at herself. The very idea that she would have obediently fallen asleep when there was so much to discover without the mage frowning over her . . .

~*~

The Bookminder

The sound of the forest waking called Liara back from slumber. Early morning had come, and she had done nothing more exciting than sleep.

But such dreams! Or rather, the same dream, thrice over. Each time, she'd left her rooms in the company of moonlight, intent on discovering the mage's secrets. And each time she awoke to find that she had but dreamt the nocturnal journey, the moon's passage across the night sky evidence of her wasted golden opportunity.

More than ever, Liara burned with a desire to uncover what Nagarath kept on the third floor of the castle.

Letting the covers slip to the floor, Liara wondered if the view from her room was as magnificent as her dreams had led her to believe. The evening before had been too dark to see much more than the line where trees met sky, a jagged division of dark on dark, the top half dotted with stars.

She waited in the cool early morning light, watching and waiting for the sun to rise and bless the valley with its glow. Gazing out to the north, she could just barely see the hard lines of Dvigrad's fortifications peeking above the treetops. She recalled her first morning in Father Phenlick's company, stealing out to one of St. Sophia's upper window casings to watch the sun rise on her new life. Even at the tender age of six, she had felt that she'd happened upon something big. In spite of the horrors of losing first father, then mother, she was on the path to greatness.

Ten years later, and far across the valley of her birth, Liara repeated her ritual.

Slowly the sky grew pink, then orange, then blue, as the first rays of the rising sun struck the hills to her left.

Off in the distance, something startled a flock of starlings, and they noisily took to the air. Flashing as the sun caught their wings, the birds banked sharply, singing as they tumbled towards the upper reaches of a stand of pine.

A thin, fiery line stole over the hills to the east, growing until the sun revealed enough of itself that Liara had to look away. With the exception of a few deep pockets of lingering mist, the entire valley of Limska Draga was bathed in sunlight.

Satisfied that the world had not changed overmuch, she turned to face her first full day in the company of a wizard.

While of course Liara had rarely—if ever—been in charge of her own destiny, she did not like the feeling that she'd been pushed about from one disinterested priest to an equally disinterested mage.

How dare he keep magick from her? She was born to it. Why else would the Fates have led her here?

"It's a test." Liara smiled wickedly, feeling she'd worked out the truth. Well, she'd just have to prove herself, then. Surpass his expectations. Surely a day in his company would show Master Nagarath that she was meant for greatness.

What girl didn't know her father? What wizard wasn't granted access to magick and all its wonders? Life owed her. Such bright thoughts urged her down the stairs, but she paused outside the kitchen door, suddenly tentative.

The test begins here.

The heavy wooden door stood before her, the gentle aromas of breakfast wafting around its edges. Liara lifted

The Bookminder

her hand to the tarnished handle, jumping in surprise as Nagarath's deep voice sounded from the other side.

"Good morning, Liara."

Her cheeks burning, feeling as though she'd made a misstep by lingering in the hall, she cracked open the door and slunk in.

"More magick?" Liara warily asked.

"No. Ears," Nagarath replied, his nose buried in his book, a faint smile playing about his lips.

Liara scowled at him—magick was no laughing matter—then eyed the spread on the heavy oaken table in dismay. A fragrant array of cheeses, boiled eggs, and crusty breads beamed at her from their platters. Breakfast, it appeared, had been served long before her arrival.

Mistake number two. Liara's blush deepening, she scurried to grab the kettle off the wall so she could at least make tea for Nagarath. New master, same old chores.

"Liara . . ." the voice murmured from behind the book. Liara looked up and realized that the task of making tea, too, had already been done. Her face fell.

Pale gray eyes peeked over the top of Nagarath's book, unreadable as he stared the girl down. Liara froze, positive she was in for a scolding. Even so, her own eyes drew toward the mage's book, endeavoring to read the title of what had so engaged her master's attention.

Noting her interest, Nagarath sighed and put his reading down. "Please have a seat, Liara," he said, and began layering cheese onto thick-sliced, lopsided-looking bread. "There is hot water aplenty here. I trust that you slept well?"

Liara gave a quick, guarded nod, watching as the

mage paused to take a generous bite of his breakfast. She slid into the indicated seat, noting the place setting her master had thoughtfully laid out for her, and waited wordlessly while he poured her a mug of steaming tea. Nagarath continued, "Your duties while you are here will be somewhat different than those you had when residing with Father Phenlick. I assume you can read?" He waited for her all-purpose shrug, then went on. "Good. We start today, then. This is yours."

He handed the book to her over the table. Liara gently grasped the tooled leather cover with trembling fingers, trying not to let her face lapse into the simpleton stare of openmouthed wonder. Even so, her pulse quickened, and she felt the telltale rush of heat in her neck and cheeks, the beginnings of a blush, as her thoughts strove to betray her.

Books were precious items indeed, and a wizard's book—Liara hardly dared breathe! She eagerly opened it and read the title page:

Various Techniques and Remedies in Book Repaire:
Methods of the Professional Working
In Libraries, Archives and Other
Precious Collections
and Book Rooms
of All Sizes

"Sir?" Liara held up the book. Seeing her master's approving smile, she thumbed through the dense text, occasional woodcuts illustrating mundane operations such as the threading of bindings and the collating of papers.

The Bookminder

To put it quite simply: it was the most boring book she'd ever seen.

Not that Liara had seen many, of course. Mostly religious texts handled in St. Sophia's as part of her cleaning duties, allowing her an occasional glimpse at the sumptuously illuminated family prayer books of the more wealthy families—as well as the opportunity to take one from time to time.

Perhaps she had misunderstood. Heart sinking, Liara rifled back through the heavy text, again read the cover. It seemed to her as though a drier topic could not be found in all of human knowledge. Battling to shove down a grumble of disappointment, she opted instead for blank ignorance, blurting flatly, "What exactly do I do with this?"

Nagarath's eyes sparkled for the first time since he'd put down his reading, "Why, read it, of course! Read it, learn it, and I'll give you another." He smiled happily at his new ward, as if this answered everything.

Well. That went splendidly. Nagarath congratulated himself as he ran his hand over the edge of the kitchen table, sweeping the crumbs of breakfast off onto the floor. The wizard had expected a protest, complaint, something from the girl when he started her on her studies. That she had simply accepted the book and moved off to another part of Parentino to read it was a very pleasant surprise. She had, in fact, looked almost eager—or at least that's how he chose to read her alacrity in leaving the kitchen.

"Yes, there's a lot of promise in that one." Nagarath

smiled, thinking of how concerned he had been just the night before on the tense walk from Dvigrad. Father Phenlick's letters had prepared him for a rebellious, disrespectful girl. Not that the priest had been unkind in his words, but Liara had been challenging.

Of course, so was her father.

Nagarath's smile clouded over, replaced with a troubled frown. Bringing Liara to Parentino had not been his first choice. If he could have had it any other way, he'd have seen Liara reared in Dvigrad, far away from the reaches—from the temptation—of magick.

Thank the gods that Phenlick is a good man. The girl could have hanged for her actions, unconscious or not. Nagarath couldn't believe how quickly things had happened. He himself had only learned of that morning's events when Dvigrad's idiot guards ransacked Liara's 'nest,' disturbing the magick that she had lain upon the place—enchantments Nagarath himself had quietly gone about enhancing once he had discovered what she was up to.

Magus, you're getting soft. He wasn't sure if Liara's naïve use of her Art was amusing or frightening. She honestly hadn't known what she was about—that much had been clear. Untaught and unsupervised, that girl could call a lot of unwanted attention to the valley with a wayward spell, exposing the power at work in Limska Draga. But step in himself? That option had never entered his mind. Although, with Liara landed on his doorstep, clearly the Fates had decided to hold him accountable in a very direct way. No shirking for him. No more lurking about in the shadows.

What choice did I have?

The thought was uncharitable. *What choice did Liara have?*

It still bothered him, the question of how exactly the Venetian soldiers had even discovered Liara's lair. Although the girl had not exactly used high magick on the hollowed-out bole of her tree—nothing he himself would panic over her employing—years of youthful vigor had gone far in altering the small sanctuary. Layer upon layer of Liara's intentions, wishes, hopes, and dreams had been ingrained into the wood, safeguarding her haven, the unconscious magick much like a varnish. Her will had shaped the tree's growth, had added to its vitality, and had, until then, protected the place from prying eyes.

My own sorcery should have helped, too. Nagarath peevishly defended his actions.

Or rather, his inactions. When Liara's tree had been disturbed, it admittedly had taken him a while to figure out what the twinge in his senses was even about. He'd thought it mere indigestion or a change in the weather. Like all of his work, Nagarath excelled at beginning a task but was not that adept with the follow-through. The spells he had laid over Liara's instinctive Art were six years out of date and had long been in need of renewal. Put simply, he'd all but washed his hands of her. *But then I had never expected, at this point in her life, to have the girl put into my care.*

The tree had been felled, Liara's minor magicks neutralized, the surrounding earth burned then salted. Surely the girl felt its loss. Nagarath himself had felt the small sting of the dying magick echoing within his own aura. But then again, Liara so far seemed to be the sort more interested in protecting her own hide, and wouldn't have known the pain for what it was.

Poor Liara. He'd come as quick as he could—although he'd have preferred a private audience with the priest over his public adoption of the fey child. Granted, his sentiments would have been the same either way. The girl would have no magick of him. Too dangerous.

No, at present, quiet contemplative study was the perfect occupation for Liara. With the mind of a mage and the fingers of a thief, she was perfect for the job Nagarath had in store for her.

After years of invisible skulking, Liara had found that most other people simply annoyed her. And as the wizard had seemed disinclined to leave his bright, comfortable kitchen, Liara turned elsewhere for her customary solitude, going as far as one of the upper hallways—clearly unused, per her quick look around.

A mouse working his way down the dim hallway momentarily roused her from her reading. He progressed slowly but with thoroughness of purpose, stopping to examine the threshold of each darkened door, looking for ways in. Liara sighed and watched his zigzag path, glad for the reprieve from deciphering the tedious words marching across each page.

A small part of her wondered if she mightn't have been more comfortable had she remained downstairs in the cozy kitchen, where there were at least chairs instead of a stone floor. It felt as though she'd been reading for days, although in reality, it had been only a few hours. The sun no longer shone through the narrow window, leaving Liara and the mouse in an eerie half-light. Shaking her head to clear out the folios, quartos, quires, and casings cluttering her mind, Liara addressed her tiny companion.

"You and me? We've got the same problem right now. He won't let me through most of those doors, either." Liara reached into her vest pocket, crumbling off some of the bread she'd secreted during breakfast. Tossing her new friend a few choice pieces, she scolded, "I'm not sure if Master Nagarath keeps a familiar or anything, but I don't think I'd want to get caught poking around, mouse or not. He's a wizard, and he's liable to turn you into something nasty."

The mouse ignored her whispered warning, nibbling at her offering before scurrying away. Footsteps sounded at the end of the hall.

"Come, come, Liara. I would never dream of turning someone into something *nasty*. Mice are quite clean animals . . ."

Her heart jumped in her chest as Nagarath approached her study corner, his sentence trailing off. Liara felt lucky she hadn't been caught prying; she hadn't known the mage to be so close. She looked up at him, her book forgotten on her lap.

"I suppose I ought to have introduced you to my last apprentice." Nagarath gestured in the direction of the mouse's escape, the corners of his mouth twitching with a suppressed smile.

"Wait . . . you didn't . . ." Liara scrambled to resume her scowl, the habitual expression having fled in the split-second it took her to catch on to the mage's joke. He almost had her, too.

"No. I didn't. But your face was worth the ruse." Nagarath chuckled. "Come, girl, why oh why are you sitting up here in the dark? I haven't done anything to offend you, have I?"

His concern was a surprising shift from the sarcasm and good-humored superiority he had displayed thus far. Liara gave one of her half-hearted shrugs in reply, weighing her words. How could she explain? Everyone hated her, so it was natural to slip away to out-of-the-way places, secret spots where nobody could tease her, hurt her, just for being different.

"I like this corner. It's cozy."

"It's dark. You'll strain your eyes." His shrug mirrored her own.

"Well, can you—I don't know—conjure up a light or something?" She smiled up at him, trying to at least meet him halfway.

Nagarath laughed, a sharp, clear sound that made her jump. "Come downstairs. I don't think we quite understand one another."

He talked while they walked down the hallway, down the stairs, and out into the gardens that provided an organized buffer of vegetation between the castle and surrounding woods. "Liara, you must know I do not ascribe myself to the company of illusionists, combat mages, or warlocks. The spells on Parentino, while impressive, are only designed to keep me—us—safe from prying eyes. And within this haven, I work the wizardry of life and nature. It has made my solitary life possible. Practical magicks, Liara. When I move the earth with my spells, it is to grow things rather than make a show of power." He cast a fond eye over the wild banks of begonias and ferns,

The Bookminder

bright stars and purple irises.

"So . . . you're a gardener?" Liara asked, her voice heavy with disappointment. "But why would you need the workrooms upstairs—"

She bit her lip, remembering belatedly that, as of yet, he had made no mention of the contents of the third floor. Nagarath gave no indication he'd heard anything beyond her first sentence, seeming to struggle with his own thoughts.

"Yes . . . a gardener. Lovely thought." He nodded softly, adopting for himself Liara's careless designation of him and his Art. Liara waited through the awkward moment of Nagarath's unfocused attention on things unseen, uncertain of what he might be getting at, until he shook himself and turned again to her.

"You know your herbs, yes? Please gather an ample amount of rosemary, sage, and . . ." He paused to think, adding, ". . . and marjoram, I believe. Yes, that will do. A few fistfuls of each, please, then meet me inside."

Liara flushed with pleasure, glad to be doing something other than read. She wandered the garden, taking in the myriad scents and colors. Although she did not quite dally in her task, neither did she hurry, examining each specimen with care before making her selection. It wasn't the way she'd spend her power—*once I get it, of course*—but Liara had to admit Nagarath's garden was impressive.

Herbs gathered, she entered Parentino's kitchen to find Nagarath sitting at the table, reading. *Honestly, does the man do anything else?* Liara frowned, hoping that a lifetime of studying together in the kitchen wasn't what the mage had in mind for her when he'd given her that book.

Without looking up, Nagarath pointed down to the one clear spot on the table, indicating she should leave her fragrant bundle there. An array of vegetables and roots lay piled to the side, and dried meat occupied a platter towards the table's center, while, pushed up against the back wall, a grouping of jars containing sauces and oils jostled for attention under a layer of dust.

"Liara," he began, distractedly licking his finger and turning a page. "Would you like to work a little magick for me"—Liara's heart leapt!—"and come up with a suitable dinner?"—and fell.

Ears burning, and for once glad that Nagarath's nose stayed buried in his book—he hadn't seen her false hopes dashed—Liara waited while the mage continued. "I'll help, of course, but I admit to being an absolute idiot when it comes to cooking. Thank you. Oh, and make sure you make enough so that you can eat your fill and not have to squirrel away morsels for later . . . the mice in my house are fed well enough."

And with that he returned his full attention to reading.

Liara did a slow turn in place, noting the heavy iron pot that hung on its crane over the hearth. She was supposed to cook in that? She wasn't even sure she could lift it. Risking a glance, she watched as Nagarath simply turned another page, his eyes fixed on his precious book. Whatever offer of assistance he had made, it wasn't immediately available for Liara to call upon.

Shrugging again, Liara leaned across the table to gather a generous amount of potatoes and beets for the heavy iron pot. Now was not the time to shirk her duties. Not when it occurred to her that perhaps *this* was the test

The Bookminder

she'd been expecting.

Liara pursed her lips, determined that she show efficiency to her lazy master of a mage. Grabbing a wooden pail, she turned toward the well out back, then stopped as she saw a larger bucket that clearly had received much more use.

She shot another sly glance at Nagarath, certain that he was peeking out from behind his book. Like the pot over the fire, the well-worn bucket was almost comically oversized.

I'm going to win at this game, Liara vowed, wiping her hands on her skirt and bracing herself. If her rail-thin, scholarly master could haul water in this thing, so could she.

Liara walked out to the well, hoisting the bucket up onto the hook and lowering it into the water. With a bracing grimace, she gave the rope a big tug, gasping as it flew up toward her, light as a feather.

So that's how he manages, she mused, hefting the sloshing bucket thoughtfully. It seemed her mage was full of magickal little surprises.

Liara risked another peek at Nagarath as she reentered the kitchen. Still absorbed in his book, he ignored her preparations entirely. Filling the pot over the stove to her satisfaction, Liara turned around to gather another armful of potatoes, but stopped as a strange sound popped behind her. Whipping around in surprise, she found that a crackling fire had lit itself under the pot.

Scattered potatoes hit the floor, the rumble of their impact ineffective at covering up Liara's startled shriek. She stooped to gather the fallen vegetables, complaining, "Look, can you stop that? I appreciate the help with the water bucket, really . . . but now you're overdoing it."

Nagarath continued to read, a slow smile spreading across his face. "Yes, Liara."

Wizard, indeed. Hmph. Liara decided that, no, once she came into her own, she would certainly not waste her power the way Master Nagarath did.

DVIGRAD

Đerkan Babić was not a big man, nor a loud one. But, like his mother Zarije, Đerkan had spent his life making sure that he had ears in all sorts of places, which made him as effective as any man bigger or louder than he. He played cards with the soldiers, dice with the woodsmen, and prayed at St. Sophia's like most everyone in Dvigrad. There was not a one among them who did not count him their friend.

It did not take long for him to hear that his mother's stirring up trouble regarding the "magick situation" in Dvigrad extended beyond his own patient ears. But then, his mother had always been one to gossip and complain. There was no harm in her, really. And so Đerkan ignored the hearsay at first.

But there they were, just shy of two months following that fey child's exile into the wizard's hands, and reports kept coming in of Zarije's continued badgering. Bad enough that she'd complained to the priest, prompting homilies on the sin of gossip. Far worse for the captain of the guard to make mention of her repeated pestering, when all Đerkan wanted was a quiet hand of *briscola*.

It was time to confront Zarije.

Đerkan did not want to hurt his mother's feelings, of course. But he was worried. Such talk as she spread, in an

The Bookminder

area like theirs that had seen so much political turmoil, could be viewed very badly by the authorities. Especially as Phenlick's authority and that of the Republic's assigned guard were currently pitted against one another, egged on by the woman's harassment.

"Oh, hello, my dear." Zarije was at the door before Đerkan placed even one foot on her front step. While he'd seen the rustle of curtains at the window, she still surprised him with the quickness of the greeting.

"Hello, Mother." Đerkan kept his smile broad, covering the foreboding in his heart. He'd never been any good at confrontation with her. The woman had an iron will.

"Come in, come in. I was just finishing up some supper. And how are my girls today?"

"Fine, Mother. No change since yesterday." Đerkan's face fought against the smile he pasted there. Zarije flitted about the room, her nervous energy putting him on edge. It seemed to him that she knew full well he had come to talk of something unpleasant, and so did everything to prevent that conversation's blossoming.

"Mother, please. I need to talk to you."

Zarije stopped mid-stride, her hands placed emphatically on her hips, her face growing forceful. Yes, she knew something was coming.

Đerkan took a deep breath. "Mother, there's talk. About some of the things you've been saying since Liara left town."

Zarije was sharp in her correction. "She did not leave. She was kicked out."

"Yes. Yes she was." Đerkan knew better than to argue semantics. "And now she's gone. And from what I hear, you keep going on about it."

"Is that so?" Zarije's hands left her hips, folded defensively into her crossed arms. "And you'd let them talk poorly about your own mother?"

"No, I would not. But neither can I keep people from saying what is true—that you've challenged everyone whose ears you can get a word into."

"I've a right to speak my mind. I have a right when the safety of the town—nay, of this entire region—may well be at risk over Phenlick's mistake."

"Shh. Mother, please." Ðerkan fervently wished he hadn't brought the matter up at all.

"I'll say what I like, if it's the truth. That girl was bad news before and she's bad news now. She'll be bringing the curse of magick back down on all our heads, mark my words. It'll be the Uskoks all over again." Zarije settled into a chair, her voice lowering to a gentle croon. "But then, perhaps you were too small to remember those times."

Ðerkan remembered. He'd been a young man when last the Uskoks came through, burning, raping, and terrorizing. He remembered the fiery words of the priest—himself a younger man those seventeen years ago. And Ðerkan remembered the soldiers, gallant and brave in their defense of the city. At the time, he'd wanted to be one someday.

Now someday had come. Ðerkan had grown to be a husband and a father. And the heroes of his youth, those selfsame soldiers, sat idly in their barracks growing fat and old and playing cards. Indeed, they went out on the occasional patrol to satisfy the edict of the priest—only to have that very priest call them off when they found real danger right in their midst.

The Bookminder

Ðerkan felt his mother's eyes on him. Lost in memories called up by her words, he hadn't really heard the rest of her impassioned speech. But his conclusions were along the same lines.

"Yes, now you see, son," said Zarije, her voice grown bitter. "But so be it . . . I can close my mouth, look the other way. After all, I'm just a stupid old woman. Just like Liara is only a quiet, strange little girl . . . No, think nothing of it, Ðerkan. I'm sure that the problem is all in my silly old head."

Ðerkan grimaced. He most certainly regretted having brought it up. But he'd come, said his piece. And who was he to argue further? The Uskok raids were but a distant memory for him, only so terrible as a story told to frighten children, magick a myth rather than a real threat.

But that girl . . . Liara made the stories come to life. Dvigrad's orphaned exile, the living embodiment of the trouble their town had once faced. Nay, might still face, if folk's grumblings were to be believed.

Mayhap his mother was right after all. The girl was a threat, the power that ran in her veins a siren call to he who'd fathered her through his magick. And while Ðerkan had initially trusted that Father Phenlick's handing her off to the harmless young mage down the road had been a tactical move to protect them all, Zarije's words had worked a magick of their own: doubt and fear, Liara's legacy.

Chapter Four

Three more to go. Liara shakily lifted one foot to advance up the next step, her mind resolutely on the books in her room, the words of one of Father Phenlick's prayers, a memory of Krešimir laughing with her over something she'd said—anything but on where she was and what she was about.

Today's attempt was the closest Liara had come to accessing the forbidden third floor of Parentino. There was no question that it was off-limits. And full of magick. It was the place that Nagarath spent many an hour, not mentioning afterward exactly what he'd been about. And it was the one spot that Liara could not seem to get into.

Although at first Liara had chalked up her strange dreams her first night in the mage's castle to an overwrought brain, subsequent efforts to storm the stairwell had produced nothing save bewilderment, followed by frustration, turning to Liara's fear that she might be going mad. Because every attempt to broach that mysterious third floor concluded with her ending up somewhere else. Instantly.

It hadn't taken her long to realize what was happening, though. And the challenge of tricking Nagarath's spell-work was too tantalizing to let go.

Liara experimented, finally concluding that the third floor's defensive spells seemed to respond to the state of

The Bookminder

her mind, or perhaps her heart. For she'd found that thinking of anything *but* trying to get up into the third floor—while she was, in fact, doing exactly that—got her much further.

An interesting exercise in concentration.

Liara carefully breathed out. Two more steps.

From her vantage point near the top of the stairs, she could almost see down the darkened corridor. Walls made of gray, craggy stone and floors of dark, polished wood, it looked much like the rest of the castle. Tempted as she was to peer around the corner and get her first good look at the magicked hallway, Liara held back, carefully blanking her mind.

It wouldn't do now to have to start over. Especially as the antagonizing spell seemed to be depositing her in more exotic locales every time she triggered it. Liara half expected to land in the garden, square in the middle of Nagarath's turnips and potatoes, if she made a wrong move, gave vent to an errant thought. And as he was currently out in the gardens . . .

Thinking of Nagarath, of his quiet tolerant smile each time she'd failed at her illicit explorations, brought a flush of guilt to Liara's face. He certainly knew what she was up to. It had become a game between them. But, she didn't know if he knew how close she was to tricking his spell at long last. She—

She looked around the kitchen in dismay. *Oops.*

Liara padded over to the open doorway. Nagarath was still out by Parentino's outer wall, fiddling with some sort of plant that had taken root at the base of the stone barrier. She smiled to herself, watching him work for a moment, the wizard finally kicking at the stubborn shrub.

She wondered why he didn't just magick it out of the ground. That's what she'd do. *If you ever let me have any magick.* She glared upwards to where the third floor lay, an itch in her mind.

Liara turned back to the empty kitchen, debating whether she had time for another round with the magicked hallway.

Or I could wash the dishes. Her eyes tried not to see Nagarath's latest mess.

Instead, they spotted something infinitely more rewarding. A silver chain dangled off the edge of the kitchen table, curling upwards and winding through the pages of a closed book, finally ducking out of sight behind a teacup.

Curious, Liara approached.

An amulet. Plain, silver like the chain, but archaic in appearance—or so it seemed to Liara's unpracticed mind.

She reached for it quicker than thought, jumping when the clomp of Nagarath's footsteps echoed in through the doorway behind her. Whirling around to face him, grateful that his coming from the bright outdoors meant he would need a moment to adjust his eyes, Liara greeted him with her hands clasped behind her back.

"I was just about to make some tea and saw your cup on the table from this morning. Did you want a new one?" Liara moved to the side, lifting the teacup in illustration. Nagarath's book lay closed upon the table, a napkin thoughtfully holding the place where he had left off reading. The pendant and its silver chain were nowhere in sight, deftly tucked into the folds of Liara's waistband for later retrieval. The little scene was perfectly positioned for innocence.

The Bookminder

He bought it.

"Yes, Liara, how thoughtful. I take it that your eyes were in need of refreshment as well? Too many Hebrew verbs for one afternoon?"

Liara smiled, nodding. This past week had seen her buried in the foreign and difficult tongue of Hebrew (or, as Nagarath called it, the Green Language). It was the language in which most magick was written. Why he thought it prudent for her to learn was beyond her. But she certainly wasn't going to argue, as it cut very close to her still-ardent desire to learn magick—even though it was difficult, and even though it meant less time for herself and more time in the company of her warden.

The Hebrew lessons also provided an unexpected side effect. Liara found that she rather liked being around the wizard. He was . . . fun. Of course, when the alternative was slogging painfully through more boring books about books, it was easy to instead get lost in the quick banter of the breakfast table or find any excuse to sit and watch the mage while he worked.

Nagarath sat down, reaching for his abandoned book, then paused as if perplexed.

Liara rushed to fill the silence, sitting opposite him. "Nagarath, how long have you been in Limska Draga?"

The question removed the thoughtful look from Nagarath's face as Liara had intended. He lowered his book, thumb holding his place. "Now, what on earth brings that to your mind, Liara?"

"Well, Father Phenlick has been really strict about there being no magick in Dvigrad. Not that his edict did any good when my father attacked. But they almost hanged me for doing it. And I wasn't even doing it on purpose. But, then you're here doing it, so I wondered if Father Phenlick's ban was here before you or if you started doing magick in Limska Draga, back when it was allowed." Liara let the words tumble freely, making up her reasons as she went, eager to manufacture any opportunity to hide away the pendant Nagarath had almost noticed missing.

"And why the conclusion that I had lived here before all of that?" He sat back, seemingly amused.

"Why else would you be allowed to do magick?"

Nagarath seemed nonplussed by the question, though his eyes glimmered. "Because George Phenlick and I have an arrangement."

"What sort of an arrangement?"

"Never you mind the details. Let's just say that it isn't mere coincidence that the Uskok raids on Limska Draga have ceased."

"Magick." Liara's smile became a wicked grin.

"That, I couldn't say. Per the terms of the arrangement." Nagarath winked, burying his own grin in his mug of tea.

"But laws, Nagarath! How do you get away with breaking the law of 'no magick in the Limska Draga valley'? Surely people know something. Even children call you 'the Wizard.'"

"That's the beauty of it. Nobody listens to children," he drawled. "Besides, people are eager to welcome the *zvončari* when they come to scare away winter. Even Zarije Babić leaves a food offering in her front window sill for the *domaći*."

"That's different. They aren't doing real magick," Liara countered uncertainly, unused to an opponent who sparred. Father Phenlick would have shut down her impertinence long before now. She felt outflanked.

"Real magick?" Nagarath cocked an eyebrow.

"You know. Like hiding the castle and things."

"Big magick or little magick. Clean or sloppy. It doesn't matter so long as the Art is in it and it works, Liara." Nagarath had the grace to keep his admonition gentle.

"Ha! So you are subverting the law. Which means Phenlick is by allowing it. Which means you should be allowed to teach me magick."

Nagarath put down his cup of tea, the playful light in his eyes extinguished. His words bit. "I'm sorry, I wasn't aware I was in the presence of one who knew how to govern a town. Please, Liara, enlighten me with your wisdom. What does a sixteen-year-old thief and liar know about truths that go beyond words and edicts?"

Liara found herself surprised by the sting of tears, and only barely kept them in check. She wondered if Nagarath even knew how much his words had hurt her, for he continued a moment later, his words coming from where he'd hidden his face back behind his book.

"To your initial question, the inhabitants of Dvigrad are carefully kept unaware of the extent of my magickal assistance. And to the best of their knowledge—per the castle's clever concealment—I don't even live within the bounds of the Limska Draga valley."

A thief and a liar. The pendant shifted heavily in her pocket. Distracting guilt blossomed anew, and she wondered if he knew how close to the mark his words had been. But no further accusation came.

She rose after a long moment, her gaze catching on

the open garden door and reminding her that she still had one more question for the mage. She was, quite frankly, curious. "Nagarath, why didn't you just magick that bush out from under the wall?"

With a sigh, Nagarath pushed his book from him, fixing the girl a stern, warning glare. But seeing nothing but innocent curiosity, he indulged. "It had grown to interfere with the warding spells for the castle. And as I did not wish to undo the spells that keep Parentino looking like a big, tired mess of stone, I had to resort to a nonmagickal means of tree removal."

He reached again for his book. A playful insolence guiding her words, Liara said, "But it's not like it just got there. Why didn't you just remove it when it was a lot smaller?"

Nagarath's mouth twitched with good humor, though he kept his face arranged in a mocking frown. "Because I am a lazy man."

Liara giggled, the tension between them broken at last. "Oh."

She rose to get the kettle now dancing over the fire. Nagarath's voice at her back stopped her.

"The pendant, please."

"The—?" Liara turned around slowly, her neutral face coming with practiced ease.

The wizard looked up from his open book, his gaze locking with hers.

Liara faltered, finding she could not lie to him.

"I . . . I moved it. When I went to clear off the table. Because it seemed a dangerous place to be left." Okay, so she could give a *little* lie.

Nagarath nodded, as if processing the words. He bent

The Bookminder

his head back to his book, hand outstretched to receive the pendant she let drop into his palm. "Calligraphy this afternoon."

"Calligr—?" Liara was puzzled.

"Yes. Penmanship." Nagarath looked up again, annoyance lining his face. "If you're going to read the Green Language, you'd better well know how to write it as well."

Liara beamed at him then, thinking that perhaps she understood at last. Nagarath had promised not to teach her magick. But what if he was dancing around that promise with all of these mysterious lessons?

This was a game at which Liara had long excelled. Careful promises. Careful working around the edges of said promises.

She couldn't wait. Calligraphy!

Nagarath was losing patience with the girl. They'd only been at calligraphy for five minutes and already Liara had petulantly thrown her pen down and walked away. He addressed her back, "Well, sulk if you want, little magpie. But, honestly, for someone with such skills as are needed for pickpocketing and pilfering, you're certainly blundering your way through your penmanship."

Liara flushed from the roots of her hair to the tips of her ears, muttering something. Nagarath was pretty sure he caught the word 'difficult' and smiled in spite of himself.

"If you preferred the boredom of simplicity. . ." he began, and was rewarded by his pupil's return. Soothing her ruffled pride he added, "You know, there's a point at which you can't rely on luck and raw talent. I, too, have been where you now stand."

Liara blinked in surprise. "You were caught stealing?"

"Goodness, no." Nagarath let out one of his booming laughs. That hadn't been the response he expected. But then, he'd come to know that most everything with Liara was unexpected. "I was referring to my education. Did you know, I actually failed my first magick test?"

"What?" That got Liara's attention.

"Yes. There I was, a first-year magus far from home. Youngest in my class. And failing at magick." He paused, suddenly unsure whether he wanted to share with Liara too many details of his past. Some particulars came dangerously close to the answers she sought. Remembering those heady days of youthful impulse, the events that had conspired to bring him to the Limska Draga valley, he cast an involuntary glance at his young ward and blanched.

"So what happened? How did you become a wizard if you failed at magick?"

"One mistake does not a failure make, Liara," he reproved. "I kept at it. But only at the urging of a dear friend of mine. . . . You see, I was apprenticed at the age of eight, making me at least two years everyone else's junior. I was also the youngest apprentice that Archmage Cromen ever took. My family lived in Italy at the time, but my father was in a position to know of such things as a French mage taking on apprentices. He believed I had a talent for the Art. You can imagine the pressure.

"Archmage Cromen was a hard teacher. Failure un-

The Bookminder

acceptable. But success had its rewards. His was an interest in the natural arts—in the workings of human anatomy, to be precise. We learned to heal and maximize the body's potential. . . . It led to my own deep-seated interest in magicks of the natural world, namely plant and animal."

Nagarath let his short tale wind to a close, mentally reviewing his carefully chosen words. No, he hadn't said more than intended. But then, the girl wouldn't have cause to be suspicious over something like that.

She, in fact, seemed quite distracted by her hands. Nagarath watched with interest as Liara carefully picked up her pen, checking for splits in the nib before re-inking it and applying one broad, beautiful line to the waiting parchment.

Nagarath bent close. It wasn't perfect, but it was a start. He moved to point out the small wiggle at the end where Liara had prematurely lifted pen from paper.

Acquiescence was still foreign to her, but, after a pause and sharp intake of breath, she managed, "The difficulty of what we've been working on is sometimes a surprise to me. I'm sorry."

These last words seemed to carry extra weight. Nagarath smiled his approval. Maybe this was less of a waste of time than he'd thought.

The afternoon had waned at long last, giving Liara leave to pursue her own ends before dinner. Though she would not have minded spending more time in the company of the wizard, it did feel good to flop down onto her bed with her latest stack of books. She scanned through the text lazily, so much so that she nearly missed it when she saw it:

A magick word.

Liara was staring at a magick word. Right there. On the page of her book.

These last few days, in addition to Hebrew, she'd been learning runes, Nagarath putting the letters together in nonsensical combinations so as to avoid forming magickal words that could be used in practical spell casting. But here it was. An actual word in an actual book.

She looked around at the silent room, barely daring to react for fear of spoiling the moment. Did Nagarath know he'd given her a book that had magick in it? Surely it was not a mistake. Nagarath didn't make mistakes.

Letting her eyes run again over the heavy lines of the complicated word, Liara allowed herself to become excited. Now, she felt certain that he intended her to learn magick after all.

She made sure that she had the pronunciation correct. Then, alone in her bedroom, Liara opened her mouth, cringing involuntarily, lest something terrible come of her saying the word aloud. "*Sh'lemull.*"

Nothing happened.

"Well, that was disappointing." Grateful that nobody had been witness to her ill-conceived attempt at spell-casting, Liara reread the page. Maybe she'd gotten the inflection wrong.

"Oh," she murmured, feeling foolish. The word was the magickal derivation of the Hebrew for wholeness, perfection, and was the magus' way of exploring the soundness of a magickal artifact. The word had no power outside of its practical purpose in testing objects.

Her embarrassing disappointment from a moment ago all but forgotten, Liara felt her palms itch and her skin prickle. Important or not, powerful or no, the word meant something to her.

She had discovered a way to see if the artifacts she'd picked up and hidden under the loose board beneath the bed were magicked. The items that Nagarath *hadn't* caught her pocketing. She quickly rose to see if one or another of the items in her small stash had any power to them.

"Liara? Could you come here, please."

The call rang out from the garden, freezing Liara mid-stride with sudden guilt. She looked back and forth from the doorway to her waiting cache, irresolute.

"Liara?" The summons came again.

Bah. "I'm coming," she shouted through the open window.

Liara hastily found a marker for her page and closed the book. Her magick would just have to wait.

DVIGRAD

"Father, I would speak to you about Liara. Was she or was she not practicing witchcraft?" Krešimir stood apprehensively at Father Phenlick's garden gate. For a long moment, he received no response, no acknowledgement that his words had even been heard. Even so, Krešimir wasn't all that keen on repeating such a query, and so waited.

At last the old priest straightened from his weeding, shielding his eyes from the bright sunlight as he squinted at his visitor. His face, his whole body language seemed to admonish the bold question he'd been posed.

Krešimir stood his ground, patiently waiting through the priest's silent assessment. He knew what Father Phenlick thought of him, a young man with fire in his veins and a cocky attitude. But daring got things done. His brazenness had earned him a decent living and a good number of friends within the village. At eighteen, he'd had any number of romantic prospects—some of which had earned him his less than stellar reputation with Dvigrad's priest—and was considered by most to be a good catch.

"Come inside. We'll talk in the vestry."

Krešimir gave a pert nod and followed, surprised by the spryness of the older man. In fact, it seemed as though the priest was eager to get beyond the reach of prying eyes and ears. That, or he was terribly angry. Phenlick's face was closed and dark, and Krešimir couldn't tell what the man was thinking. At least, not until they'd entered Phenlick's inner sanctum, the door slamming shut behind them.

"Young man, what in heaven's name were you thinking, bringing that up out there?"

Krešimir was taken aback. "With the rumors swirling around, I thought it best to speak openly about such things."

"Then you're a greater idiot than I thought." Phenlick sat, gesturing that his guest do the same. He seemed to collapse into himself, now looking frail and small, his momentary vitality all but gone. The priest passed a bony hand over his mouth, as if wiping away the sudden fear that had crept into his voice. "Don't you know what danger the girl is in?"

"Well, if you hadn't let her go with that wizard—"

"Yes. Yes, she was practicing magick," Phenlick thundered.

Krešimir was a good man in a fight, but he'd had his fair share of wind knocked out of him. To hear this news felt much the same. He didn't quite know what to say.

"Well, she was your friend, wasn't she? Did you not know what was going on with her?"

"We were friends—after a fashion." Krešimir managed to find his tongue, his head still whirling from the priest's admission. "But you know Liara. She wasn't . . . wasn't going to confide in anyone. Except for maybe you, Father. Which is why I sought you out for the truth when the rumors just wouldn't go away."

"When accused by the guard, the girl denied it. Vehemently."

"But the truth is?"

"The truth is she likely did not know herself."

"And you let her go with that wizard. Knowing that."

Now it was Krešimir's turn to get angry.

"She's safe with him, Krešimir."

"Safe? How could she possibly be safe with someone like him?"

"Perhaps you had a better offer for her?"

Phenlick's words cut deep. Krešimir had considered making such an offer. After all, he lived outside of the town walls, having years ago followed in his father's footsteps by making his livelihood amongst the trees of the Limska Draga forest.

But being young and reluctant to settle just yet, Krešimir had hesitated. And that hesitation had cost him. Succumbing to the fears that the villagers had long sown in his heart, Krešimir had ignored his own conscience.

And somehow the priest knew all this, even without the young man having to confess aloud the shortcomings of his soul. For Phenlick offered, his voice heavy, "I too, feel that we did not do right by Liara, for fear of losing control here in Dvigrad. I did what I could, Krešimir."

Even so, I am losing control of Dvigrad. Phenlick's conversation with Krešimir continued long after the young man had taken his leave. The words of Liara's friend had renewed in the priest the fears that had been growing throughout the summer. Stirred up by that old

The Bookminder

busybody Babić, and now even her son, people had started to complain outright that the Venetian soldiers were not being allowed to do what they'd been called to Dvigrad for. Not only was his judgment under scrutiny, so, too, was his authority.

He'd felt the effects during Mass—shifting, untrusting eyes of a congregation that had begun to put their trust in the sword rather than the Word.

Perhaps I've grown too old. Phenlick stared at the blank parchment on his desk. The standoff continued, as it had done all afternoon. He wished to write to Rome. Beg assistance. Support. Granted, it had been the doge who'd put him here in this backwater holding, and he thought he had done rather well, considering what he had to work with. Were they not responsible to provide aid in the event of a potential coup? But Rome had the power to send someone of the cloth. Venice would only send more soldiers.

But would Rome help me in a matter that concerns Venice's holdings?

"Yes. In matters of morality, they would. But everything I write must be absolute truth," Phenlick murmured, picking up his pen and uncapping the ink. "There can be no shirking of what happened here, else I am not worthy of my post or the aid I request."

Closing his eyes, Father Phenlick searched his soul for the certainty of thought that would guide his words. Again the accusation that he had mishandled the "Liara situation" rose to torment him. By rights, the girl should have been subject to the punishment dealt those who practiced magick—but then, so should have Nagarath, many years before that.

"But their hearts are good. They are good people. Is that not more important?" Phenlick argued aloud with himself, anguished.

And with that, he had his answer and what he would write to Rome.

~*~

Krešimir heard the tentative knock on his door, but didn't bother rising from his task. Whomever it was could either wait for him or enter of their own volition. Đerkan's youngest had broken her doll's cradle, and Krešimir had been commissioned for the replacement. And since his chisel was making enough racket to announce to even the wizard across the valley that he was home and working, Krešimir figured he'd effectively bidden his visitor enter.

It was the priest.

For him, Krešimir could hold off his work on the fine and fanciful carving he was adding to the footboard.

"Good afternoon, Father." He put down his chisel and, wiping his hands on his trousers, gestured to an open chair.

"You do beautiful work, Krešimir. And is that—?" The priest admired the chair before he sat, then gave Krešimir's current project an inquisitive look.

"For Đerkan's daughter's doll, sir." Krešimir smiled his thanks at the gentle compliment. He couldn't remember the last time Father Phenlick had gone outside Dvigrad's protective walls, but the priest's calm demeanor put all worries from his heart. Mind flashing back to the morning's conversation, Krešimir crossed the room to

The Bookminder

gather cups and drink. "What brings you visiting?" Phenlick declined Krešimir's silent offer of hospitality with a shake of the head. "I have a commission of my own for you. But it will not require chisels or hammer. I hesitate to even ask, but I had nobody else I could trust." Krešimir sank into the chair opposite his visitor, curious but wary.

"Things in Dvigrad are worse than even you know." Phenlick's voice grew shaky, and Krešimir knew it cost the priest much to open his heart. "The soldiers are dangerously close to open rebellion of Church rule. If Venice knew, they could likely assist. But I trust Rome, and so to Rome I write."

Phenlick now drew forth an envelope, holding it out to Krešimir. "I am not young and hale, like you. I know you wish to do something to help our friend, Liara. Would you undertake the delivery of this letter and await its response? You only need go as far as the sea, of course."

"Of course," Krešimir agreed. He hesitated a moment before venturing, "Do you expect..."

"That they'll be sending someone younger and more dynamic to replace me?" Phenlick chuckled, saving Krešimir the embarrassment of asking outright. "That is my hope. And maybe an official-looking, strongly-worded letter of admonishment to those who've nothing better to do than stir up trouble."

"Thank you for trusting me, Father," said Krešimir, ardent and eager. "I will leave tomorrow morning."

Father Phenlick smiled his thanks, rising to his feet. "Tomorrow. The next day. Just make sure you finish that little cradle for Zarije's granddaughter first, or she'll have my head."

Chapter Five

On at least three occasions that morning, Liara felt guiltily certain that Nagarath would stop her on her way out of Parentino. For, at the bottom of her herb basket, concealed beneath its cream-colored cloth, lay a scrap of parchment with four words on it.

Four words that Liara didn't quite trust to her memory just yet, each painstakingly gleaned from her heaps of reading, incidental knowledge given to her by the mage.

Four words of magick.

However, as Liara at last crossed the threshold of Parentino's outer wall, she gave in to a different sort of trepidation—self-doubt. In spite of her best attempts, the trinkets she'd been squirreling away had proven non-magickal. Or broken. Or maybe she just wasn't able to test their soundness because she wasn't getting the pronunciation of '*sh'lemull*' just right.

But that hadn't stopped her from combing through texts, collecting the handful of arcane terms as eagerly as she had once acquired 'lost' items from her fellow townfolk. And it certainly didn't mean she wasn't going to try again. This morning was to be her first real experiment.

Hiking through the undergrowth of the quiet, watchful wood, Liara struck out for a spot well known to her from past explorations. In the exact opposite direction of

Dvigrad, and far from her own long-abandoned haven in the woods, she figured that the chances of seeing anyone else were next to none. It was the perfect plan. The way was easy, and Liara found the spot she sought within half an hour of her having left Parentino. Smiling, she scrambled up onto the rocky outcropping that hung over a small stream. The place held a special sort of magick for Liara. It was here she and Krešimir had often played as children, and to where they escaped for long afternoons as young adults.

Putting the happy memories aside, Liara pulled herself fully back into the present, musing aloud, "What I need is a dead tree."

"Liara, Liara. Always looking for a tree in a forest."

Whirling around, heart in her throat, Liara tried to espy the speaker. *Krešimir.*

And there he was—skipping up onto the rocky outcropping beside her, a coy smile gracing his handsome face.

She swallowed. "What are you doing here?"

"I should ask you the same. Aren't you supposed to be off wizarding or something?" Though playful, Krešimir's words held a layer of pain that even Liara could hear. Same old Krešimir. He was nothing if not glib.

"I'm gathering herbs." She lifted the basket by way of illustration, her heart skipping another beat as her boy flashed another smile, this one warmer than his first.

"Sure you are. Demure Liara. Quiet and obedient Liara gathering herbs." Krešimir sat down at her feet. "Teach me some magick, Liara. Don't make me beg."

She countered his smile with a petulant frown, not really all that annoyed with her old friend, but wishing he'd talk seriously just this once. Perhaps the man was incapable of such. She sat down as well, sizing him up. "What are you doing this far south?"

Krešimir's face grew stony, then softened. "I'm doing something for Father Phenlick in Vrsar. Things have ... not been the same since you left."

With a thrill, Liara saw that Krešimir was not referring to just events in the village. The realization pulled her mind away from questioning the assignment from Father Phenlick. They sat in silence for a long moment.

'Liara, I'm sorry for what happened.' Come on, say it, Liara pleaded with her eyes.

Krešimir said nothing, his gaze on the rock, the stream, the trees—anything but her.

'Liara, I'm sorry for what happened.' She wanted to scream it at him. *Say it, you fool. Say you miss me.*

"So you needed a dead tree. For herb gathering." Krešimir's eyes were back on her, skeptical and teasing.

"Oh, all right. I was trying something magick," she admitted. Liara fished in her basket for the scrap of parchment, suddenly very self-conscious. Her words tumbled out over themselves as she explained. "Nagarath isn't teaching me any magick because he promised Phenlick, so I'm trying to do it myself. Only he keeps it all hidden away and locked up. I can't even get into the third floor of Parentino—"

"Parentino?" Krešimir cut in.

"Oh yeah, I forgot. You can't see it properly." Liara breezed over the detail, pride creeping in. "Nagarath has it magicked so it looks like ruins. Only he and I can see it as it really is. Anyway, I've been reading and collecting as many words of magick as I can. See?" She handed her scrap of parchment over to Krešimir.

"*Atsm—*"

"Don't!" Liara snatched the words back. "This is highly powerful magick and has to be pronounced just so. I've been practicing so I could get it just right."

"What's it do?" Krešimir leaned in, eyes searching for another peek at the forbidden words.

"Brings something to life," said Liara. "Hence the dead tree."

"Can I . . . can I watch?"

She had hoped he wouldn't ask that, though some part of her quivered with delight at the thought of sharing this moment of triumph with him.

"Only if you stand back and stay quiet." Liara arched her eyebrows imperiously, raising her hands as if ready to incant.

Krešimir scooted backwards, grinning, a parody of perfect attentiveness.

Just like old times. Liara grinned back. *Here goes nothing.*

"*Atsmi'i shinah ata yal'ad.*" Her words rang out in the forest. Somewhere, a bird squawked. A leaf fell. Other than that, nothing happened.

"Well . . ." Frustrated, Liara looked again to her parchment.

"Wow!" Krešimir's exclamation recalled her attention. Puzzled, Liara followed his gaze upward, starting at what she saw.

In the leafy canopy directly above their heads, an oak branch sported beautiful pink leaves. Unfortunately, during the space of time it took Krešimir and Liara to note the unexpected change, the branches adjacent also faded and turned a lovely shade of rose. And then the ones next to that. And the ones bordering those . . .

"Um, Liara. Was that supposed to happen?" Krešimir was on his feet, his own face as pale as the trees were bright.

"No," Liara breathed. Her eyes darted from one transformed branch to the next, praying that the spell would stop there. The uneasy feeling that she was in very deep trouble grew within the pit of her stomach. "No, it wasn't. And I think you should go."

"They're quite pretty. . ."

Pretty or not, looking at the pink trees, Liara feared she might cry. And she really did not want Krešimir to see that on top of everything else. What if her spell didn't stop until it reached every single tree in Limska Draga?

She cast frantic eyes over the garish canopy, shuddering with relief as she caught sight of familiar deep summer greens ringing the edge of her spell, the magick's effects fading at the edges, like ripples in a pond.

The damage was localized—a dozen trees, maybe more, maybe less. Even so, she could almost feel the noose tightening around her neck. Father Phenlick's guardianship had been withdrawn from her. And Nagarath? He seemed a nice enough man, but she knew better than to count on his protection.

Those trees. *What am I going to do?*

"It'll be fine, Liara—" Krešimir began.

"Just go, okay?" Liara hurled at him, her insides quaking.

"I won't tell—" he started again, then stopped. Liara could see the argument forming on the tip of his tongue. Her heart leapt, tumbling past the words she already regretted. *Stay, Krešimir. Or take me with you.* He turned away. "Okay, I'll go. Just, please. Take care of yourself. It was . . . good seeing you." And with a jump down from the rock, he strode off into the still-green undergrowth.

Turn around, her mind begged. *Change your mind and turn around. Come back and say you've missed me. That it will be all right, and that you wanted me all along.*

Unseen by the man walking away, Liara's tears began to fall.

"Oh, Liara, was there any rosemary?" Nagarath eyed Liara's basket of limp herbs with dismay. He certainly did not wish to scold the girl, but an afternoon in the woods with nothing to show for it but a handful of wilted mint was a bit of a disappointment.

Liara's voice echoed back down the stairs. "Not yet. They were too little to transplant."

The girl had come in but moments before, dumping her basket onto the kitchen table and disappearing up into her room without a word. Strange. Nagarath would have followed—even he knew something was bothering her—but the bedraggled herbs needed to be planted before much more time passed.

Grumbling about leaving tasks half-finished—a crime of which he was not totally innocent himself—Nagarath stepped out to add a new row to his garden, only to find a bright-eyed sparrowhawk perched on the low wall, waiting.

"Yes?" Nagarath opened his mind to the bird, recognizing it as one of his own. Unbeknownst to most, he employed a large contingent of birds of all breeds and temperaments to keep an eye on the valley. The wizard let the familiar feeling wash over him, the trickle of ice water in the veins as his aura connected with that of the sparrowhawk. A bird's-eye image of the woods formed in his consciousness.

"What are we seeing here . . . ?" Nagarath murmured, leaning on his hoe and closing his eyes. Treetops flashed by beneath him, the greenery of summer already turning over to the brilliant hues of autumn. Interesting that an entire stand of oak should turn so early. . .

"Pink! Those trees are pink!" His eyes snapped open and he jumped, startling his messenger bird to ungainly flight. "Sorry."

It didn't hurt to break a mental link like that, but Nagarath hated to be rude.

Wilted mint forgotten, the mage stormed back into the castle. Face dark with wrath, long strides taking the stairs two at a time, Nagarath reached Liara's room within moments.

"Liara!" He banged on her door. "Liara!"

She didn't answer.

Nagarath tried the knob. Locked. Of course. Further incensed, he barked the spell of opening and burst in, demanding, "Tell me you know nothing about pink trees."

Though she gave a startled shriek, nearly tumbling from her bed in surprise, Nagarath could see that Liara had been expecting him. She shot him her own affronted look as she hunted about for a marker for her book, exuding annoyance over the interruption. He waited through

The Bookminder

the half-second it took the girl to note his fury and consequently wilt. She mumbled, "I'm . . . I'm sorry."

"You're—you're *sorry*?" Nagarath sputtered. "How did you even—never mind how. What I'd like to know is: whatever possessed you to do such a thing?"

"It was an accident." Liara shrank further, her words carrying the high pitch of one near tears.

Taking a deep breath, Nagarath closed his eyes. He forced his tone into calmness, abashed at his outburst in the face of Liara's fear. "Very well. *Now,* I want to know how you did it."

Liara held out the scrap of parchment that contained her ill-conceived spell-work.

"*Atsmi'i shin*—" Nagarath read the words, his eyebrows knitting together in surprise. "What on earth is this supposed to mean?"

" 'I give you life'? I was trying to see if I could make something dead grow." Liara squirmed under Nagarath's incredulous gaze. "I . . . I don't know why the oak leaves turned pink."

Nagarath couldn't begin to guess where the girl had gotten those words. They were, indeed, words of magick. Arranged in an admittedly odd sentence. Trying to keep himself from laughing, he translated for her. "It means, 'I change what you bear.' "

"Oh." Liara's face fell.

"You know, Liara, that what you tried was very dangerous. First, what you were attempting—poorly, I might add—is technically a form of necromancy. Not a good idea for the most accomplished mages, never mind someone not trained in the Art. Second—"

"Then train me!" Liara cried. "Why am I even here?

So I can sit all day reading books about nothing, writing words I cannot use, doing nothing at all of importance? You might as well just lock me away in the tower—"

"Second," Nagarath thundered over his ward, "if anyone from Dvigrad saw this—anyone at all—both our lives would be forfeit. Magick is forbidden. Understand? I get away with what I do because nobody here even knows I'm doing it!" The claim wasn't entirely true, but he'd had his fill of that recurring discussion. "Right now, I have half a mind to march you straight back to that damnable village and let you fend for yourself. But first I need to go undo your mess before anyone sees those ridiculous pink trees."

Nagarath managed to keep a stern eye while he swept out the room, escaping to the solitude of his workroom. The shocked and ashamed look on Liara's face at his explosion was almost too much for him, but he stopped himself from turning back. *Better to let the words lie for a while.*

Nagarath did not hear so much as a peep from Liara for the rest of the afternoon. Surprisingly, she stayed where he'd left her: in her room. He knew because he'd checked on her aura several times.

It turned out that restoring the trees to their natural coloration was rather easy, making him wonder if perhaps he'd overreacted. After all, the girl had a point. He'd been so busy keeping every possible thread of magick from Liara that he'd not really explained what he had in mind for her. No wonder she was acting out. He'd do much the same, in her position.

Enough was enough. Nagarath decided he needed to make amends. He knew that his threat to give Liara back to the village was an idle one. But did she? He'd gathered from small talk over meals that the fear of abandonment had been a constant in her life at St. Sophia's. It occasionally came to temporary fruition, but then the good Father Phenlick would discover he hadn't the heart to throw her out. Nagarath did not want to be a similar source of fear and instability in Liara's life. Though unknown to her, he had a good deal at stake in keeping her safe.

~*~

The knock on her door was much quieter than the one that had preceded it scant hours before. Liara considered not responding, even so. *Let him break the door down this time. I don't care.*

"Liara?"

She sniffled and answered, "Come in."

She had dreaded this moment all afternoon. Maybe her mistake had been un-correctable. Perhaps the villagers were coming any minute to burn Parentino to the ground. Mayhap she was about to once more find herself without a home. She rose to meet the mage, then stood, puzzled. The contrition on Nagarath's face was a rather new look for him.

"If you please, I'd like to apologize for my behavior this morning. I was rude and acted out of my own selfish reasons." Nagarath paused, running his hands through his untamed hair, and Liara sensed a brief moment of indecision within him. He then added, "I'd like you to come downstairs to the main parlor. I've something to show you."

Liara stood in stunned silence for a moment. She had been waiting for punishment, and in some ways thrilling at the prospect of having to not face deciphering another dull book. Krešimir had all but promised to take her in, after all. Or so she'd wished to believe.

You can wish all you want, Liara. But Krešimir had no trouble walking away from you this morning.

That thought, the fear that Krešimir didn't want her—that nobody wanted her—had been too much for Liara. So she'd hidden away, retreating from ugly truths and magick gone wrong, awaiting judgment from the stern-faced Nagarath.

Nagarath, whom she had grown fond of, in spite of herself.

Nagarath, who had finally returned, not in rage, but with remorse. *If you please, I'd like to apologize for my behavior . . . I was rude and acted out of my own selfish reasons . . .* She played the words over in her mind, savoring the sweet relief they brought.

What were his reasons, anyway? Liara puzzled. Resolving to ask about it later, she went down the stairs after the wizard.

He sat in a chair by the hearth in the parlor, gesturing to its twin as she entered the room. Without preamble he began, "I've seen your—ahem—handiwork. You're a very good thief—" Nagarath smiled as Liara opened her mouth to protest, stopping herself only as she realized the accusation's accuracy.

"You've clever hands and a sharp mind," the mage

continued. Reaching over to a shelf by the fireplace, he pulled down a dilapidated book.

Oh, great. Another one. Liara accepted the sad specimen of a book with an appraising eye. Her studies had not been for nothing. Already her mind began calculating what would need to be done to rehabilitate such a book.

She only half listened as Nagarath went on, "Put simply, a large portion of my collection has fallen into disrepair and needs to be put to rights. I can start you restoring books, such as that one, as the next step in your education."

He paused, waiting for Liara's eyes to meet his. "Should you prove capable, I would like you to refurbish all the books of my library—"

Magick . . . Liara mouthed the word unconsciously, her pulse quickening.

"Yes. As you proved to us all this morning, you have a magickal signature of your own, which makes you the perfect person to act as my librarian." As was its wont, Nagarath's exuberance immersed him in theory. "You see, a book used for magickal purposes must be both physically and magickally sound for the spells within to work. Per the First Law of Magick Transferre—"

"But—magick." Liara gaped at the wizard, unsure if this was some sort of a trick. After the events of this morning, shouldn't he be keeping this sort of thing from her? Liara's whole world seemed to be opening up before her, the possibilities growing alongside her excitement. Did this mean she would become a wizard after all? She stared at the bedraggled book in her hands.

As if sensing her confusion and unspoken hopes, Nagarath said gently, "Liara, the skills that you will learn are nothing like what I possess. Actually performing magick and knowing the properties and principles of the Art are two very different things. Understood?"

He waited for her affirmative nod.

"You'll learn that the very fiber of a page, the exact stitching pattern of the binding, affects the workings of the spells within. You'll learn how to manipulate these elements to control how well a magicked book performs. No more. Theory and methodology, Liara."

"Yes." She understood. And though the limitations of her education were laid out in a clear and disappointing row in front of her, nothing Nagarath said could upset her at this moment.

I have magick in me! Positively glowing, Liara smiled up into Nagarath's eyes. "Thank you."

There was a place in the world for her after all. Work—important work!—suited to her skills. *And,* Liara whispered to herself in the back of her mind, *I have magick!*

"The Laws of Magick Transferre. Recite." The mage roamed the parlor, hands clasped behind his back, more or less ignoring his pupil.

Unless, of course, she made a mistake. Nagarath's apparent distraction more unnerving than his direct attention would have been, Liara's dutiful recounting of the two laws started strong only to falter towards the end. "Laws of Magick Transferre. Being the Laws of Magick that predict and control the functioning of non-sentient magicked items. Law The First of Magicked Artifacts: A

Magicked Artifact must be sound both . . . both—"

"Both physically and magickally . . ."

". . . both physically and magickally in order to function as intended," Liara rushed over his prompt.

"And the second?"

"Law The Second of Magicked Artifacts." Liara paused, screwing up her face in concentration. This was the law that would most impact her own work as the wizard's librarian. She tried again. "Law The Second of Magicked Artifacts: Damage . . . damage to either condition—"

"Physical or magickal . . ."

"Yes, sorry—the physical or magickal condition of a Magicked Artifact will affect the outcome of Magicks performed through said Artifact." Liara finished her patched-together recitation on a triumphant note, despite her lackadaisical attempts at memorization. What was left of her breath rushed out in relief.

Nagarath had stopped his pacing, his back still toward her. "Liara, these Laws . . ."

"I know, I know. I just—" Liara bit her lip, eyes brightening as she added, "But I know the Laws of Magick Creatio. They are—"

"Stop." Nagarath raised a hand, now turning to fix his piercing gaze upon her. She withered under the scrutiny. "I did not ask for the Laws of Magick Creatio. The Laws of Magick Transferre. Again."

Liara opened her mouth to argue.

"Again."

With a sigh, Liara closed her eyes and began to recite. Again.

Carefully moving the magnifying lens out of direct sunlight so as to avoid adding any more scorch marks to his table, Nagarath frowned toward the open door of the kitchen. He'd set up just beyond the outer door, alongside the low wall surrounding his garden. This unique arrangement had a twofold purpose. One, he had the easiest possible access to the plants he'd be experimenting on. And two, he sincerely hoped that working his magicks here in the open might draw Liara forth from her studies.

For, while he still wanted to keep magick from the girl, Nagarath had come to realize that a practical demonstration of the Laws might be in order, especially as Liara was so insistent in her questions regarding the Laws of Magick Creatio. Appreciative of her application to her task of memorization, but also eager that his ward have the opportunity to watch him work, Nagarath let several minutes slip past. But no amount of procrastination, it seemed, would conjure the usually inquisitive girl today.

Nagarath turned back to his project. The flowers and shoots arrayed on the massive table had wilted during his short delay, but would still serve their purpose. Or not. Like most theoretical magicks, there were no guarantees the spell would work.

Which was precisely what Nagarath had been hoping Liara would witness. Placing his tools back on the table with a petulant rattle, he turned once more to the door. But, no. It was one thing to "accidentally" perform magick within Liara's sight, another to bodily drag her over for a demonstration.

Satisfied that he still knew the difference, and could

therefore continue lying to himself that he was keeping his promise to the priest, Nagarath decided to ignore Liara for the moment. After all, she had a penchant for showing up when she felt herself most ignored.

Nagarath found the observation amusing. He'd had some experiences with cats . . . Liara's behavior was often more or less in line with the capricious creatures. *She's practically a familiar.* He chuckled to himself, wondering whether she'd find the comparison flattering or not.

She certainly was an inspiration. Looking to the sheaf of notes in the corner of his table, Nagarath wondered how long it had been since he'd worked seriously on the ideas begun back when he was but an apprentice. Oh, he'd dabbled in a few theories since that time. But no real progress had been made.

And why bother? His peers in the Art were either scattered to the wind or dead. The only one who'd likely ever benefit from original spell-casting would be himself . . . and now Liara. Liara, whose joy and curiosity over magick reminded him why he had loved the Art in the beginning.

Nagarath had to admit, the girl had a spark that went beyond a talent in the Art. Being more or less a hermit and having had to grow up at an early age, he'd forgotten that, at one point, all young people would have that gift.

His hands' motions casual but exacting, Nagarath was rewarded when the pile of flowers under his fingers stiffened, then grew vivid and fresh. However, a second pile further down the table withered and browned, their inner magickal fire gone.

Not an entirely unexpected result. He frowned, placing his hands on his hips and clicking his tongue reflectively. *But why had it happened?* Undaunted, he made a mark on one of his pages of scribbles.

His goal was to harvest the innate magickal power of one organic item and channel it into another, but without harming the first. He'd accomplished the first half of his objective, but botched the second. *Which, admit it, was exactly what you hoped Liara to see.* Nagarath smiled to himself. *A mistake. That not all magicks are perfect and researched and written down in books. That the true Art lies in the finding, in the making.*

Nagarath swept the spent flowers off to the ground. No matter. He had an entire garden to raid for his experiments, and an entire afternoon to tweak his technique in making an Artless variety of rose.

Perhaps in his next trip into the garden, he'd draw Liara's attention. After all, whether she knew it or not, it was she who had inspired him to take up his old studies once more. And it was she who would likely reap the benefits of Nagarath's line of experimentation.

Liara entered the kitchen and addressed the wizard without preamble: "The Laws of Magick Transferre. Law The First of Magicked Artifacts: A Magicked Artifact must be sound both physically and magickally in order to function as intended.

"Law The Second of Magicked Artifacts: Damage to either the physical or magickal condition of a Magicked Artifact will affect the outcome of Magicks performed through said Artifact. Also, purposeful damage to a Magicked Artifact for experimental purposes is not recommended."

Finishing her triumphant—and flawless—recitation of the two laws with a grin, Liara awaited the mage's reaction.

"Very good, my dear." Nagarath put aside his book, adding it to the growing pile next to him.

Liara raised one eloquent eyebrow in a silent scolding. If he added one more book to the groaning table, there would be nowhere for them to eat.

"Again?" she prompted, ready to recite anew.

Nagarath shook his head. "No, that was said perfectly. Now, explain these laws to me. Pretend I know nothing about them." He folded his hands and leaned forward, ever the attentive student.

Liara looked at him blankly. "As in . . . ?"

"As in, why do these laws matter? What is subject to them?" Nagarath's warm voice urged her on.

"Any physical item that has been imbued with magick is subject to these laws. And they matter because . . . because that's just how magick works," Liara concluded, frustrated. She had come down from her work rememorizing the laws, excited to share what she had accomplished, only to feel inadequate again.

Whether he sensed her irritation or simply liked her answer, ill-said as it was, Nagarath nodded.

"Nagarath, do books have magickal signatures?"

This got his attention more than her perfect recitation had. Nagarath eyed her sharply, his reply measured. "What do you think, Liara?"

"I don't know." Her words carried none of the brash brightness from a moment before. "But someone had to create them. Someone is responsible for their existence."

"Are we still talking about books?" It was Nagarath's turn to raise an eyebrow.

Eyes lowered, Liara squirmed.

"If you must know, the answer is yes . . . and no. Anything a mage touches with his magick leaves a mark, a ghost of his—or her—magickal aura."

Liara looked up at her tutor, questions in her eyes.

"Yes, Liara, this pertains to the Laws of Creatio," Nagarath confirmed. "But as artifacts—ones that are well cared for—are typically meant to last for many ages, the signature of the original mage tends to fade over time, blending with the subsequent signatures of those that handle the object long after his death. And then there are the neutral magicks, very rare and very powerful—"

Lost in his lecture, Nagarath missed the look of excitement that sprang to Liara's face.

She interrupted, "The Third Law of Magick Creatio: The destruction of an originating power subsequently destroys the magickal properties of its surrogate. In the case of Magicked Artifacts, the Second Law of Transferre applies."

"Something like that, yes. But usually, artifacts are designed to be self-sustaining, in which case the Laws of Creatio do not even apply. It wouldn't be that useful to have spell books stop working every time the mage who made them dies. And this we can do because inanimate objects don't draw power the way a living being does when we—"

"What about my trees?" Liara interrupted again, a new thought striking her.

"Your trees? Oh! The pink ones." Nagarath waved

off the concern. "I fixed that. Counter spell."

"But my signature—"

"Safely tucked away inside of you," Nagarath laughed. "There's no residual Liara-magick running amok."

That hadn't been what she was getting at. Liara frowned, trying another tactic. "Have you ever seen a dragon?"

Nagarath blinked at the turn of conversation, then sighed. "I suppose it would have been too much to hope that you would be better informed than that. There are no dragons, Liara. They're mythical. What made you think they might actually exist?"

"Well, people don't always believe in magick, but it exists," Liara challenged.

Nagarath shrugged, rattling off a list of purportedly magickal things that also "did not exist." Leprechauns, elves, fairies, gnomes, sprites, unicorns, mermaids . . . he hesitated and added griffins and centaurs: while they *had* existed, they had since gone extinct.

"But where do the stories come from?"

"Rumor. Or a need to explain a phenomenon. Some people think I sacrifice animals and eat small children."

Liara looked at the gangly, book-clutching scholar before her and laughed. "Well that's silly. Some wizards might do something like that, but never you!"

"Yes, some might somewhere . . ." Nagarath conceded, his eyes far away.

Liara leapt on his comment. "Hah! So too there might be dragons . . . somewhere."

Exasperated, Nagarath threw his hands up. "But there aren't!"

"Why?"

"What do you mean 'why'? You might as well ask 'why not anything'!" Nagarath shook his head and stamped over to the hearth to pour himself another mug of tea.

"Well, exactly! Magick can, technically, make anything possible," Liara countered, feeling she'd gained the upper hand. She added smugly, "For a wizard, you've a stunning lack of imagination sometimes."

Nagarath fixed his ward with a stern glance, the one that told her a lecture was forming on the tip of his tongue. Liara smiled back, welcoming the answer, whatever it might be. *Now we're getting somewhere.*

Nagarath sat back in his chair. "Liara, you know as well as I that there are rules, besides the Laws that I am having you learn. For example, I could create a small being to do my bidding—a goblin, if you will. But in doing so, the magicks I'd employ would likely create side effects of some sort or another." Nagarath waved off Liara's question. "No, I do not know specifically *what* sort of side effects, offhand. A study of the spells I would employ would reveal a likely outcome. And so, if I were to perform my hypothetical spell, I'd be measuring the benefits and risks . . . which does make the impossible possible, yes, but highly ill-advised at times. So much so that it's best to think of the aforementioned hypothetical spells as unusable. If magick were limitless in power except for the strength and ability of the caster, would not the world be full of marvelous things? Would not wizards rule the land? Consequences, Liara. . . . Consequences."

Liara frowned. The pink trees had seemed innocent enough. But even that wasn't quite right . . . Liara remembered the fear in Nagarath's voice as he'd scolded her, yelled at her for potentially exposing them to the wrath of Dvigrad's soldiers.

Nagarath hesitated before adding, "You, little magpie, are in some ways a consequence. Likely unintended and unforeseen—and a lucky boon for me and all who know you!—but a side effect of another spell, intended for another purpose."

Liara swallowed the lump rising in her throat, now seeing the truth of his words, the necessary precautions to be taken when wielding such power. *Or you could end up with a mistake.*

With a fond smile, Nagarath reached across the table to pinch Liara's nose. "So you're living proof that I'm not altogether right. Sprites, at the very least, do exist."

"I'd rather be a dragon, thank you very much," Liara quipped, her smile hollow, the lesson over.

VRSAR, coastal city at the mouth of the River Pazinčica

Well, this trip has been fortunate for me, if long. Krešimir gave a wave to the inn-keep as he claimed his usual spot in the corner of the common room. When he'd left Limska Draga for the coast, he'd counted on easily finding a ship willing to carry Phenlick's letter to Rome. But here he was, nearly two weeks later, having found that his forest-bound living had left him much mistaken on how shipping actually worked.

Krešimir wondered how long he would have to wait for Rome's reply once his letter was finally delivered. *They couldn't ignore the plea. Could they?*

Although it had seemed that the tide had begun to turn on Old Woman Babić's gossip when Krešimir left Dvigrad, the vicious lies ebbing when the wizard and his charge did not turn up to wreak havoc on the town, Krešimir had learned never to underestimate the superstitions of Dvigradians.

At any rate, Phenlick seemed beyond tired, and Krešimir agreed that the town needed new leadership to put the Zarijes in their place. And besides, his trip had more than paid for itself. Krešimir's pack of hand-carved trinkets and toys was nearly empty. It had felt pretty good to have his goods snatched up by eager ladies and children, especially in a town where exotic ships came and went on a semi-regular basis.

If I could continue my living here . . . Waiting for his breakfast, Krešimir basked in sunny thoughts of wealth and healthful coastal air. It had occurred to him on more than one occasion over the past ten days that a woman like Liara could disappear very easily into the bustle of this fishing town. Nobody would care about her past, not if Krešimir had any say in it. After all, the few strangers who had inquired after his own origins had either shrugged or looked blankly at him when he replied, "Dvigrad, of Limska Draga." It seemed that, even if they caught on to the fact that he was from somewhere further upstream, they couldn't care less.

The inn-keep stopped by his table, leaving a heaping platter of hardboiled eggs, breads, cheeses, and fish freshly caught from the sea. Another perk of a coastal town. Krešimir dove into the food, eager to finish breaking his fast before his first customers came calling.

". . . just up the river. Past the old ruins and up on a hillside. Twin-town."

Twin-town. Dvigrad.

Krešimir's head shot up, his eyes scanning the room, his attention settling on two men had just entered the room, one of whom he recognized on sight. Đerkan Babić.

"Dvigrad," the other man said. "There are no wizards there. Not since the edict. The doge even sent soldiers there—Uskoks kept hammering the valley. I'd always heard the old fort was nothing but on the wayside to bigger and better places, no offense."

"Well, friend. Would you like to see some proof? I saw the enchanted wood, those accursed pink trees, with my own eyes—" Đerkan's words were cut short as Krešimir's fist slammed into his mouth.

"What the—? Hey, you! Stop!"

Angry words followed the two men out of the inn, Krešimir grappling with the man he'd struck. He was rewarded with a bloody lip of his own as the man took a swing. The brief scuffle ended with the two combatants wrestling in the dirt of the street.

"What are you doing here, Đerkan? Tell me." Krešimir had a fistful of his victim's collar, his hand held ready for another blow.

"Hold." Đerkan shrunk within Krešimir's grasp, raising his hands in surrender.

Krešimir let his hands fall to his sides. He rose to his feet, breathing heavily. "So what—? Damn it!"

Đerkan took off at a run. The maneuver cost Krešimir precious seconds as he lurched into motion. Though older than the woodsman by over fifteen years, Đerkan Babić was still young enough to be fleet of foot. Disappearing up a winding alley, he tried to outstrip his attacker.

Krešimir gained on the older man, earning him a glimpse of Đerkan's elbow, a flash of his purse, as he rounded the next corner. Stone archways and flower pots passed in a blur, angry shouts following behind, the fleeting remnants of collisions narrowly avoided.

Through the chase, Krešimir replayed what he had overheard. Đerkan claimed to have proof of the magick in Dvigrad. *What proof could the man possibly have?* The thought goaded him onward.

Though he did not know the area well, Krešimir saw his chance as he skidded round the next building. Đerkan

The Bookminder

went left, Krešimir went right, the two narrow alleys coming together shortly thereafter, just as Krešimir had anticipated. And Krešimir got there first.

"Ha." The word was both confirmation of his victory and an ineffective attempt at catching his breath. Krešimir pinned Đerkan to the wall, his eyes positively sparking with anger.

"Krešimir." Đerkan's voice came out little better than a wheeze.

"Tell me what you've been telling people," Krešimir yelled.

"Kreš—"

"Tell me!"

Đerkan nodded, his head sagging with the motion. "Someone needed to know."

"Know what?"

"Someone needed to know what was happening in Limska Draga. Once that little witch left our town," Đerkan spat.

Krešimir pressed harder, grinding Đerkan's shoulder into the stone wall. "You said something about pink trees."

Đerkan started to laugh. "You'd protect her, wouldn't you? Even if she destroyed us all. Here. Here is what I saw, Krešimir." He shoved his hand into his pocket, pulling out no less than six crumpled oak leaves. They were a garish shade of pink.

Krešimir sucked in his breath. He hadn't known there were other witnesses to Liara's folly. He forced his tone to stay even. "Where did you get those? Why are you here?"

"Why, I was following you. Wanted to know what Phenlick's lackey was up to." Đerkan laughed in Krešimir's face.

Phenlick's "lackey" punched Đerkan, this time making sure the man stayed down. Kneeling, Krešimir wrested the incriminating leaves from Babić's limp hand, grateful that the skirmish had concluded in an empty alleyway. With a quick look around, he searched Đerkan's pockets for more of his "proof" of the magickal doings in Limska Draga.

Krešimir straightened in alarm as a whispering note caught his attention. Soft and nearly unnoticed under the sound of his own hard breathing from the scuffle and chase, the footfall presaged discovery. Assault and now theft? To be caught—and with Liara's leaves—was unthinkable. But no shouts of discovery, no rushing of angry guards followed the noise down the narrow and twisting alleyway.

"Try getting people to believe you now, Babić." Krešimir grunted, finding no further evidence of Liara's folly tucked inside Đerkan's purse. The shuffling, sighing sound caught his ears again, this time forcing him to his feet. A slight shifting of black in the deep shadows of the close-leaning buildings now caught his eyes and Krešimir fled, confident he'd finished his business just in time.

Đerkan Babić came to with a groan, but decided against moving straight off. It felt like the daylight poured directly into his sore head. Experimental fingers on his jaw proved no breaks, however. That was fortunate.

What rotten luck, Krešimir finding him in Vrsar.

Đerkan had thought he'd been doing a halfway decent job of seeing but remaining unseen. He knew that the woodsman was under some sort of commission from the priest—something involving a letter to Rome. And while Đerkan had hated having to stay long in this coastal town while God-knew-what was happening in Dvigrad, he had hoped he might have luck intercepting the response when it came.

Blinking as the gray-brown of the alley came into focus, Đerkan realized that the dark shadow before him was not some dim doorway, but a man. A man cloaked in black.

"Shhh . . ." The man approached, Đerkan emitting a groggy groan in reply. "Did I hear correctly that somebody has been spreading stories of magick from Limska Draga?"

The tall man bent, his dark robes swirling around him, as he reached a hand towards Đerkan. Foreign words, sharp and eerie, hissed from beneath the stranger's hood. Đerkan felt a gentle tug on his purse, the strings loosening and the little pouch removing itself from his belt by some unseen force. Terror replaced soreness in his inability to move and he trembled helplessly as the contents of his purse emptied out onto the ground in a discordant rattle.

The cloaked stranger stopped his speech, reaching down to sift through the leavings, picking up a small, parchment-thin item from the cobbled stone. Pink against black, the little leaf seemed to draw a fair bit of the man's interest. Enough, at least, that he did not bother to assist

Đerkan, now croaking his protest as he attempted to right himself.

"That's mine—" Đerkan began.

They were his last words.

Chapter Six

"Hmph. Mine, now." Liara was supposed to be organizing Nagarath's cellars. Instead, she was pocketing whatever small and interesting items came within reach—such as the bundle of sage claimed a moment ago.

Her purpose for the task was twofold. Once she discovered that the mage kept the food they ate directly next to deadly poisons, with little to no system of order and labeling, nothing was going to keep her from remedying the potentially dangerous situation. (When pressed, Nagarath had sniffed disdainfully at Liara's concerns, insulted that his "acceptable system of piles" had been called into question.) Her second reason was, of course, one she kept to herself: snooping.

As Nagarath had seemed singularly uninterested in joining her at cleaning up Parentino's cellars, Liara assumed his tacit approval of her purloining anything she found interesting, magicked or otherwise. She looked upward to the dark ceiling, addressing the wizard roaming the floors above. "Serves you right for not helping me."

Shaking her hand to clear the cobwebs that clung to her wrist, Liara wondered if and when she could attempt something with the small herbed bundle in her pocket. That it was magicked she had no doubt. A word of power had confirmed it.

Which was odd, considering a sage sachet seemed a useless thing to imbue with power. Unless . . .

Turning back, she again espied the glint of metal that had caught her eye in the first place. "Aha."

In the dark recesses of the low shelf, a strange gilt cage of copper wire winked at her in the lantern light. No bigger than Liara's hand, the wire box had held the sage bundle safely tucked in her pocket.

"*Sh'lemull.*" Though her voice came out a near-whisper, the word still proved potent. A blue-gray haze of light rose from the copper box, fading as fast as it had arisen.

Liara's hands itched with excitement as she carefully lifted the small copper cage. She didn't know what the box did, necessarily, but the reaction from the enchanted sage bundle had been much the same when tested. Liara pocketed the fascinating item. *Perhaps it magicks what we put inside of it.*

"Liara?" Nagarath's searching call startled Liara from her pondering.

She jumped, quickly slid a barrel over to hide the now-empty space on the shelf, then crossed the room, putting distance between her and the spot of her thievery as the mage's feet sounded on the cellar stairs. She feigned a tired smile, wiping her hands on her skirt as she went to greet him.

"Looks lovely down here." Nagarath peered around, an approving smile on his face. His eyes lit on the racks of hard cheeses, and he strode over to liberate one. "Come. I think we need a break from all of this darkness and dirt."

Liara nodded, following him up the stairs and into the kitchen, her hand straying guiltily to her pocket. The little box nestled comfortably at her side without so much as a telltale clink.

Working the day away in the lamplight of the cellar, Liara blinked hard in the sudden brightness of the sunlit kitchen. When she could open her eyes a moment later, the contents of the table gave her quite a surprise.

"Olives." Liara frowned her confusion at the basket of gleaming fruit.

"And truffles." Nagarath indicated the cloth bundle alongside, its contents less enchanting to behold, but valuable nonetheless.

"Where did you . . .?" Liara's brow furrowed further. She hadn't even known Nagarath to be gone. And here he was, returned from goodness-knew-where with two amazing finds. She crossed her arms, annoyed that he'd gone on an adventure without her. Truffle hunting was exciting—doubly so when there was no dog to help you, she assumed. Nagarath would have had to resort to magick. And Parentino was situated too far inland for the olives—those were a seaside treat.

"Never you mind, little magpie." Nagarath tweaked her nose as he strode past. Liara couldn't tell if he purposefully ignored her scowl, or if he was simply oblivious as he continued brightly, "I was thinking the cheese would go well with the mushrooms. And then—if you are done in the cellars, of course—we could try preserving the rest this afternoon. Along with the olives, obviously."

Liara nodded, distracted as a new thought itched at the back of her mind. Nagarath's tone was off. Too bright, too glib, even for him. She wondered at it.

The Bookminder

He turned back toward her, finally seeming to notice her ill temper. "What?"

Liara shook her head. "Nothing."

It wasn't nothing. But until she figured out what it was, she wasn't going to bring up her half-formed thoughts and growing feeling of unease. For a moment, Nagarath seemed a stranger to her. Liara found she didn't like the distance. And, she realized, she didn't like feeling shut out. Of late, she had been increasingly involved in the running of Parentino; had learned that it took more than magick to put food on the table, firewood in the bins, and clothes upon their backs. Her organization of the cellar was one such way in which she was slowly claiming Parentino as her own. Why hadn't Nagarath told her where he'd been?

Nagarath shrugged, accepting Liara's non-answer, and the moment was gone before she could transfer her complaints from brain to tongue.

She sighed and grabbed the bucket for water. In spite of her annoyance, she had more pressing concerns. The magicked box and sage still sat heavily in her pocket, and Liara needed a way to get them securely tucked elsewhere before Nagarath noticed.

Not that he would, since apparently he doesn't notice me enough to bring me anywhere. Liara sulked her way over to the well, seeking a hiding spot for her ill-gotten gains. However, by the time she had drawn the water, she decided to keep the items on her person, her guilty conscience eased by the idea that his infraction somehow made them even.

She entered the kitchen.

"Liara, are you mad at me?"

She ignored the question, going instead to the fire to start the water boiling.

"Because I didn't take you with me."

At least he figured that out. Liara nodded, refusing to look at him.

"Oh."

Oh? Liara felt her annoyance grow. *A monosyllabic answer—not even an apology!*

She snapped back, "You declined my request for help in the cellar fixing your mess. And then you spent the morning going goodness-knows-where on this beautiful autumn day, leaving me to muck around in the dust and the dark."

Liara stopped herself from saying anything further, his stricken look adding another layer of guilt to that which she already bore. Nagarath looked ashamed, and Liara hated herself for having put him in that position just because she was in a bad mood.

"I . . . I don't know what to say, Liara." The words tumbled from Nagarath's mouth. "It just slipped my mind that you would have wanted to go. I was being . . . efficient. I'm used to going places by myself. Doing things on my own, even now. And with you in the cellars, seeming so busy . . ."

Liara shook her head. "No. It's not a problem. I'm sorry. I was just frustrated. And surprised to know you'd even gone. And then you wouldn't tell me where you went."

"Tell you what: the next time I do anything even remotely magickal and exotic, you can come with me. Well enough?"

Liara nodded. She felt silly for having made such a

The Bookminder

big deal of the mushrooms and olives, whining over something so stupid as him leaving her behind. Flashing what she hoped was a reconciliatory smile, she excused herself to her rooms, citing the need to rid her person of the dust of the cellars.

Prying up the loose floorboard under her bed, Liara deposited the copper box and sage sachet. Safe at last. At that moment, Liara realized that perhaps the guilt she'd imagined on the wizard's face had been little more than a projection of her own.

"Too late now." Liara slid the board back over her little cache, the temptation to come clean and return the items drowned out by the simple voice of reason. She hadn't the strength to answer for her actions that day.

The storm of Liara's temper having passed and the remnants of the wizard's afternoon of brining olives and salting truffles having long been swept from the table, Liara settled down in the sunny kitchen for a few hours of quiet writing.

Out of the corner of her eye, she saw Nagarath enter the kitchen with another stack of his tired and tattered books. She sighed, for her pen seemed to waver every time the mage watched. *Couldn't he read somewhere else?*

The morning's desire to have Nagarath nearby forgotten in her quest for silent study, it was tempting to simply walk out into the garden in protest. Instead, she fixed upon him a playful glare, hoping that would hold him at bay until she had finished with at least that page of copy work.

It would not.

The books thumped onto the table by her elbow. Liara's ink jumped in its bottle, jostled by the impact of the heavy reading. Nagarath said not a word, raising an eyebrow in equally good-humored challenge and lifting his index finger to his lips. He had, apparently, opted to play along with her afternoon vow of silence.

Curious, Liara gave the books a sideways glance. Though none of the Nagarath's books were in what Liara would call stellar condition, this group seemed to be in worse shape than usual; hence her assumption that they had been intended for the mage's every-day use.

Nagarath would call them careworn. Liara considered his mistreatment of books to be downright criminal.

With a sigh, Liara pushed the books away from her and gazed resolutely at her page of crooked runes and jagged letters. To her eyes, they looked terrible. But then, that was how the language of magick was written. Pointy. Eye-catching.

Nagarath stared at her from his place across the table. The fact that he had not bothered to grab a book for himself made his meaningful look all the more distracting.

Liara squirmed in her seat. *What does he want from me?* She opened her mouth to ask as much when Nagarath flicked his eyes over the books at her elbow.

"Look. Can't these just wait until I—" Liara cut off her protest and gave in, lifting the cover on the top book. Her blood tingled in her veins as she tried to read the words. Tried and failed.

Deep black lettering covered the frontispiece. Heavily inked, the words ran end to end, margin to margin.

The Bookminder

They had presence, demanded to be read. Or maybe it was the magick they proclaimed.

Nagarath had just placed a stack of spell books in front of Liara. Her mouth dropped open, penmanship forgotten.

"These are . . . books of magick."

Nagarath nodded, clearly finding amusement in her delayed reaction. "Would you like to see where the rest of my collection is housed?"

Liara didn't say a word, only nodded her assent, afraid that more words would spoil the moment. *A real wizard's library. At last.*

In her excitement, for that brief moment, she forgot the future, did not think of her plans and her questions or how she could gain an advantage. She was simply Nagarath's librarian—a title that was itself an honor, not some stepping stone to something greater.

Black cloak of power flapping about his ankles, Nagarath swept from the kitchen, not bothering to ensure Liara followed. For of course she did. He really couldn't go fast enough for her now that she was to see his library.

Liara wondered where he'd concealed it all this time. But remembering how Parentino appeared to outsiders, and recalling her own failed attempts at accessing areas forbidden her, she figured the library to be close by but well hidden. It would be interesting to see what Nagarath had done with his books. Interesting, if not all that surprising.

But she refused to be jaded. Magick was magick, after all. And it never got old to her. Following in Nagarath's footsteps, down the hall and up the familiar stairs, Liara allowed herself a brief indulgence in her favorite daydream. Flickering candlelight, arcane symbols marking doors and walls, perhaps an ancient skull gleaming from out of the darkness . . . this was what Liara had long envisioned. And in a few short moments, it would be hers to explore.

No longer would she have to prove herself worthy of Nagarath's trust. He was opening his library to her. She was to be given access to powerful secrets, custodianship of the mage's beautiful and cherished collection of spell books. Nobody in Limska Draga could compare to her own consequence, save for Nagarath himself. From there, it was surely but a short leap to apprenticeship.

The farther they ascended, the more her idea of a deep, dark dungeon of books sputtered and died. Up past the third floor with its locked secrets, the stairwell had gained a distinct spiral bend. Liara tried to picture where they were in the castle. A tower, perhaps?

Liara's training spoke up. *Such a library would be beyond impractical. Too hard to store books properly below ground level.* Eyes devouring every detail of their passage, she noted the dust of disuse coating the steps and narrow curved walls. Sconces, though lit, flickered dully, ineffective at driving back the gloom that haunted the stairwell.

Cresting the final landing, Liara nearly lost sight of her guide in the dimly lit hall at the top of the stairs, his cloak only a shade darker than the surrounding blackness. Liara thrilled to see a solitary door at the end of the passage.

Nagarath strode quickly to the solid oak door, grasped the large, ancient lock with his left hand, and signed over the apparatus briefly with the knot atop his

The Bookminder

staff. A deep red glow, barely apparent even in the murk of the hallway, signaled the spell of opening. With a solid shove, the heavy door groaned awake, gliding open into the dank and musty air of the wizard's library.

Liara peered anxiously into the darkness as her master waved the globe wall lights to life.

"Well?" Nagarath stood to the side, grinning.

In every daydream of the grand moment she would finally enter the wondrous library, Liara had never imagined the scene that lay before her.

It was a smelly, old, dusty. . . room. Though smaller than the great room downstairs, the space was still one of the largest she had ever seen, save for St. Sophia's sanctuary. Ringed by no less than two balconies—the topmost of which their doorway had entered onto—the library seemed to require the stacks of books within to support itself, such was its dilapidation. Craning her neck, almost afraid to enter, Liara struggled in vain to hide her severe disappointment.

From the smell of things, the place hadn't been aired since goodness-knew-when, and had clearly never seen a dust rag or broom. The tracks of small animals could be seen winding between the staggering stacks of books. And the books. The poor books! More on the floor than on the shelves, they were stacked in every available space, all higgledy-piggledy.

Nagarath, still standing to the side, eagerly awaited Liara's approval . . . awe . . . or whatever she was supposed to show to this—this *mess*.

She thought quickly. "It's like . . . nothing I could have ever conceived!"

"I know, isn't it glorious?" Nagarath took two of his

long strides over to the balcony's edge, motioning her over. One hand dove into a pile of books that sat on a three-legged stool and pulled out a ragged jumble of parchment, knocking several other sheaves to the floor in the process. Liara cringed as she saw bindings sag and pages curl on impact with the flagstone.

Does he expect me to fix this? Or is he happy with how it looks? Liara feared the answer. Knowing Nagarath's other tendencies, he likely hadn't even noticed the sad state of his collection until various spell books stopped working.

Nagarath had picked his way down to the main floor of the room—Liara refused to call it a library just yet—and was gesturing for her to follow. More books tumbled to the ground in her wake, despite her careful attempts to not disturb the piles. Even the metal spiral staircases that gave access to all floors were piled in parchment and weathered codices.

Now here is a sight. Liara finally found something of interest. Near the wall, next to another door, two long benches flanked a gently sloping table. The convenient arrangement allowed for use of the books right where they were chained. Yes, chained. In her studies, Liara had come across descriptions of such systems, generally used on rare texts to prevent theft. Smiling, she bent to inspect the codices, glad that Nagarath had at least cared for the wellbeing of *some* of his collection.

She leapt back with a short shriek as one of the books jumped and tumbled onto its spine, pages fluttering and emitting a low snarl—well, a bookish equivalent of a snarl.

Blushing, Liara turned to find Nagarath laughing.

The Bookminder

"Well, I didn't know it was going to do that!"

Nagarath nodded, still chuckling in spite of his best efforts to quell his mirth for her sake. "I'm sorry. But your face just now . . . Yes, little magpie, these books know their own. I can't even use them, some days. But they do make a good deterrent for thieves." He turned and opened the door behind him, revealing a bright foyer.

Blinking, Liara stepped into the sunlit hallway, noting that they had returned to the main floor of Parentino and were, in fact, standing just outside the great room.

How many times have I passed this by?

"Don't worry. It was a wall for you," Nagarath answered her puzzled stare. "Well, sort of. Remember the tapestry?"

"The one depicting Saint Jerome and the lion?"

"Yes. Come." Nagarath indicated that she stand clear of the door, shutting it behind her.

Liara looked from the door to the wizard. "What?"

Nagarath pointed back to the door behind her and Liara turned, surprised to see the familiar tapestry and stone wall she'd passed nearly every day.

"So how do we—?" She shifted the heavy curtain aside, revealing the library door. "It's as simple as that?"

"Yes and no. Technically the door has always been there under the tapestry. Only I could see it when Saint Jerome was moved aside. Now only you and I can see it." Nagarath shrugged.

"So all that song and dance coming up the winding stairs?"

"The back door, yes. Admittedly, it was much more aligned with your expectations, am I right? That, and I did not wish your first impression of my library to be one

of snarling books straining to break free of their chains."
Liara scowled playfully. The mage knew her well.

Not wishing to hover, and having some work of his own to complete, Nagarath now let Liara tour the library in peace. Which was fine with her, for it left her free to unmask her true feelings of revulsion and disappointment as she gingerly picked her way through yet another example of Nagarath's disastrous lack of organization.

Where do I even begin? She looked around helplessly, acknowledging that any first move she made against the chaos would at least be a start. Turning 'round the room in a slow circle, Liara tried to concentrate, but found that her mind wouldn't settle. It was as if the books were whispering to her. Not just the chained books, though those still made her skin crawl, but the whole collection of dilapidated material. She could nearly hear the quick hushing of a pile if she looked fixedly at it.

"Well, of course it's an interior room," Liara grumbled aloud, determined to drown out the whispers of the collection as she looked, unsuccessfully, for a way to bring fresh air and light into the windowless library. She thought she'd gotten used to the smell of books. But this many, in this close a space, with this much dust? Liara did not feel ashamed ducking out into the comparably airy hallway.

Her indecorous exit seemed to amuse the books, the whispering sounds increasing.

"Oh, shut up," she growled. The complaint made her feel better, though slightly crazier, as she stood outside the door, pondering her next move.

~*~

The Bookminder

If seeing Nagarath's library was a disappointment, cleaning it was far, far worse. But there was excitement in it, too—far more than the monotony of dusting St. Sophia's. Nagarath had the sense to stay out of Liara's way as she scoured and scraped, and hauled and heaved, the tipsy towers of the library's contents shifting about the great room as she tackled each corner with ardent fury.

It was fulfilling to see the change come over the place, and over the days it took her to put the great room to rights, Liara found herself rising early and staying late. There were carvings on the bookshelves, tiny engravings set into the stones of the outer walls. Even the balustrades were molded into fantastical shapes and patterns. Here was the magick Liara had looked for, even if it was only whimsy.

And just when she thought her arms would snap off from dragging countless buckets of water in and out of the library, Liara found that she'd scrubbed and swept her way past the patina of dirt and grime and into a new dilemma: she now had to confront Nagarath's maddening collection.

For the whispers that Liara had imagined she'd heard on the first day had continued, growing louder, rather than diminishing with her increased familiarity with the library.

It was odd how some of the wizard's books seemed to call to her, demanding her attention, while others seemed patient to wait their turn, complacent in their tottering piles. Of course, Liara decided to attend to the former first, hoping to stem the chatter that she seemed to hear only in her mind. But that seemingly logical approach soon proved her undoing, for Liara realized she'd have to familiarize herself with the contents of each book in order to determine a general cataloguing scheme.

Glad that she had developed a plan of attack, at least, she picked up her first book, the one that seemed to be clamoring the loudest.

Quietly turning to the title page, she felt her heart quicken as she began to read. For a moment, Liara was convinced that she was falling. The words swam before her eyes, the ink bleeding into her brain, screaming gibberish at her. Magick pulled at her eyes, whispered into her ears. Her hands, her spine tingled as the magick inside of her flickered to life, compelled by the words on the page—

With a shriek, Liara threw the book from her.

Pulse pounding, she sat on her chair in the stillness of the library, unsure of what had just happened, knowing only that it had been decidedly unpleasant. She eyed the book with misgiving. Lying where it had fallen, pages fanned open, place-marker ribbon knocked askew, it certainly looked innocent enough.

Convinced that it had been the excitement of an overworked mind, but not eager to repeat the experience, Liara turned to a new book. A smallish tome, decorated in unassuming swirls and declaring its contents a discourse on basic weather working, it seemed safe enough. But this one was worse than the last.

Words everywhere. The barbed black runes snagged at Liara's eyes as she scanned the page, whispering their horrid syllables out from under the cover when she closed the book in terror and fled the room.

She could still feel the pull of the books even as she gently lowered the concealing tapestry over the door from

The Bookminder

the safety of the hallway. She ran to her room hearing, even now, the books calling to her, beckoning with fanciful tooling on leather covers, the feathery edges of parchment easing their way out of their place to greet her, words that swam over pages mottled with age and rot and danced in her head long after a cover was firmly closed.

Tears in her eyes, Liara hastily packed her few belongings. What good was a librarian who couldn't be around books? The world seemed to crash around her, the noise of her dreams shattering drowning out the clamor of the books at long last.

A knock on the door made her jump. She turned to find Nagarath waiting on her, a puzzled and hurt look in his eye.

"Have I missed something?" he asked.

Sniffling, Liara explained the problem in one heartbroken gush of words. "I can't be your librarian, Nagarath. I cleaned the library, but couldn't—I can't—can't organize it, much less repair it for you. So I'm leaving. Before I'm kicked out, as I'm sure I will be, because I can't be around the books. Things . . . happen." *I'm hearing voices and using magick without intending to.* She swallowed back the admission, unable to trust such a terrible truth to him and feeling all the more miserable for it.

"Oh, my little magpie." Nagarath approached, offering a consoling arm. Sorrow tinged his voice as he continued, "I am so sorry to have forgotten."

"Forgotten what?"

"That my books might be . . . difficult."

Liara shook her head, shrinking from the mage. "No, it isn't them. It's me. I guess. I can't seem to get near enough to them without being pulled in—into them. And my eyes just fixate on those words. I feel as if—it's so silly, but—it's as if they're working on me instead of the other way around."

"No, I should have warned you about spell books. They know their own." He sighed and fixed his sharp eyes on hers. "You did try introducing yourself, right?"

Looking up abruptly, Liara found herself transfixed by Nagarath's bright, penetrating gaze. The sorrow in his face had faded, replaced by the familiar spark of humor.

"Introducing myself?" Puzzled, she wasn't sure if Nagarath was playing a trick on her. The idea was odd, to say the least. *Introduce yourself to a bunch of old books? How?*

"How you do it is no real matter. Just see that you do, so that they know you and stop pulling at your innate art, your inborn magickal tendencies. The books are simply trying to figure you out, and will draw the magick from you if you don't put them in their place. A proper introduction would also help you to be comfortable around them."

"But they're just books—" Liara interjected, feeling more foolish than ever.

"Ah, but they aren't. Come now, you mean you haven't been at least a little awed by the promise of what lies behind each cover? You haven't felt the pull of that incredible power, each tome with an aura of its own, a distinct flavor, making you feel somewhat uneasy but also entranced? Seduced? Not even a little? Don't disappoint me, little magpie. The books know their own." The smile was kind and Liara relaxed; at least he wasn't mocking or testing her.

She smiled back shyly. "Well. A little. I just didn't

The Bookminder

put it down to that. I really thought it was me. So . . . how do I introduce myself? Is there a proper way?"

Nagarath waved his hand. "No, no. There's no proper way to do anything when working with a power not your own. You make your own path or turn back. In this instance, you're simply working to find common ground, an understanding. Acclimate them to you, and yourself to them. I'm sure you'll be fine after that."

It was with a lighter heart that Liara reentered the library. And though the books still whispered at the back of her mind, she found that confidence went a long way in subduing their pull.

By mid-afternoon, she had managed to clear a good portion of the western corner, just by reading the covers and sorting them into fresh piles for later perusal. And that night, having no better idea in her head on how to achieve acclimation, Liara slept on the floor of the library, the shelf next to her holding her stash of stolen goods—items she now had technically returned to the mage.

Chapter Seven

Nagarath stood in the garden, reading the wind. The smell of snow was in the air, though it was still some way off. With luck, it would not fall until after the crisp November morning's spellwork. If not, he would just have to work all the harder at maintaining the illusion, something he hated having to do.

He went inside to summon his ward. It was funny to think that scarcely a month ago, he'd been hard-pressed to get Liara back into his library after her scare. Nowadays, it took a fair bit of effort to draw her out.

"Good morning, Nagarath," her cheery greeting echoed down from the library's second floor balcony.

"Good morning, Liara. I—" Nagarath paused, noting with a frown the small shelf by the door that contained only about half of the books of notes, scrawled experiments, and jottings of his personal projects that it should. "Liara, where are the rest of my—? Oh, never mind."

Spying the rest of the items in question, he crossed the room to where they lay in a series of small piles. Shaking his head at Liara's sense of organization, he endeavored to carry them all back over to the shelf by the door, taking no care as to their order. Several armfuls later, he was stopped mid-stride by a very angry, very annoyed librarian.

"Just what do you think you are doing?"

Hands otherwise occupied with the books he carried,

Nagarath indicated as best he could the shelf he was restocking.

"Liara remained rooted in his path. "Those haven't been indexed yet."

"They're my work books, Liara. I use these on a near constant basis. I have no need to index them." Nagarath moved around the girl and continued on his way.

"Then why are they in here and not in your work room?" Liara raised her eyebrows, skeptical of his claim.

"If I wanted them ruined, Liara, I'd have taken them in there with me a long time ago."

Liara pursed her lips, watching in silence as Nagarath cheerfully undid most of her morning's work.

"Now,"—he dusted his hands triumphantly—"would you like to accompany me on a little sojourn into the woods? It's delivery day."

At Liara's blank face, he chuckled, then beckoned her out into the hall. "You'll be needing a coat and a hat. There's ice on the wind."

Nagarath let the girl puzzle over his words, enjoying the little mystery he'd created for her. He was rather impressed, in fact, by the quiet acquiescence with which Liara followed him out the gate and into the woods, never even questioning the fact that he demanded they each grab a sack, one empty and one not.

Crunching over the hard ground, the last of the autumn leaves blowing fitfully amongst the silent, barren tree trunks, Nagarath and his ward barely had time for their hands to become chilled when they came within sight of a cozy hut. Wood smoke drifted from the little, twisted chimney in its hunched roof, and a small window declared cheer and warmth within.

"Whose is that?" Liara breathed, hastening to fall alongside as they approached the cottage.

"Ours."

"Wait, what?"

Upon reaching the diminutive door, Nagarath held it open for Liara, then stooped to follow her inside. Watching her eyes roam over the comfortable interior, he explained, "It is one thing to allow you to see Parentino as it truly is. It is quite another to have that secret compromised by accepting deliveries from town there."

Liara answered with a blank face.

"Once monthly—save for in the heart of winter—I receive goods from Dvigrad. Items I would be hard-pressed to come by myself. The ink and parchment you have been using, for example, is something I have gotten from town in exchange for small favors."

Nagarath's mouth twitched an aborted smile as Liara answered, "Magick."

"I cannot say. After all, there is a ban on all magick, yes?"

He winked. Liara grinned.

"So, when Piotr arrives, act like this is home. Until now, I've convinced him that you've always been out when he and I met."

Liara nodded slowly. "Why the change?"

"Why bring you with me?" Nagarath was confused. "You asked that I take you along for such things. Besides, it did not feel right keeping this place from you any longer."

There was little time for his words to sink in and for Liara to explore the cozy dwelling before a knock at the door called to them.

The Bookminder

"Enter, Piotr," Nagarath bade their visitor, but not without a forlorn look at the book with which he had intended to pass the time. Liara rolled her eyes.

Dvigrad's apothecary came in, stamping his feet to warm them. "Greetings, wizard. Oh, Liara! You're here as well." It was hard to tell from his look whether he was glad to see the girl or not.

"You need to do something about this cold, Nagarath," said Piotr, his words gruff with chill.

Ah. Deciding that the dour look on their visitor's face was due to the weather, Nagarath fixed Piotr a warm smile and offered him a chair, bidding Liara to fetch a warming beverage.

The girl slid into the subservient role nicely, quietly nodding and bustling about by the fire, her face unreadable.

"Letter for you from Father." This Piotr delivered himself, his eyes darkening with hidden meaning. It sounded urgent and, at Piotr's nod, Nagarath opened and read it.

His eyes widened, then narrowed as he strove to master the unexpected stir of emotion at the priest's words. He shifted his gaze quickly to Liara and then back to Piotr, speaking without directly alluding to the letter's contents. "I'm not entirely sure what he wants me to do about it. Does he expect a reply?"

"I presume so, sir," Piotr answered, his voice low.

With a curt nod, Nagarath put pen to paper, leaving Piotr and Liara a moment to catch up.

"I hadn't expected to see you today, Liara. You're looking well."

Liara ignored him, her eyes on Nagarath. Although

engrossed in his letter writing, Nagarath kept half an eye to the exchange, gauging her response. *Speak with your kinsman, girl. Don't look to me.*

Not one to be deterred easily, Piotr pressed further for conversation. "Nagarath says you've been doing quite nicely."

"I like it well enough here," she conceded awkwardly. "Er, so . . . this is where we've been getting our yarn?" Liara gestured to the sack on the table, and Piotr nodded.

Nagarath could feel Liara's continued gaze upon him as he put the finishing touches on his reply to Father Phenlick, concealing his letter amongst the cloth bundle he had readied for Dvigrad's apothecary.

Liara waited in the doorway while he saw Piotr off, she merely nodding shyly in response to Piotr's cheerful goodbye. From the corner of his eye, Nagarath watched his ward retreat back inside. She glanced sideways at the delivered bundle, then lifted the edge of the bag to better see the spoils. Fresh cheese, milled flour, and spun wool peeked out. Phenlick's letter lay open on the table.

Nagarath ducked his head in the door just in time to stop her from reading the priest's correspondence.

"Come. It's time we leave." In one smooth motion, Nagarath snatched up the letter and hefted one of the packages left by Piotr, leaving the other to Liara. Confirming first that Dvigrad's apothecary was indeed out of sight, Liara ventured out the door, Nagarath following soon after.

With a wave, he dismissed the illusion, and the little hut disappeared in the blink of an eye. Nagarath turned to find Liara staring at the space where the cozy cottage had stood but a moment before, her face white with shock.

The Bookminder

~*~

Realizing that the mage was looking at her, concern lining his face, Liara quickly got hold of herself. Feeling stupid for having grown attached to the illusionary cottage in the space of an afternoon, she forced her thoughts back to Phenlick's letter.

"What's in the letter?" she asked, taking the direct approach.

"News from Dvigrad." Nagarath's face was carefully closed off to her. Unreadable. "He sends his regards to you."

Liara flushed, though not with pleasure. "Checking up on me. What business is it of his?"

"Liara." It was Nagarath's turn to be shocked. His look told Liara she'd just crossed a line.

In her anguish, she paid no heed, her words tumbling onward. "Does he always send secret letters to you? Has he been using you to spy on me?"

"Enough, Liara. If you cannot see that other people care for you, then that is your own problem. Do not make it mine."

"What about the people I care for?"

These words stopped him. They walked in silence for a long moment. Through the deepening gloom of the late afternoon, one small snowflake fell, then another.

With the snow came an admission, though she kept it to herself. She couldn't have cared less that Father Phenlick was checking up on her. If anything, it was comforting to know the priest still cared what happened to her. But it served to highlight the cold fact that Krešimir had not looked after her, not once since their accidental meeting almost three months back. And while they had often gone months without seeing one another when she lived in Dvigrad, Liara found the silence hurtful.

"You never asked if I had any messages I wanted to send along." There. She'd said it as best she could—come as close as she wanted to confessing her feelings regarding the life she had left behind.

~*~

Nagarath found himself shamed by Liara's words. He looked down to the young woman marching stolidly at his side, and realized how much he had wronged her. Until now, Liara had been less a living, breathing, feeling human and more an interesting challenge, a project, or some abstract idea.

At times, he had caught glimpses of the girl's heart—only to discount them. Liara's keen desire to learn magick, to discover more about her mysterious origins, drove him to close off all discussion stemming from those two topics.

Nagarath hadn't been cruel, hadn't even ignored her. He just hadn't understood. What's more, he hadn't even known he should try.

"I'm sorry." He realized the words were inadequate. Months of companionship, believing they'd reached some semblance of friendship, and he'd been so paranoid about the issue of magick that he'd not bothered to find out who she really was.

Where to begin? Nagarath didn't know.

He again glanced down at Liara. "Did you want me to send a message to somebody in Dvigrad?"

The Bookminder

The girl shook her head.

Nagarath prodded, "Liara, it was your home. If you need—"

"Dvigrad was never my home. Just let it go."

Nagarath likely saw it before Liara did. The real reason she was upset. He let play in his mind's eye the memory of Liara flitting about the cozy cabin. For all that she seemed to thrive in Parentino, she had positively glowed upon entering the little magicked hut in the woods.

'Act like this is home,' he'd said of the cottage. *'Ours'* he'd called it, then hours later he'd made it vanish with a mere gesture. He recalled the shock on her face. It was not the shock of a girl who lived in illusion, dwelt in magick. No, Nagarath had inadvertently given Liara her heart's true desire, then glibly snatched it away.

He opened his mouth to apologize anew. But Liara had already steeled herself, her face having lost its pinched, sullen look. Nagarath realized he had again overlooked one of Liara's other qualities: she was resolute.

Liara screwed shut her eyes, finding the tension of the black on black nighttime a deterrent to sleep. Huddling deeper beneath the covers, she tossed in her bed, trying to drown out the noise of her thoughts. But her mind refused to settle, still caught up in the emotional events of the day before. She thought she had already made her peace with her feelings. Why couldn't she sleep?

Her eyes fluttered back open and she debated getting up, doing something to quell her restlessness. Anything but to lie awake all night staring into the black. Sighing noisily, she tossed back to her other side, stiffening in concentration as she again shut her eyes, but opened her ears. A subtle squeak sounded from the garden. She waited.

There it was again.

Throwing off the covers at last, Liara softly padded over to the window, braced herself, and pulled back the drapes. Stiff fingers wrestled with the latch on the shutters before the window opened to her. She looked out, seeking the source of the mysterious noises. The brightness below was dazzling, and she leaned forward intently, cold almost forgotten. The first winter's snow had blanketed the garden during their walk back to Parentino, aiding the illumination already provided by the full moon above. Waiting a moment, Liara was rewarded by the sight of a dark figure emerging from the kitchen door. She watched as, stopping at the low stone pillar that graced the center of the courtyard, Nagarath straightened and impatiently threw back the cloak that had fallen across his hands, impeding his work.

Puzzled, Liara settled into her window-side perch, any thought of returning meekly to bed overpowered by her interest in what Nagarath was up to at such an odd hour. A flash of light in his hands caught her attention, and she peered across the dark, trying to see what the mage was fiddling with—rather unsuccessfully, judging by the sound of his muffled curses.

Rousing herself, Liara made up her mind to brave the cold night, quietly whisking herself down the stairs and

The Bookminder

into the kitchen. Halfway out the door in only her nightgown and boots, she nearly collided with the wizard who had apparently decided to run back inside.

As she guessed it to be several hours before dawn, Liara was surprised to see the man so alert. But not as surprised as he was at her wakefulness, it seemed.

"Goodness, Liara. What brings you down at this hour?" Having swiftly sidestepped the collision, Nagarath stood looking over her hurried state of dress with bemusement. "I didn't wake you with my messing about outside, did I?"

Liara shook her head and followed the mage, taking an appreciative sniff of the steaming pot over the fire. Peppermint. No wonder he was awake.

"What is it you're doing?" she asked, craning to see if the dark garden held any further clues.

Following her gaze, Nagarath excitedly poured a second mug of tea. "Studying tonight's full moon." He gestured for her to follow as he strode out to the garden. "Come on."

"What, right now?" Liara hung back, suddenly reluctant to leave her warm spot near the fire.

"No, tomorrow at midday when the sun's up. Of course, now."

"But it's cold out."

"Well, that's what the tea is for." Nagarath stomped the snow off his boots as he reentered the warmth of the kitchen. "Hang on a tick."

He left Liara yawning over her tea. A brief clamor moments later heralded his return, a thick woolen blanket and an unevenly knit scarf bundled in his arms.

"There." He dumped the soft heap unceremoniously

onto a chair. "Meet me out back if you'd like. I'm hoping to see the oceans tonight!"

And with that, he was gone.

Staring grumpily at the misshapen pile of wool, Liara debated marching straight up to her room and leaving the mage to his adventures in the cold, dark night.

But of course, she wouldn't.

What was it he said he'd be looking at? Oceans on the moon? She lifted the comical scarf and chuckled in spite of herself, certain she'd misheard. Something about the lopsided knitting pattern touched her heart, warming her as she pictured Nagarath hunched over a pair of needles, a determined frown drawing his eyebrows together.

Wrapping herself in the blanket, Liara braced herself and went out to the garden. The sharp bite of the midnight cold hit her like a bucket of icy water, dampening her short-lived burst of curiosity. Determined, for she liked to think of herself as hardy, Liara waited a moment for her eyes to adjust to the light of the crystalline moon, and then strode over the tramped-down snow to where Nagarath stood with his face pressed up to the top of the stone pedestal that had long stood at the edge of the kitchen garden.

The odd sight prompted Liara to raise her eyebrows in skeptical surprise. Hearing her approaching footsteps, Nagarath straightened and, stepping aside, revealed the object of his scrutiny.

Glinting in the moonlight, an intricate mechanism of glass, iron, and brass sat atop the stone pillar. Liara felt a shiver, this one not from the cold.

"What's that?" she breathed, eyes on the fantastic device. Gleaming knobs and loops of brass, sparkling

The Bookminder

glass plates—the fineness of the design made it as remarkable as the guard's own armaments, while the object's delicacy made it the most beautiful manmade item she'd ever beheld.

"It's a telescope." Nagarath beckoned her nearer. "Well, half of one, technically."

He gestured to the corresponding lens atop Parentino's parapet. Liara gazed up in wonder at the fantastically large glass window shining atop the tall tower where Nagarath worked his magicks.

"But how—? What—?" Liara looked from one part of the telescope to the other, her quick mind calculating that the bright orb of the moon would shortly come into alignment with the two sections of telescope.

Following her gaze, Nagarath confirmed her suspicions. "In a few minutes, the moon will arc far enough along its path that the lens atop my tower can catch it. Then we'll be able to view it through the eyepiece down here." He patted the mechanism.

"But why have I never seen the . . ."—she wrapped her tongue around the unfamiliar word—"telescope before?"

"Ah, well," Nagarath said with relish, "I've designed the two pieces for easy placement and removal. A lens that size"—he gestured up to the object on the castle wall—"could do some real damage if it collected any sunlight. So I only put it up when I plan to use it. Plus, something so delicate could be easily damaged by rain, wind, birds . . . Though of course, I magicked it to keep it relatively safe from the elements, as well as made it lighter, stronger, clearer, purer—yes, I cheated a bit." Nagarath broke off from his explanation with a sheepish smile.

"Cheated?"

"Used magick to enhance the telescope's ability beyond what would normally be feasible. You'll see what I mean when you look through it."

"Cheated." Liara snorted. "That's like saying tall people cheat when they use their height to pick the better apples at the top of the tree."

The wizard opened his mouth to argue, but stopped short, exclaiming, "Goodness! I'd say it's time!" He bent to the eyepiece, his triumphant 'ha!' telling Liara that it was, indeed, time.

Nagarath delicately manipulated knobs and made other minute adjustments. Then, with a flush of excitement, he reached out, eye still pressed to the mechanism, and gently drew Liara towards him.

"A-a-and . . . there we go!" he breathed softly and straightened, indicating that Liara should take a look.

Gingerly, she put her eye to the device, afraid that her clumsy touch would disturb the sensitive instrument. Then she whistled her surprise, nearly drawing back in shock.

Suspended in the middle of the viewing piece sat the silver orb of the moon, but unlike she had ever seen it before.

To begin with, it was huge. So much so, that Liara removed her gaze from the telescope long enough to ascertain that the moon had not, in fact, suddenly grown. Ducking back to the eyepiece, she drank in the sight.

"My goodness," she breathed, "It's as if . . . we got closer to it."

New details were brought into sharp relief, mere

The Bookminder

smudges of dark and light revealing themselves in greater contrast, and she reluctantly pulled away once more. "I think . . . I think there are lakes up there," she whispered excitedly, wanting to crow about her discovery, but somehow feeling she oughtn't disturb the calm quiet of the moonlit night.

"Oceans, Liara," Nagarath corrected. "And yes, I think so, too."

He pinched the bridge of his nose, his common gesture of deep thought. The mage looked from the girl to the moon adding, "The distance between here and Dvigrad? From here to the moon is eleven thousand times that distance. So your lakes are oceans, and the hills, mountains."

Looking up at the moon, small and distant without the aid of the telescope, Liara debated stealing another peek through the lens. While she hesitated, Nagarath bobbed his head back down to the eyepiece and, first blowing on his hands for warmth, withdrew a small empty book from a pocket of his robes, along with an ink bottle and pen. With quick, darting glances, he tried to write and watch—succeeding at neither.

Frustrated just watching the man try to coordinate the two activities, Liara reached out to take the writing instruments. With barely a nod and murmured thanks, Nagarath started uttering his observations aloud so that she could commit them to paper.

This went on for only a few minutes. Then, "Switch!" Nagarath said abruptly, and straightened, taking the paper and pen from her hands. Startled, Liara looked dumbly at the mage as he moved to the side, his smile encouraging but unhelpful. Bending down to put her eye to the piece, she felt Nagarath lean close and speak softly in her ear. "Just tell me what you observe, Liara."

The whisper, spoken so near to her, so intimately, sparked in Liara an unexpected thrill. For a moment, she gazed mutely through the telescope, feeling more than seeing. As Nagarath bent close once more, however, she found her tongue, as fearful that he might note her blush as she was that her turn at the telescope might have ended before she got to really see anything.

"It has stars on it."

Clearing her throat, sticking her frozen fingers deep inside her woolen blanket, Liara clarified further. "I see lines, radiating outward like stars. Roads, perhaps? Leading to and from impossibly large cities—round cities with walls ringing their edge."

Liara glanced away to see Nagarath nodding and smiling, his pen scratching at his book of notes. She wanted to ask if she was correct. The mage's hasty writing ceased and his eye caught her own, questioning.

Blushing in earnest, Liara ducked back to the telescope's eyepiece. Beginning her observations anew, she distanced herself as much from the moon as from the press of Nagarath's gaze. "It's like a big pearl. Luminous. Floating in an inky expanse of black velvet. A lost jewel. Lost but not forgotten, just out of reach."

She took a deep breath, the moon filling her vision and tugging at her mind. She couldn't remember the last time she'd been allowed to give vent to flights of fancy, to speak from deep within herself and have her words noted. "It has scratches. And dots. Slashing across the middle, I can see a mountain ridge—"

At this Liara again looked nervously to Nagarath. *Mountains. On the moon.*

"And at their edge, I see two oceans ringed with more of those curious circles, perhaps more walled cities. The water of the moon's oceans is dark, the cities and mountain peaks tinged with white. Like snow. I wonder if the people there are cold and wear mittens and hand-knitted scarves." Liara's fingers fiddled with the warm scarf about her own neck, and she thrust them back into her pockets, hastily putting a stop to the unconscious gesture. "Are they like us? And does Father Phenlick know they're there? Do they have the same God as us? Do they have magick? Families?"

"Father Phenlick is actually how I acquired the pieces I needed for my telescope."

Liara jumped back from the eyepiece as Nagarath spoke, his arm moving into her field of vision to adjust a dial on the telescope. He let her continue onward, Liara noting a strange, quiet smile on his lips as she eagerly moved to view the moon once more.

"I can't see any trees." She frowned. "But then, we're really far away. Or perhaps they're all silver and black with wintertime. After all, the moon gets orangish in the autumn—although I don't remember it ever seeming greenish in the summer time. Perhaps . . . perhaps—"

Her face contorting with the effort to puzzle through the oddity, she looked back to her mage, impulsively blurting out, "I want to visit it. Tell me there's enough magick in the world for us to visit it someday, Nagarath."

At this, Nagarath appeared nonplussed, as if it hadn't before occurred to him to do anything other than gaze at the moon from afar. Again that curious smile as he answered, "If there is magick enough in the world to get us there safely, Liara, I promise that you are who I would take."

Satisfied, Liara pressed her eye back to the telescope, positively enchanted by the sight, by the idea that Nagarath would give her the moon. Nagarath, who wouldn't even give her magick.

But there's magick in this. Doesn't he see that? Again, she let her eyes drink in the pearl-white moon. So intent was Liara on the rare sight before her eyes that she barely noticed the long moments passing. It never occurred to her until much later that the moon stayed centered in the viewing pane, and that Nagarath did not again take his turn at the telescope. For at the time, it felt as though time had stopped.

In fact, it wouldn't be until the next morning, when they read their notes over breakfast, that Liara would hear how she waxed poetic. While moongazing, Liara forgot the cold and the dark and the very words she spoke as she attempted to describe the beauty of the moment, conscious only of the moon and the wizard who stood close by in the night, sharing his discoveries with her.

DVIGRAD

A rumor was flying about Dvigrad: something terrible had befallen Zarije Babić's son.

Of this rumor, Zarije had much to say, having started it herself.

But as the winter snows began, Old Woman Babić really did fear that something bad had happened to Đerkan. And as Father Phenlick appeared quite reluctant to admit that he, too, had sent a man on a mission, Zarije found little to no opposition to her loosened tongue. The tide had turned in her favor at last.

Bypassing the priest—for he had proved singularly unhelpful ever since he'd let that girl go off with the wizard—Zarije went straight to the Venetian guard for help. They were only too willing to exercise their power, having had months to think on the events of the previous spring.

"Please, you must help me find Đerkan," Zarije begged the captain of the guard. "We can patrol the forest far and wide. My son must be found."

The man twirled his mustaches thoughtfully. "This is a matter for Father Phenlick. Our orders come from he who Rome has placed as protector of Limska Draga."

Babić gave the man an arch look. "You don't think I've tried? That man has had it out for me and mine ever

The Bookminder

since that problem with Liara. But mayhap you haven't seen that side of him."

The poisoned words did their work. "I'll get a patrol together." The captain nodded to one of his men. "Did Ðerkan tell you where he was going when he left?"

Inwardly, Zarije rejoiced. "Just that he was following the river to the coast, as he often did." She paused and leaned in close, as if fearful of saying the words aloud. "He was of a mind that the priest was in league with the wizard and may have sent him word of Dvigrad's doings via a messenger, a man of the woods who may have done harm to my son rather than become exposed."

For a moment, Zarije thought she might have overdone it, that her hasty words would expose her to the priest whom the guard would have to consult before leaving on exercise.

It seemed to her that the captain of the guard weighed similar thoughts. "If what you say is true, this matter is more serious than previously supposed. Already the priest has disobeyed his own authority by letting the girl go free. Do not worry, lady, about your confiding in us. We have no love lost for the priest. We who would remain loyal to Venice will investigate and make these matters known publicly. Until that time, remain strong in your hope."

The soldier rose, dismissing Zarije.

From her front window, the woman watched as several patrols of fully outfitted soldiers left Dvigrad that afternoon, their faces grim. From her vantage point, she could see Father Phenlick, equally grim, arguing with the captain as each watch left town.

~*~

"But it's the middle of winter and you're needed here." Phenlick was obstinate. And though he felt the gesture futile and petty—*like a child's*—he stamped his foot in emphasis. *Dvigrad's priest, throwing a tantrum in the street. Is that what we have come to?*
The captain seemed to think so. His impassive patience was maddening. George Phenlick would have much rather had this conversation tucked away in the sanctitude of the church, instead of losing his temper here in plain view of everyone . . . and in sight of Babić, undoubtedly watching from afar. He felt the hair on the back of his neck prickle.
Something was wrong. Zarije was right about that much. He could feel it, too. Not a premonition, no. But something. Something in his bones told Father Phenlick that trouble was afoot, and it would be better if the captain did not send all his soldiers out on some chase after Babić's son.
Especially as I know why he left and whom he was tailing.
"Zarije has the right to see her son safe. As you yourself have said, it's winter." The soldier frowned and leaned in. "Or do you have information that we don't, Father? Seems you're still on pretty friendly terms with that wizard."
Phenlick could tell the captain's words and accompanying gesture hadn't been meant as a threat—not a creditable one, at least—but he drew himself taller all the same, returning the imperious look with one of his own. "What I know is my business and that of Dvigrad's. If

you have something to say, just say it."

"I did say it. I said it when we found that girl's witchcraft—magick you denied she had. I repeated it when you changed your mind and found fault with her, kicking her out only to have her take up with that wizard—"

"There was no change of mind. The girl was guilty of theft and showed no remorse. I did listen to you and your men—it is your report that showed the depths of Liara's thieving ways. Even so, I wasn't about to let a girl of sixteen years wander about the woods, prey to anything, when Nagarath was so obliging as to take her under his wing."

The words grew of their own volition, carrying Phenlick along. As he spoke, he realized the truth of his convictions, that he'd done right by the girl in spite of all. He even found that he had to suppress a twinge of pride at the guard's frown over use of Nagarath's name. *Yes, I know the mage's name, you pompous, sword-carrying, hardhearted fool of a man.*

The unmistakable rattle and clank of armored trappings caused all eyes to turn. Watching his companion's gaze shift, Phenlick wondered if he'd made his point well enough. He was not going to beg. Not on the vagary of a mere 'bad feeling.' Nor did he want it known that he had already appealed to Rome and the Republic for aid and advice, though if rumor was to be believed, it seemed as though perhaps Zarije had put forth her own guesses.

The captain of his guard turned back, military starch back in place in shoulders and stance. "You serve Dvigrad. I'll serve Venice."

With a barked command, the last of Venice's defensive aid marched in double-file towards Dvigrad's gate. After a curt nod, their commander, too, turned on his heel and strode towards the outer wall, leaving Phenlick dumbfounded and frustrated in the cold, snow-specked street.

He tried to bury the rising apprehension as he watched the uniformed men leave. The last of ten such patrols. None of whom had so far returned. *Though they haven't been expected back, as yet,* Phenlick reminded himself. Which meant they'd found nothing to the rumors, no truth to Zarije's judicious whispers.

Which ought to have made him feel better, surely? And if Krešimir returned with a competent replacement . . . yes, all would be well, so long as he had the patience to ride out the worries, and so long as there was authority enough for Phenlick's replacement to grasp. Liara was safe with Nagarath, the valley tucked in the safe embrace of early winter.

Even so, as Father George Phenlick, too, turned on his heel to walk back into the winding inner alleyways of Dvigrad in search of Piotr, he felt anew the twisting knife of contradiction in his soul. He was right to help Liara, to trust Nagarath—he was certain of it. And yet the indefatigable apprehension remained at the back of his mind, and for the first time he wondered if his charity and righteous heart had spelled doom upon them—if perhaps there had never been a correct path to choose in regard to Dvigrad's orphaned magick girl.

Chapter Eight

In her weeks of working amongst Nagarath's collection, Liara discovered that there was far more involved in putting a library of thousands of books, scrolls, and other ephemera to rights than cleaning, or even indexing. And so she had begun a secret work of her own.

Liberating parchment and ink, she'd spent countless hours working in the quiet of the library, jumping at every sound lest Nagarath come unexpectedly upon her project. But now, at the turning of the season, Liara had finished her masterpiece.

With triumph and trepidation—and a small bit of drama to which Liara, being Liara, could not help but succumb—she bade Nagarath close his eyes. Then, shuffling forward gingerly, she led him to the center of the room, where a large book lay in state on a heavy oaken podium.

A good five inches thick, the book had required every ounce of her skill to bind. The covers were solid maple, their width longer than her forearms.

"It's okay to open your eyes now." Liara held her breath excitedly as Nagarath's eyes fluttered open.

"What in the world?" He didn't seem to know what to make of the massive codex, by far the largest book he had in his collection. Hefting it open, he discovered a bound pile of blank parchment. Shooting a puzzled look

The Bookminder

to Liara, he waited for help.

Bursting with pride ill-contained behind her superior smile, Liara sauntered over to her creation and laid a hand on one of the blank pages. Eyes closed, she waited calmly for several moments. Then, eyes open once more, she quickly flipped through the book, coming to a stop as the text manifested on the page, seemingly writing itself as the mage and his exultant librarian watched.

"Amazing . . ." Nagarath whistled his appreciation. Liara's massive book had referenced the one he'd been reading at the kitchen table just that morning. "Explain."

Liara stood back from the book and let the words fade. "Per my studies, I began fixing your collection in the usual way. I put things to rights, sorting, organizing and making an index. A shelf list. But by the time I'd started filling a third shelf, I realized that such a list would run several volumes in length were I to give each scroll and book its own notation. The index was going to need an index! Based on what I had seen of the shambles in the library before I got here, I figured I mostly knew how you searched for a book. And so I concluded that what you really needed was a master book, one that not only told you where I'd shelved things but also what items you had on any given topic. So my index became a catalogue."

"It is remarkable. But Liara, I must ask how you—"

"So all you have to do is concentrate on what you're looking for and, poof, the book tells us where to find it in the library." She brushed past the inquiry, blushing guiltily. "But it's hard to get it fine-tuned. You can't just think of anything—it'll only recognize certain ideas, and sometimes it takes a few times to adjust what you're asking to find."

"I—"

For a moment it appeared as though the mage meant to return to his question and Liara cringed inwardly, for she was fairly certain he would not entirely approve of the 'how' in the catalogue's creation. But Nagarath's scholarly interest had been incensed and his eyes returned to the massive book.

She gestured for him to give it a try, which he did with alacrity. Placing his hand gently on the open page, he shut his eyes and waited for a moment, then jumped, removing his hand and opening his eyes with a snap.

"Go on," Liara encouraged, excited to see the book working on the mage. "You feel it, right?"

"What a strange spell you've devised, my little librarian," he murmured. Looking down the page, his eyes dancing as they watched the parchment fill with dark, slanting text, Nagarath pinched the bridge of his nose thoughtfully. Liara could practically feel him concentrating, and laughed out loud.

"Oh." The wizard let the disappointed little word sneak out.

Her face falling, Liara craned her neck to get a good look at the book. Nagarath obligingly shifted to let her see what he'd gotten as a result.

The page held a description of one of the mage's lesser-used books, a history of magecraft with chapters on each of the greats. Liara recalled having had a discussion about the book—he wanting to toss it in the 'discard' pile, while she had defended its possible uses. The look on Nagarath's face told her this was not the book he'd hoped to conjure up.

The Bookminder

"You did that on purpose," he accused with a grin.

"No, I didn't," Liara answered, completely earnest and more than a little disappointed in the results. "I knew that we'd have to calibrate it a bit, but. . ."

"Try again?" Nagarath seemed eager to remedy the early failure. "This time I'll speak my thoughts aloud as best I can, to see where I might be going about it wrong."

Nodding, Liara stood next to him as he again placed his hand palm down on the blank page. She was grateful for the small gesture of kindness, the mage having laid the blame on himself rather than the catalogue.

"So, book, what I would like to get is that spell employing spiders that I used last week . . ." Nagarath began, immediately prompting a correction from Liara.

"The book doesn't know what you used last week," she chimed in gently. "Think in terms of the spell's details—what it's meant to accomplish, important components, who developed it perhaps."

"So, really it's me we're calibrating here," Nagarath muttered slyly, with a wink.

"Nagarath, I—" Liara began, only to realize that he was teasing her.

"All right, all right. It would be a useful feature, though." He drew his hand back with a confused frown. "I think I need to start over. It felt as if I could open this book at twenty different spots as an answer to my query." He cracked his knuckles and wiggled his fingers before giving it yet another attempt, waving his hands with a flourish. "I *think* I've got the hang of it now. . . . Can't let the mind wander."

"So *you'll* never be able to use the catalogue," Liara muttered mutinously, sitting over by the wall to wait for the wizard to stop fooling around.

"Ha!" Nagarath's booming voice echoed sharply about the room. "I heard that."

A few silent moments ticked by before he shouted again, this time in triumph. "There, that's more like it. Liara, this is really quite marvelous!"

Blushing, she rose and approached the mage, his hand still on the open page. Beaming, Nagarath gestured with his free hand, and lo, there on the parchment was the spell he'd been asking after—complete with location information for the book in which it was found, as well as a description of related spells.

"I really would like to know how you did it, however." Liara shrank under the dark knitting of the mage's eyebrows. "If only so that I could add in the aforementioned recall functionality without damaging the spells already at work in this book."

"Hold on. You don't care that I . . . that I . . ." She paused, trying to find a way to say she'd performed magick without actually admitting to it.

The answer was a smile and gentle pat on the back. "Oh, Liara, whatever am I going to do with you? I give you the simplest of tasks and still you find a way to weave spells through it all.

"I care, of course. But in such a way as I cannot argue against it. Or are you not also willing to see this as a perfect carrying out of one's duties as my librarian? Penmanship and bookbinding. As you yourself said, I needed this volume, which means your project could be viewed as a bit of—" his lips twitched with humor "—repair work."

With a grunt, he lifted the heavy cover back into

The Bookminder

place, shutting the catalogue until the next use. "I do still have one question, Liara."

"Yes?"

He turned to her with a raised eyebrow. "Did it have to be so big?"

Liara held back a grin. "Well, you've got a lot of books, Nagarath."

~*~

Nagarath waited until Liara was long abed before he returned to the catalogue in the library. It wasn't that he didn't want her to see him use the gift. He was, in fact, so grateful—so astounded—that he needed some time alone to think.

"*Maa'ome.*" At his muttered command, the globe lights of the library stirred to life. Approaching the pedestal with its massive book, Nagarath let his fears and worries wash over him.

The girl was special, no doubt. Taking the small morsels of magick that he'd been forced to throw into her education, Liara had digested them into a work of art of which he could never have even conceived. Daunting. Indomitable.

The question was no longer whether he should keep magick from her, but whether he could.

Angrily, Nagarath paced the room, his eyes seeing only the wonderful things Liara had brought him. She had—quite literally—taken the broken pieces of his life and put them back together, reimagining them better. She'd done more for him than she'd done for herself.

Guilt redoubled its attack. She'd done more for him

than he'd done for her.

"But I could not give her more. Not yet." He spoke to nobody in particular, or perhaps he addressed the Fates. After all, it was their fault that Liara had been dealt the hand she held.

No, you dealt her that hand, Nagarath. He argued with himself, *But I'm working to fix all of that.*

"By lying to her?" His anger became anguish.

The silence rang its non-answer back to him.

"Nagarath, you may well be the only person on this earth who knows what is right." He approached the podium once more. These last words gave him some small measure of comfort, returned him to himself.

He gently lifted the cover of the catalogue book and, opening to a random page, placed his hand on the parchment within. He let his questions guide his thoughts. So engrossed was he in his dilemma that he almost didn't notice the words bleeding to life beneath his hand.

He read them aloud, reassured by their simple wisdom, and smiling at the tidy interconnectedness of things:

"The Laws of Magick Creatio. Law The First: Magickal power mimics the Magickal signature of the originating or altering power. Law The Second: Once the age of twenty has been reached, a subservient power gains autonomy and its signature is fixed. Law The Third: The destruction of an originating power subsequently destroys the magickal properties of its surrogate. In the case of Magicked Artifacts, the Second Law of Transferre applies."

In the silence, the Fates had spoken.

Four years. I can tell her everything in four years. Nagarath shut the book, his doubts quelled for the moment. *In the meantime, I think I will see if we can cook up a way to recall what books were summoned via the catalogue. Could be useful for a forgetful mage like myself.*

He chuckled, snuffling out the globe lights with a snap of his fingers.

Chapter Nine

Nagarath crashed heedlessly through the underbrush of the wood, his black cloak of power marking a wide swath in the snow. There was no need for secrecy. The light had only just begun to sneak its way into the morning skies, a lighter grey upon the dark. There would be nobody about at this hour, not in this bitter cold.

Besides, he had bespelled himself from prying eyes. The charm repaired the damage he left in his wake and dampened the sound of his passage. For though he hated using his power for such things, the urgency that drove him out into the woods of Limska Draga on this early morning was greater than his reluctance to employ the spellwork.

The squirrel he chased simply moved too fast for any other option.

While he felt a pang of conscience for having purposefully left without telling Liara, Nagarath tried to argue it away. Telling the girl would have necessitated any number of problematic explanations, for one thing. And disclosing the contents of Phenlick's letter, with its rumors of unrest stemming from Liara's exile, was not something he wanted to do just yet—if ever.

Then there were the creatures of the forest, the mage's eyes and ears. The varying reports of armed men in the woods had so far been discreet enough so as not to draw Liara's attention, squirrels and birds having come to

The Bookminder

him mostly to complain. Nagarath was certain Liara would not take kindly to the revelation that he had magicked the animals. They made regular patrols of the forest, and had done so, in fact, for many years.

Satisfied that he was in the right, Nagarath continued trailing his informant through the trees. The gray squirrel slowed, scratching and skittering along through the underbrush. Gently, so as not to disturb the flighty animal, Nagarath crouched and peered about the small clearing. Informant for the mage or no, squirrels were always both easily frightened and angered.

At his feet, the last of the year's ground cover bent under the weight of the previous week's early snowfall. But beyond that, partially open to the gray swirling skies through the trees, the little clearing was trampled flat. Booted feet had cut into the snow. A broken branch lay here and there. Whoever had been there had been of sufficient number that they had not bothered to cover their tracks.

With a heavy sigh, Nagarath reached into a pocket of his robes and drew forth a nondescript pebble. Dropping it, he murmured quick words of magick and rose to his feet. He looked inquisitively to the squirrel and again they were off, crashing through the crusty snows and brittle foliage of early winter.

They visited five such sites before the skies had brightened to a polished gray-white. And at each, Nagarath repeated his ritual of words and pebble. Satisfied, he thanked the squirrel and bid the little creature farewell.

Alone in the wood, Nagarath turned a slow circle, closing his eyes in readiness for his spell, gripping his staff tightly as the hair at the nape of his neck prickled and stood to attention. Spellwork made him vulnerable, and he could feel other eyes upon him. *Could I possibly bring myself to attack Dvigrad's soldiers?*

If it proved necessary. The thought came unbidden as he sought to settle his mind for the magick. Yes. Yes he could. The truth of the revelation sparked a shudder that went beyond the cold of the winter air.

Resolve strengthened, he muttered a few of the sharp words of the Green Language. In his mind, five points of green light flickered to life. He could feel that he stood over the fifth, the pebble at his feet glowing the brightest to his magickal senses. Widening the gaze of his mind's eye, Nagarath sought the two blue-white points that marked Dvigrad and Parentino on his mental map. He thought he ought to have located them by now . . .

There. Parentino, glowing steadily in his mind. He hadn't realized that he'd traveled so far afield. He loosed the breath he'd held, feeling the sudden squeezing sensation in his chest ease.

Even so, the flicker of fear remained. His eyes snapped back open. He couldn't 'see' Dvigrad. Luckily, the squirrel's zigzag path through the forest had not disoriented him so much that he couldn't get his bearings based on his position relative to Parentino's. Pausing a moment on the path, he gently raised his staff in a protective gesture.

Surely there was nothing amiss in Dvigrad? It was only last week that Piotr had come to see them, only days since the town guard had made their various camps that so disturbed the squirrel. Not entirely reassured by his logic, he set out once more, favoring speed over silence until he could finally make out Dvigrad's familiar, reassuring form through the winter-thinned trees.

In the short walk, Nagarath had decided that, early or not, unwelcome or no, it was high time he talked face to face with the priest about the goings on in Limska Draga. If there wasn't a need to be in the woods, then the guard should be back within Dvigrad's walls by sundown, not camping in the forest like vagabonds. On the other hand, if they were patrolling against some unknown trouble, then it was Nagarath's right to know so that he could prepare his own defenses accordingly. *And perhaps provide some of my own to Dvigrad.*

Almost immediately, he retracted this last thought with a shiver. He, of all people, was not the one to offer a good defense against trouble. Breathing heavily, for the cold and the fear had both been growing on him as he traveled, Nagarath walked round Dvigrad from the backside.

He was doubly thankful for the charm that had rendered him invisible throughout his investigations. If there was real trouble afoot in Limska Draga, the soldiers he sought might well still be scattered amongst the trees, even further than he'd looked. Even so, the time for stealth was over. It would not do to approach the wall and catch the guard unaware by means of magick.

"*Her'ah.*" The spell of revealing came out as an exhalation, Nagarath pressing forward into the path in the space of a breath. Shading his eyes from the brightness of gray stone against gray skies, he looked upward to the battlements.

"Good day," Nagarath shouted. The wall gave nothing save a stern-faced silence. "Good day?"

When his second call aroused no further activity

from the empty walls, he gave the gates a push. They yielded only as far as the bar on the inside allowed.

So, we're playing this game now, are we? Nagarath stood back from the wall, again craning his neck upward, looking for any signs that his greetings had been noted. Early or not, someone must be up. The days simply passed too swiftly at this time of year. Annoyance turning to ire, Nagarath turned back toward the town gates, his staff raised anew to draw, most carefully, the required opening rune upon the impenetrable gate. Though he much preferred his wand for such purposes, it would not do to come charging through the city's entrance, weapon drawn.

With a quick and quiet spark, Nagarath's magick forced the barrier's locks and bars to give way and the mage entered, fearful of what he might find.

Out in the garden, Liara fitfully overturned clumps of dirt, looking for signs that any of the root vegetables had survived the early snow. While winter storms and cold snaps were not uncommon—Liara could remember half a dozen such winters in her own short lifetime—a thick blanket of snow this early had come as a surprise.

Nagarath had, of course, shrugged off her insistence that they hurry out and harvest what they could. Which was why she had decided to do exactly that. If the mage was going to wander off without so much as a word, then he couldn't complain about what happened in his absence. Besides, she'd worked too hard on the kitchen garden to have the fruits of her labor ruined by lazy stub-

The Bookminder

bornness.

Stretching her arms in an attempt to free herself of the crick in her back, Liara paused. Limbs akimbo, she stared, frozen, up into the bleak winter sky, listening intently as bird twitters silenced and the air became unnaturally still. Rising to her feet in alarm, she darted a glance at the gate, confirming that it was indeed locked. But the building pressure in the air told her that it would not help.

Whatever was coming was not coming through the gate . . .

Liara ran for the safety of the castle, fleeing into the cellar. Covering her ears, she tried to fight the mounting pressure in the air, like a giant fist squeezing her lungs. She could almost hear the walls screaming. The air positively danced with magick. Panic rising, she ran back up the stairs, debating whether to try her bedroom or the library. She chose the library.

Pushing aside the tapestry that hid the door, Liara ruled out the possibility of a misfired spell or experiment. Whatever was in the air felt purposeful. Menacing. Forbidding. Like it wanted to crush the life out of her.

With a quick, guilty glance over her shoulder—*where are you, Nagarath?*—Liara slammed shut the library door and, running over to a nearby shelf, grabbed a recently catalogued book of wards.

"Please work," she mumbled, not quite sure whom she addressed, frantically turning pages as the room swam into focus around her. A trembling breath, and the spell was cast.

Liara swayed and sat down hard. A long, breathless moment passed before she rose slowly, shaking, to her feet. Feeling a trickle of wetness above her upper lip, Liara wiped blood from her nose, wincing as her heart skipped a few beats. Still, the room had ceased to ripple, the air becoming breathable and quiet. A soft, bright sensation settled in her mind as she realized that her casting might actually have worked.

Liara, magus of Parentino, she crowed inwardly. She barely had time to register the thought before a whoosh of wind stirred the pages of the book in her hands to life and, with a loud bang, Nagarath appeared in the center of the room.

Startled, Liara watched unmoving as the mage stumbled towards her, his face gaunt and pale. And then she was in his arms, Nagarath murmuring into her hair, "Oh, thank you. Thank you, gods."

Caught in the impromptu bear hug, Liara's spine stiffened as she caught the smell of death upon the man, death and the fiery scent of burned-up magicks. Remembering himself, Nagarath let go of his ward and walked in a daze to the wall, slumping down against it, as if exhausted, spent. His staff clattered to the ground beside him, momentarily forgotten.

Liara still hadn't moved, had not said a word, stunned as she was by his abrupt entrance and even stranger display of affection.

He looked up at her, his eyes haunted. "They're all dead. All of them, Liara."

She shifted uncomfortably. He was near tears. To her dismay, her mind dislodged from his words, traveling back to Nagarath's impulsive embrace, stuck on the confusing and embarrassing clutter of feelings it sparked. She wanted to relive the moment again and again. She wanted to wipe it from her memory. It was awful. And distracting. Unsure how to react to Nagarath's pain, she opted for the safe route, gently claiming a spot on the floor beside him, forcing herself back to the present and searching his face for answers. *What in the world had just happened? Why did he look like, smell like . . . death?*

"Who's dead?"

"The town. Dvigrad." A weak hand gestured to the outside world.

The room tilted and swiftly righted itself, leaving Liara gasping for breath. *Dead. Everyone is dead.*

"How did—?" Her voice cracked, betraying emotions she could not yet comprehend. Her brain told her it wasn't possible, that Nagarath was mistaken or exaggerating. But her heart, frozen with shock to the point of barely beating, told her the truth of it. She could feel Dvigrad's absence even here in Parentino, could see it in his face. Suddenly, Liara missed the numb sensation of a moment before, finding she did not like the new, terrible fear that had taken its place. "Was it—?"

Fire, her mind wanted to say, wanted to supply a reason for it all to add up. But a daughter of the woods, she knew better. Nagarath had smelled not of ash and heat, but of spent magicks. Her heart squeezed again at the thought. *Too much magick used. Nagarath, why?* Perhaps it had been the abrupt manner in which he had returned? In all her time with the mage, she had never seen him use his Art in so dramatic a fashion. She hadn't even known he could.

Thinking of Nagarath's display of power, mentally dissecting his scent, called back into sharp focus the memory of him holding her close, however briefly. She could almost feel the comforting warmth of his arms, the desperation of his embrace and the emotions riding high underneath the intimate gesture. Her own tumble of emotions swelled with the recollection. Liara turned away, overwhelmed.

"Plague." The word, barely a whisper, drew Liara out of her spiraling thoughts. "It took the whole town. Save for the soldiers, I believe."

"Soldiers," Liara repeated dully, as if by so doing she might bring some sense of order to her reeling mind. The smell of burnt magick wafted again to her nose, her heart skipping an anxious beat. "Wait, did you . . . did you fight them?"

Nagarath stirred, his eyes gaining back some of their steely focus. "No. They were just gone. I'd been looking into it. They've been patrolling further and further from Dvigrad, of late."

Liara tried to think of why else Nagarath would have used so much magick at once. He looked about done in. It was terrifying, seeing his face so ashen. What if he died on her? What would she do then?

As if sensing her unspoken worries, Nagarath smiled and reached for her hand, his voice rough with emotion. "Someone needed to honor the bodies before scavengers defiled them. Not that animals would have taken much interest in a place with the smell of sickness so thick in the air. I used a good deal of magick to make sure that each was properly mourned."

Liara turned away, shrinking from the mental picture of her friend building the large funeral pyre. "I'm sorry," she said simply, not knowing what else to say.

Nagarath squeezed her hand. "They were your people, Liara."

Reluctantly, she nodded her assent, unsure of how she felt about it. True, she'd been closer to some than others, but . . .

"Liara, there's blood on your nose." Nagarath's voice came sharp, interrupting all thought.

"Oh. That." Liara moved to wipe the blood with her sleeve, but stopped. Father Phenlick had taught her better than that. Blanching at the thought of the old priest, she hid her face under her handkerchief. "It's nothing. I . . . I got scared. There was something in the air. Squeezing me. I ran inside. Here. And did the first thing I could think of."

Nagarath's eyes shot to the cover of the book that Liara now held up, his face a mix of incredulity and anger. Liara would have rejoiced to see the mage show so much spark had he not looked so forbidding. "Did you . . . did you attempt a warding spell?"

Liara nodded. "I thought something was attacking Parentino."

Nagarath blinked in surprise, his look changing from one of danger back to one of keen alertness. "How so?"

"Something just felt . . . scary . . . all of a sudden. Like the air was all crackly. And the pressure? Oh, I thought my heart would burst from it. So I ran inside, thinking I'd at least try to stop whatever-it-was from getting in here with me and the books and things." She shrugged. "I just sort of reacted."

Nagarath sat back against the wall, stunned. "You 'just sort of' performed complex magick."

Liara blushed. "I . . . was worried I'd locked you out."

"Me?" This seemed to amuse him. "I don't think you

could. Not out of my own castle."

Liara pouted at the immediate dismissal of the first high-level magicks she'd performed.

He waved aside her reaction. "No, no. You see. . . I've got so many spells at work within these stones. I felt the defensive wards trigger all the way from Dvigrad. You saw me rush back. I was afraid . . ." He shook his head, as if clearing a thought.

"So, you're saying it was our defensive spells that tried to crush me?" Liara recoiled.

"That tried to cr– what? No! That's preposterous. You must have done something to trip them."

"I was gardening." Liara's response came flat, her annoyance hanging as thickly in the air as the adverse magick she'd suffered through.

"You were out in the gardens?"

Liara nodded.

"Yes, well." Nagarath tugged at his nose. "Outside the walls, the spells defending the castle had no way of really knowing if you were an enemy or a guest. They're rather good enchantments, if a mish-mash."

"Like everything else you do?" Liara interrupted blackly.

"Yes, but over time, they have become quite effective, clearly."

"I could have been squished!"

"Goodness, no." Nagarath shook his head against the cool stone wall. "Ended up with one whopping headache, perhaps. But nothing worse than that, once the spells saw into your head and heart, saw that you were allied with me. I'm sorry for the fright, little magpie. You did well."

Together they sat in the silence of the library, neither

eager to return from their brief sparring match to the bleakness of reality. Liara's mind was abuzz, unable to settle in the tumult of magick and questions pummeling her. Dvigrad dead. Her blood, singing with the power of her first advanced spellwork—for, oh yes, it would be the first of many. Phenlick, Piotr, Babić . . . Krešimir, all gone.

Her eyes prickled, sour tears that refused to do more than stab at the backs of her eyes. But why? How? And was Parentino safe under Nagarath's hodge-podge illusions and wards? Something had to have triggered them. She'd been outside countless times over the past eight months with not so much as a twinge from the wizard's patchwork enchantments. No, something else had tripped Parentino's protections. But what? And had it anything to do with what had happened in the town?

With that, Liara's mind returned to Dvigrad, starting the circuit of fretting and fearing anew.

"You say that you were gardening?"

Nagarath's statement came at her again, with that same dreamy distance he tended to put between emotion and academia. Liara fought the urge to snap her response. "Yes."

"And not with magick?"

Liara noted the slip of Nagarath's gaze back to the book of wards, still in her hand. Annoyed that he'd question the matter—*again*—especially considering the fright that his spells had given her, she opted for tightlipped silence.

"Liara, if we have to discuss anew the dangers of you performing illicit magicks . . ." Nagarath gently reached over to take the spell book from her.

"I didn't do it, all right? *They* attacked *me*." Liara snatched the book to her chest, then relaxed her hold, feeling stupid. It was Nagarath's book. And the mage look positively wounded by her words. "Or something did."

The inherent question in the admission died unanswered between them, as Nagarath turned to stare at the tile beneath his feet, seemingly spent, his mouth set in a hard line. Liara sat through the silence, waiting for acknowledgement of her last statement, her hinted fears.

Nothing from the mage. He continued his moody stare at the floor.

She prodded, unable to let the matter drop, "I draw water, I use the privy. It's not the first time I've been outside the keep. And before you ask, no, I wasn't outside Parentino's outer wall."

"I don't have spells beyond our perimeter. You know that." His eyes darted to her briefly, the fierce anger in them kindling Liara's own. "Listen, the only way the inert spells that protect the courtyard would activate is by them sensing an adverse force—either a trespasser harboring ill-intent or a magick other than my own."

"I didn't touch your horrid old spells. I told you what happened."

"Even now. After everything that happened today." Anger turned to hollow bleakness and Nagarath's accusation came hoarse, sorrowful. "Liara, when are you going to stop lying?"

"When are you going to believe me?"

Liara was angry. She was hurt. Today should have been a banner day. She had cast a serious spell, unaided. A hero. She'd been frightened out of her wits, more than

The Bookminder

she could ever remember from her own ordeal in the garden. The fears she'd known as a child had been visible threats, easy to identify and anticipate. But magick? It was terrifying, exhilarating. And she'd mastered it, only to have old sins thrown back in her face, instead of congratulations and thanks for saving the castle.

'After everything that happened today.' The tang of spent magicks was fading from the air, carrying with it the sting of Nagarath's thoughtless accusation. Oh, the things that her mage had been through today. The memory of his first words, whispered into her hair as he held her, returned full force. She was still mad at him, to be certain—him and his stupid patchwork spells. But she owed it to her friend to swallow her pride, bite back the retort that old habits had formed on her tongue. Because, in spite of his hurtful words, he cared. Cared so much that he'd burned through incredible amounts of power to return and assure himself of her safety. So much so that she could see the tense alertness under the exhaustion, and she knew that, even now, he was actively sustaining his "horrid old spells."

"Do you have to work hard to maintain them?" She looked again to Nagarath's hooded eyes, the gray pallor of his skin. Her fears sharpened, crowding out her anger. What if he had caught the plague? What if it wasn't just a drain on his magick that was hurting him? Or worse, what if he ran out of magick? Liara knew from her studies in magickal theory that large amounts of casting or long-term maintenance of a network of spells could very well drain all magick from the caster—if it didn't kill them first. A wizard who became incantate lost their magickal signature forever, their ongoing spells often ending as well.

Nagarath saw her worried frown, followed her unspoken thoughts. "I am far from incantate, my dear. Just . . . tired. Believe me, I'm nowhere near dropping, but I will say it would take a great deal of peril before I'd attempt any more casting at present. Granted, I shouldn't have left you defenseless—near defenseless"—Nagarath corrected himself at Liara's quick glance—"with only the castle spells to protect you in the event of disaster. But I couldn't very well leave all those poor souls in Dvigrad like that."

Liara knew she should feel guilty over having bothered him about the spells. He'd had to deal with so much in those last few hours. But, the awfulness of that moment in the garden hung around her like an unwelcome fog. His questioning of her account made sense, in light of past actions and today's stunning demonstration of power. What if she had unconsciously done something to his wards? And what if they hadn't, in the end, functioned as the wizard promised, reading her heart or whatever it was he'd said?

She glanced at Nagarath, laboring under the maintenance of the spells, and an even darker fear snaked its way into her spine: what if her warding of the castle had saved her from a real threat? Cobbled together defenses or not, what had happened in the garden hadn't felt like Nagarath's magick. Liara shuddered, wishing he'd say something else.

Dvigrad, dead. The thought returned to her, unwelcome and pressing.

His face darkening, Nagarath eased himself up off the ground. Leaning heavily on his staff as he limped towards the doorway, he called back over his shoulder, "Liara, you'll find that all parts of the castle are now open to you. However, I would ask that you refrain from going out of doors until I can sort out what happened to the enchantments at work outside Parentino. And please, try not to do anything stupid while I am in my workroom looking for a way to better separate my personal magick from the direct maintenance of our defensive spells."

Liara obeyed. In fact, she did not move at all, in spite of Parentino with all its exciting nooks and crannies fully opened to her at last. Instead, she looked in on herself and frowned.

Dvigrad, buried and gone.
Why could she feel nothing? Not even shed one tear?

Chapter Ten

Never had the walk up the winding steps to his workroom tower seemed so long. In spite of his urgency, Nagarath stopped no less than three separate times on his way up. Finally gaining the landing, he raised his hand to lift the wards from the room, then stopped. He'd already undone them with his promise to Liara.

What in the world were you thinking, idiot? Letting that curious cat wander about freely, after all you've done to dissuade her from it. Nagarath entered his workroom, shaking his head at himself as he crossed the room and sat at his large work table. *Well, you oaf, you were thinking that if you were going to trap the girl inside, she might at least have the most inside to inhabit.*

"Do you have it in you, mage?" Nagarath muttered, finding that the challenge of animosity, even self-created, often did much to goad him onward. It was a useful trick for a lazy man like him to employ, though today he didn't feel indolent so much as spent. He honestly was unsure whether he had the power at hand to do much of anything after what he'd spent in Dvigrad and in returning home.

He closed his eyes, taking deep breaths to steady his mind before he launched his Art out in every direction, the dull glint of his aura gently touching every corner of Parentino. It felt good to feel the ebb and whirl of the magick through stone and soil as his mind approached the borders of his defenses. No cracks. No inconsistencies.

The Bookminder

That, at least, was something. With Liara's description of how the spells had hit her when they'd churned into motion, he'd been concerned that something had gone wrong, that perhaps there was a chink in the armor. *Or something worse.*

A niggling thought circled the edge of consciousness, a complicated arithmetic of minutiae: the positioning of bodies, the smell of the air, the casual absence of at least one patrol of Venice's soldiers. Details he'd not been allowed to fully explore once the flash of Parentino's enchantments had called him back to the castle in a rush of fear.

Withdrawing his questing mind back to himself, Nagarath let his eyes flutter open.

The defenses really were a cobbled-together mess, an ungainly grouping of ideas growing over time to become what they were that day.

"They do work, though," he murmured to himself, rising to cross the room.

Inside Parentino, he had made a veritable maze of realities—Liara had tripped more than one of them in her time there. But then, those defenses were meant to confuse and frustrate unwanted guests, not harm them.

But something had to have occurred to activate the courtyard spells . . . again, unless Liara was less than forthcoming as to the sequence of events. He recalled his tumultuous return to Parentino's library, Liara's look of surprised guilt. Caught in the act, book in hand. No, her story—vague feelings of menace and magick—simply did not add up. With Parentino's wards connected to his art, he'd be able to tell if there were an outside force that meant ill. The trouble was in Dvigrad, not here at home.

He told himself again: what he'd witnessed was natural, if tragic.

Dvigrad. *They're all dead.*

Memories of bodies, of the stench of life gone rotten, assailed him anew. Familiar faces gone still, pain written on each and every one. The silence of cook fires gone cold. Death. Death everywhere.

Too many things at once.

Weeping, Nagarath leaned heavily against his worktable. *Too late, too late. Always too late.*

"All the power in the world..."

Never mind that he hadn't taken an active role in Dvigrad's safety since securing Liara under his roof. But then, that was the problem, wasn't it? He couldn't do two things properly. Either one or the other would suffer—more often than not, both. And so he ignored what was the least pressing to him. And always: consequences.

His mangled thoughts found a voice and became a scream, raw and jagged. Jolting forward, Nagarath swept his hand across the table, scattering scrolls and spell components. Snarling, he eyed the large swath of his wrath. "Twenty years a mage and still making messes."

He arced his other arm across the table, his sleeve raking against his careful array of glittering bottles, knocking over books and spilling ink. Turning, he poured his anger out on the shelves lining the walls, blindly pulling at anything his hands caught on as he savaged the workroom. The masonry rang with the rattle and ping of porcelain shattering on stone. Paper tore and crumpled. Curios of metal and mineral rang out, crying ablution into the brief, violent dissonance. And then all was silent, save for Nagarath's own heavy breathing. The snap of broken glass underfoot drew his eyes downward, clearing his sight that had gone black with grief and anger.

Dvigrad dead and patrols of soldiers gone missing. How could Venice not look to Limska Draga and ask hard questions? The valley's sole survivors a magick-user and a girl accused of witchcraft? It was all too convenient, if you asked him.

With every knock and slight against the girl, it had long seemed to Nagarath that the town had wanted disaster to visit once more. He'd told the priest as much some ten years before. If they wanted magick to forget them, they had to let it. Stop pelting it with stones and challenging it to a duel.

But, they never listened. They discounted all Nagarath's warnings. How did one explain vague feelings of ill-boding, visions, and scrying to a people who had closed their collective mind to magick?

"But should we have dealt with the child differently? Could I have taken her in and raised her as my own? Could I have forgone magick myself to protect her and everyone else from it?"

He could not have.

And to lay waste to everything around him, to give in to despair, to weakness, would not serve anyone. Chastised, he made his way to one of the armchairs, waving a hand weakly at the mayhem he'd created. The detritus of his outburst skittered into a tidy pile; his workbench cleared itself in fits and starts.

Now was not the time to assign blame or even attempt to figure out what had happened. The priority was Liara. As it had always been. There would be time to go back to Dvigrad and see with new eyes what had really happened. In the meantime, he must first find a way to untangle the knotted snarl of spells he'd woven about Parentino, lest they should be tested further.

~*~

Night fell, and still Nagarath had not come down from his tower. Nor had he touched the now-cold mugs of tea and accompanying bread and honey that Liara had left by his threshold. Ear to the door, she could tell that Nagarath had thrown himself into his work after a brief rest. Worry about his overexertion had led her to prepare the aforementioned meals, but now it seemed as if her master was resting again. Waiting outside the hallway in trepidation, Liara finally nerved herself up to the possibility of disturbing a distraught mage at work. Creaking the door open with utter care and quiet, Liara looked in.

He was asleep.

Slumped on his stool, head lolling to the side, his was the sleep of the deeply exhausted. The shattered remains of a small earthenware pot lay at his feet, the wizard having slept through the sound of its breaking.

Leaving the precariously perched sleeper to the whims of gravity, Liara decided it was time that she, too, get some rest, though the afternoon had already proven to her that rest was not something she would easily find.

She felt dried up and empty. Lost. Her first action upon Nagarath's abrupt leaving for his workroom had been to glance back over the book of wards she still held in her hand. There had been a momentary temptation to try casting a second spell, just to see if she could. But then the words of the wizard returned to her. It would be

The Bookminder

a terrible thing if she accidentally interfered with the magicks he was working on in his tower.

Liara had spent much of the rest of the day staring out a third story window at the hint of Dvigrad's distant battlements, trying to feel something, anything, for the people who had died there. However, the hollow feeling remained, and no tears came.

The grief came at her in the night, unexpected and unwanted. Having slipped into slumber at long last, Liara awoke to find hot tears streaming over her cheeks and dotting her pillow, full of remorse and anger at herself for time wasted. She could taste the bitterness over her petty pride and stubborn determination to not simply blend in with her fellow villagers, to help them past their mistrust.

Her home. Her people.

Liara sat up in the dark night, wiping her face clear of the torrent that, once begun, would not stop. Trembling fingers grasped at the edge of the covers, pulled them up around her, as if she could bury herself from the pain washing over her in waves.

Had death come swiftly? Or had it been awful, drawn out, painful? Fresh tears flooded Liara's eyes as she tortured herself, imagining each familiar face in turn. Father Phenlick, his kind, wrinkled smile gone still and pale. Piotr, whom she had seen but days before, and given little in exchange for his kindness. Even Old Woman Babić's face sprang up unbidden, frowning at her even in death.

Krešimir's face came last to her mind's eye. He lived outside of the walls. Had he, too, succumbed? Nagarath hadn't said. And yet, he had. *They're all dead. All of them, Liara.*

With a shudder, Liara realized that the only reason she hadn't also died was because they had cast her out. *I should have been there. Then they would have understood. Understood that, deep down, I was one of them.*

Even that was a lie. She hadn't been 'one of them' when she lived there. She had been a charity case, a pity friend. She remembered the last time she saw Krešimir, their impromptu meeting in the woods and those garish pink trees that had been the result. He had walked away, then.

Her hopes for him had all been folly. He would never have been hers, not with her history. Had he, too, thought as much? Had he thought of her as he died?

The tears fell faster still.

Liara rose from her bed, crossing to the window to stare out over the barren trees. Though on the wane, the moon still gave off enough illumination on the winter whiteness that she could see nearly all the way to Dvigrad.

A thought tickled at the back of her mind, a voice shouting at her from a great distance. Something about her last meeting with Krešimir. In the woods south of Parentino.

"I'm doing something for Father Phenlick." Liara whispered the words as reverently as if they were an incantation. A tremor shot through her. Krešimir had been leaving. But why?

Hope rose in her chest, choking her. Krešimir hadn't been home. Maybe. There was no way to know. Unless he came back.

The Bookminder

New tears blurred Liara's eyes, obscuring her view of the dark trees of Limska Draga. Climbing back into bed, she let the spark of hope sing her to a fitful sleep.

Chapter Eleven

Liara grimaced as she gingerly turned another page of the book she was assessing. It was a strange old thing. Its age-brittled folios were made from some sort of pressed leaf that gave off a faint sweet odor, and the contents written in a curious, slanting hand. Since discovering it in Nagarath's library, she'd never harbored hopes of replicating the unique materials, and hence preserve the book's inherent magick, but it was worth copying the text and noting the construction, should the opportunity ever later arise for her or Nagarath to make the work anew.

Though she exercised care, a zigzag fissure split the page in her hand, reaching the bottom edge with an audible snap. With a heavy sigh, Liara placed the severed half-page into the growing pile at her elbow.

Across the table, Nagarath flicked his eyes to her progress briefly before returning to his own volume.

Neither of them touched their breakfast.

Pursing her lips, Liara fixed her attention back on the damaged book. It was tense work, to be sure. Especially under the watchful of a mage who had clearly forgotten how much damage had come to books at his own hand.

But it was a tension born of concentration and care rather than that of the fear that Parentino had lived under of late. Though he'd meant the gesture kindly, Nagarath had taken to sharing, and it was driving Liara's imagination into all sorts of dark corners.

He shared his workings and the results—disappointing, more often than not. He confessed his fears: it turned out that Liara wasn't the only one questioning what had really tripped Parentino's defenses, though Nagarath had come to blame himself. Together, these revelations had served to raise tensions within the castle and force both wizard and ward to stay inside the keep's protective stones. The mage still hadn't found any sign of the missing soldiers from Dvigrad, leaving greater and more terrifying what if's hanging over their heads.

What if the soldiers had been attacked? What if whatever killed Dvigrad came back? Nagarath maintained that there was something unnatural in the way plague had taken the village. It was so sudden, so absolute.

What if it was all a trap, a manufactured excuse to come down upon the magick users of Limska Draga with the might of the Republic? Or, perhaps it was something infinitely more sinister, the workings of a rival mage, intent on the wonders of Nagarath's library now that the collection was slowly being restored. He could even believe that rumor of Limska Draga's recluse mage had reached far-off ears. Questing magicks, being blanket enchantments, could very well account for both the death in Dvigrad—a sort of poisoning or curse—and the triggering of Parentino's outer defenses.

This latest theory was Nagarath's favorite. The mage explained to Liara that the wizarding world was small. Most every sorcerer of pedigree knew from where his fellows hailed. And many of them stole the secrets of his or her magely brethren. It was how the craft advanced, in fact. Fear of theft provided no better impetus for honing one's skills in hexes and counter spells. And Nagarath's secrets were most definitely worth stealing.

But now, nearly a week after the discovery of the tragic circumstances in Dvigrad, none of the mage's dire predictions had come true. Not that Liara wanted a troop of soldiers or an avenging wizard storming Parentino, but it made being stuck inside the castle seem . . . silly.

Although of course, the recent events were no laughing matter. Even now, Liara had yet to bring her profusion of tears under control, but these she took great pains to conceal from Nagarath. And so they had entered the days of hidden tears and brave smiles . . . and working at the breakfast table. Another page cracked under her gentle fingers. She had to grit her teeth to stop herself from cursing aloud.

A loud crash rattled the table, and Liara looked up just in time to see Nagarath darting towards her. Reaching out, he grabbed her arm, pulling her to her feet. She was halfway through the door and into the hallway within the space of a breath. But she had little time for annoyance at the manhandling.

"Liara, please, as you value your life, I beg of you to go to the topmost floor and hide yourself in one of the rooms. Do not come out until I call for you. And please, for the love of all, do not even think of doing that trick with the warding spell again. For I might be called upon to do some serious hexes, in a moment, and do not desire having to adjust to unexpected magicks."

Eyes on Nagarath's face, Liara's indignation dissolved into profound fear. The wizard's wand was out. And his hands were shaking. He did not have to ask her

The Bookminder

again. Fleeing, she hitched up her skirts, taking the stairs two at a time, trying not to think about what had frightened Nagarath so deeply.

Gaining the topmost landing, she turned and looked back, hesitant. But the urgency—the desperation—in Nagarath's face, his voice, had followed her up the stairs. She ran to the nearest unlocked room, her heart pounding so that she could hear nothing outside its panicked hammering.

Standing alone in the dark, she looked to the shuttered and draped window. Her fingers fairly itched to tear open the coverings. And yet she could not, lest her action be noted by . . . *By what? What is out there?*

Fretfully, she paced in silence, ears straining for any clue as to what was going on below.

The hissing scrape of metal on metal lanced through her spine, unnerving her. Muffled grunting followed, and Liara hurried to the window. Another clank of metal confirmed it. She knew those sounds. Swords being unsheathed, the hard slap of wrist or shin guard striking stone—these were signs she knew from countless times spent slipping in and out of Dvigrad for clandestine visits to her tree. Soldiers.

Men who had torched that selfsame tree. And no Father Phenlick to defend her this time. Liara could just see them now, hard-faced men eager to finish what they'd started months before. A squad of four—no, she recalled, five—soldiers, worn but intent as they marched on Parentino's ruins, scrambling along its tumbled border stones, alert for any sign of the wizard.

But it didn't sound as if they were attacking so much as exploring. And arguing. Puzzled, she settled in the window ledge to listen, hugging her arms tightly.

"Nothing here. Like I said."

"Keep searching."

"Does this pile of stone look like somewhere a man could live?"

In her hidden alcove, a thrill fluttered up from the soles of Liara's feet. She recognized those voices. Men-at-arms she'd lived alongside in Dvigrad. Were they here for her? Or Nagarath? She allowed herself a secret smile. Weed choked and collapsing in on itself, she'd thought much the same thing when she'd gazed upon Parentino her first night as an exile, had felt the same foreboding that surely flickered over the men's helmed faces.

"Well, the witchcraft has to have a source. With evidence of his black doings all over Dvigrad, and since the only man who used to come a-callin' on the wizard is dead..."

Piotr, Dvigrad's apothecary. A lump rose to choke her as Liara remembered Nagarath's illusory but snug cottage, the last time Liara had seen anyone from town alive and well.

"Sorcery or not, remember the mage will have the girl with him."

"In any case, with no one left to tell of what we found in that village, I say we ought to report—" A man's terrified scream cut the sentence short. The sounds of boots scrambling on rock mingled with the rallying cries of the small patrol. Swords and shields raised, the soldiers rallied, crossing Parentino's tumbled borders, closing in.

"Fly at him, men!"

"The black devil!"

Nagarath!

Liara mouthed the name in the dark, raising her hands on impulse, ready to cast the spell that would give her Sight. No. Nagarath needed none of her distractions. But if he had been discovered by the soldiers, there was little point in keeping hidden. She had to know. She had to see. Grasping the heavy curtains, she leapt back as something hit the shutters, hard.

"Witchery! See how my arrow was stopped in mid-air?"

Quaking, Liara backed away from the window, her mind filled with the images of the angry men, their hatred of her and of her mage. Grateful for the wayward arrow that had stopped her hasty actions, she clasped trembling fingers together.

She could see altogether too well with merely the sounds drifting up from below. The men were gaining the inner courtyard. They were now past the stone column that stood at its center. The violent scuffle ended in the twanging of another bow. And then nothing.

Nagarath! Only her hands, pressed hard against her mouth, could keep her from screaming his name aloud. Horrified, Liara could only wait in the darkness, willing her heart to stop thumping so loudly so that she might hear more.

"It was naught but another of those damned birds. Natural causes, you'd said? Bah! The whole valley is bewitched. I bet it is that girl, mark my words. She's come back to make sure we all feel her wrath."

The rumble of sliding rocks and more muttered curses drifted up, background to Liara's shuddering relief. The soldiers were retreating, picking their way gingerly back to less rocky terrain having done little more than terrified themselves over an impetuous crow. Another of the men grumbled his discontent, "Should have gone to the cottage, not this tumbled heap of stone."

Leave Krešimir out of this. Dead or no, his friendship to her was no crime. *Finish them off, Nagarath. I want them gone.* Liara's fingers clenched and unclenched at her sides, anger burning away her fear.

The crashing clang of metal came accompanied by the dull roar of yet another small rockslide. "I'm down!"

Venice's finest, and they cannot navigate a rock pile without falling all over themselves. Liara smirked.

Pandemonium broke out in the yard below, drawing Liara once more to the dark and shuttered window, her smug smile buried under rekindled fears. Incoherent shouting rose to her strained ears. Not a retreat then, but a rallying cry: fearful and desperate men, rushing to the aid of their fellow soldier.

They had to be stopped! Didn't Nagarath see that? Her own nerves frayed to breaking, Liara sank to her knees, listening hard as the soldiers' bold challenge became a blubbering groan, punctuated with the clanking of arms being thrown aside. *Dear God, what had the wizard done to them?*

Somewhere downstairs, a door banged open within the castle.

In the skirmish, Nagarath had missed one of the soldiers!

Jumping to her feet, Liara ran for the hallway. The soldiers' noise faded behind her as she reached the top of the stairs. Another sharp report reverberated through the stones of Parentino, adding further to her urgency.

The Bookminder

"I told you to stay put until I called you!"

Nagarath's angry rebuke drifted up at her over the frantic patter of her footsteps. She could see his pale face and the gem atop his staff, glittering in the magelight that flickered at his side. She froze, moving only when he beckoned an instant later.

With a cry halfway between a sob and a hiccup, Liara flung herself into his arms. "I was afraid. I heard the soldiers. I heard them talking. They said I did this. They said the valley is bewitched. They—"

A comforting hand stroked her hair. He smelled of sorcery. And rage. It was calming, to be in the presence of that much power. Reluctantly, Liara extracted herself from his arms.

Something didn't feel right. He seemed upset. Or, more accurately, bewildered. She hurried to make amends. "I'm sorry."

"Hush. They will not return, I can promise you that. We are safe."

Can you promise safety, mage? You've been doing that for years. George Phenlick's protection from military prosecution in exchange for keeping Dvigrad safe, hidden from those who might take interest in their strange fey child. And look at all that has happened. Like the girl, you have a knack for—a history of—attracting trouble—and put countless others in danger as a result.

He hadn't exaggerated when he'd explained to Liara how closely knit the community of magick-users was. One could find even the great Merlin—famously a recluse—if he looked hard enough. Nagarath had long acknowledged to himself that finding a way to hide from his brethren would be costly. But he hadn't counted on collateral damage, such as the fate Dvigrad had suffered.

He turned hooded eyes on his workroom, whispering the word that would illuminate the sole lamp upon his table. The components for dark magicks glittered in his Sight.

Temptation. Compromise.

What he'd done to Dvigrad's soldiers was going to haunt him. But then, he'd known that when he'd chosen to cast his first spell against them. Enchantments of the blackest sort; a part of him wondered from what dark corner he'd dreamed up the demons that he'd projected into the men's minds. *Likely the same corner where fear for Liara lives.*

Outside, a simple glamour shielded the castle's true state from prying eyes—admittedly, not an effective defense. Someone with a strong enough will could easily bypass the simple illusion. It was mere chance that the soldiers had lacked the conviction to see Parentino as it truly was.

"Though, I learned today that those men hadn't a single penetrating thought amongst them." Nagarath spoke through gritted teeth remembering the men's terror, his eyes squinting to read the dusty bottles deep within a recessed wall shelf. "But that may not always be the case."

If only they'd have just gone away. Again, Nagarath lamented his actions. *It's their fault for having come upon us so suddenly, forcing my hand.* He shuddered to think how closely he had come to attacking the men outright, the appropriate curses having come readily to his mind even as he'd ushered Liara up the stairs and out of sight. *But then, mental distress can be as damaging as physical*, he reminded himself, unable to look away from the spell components on his table, a glittering line of guilt.

What was done was done. No changing it now. And with as little information as he'd been able to gather in the town before flying back to Parentino in a blink, the knowledge he'd gleaned from the men's terror-struck minds had been most welcome. He'd had no choice but to send them away as gibbering idiots once he'd found that they planned on making for the coast to report Dvigrad's fall, implicating magick.

Not that they might have been far off. If the timeline he'd witnessed in the men's collective memories was correct, the plague that had hit Dvigrad had come and gone too quickly. The soldiers hadn't caught it, for example. Additionally, he'd been able to see once and for all just how isolated the town had been. There was no logical way for such a disease to have come upon the town. In some ways, he was grateful for having taken the tack he had with the assailants.

Compromise in the service of morality. Nagarath's thoughts circled around to his early days as a mage. At one point, he wouldn't have questioned, merely acted, entitlement and need guiding his power. But then, he'd been taught that way—he and his fellow apprentices. Archmage Cromen would scoff to see where Nagarath's delicate sense of fairness had taken him.

Of this I can be proud, even if my spells are a hodgepodge mess, uneven as a poorly knit scarf.

Nagarath despised the idea that he might have to bespell the woods around him, to do outside the grounds of Parentino what he had done on the inside. Interfering with the senses of mere passersby beyond straightforward illusion was too dirty a magick for his tastes. It was unwarranted meddling, an attack rather than a defense.

Much like what you just did to Dvigrad's last patrol?

At this, he hesitated in his casting, his hand poised above the pages of his spell book.

"No, nothing so drastic as that."

Hesitation, the weighing of right and wrong: that was the difference, what set him apart from the other mages, the dark mages who wouldn't think twice before performing such a curse and would laugh at him for his sensitivity.

"And it matters, damn it." Satisfied that he still could see the shadowy border between light and dark magicks—and could weigh the consequences of both—Nagarath had his answer.

Grabbing half a dozen of the tiny bottles—spell components that had traveled the world with him, exotics he hardly dared touch in his more mundane spellwork—Nagarath crossed back to his work table. He'd already started down this path; there was little he could do to change it now.

Uncorking various bottles and carefully setting the stoppers aside, he straightened. Thinking, setting aside all other concerns save magick, he sought the proper course. The enchantments would not be all that terrible to construct. Invisibility was easy, and he could use his labyrinth of spells from inside Parentino as a pattern for what he would spread outward into the nearby wood.

"Nobody, not a single person, will be able to find us,

then," Nagarath intoned darkly.

Would it solve the problem? Would it set straight Dvigrad's soldiers, men who had leapt to disastrous conclusions and might very well expose the valley to Venice's wrath? Would it bring Dvigrad back? No. But it would keep Liara safe. And at the moment, that was all he cared about.

Would it explain what happened in the village?

Nagarath thrust the unwelcome thought from him. There would be time to sort through the soldiers' memories later. They were a fearful lot; perhaps some of what they'd sensed had been a product of inflamed imaginations, dull as theirs might be. Never mind that it played to the fears he already held.

Promises, Nagarath.

The work was slow, as he also had to maintain the old defensive spells while he wove the new. It would take some time to figure out how to remove himself from their direct maintenance later on. Right now, the important thing was Liara's safety.

Raising his hands to cast his first spell, another tremor of fear shot through him. A memory. One that refused to leave him be. That whisper of power against his own, a brush of foreign magicks as he had entered Dvigrad.

Chapter Twelve

The cellars are scoured, the library is spotless, the great room is swept and polished. And the kitchen? As tidy as it could ever be. Liara stomped about, trying to make certain that the mage heard her annoyance.

She could swear that Nagarath had moved all of his potions work down into the dining area. And each time she cleaned everything up, it came right back. Two bottles at a time, she shifted the arcane ingredients to the far end of the large oaken table, trying not to think about what they contained. Most of his spell components had a patina of contents encrusted down the sides, pasting years of dirt to their surface. She considered it a small blessing that many of the labels were obscured by the crust of Nagarath's patent carelessness.

Drawn, presumably, by her clamor, Nagarath appeared in the doorway, an inquisitive look giving color to his otherwise pale face. The scolding Liara had prepared died on her lips. Her mage looked awful. But then, he'd looked that way for weeks. Ever since he'd come back from Dvigrad, delivering the devastating news.

At her quiet smile, Nagarath entered the kitchen, giving Liara better opportunity to assess his health. She eyed with misgiving the small tremor in his hands, the skittish twitch of his eyes, as he rummaged about in everything she'd just painstakingly moved. Three weeks ago, she had come to believe he'd truly caught the plague—days of his color not improving, energy getting lower. Even his humor had gone out of sorts and not come back. But it had all turned out to be something to do with the castle defenses. Even after his supposed tweaks.

When pressed, Nagarath had tried to explain—the usual verbal flood while he pinched the bridge of his nose and stared off into the distance. His familiar behavior alone had gone far in securing Liara's relief. And although the explanatory speech felt stilted, his lecture had ended in good advice: keep busy.

And so she had, finding that even dark thoughts of Dvigrad were sweetened slightly by the idea that she was, in many ways, paying homage to Father Phenlick's memory with all of her hard work. She could imagine the look of mock-horror on the old priest's face if he saw her systematic scrubbing for days on end. His Liara, purposely doing housework? After all the effort she'd expended in avoiding such tasks for the past decade?

But that amusement had run its course when Liara ceased to find useful tasks.

Turning abruptly, Liara bumped into the mage.

"Hey." The monosyllabic complaint came out harsher than intended.

"Hey, yourself."

He was teasing her. She was certain of it. And she was not in the mood to play along—especially as she saw that he'd dumped something very foul-smelling into the cauldron she'd just gotten clean.

"Gah! You're a mess. Do you know that? Is that your plan, Nagarath? Keep me stuck inside so you have a handy servant to clean up after your endlessly unkempt sorcery?" She wrinkled her nose. "Our supper comes out of that pot."

"That was not 'my plan,' no. If you haven't noticed, I, too, am stuck inside Parentino."

"You're a wizard. Fix your stupid spells."

Nagarath opened his mouth, then shut it, turning away from her. She moved to apologize, stopping as he waved his hand over the pot, murmuring a sharp incantation. The glob of putrid potion lifted itself into the air, quivering before the mage sent it skittering out the door—also opened via his magick. "Better?"

"I meant the castle."

"I know what you meant." He still hadn't turned back towards her.

Torn, Liara held a quick, silent debate: apology, or explanation? Neither came to fruition as Nagarath took advantage of her silence, turning to her at last and fixing her with those piercing eyes of his. "Years of effort have gone into defending my position in Limska Draga. To undo it at the snap of my fingers? Not possible. As complex as my system of wards has become, most any solution I rush into would be the wrong one and could well expose us to what is out there. Or it could very well collapse the castle into the ruins it pretends to be. I opened Parentino to you. Please be content with that until the danger has passed."

Danger. The tingle at the base of Liara's spine threatened, as it always did at Nagarath's mention of the word.

She knew danger. In fact, it had so far kept her from exploring the breadth of Parentino. Memories of magick—squeezing, stabbing at her heart and lungs—still haunted her dreams. Three times she'd awoken in the night, sweating and fearful it was happening all over again. But she'd submit to a month of sleepless nights before she admitted that to the mage.

"I'm bored. And I'm bored of being bored." She bounced on her toes. "I've cleaned until my fingers have bled and read until my eyes have gone crossed. I need something to do."

"Run up and down the hallways; climb the stairs. It'll be good for you. And tire you out."

And keep me out from underfoot, is that it? She glared at the wizard.

Run the hallways. She'd as soon curl up and die.

Didn't he understand? She needed fresh air, open sky. Every time she saw a shuttered and curtained window, she could feel the ire boil up, fresh and sharp. Granted, the weather had taken the opportunity to turn bitter, snow and ice coating the castle in turn. But looking longingly at the forbidden outdoors, Liara couldn't help but wish for a little bite of frost on the nose and chilled fingers, if only for the variety.

And if only to put to rest her own growing fears.

Of the two of them, Nagarath was the talkative one. To have him increasingly lost in his own ruminations, shutting her out and shuffling her off to the furthest reaches of Parentino with his silly suggestions. . . . Again, the dark specter of Dvigrad rose in her mind: Nagarath's ill-expressed concerns that kept them trapped in the castle.

In the end, Liara ran the stairs, if only to spite Nagarath with her persistence. And because every time she did so, he had to use a different staircase lest he be trampled in her exuberance.

You see, Nagarath? This is me trapped inside. Huffing, Liara rounded the top of the spiral staircase—the one that they'd used the first time she saw Nagarath's library. Though she would never have admitted it, it did feel good to get her pulse pounding by means other than nightmares and half-formed fears. But she was still mad at the mage, anger fueling her steps as she turned to descend back to the main floor.

This is me after weeks of no fresh air. No sunshine. Nothing new save for— Liara tripped, throwing her hands out in front of her instinctively as the stairs rushed up to meet her. Pain flared in wrists, knees, hips and shoulders as she twisted, trying to catch herself and prevent a full tumble down the flight. The entire mishap was over in the space of three steps, the sharp curve of the tower doing as much to break her fall as her bruised limbs. Crumpled, she lay unmoving, tears springing to her eyes.

Predictably, Nagarath was there. She heard his echoing steps but an instant before the man himself was at her side. "Liara—!"

"It's your fault, you know." She carefully shifted into a seated position, hissing as her left wrist gave a painful twinge. Quickly assessing the damage, she noted that, in addition to her screaming wrist, both hands were skinned as well as her knees. And she was pretty sure she was about to have a very colorful set of bruises on her hip and head from where she'd glanced off the wall.

"My fa—?"

"You made me run the stairs."

Liara watched the anger roll across Nagarath's brow,

a swiftly passing storm replaced almost immediately by bright concern. Wincing, she saw no apology was needed for her unfounded accusation, as the wizard gently sent his magelight to hover between them, allowing him to better assess her injuries.

"That I did." He smiled, grim. "I did not, however, instruct that you should fall down them."

Nodding, Liara tried to smile through her tears as Nagarath gently took hold of her left arm. The fact that he avoided touching—or even directly moving—her wrist was telling.

"I'll need to see if this is broken or merely a sprain."

Closing her eyes tight, she dipped her head in acknowledgment. A gentle warmth skipped across her knuckles, swirling down along the hollow of her wrist to climb halfway to her elbow. Nagarath's magick. She opened her eyes, taken aback.

"I'm not so far stretched that I cannot do things properly, Liara." He spoke through gritted teeth, reading her surprise. "But we are lucky. It is not fractured, merely badly twisted. This I can treat with what medicines we have in the cellars. Come."

Helped to her feet, Liara descended the rest of the stairs with care. Fears allayed, she felt her restless frustration return as Nagarath bade her sit in the kitchen and went to forage the meticulously tidy cellars. She tried to distract herself from the sounds of the wizard overturning her careful cleaning by checking over which of her garments had been damaged in her tumble.

Long minutes later, the mage returned. A glance at his empty hands told Liara that he hadn't found what he sought. She waited, wisely keeping her silence, as Nagarath gave the door to the courtyard a long, sullen look. The battle waged in his face was fierce but short. He turned his eyes back on her, forcing a smile. "If you'll forgive me, my little magpie, it would appear that I must employ more spells on your sprain than I would like. We seem to be completely out of that which would otherwise have limited my magickal involvement."

"Maybe you don't have to? I mean, it's not as if there's a garrison of soldiers knocking down our gates right now. You could just go—"

"Enough. Please, Liara." The look on his face forced her silence.

A month's worth of fears pressed at her, jostling aside the pain from her fall. There was something he still wasn't telling her. Pushed to the point of breaking, why else would he be so stubborn on this point of barricading them in the castle?

Piotr could have fixed it without magick.

Liara gulped back the unexpected flood of emotions. *But Piotr is dead.*

Dvigrad is dead. And I'm alive.

Alive. What did that even mean?

Ice water flooded her veins as she looked at her skinned right palm. "Nagarath, am I a real person?"

Startled, his sharpness retreated into academic curiosity. "Whatever in the world prompted such a question?"

She lifted her hand in illustration. "Well, there's no blood. It's just pink and scraped. There's supposed to be blood. What if I'm not anyone at all? What if I'm just some sort of spell run amok, and everything that has happened is because of me?"

"Oh, my little magpie." Nagarath sat down, gently

taking her injured wrist in his hands. "You are very much alive. As much as me."

She knew that. But the rash words were out, forced by pain.

"Do you wish to know how I know that you are your own person, not some animated puppet?"

He knew her well. Glad that she didn't have to explain, Liara nodded.

"Well, then." Nagarath's eyes sparkled with that intense yet distant gleam Liara had come to associate with an avalanche of instruction bearing down on her. The warmth of the mage's healing spell crept into her fingers and bled up into her arm. Blushing, she looked away, focusing on the wood of the table so that she might better hear him speak.

"There are a myriad of spells that only give the semblance of life—a far cry from the real thing. The words of binding that infuse magick into a body, for example, are but a poor mage's substitute for spirit. A creature created thusly will be animated, but not living.

"There are many degrees between having movement and being truly alive. It takes a powerful spell to call a true soul to your bidding, and, while that gives life, such a life is incomplete when compared to you or me. Most who are called from other realms only inhabit and control the body they are granted. But a spirit in a body cannot make blood flow through veins or lungs breathe. They cannot feel pain—emotional or otherwise. It is why wizards cannot truly raise people from the dead or grant immortality."

His eyes grew hard. "This is why some choose to pervert the living. A live minion always has more self-preservation instincts than a spirit who merely controls a body. But it has its costs—a lack of complete control, for one. The mage who attacked your home seventeen years ago had that problem with the minions he summoned. Had he employed non-living, animated spirits, not only would he have retained control of them, they wouldn't have had sufficient life to bring you into the world." Nagarath trailed off.

"They weren't demons or ghosts, then?" Liara spoke without lifting her eyes from the table. "They . . . those things that attacked my mother, the village . . . they were real, living creatures?" She shuddered, looking up to lock her dark gaze to Nagarath's. "Do you know what they were?"

Nagarath did not answer straight off, clearly uncomfortable delving into the past. But to his credit, he continued, "Based on what I see in your aura, I'd guess they were something dreamt up by the mage who controlled them—a perversion of another creature, similar enough to us that they could sire a human child. Likely something akin to werewolves."

"Werewolves?" The word distracted her from thoughts of Dvigrad and her mother, and the tales of the townsfolk. "But you said they don't exist."

"I never said *werewolves* didn't," Nagarath smiled encouragingly.

"Explain."

"Well. The records are a tad muddy from the passage of time and too many historians, but the theory is that a wizard created the first werewolves and promptly lost control of them, or left them to their own devices. At any rate, the first werewolves managed to procreate amongst

The Bookminder

themselves after reaching autonomy from the mage—"

"Autonomy?" Liara grew excited. "As in, the Laws of Magick Creatio . . ."

"Indeed." Nagarath smiled as Liara warmed to her favorite topic. "Magickal Law the Second: once the age of twenty has been reached, a subservient power gains autonomy and its signature is fixed. Meaning that twenty years after their creation, the magick of the werewolves became separate from that of the mage's own and were inherent to themselves.

"As you well know, per the Third Law, before that point, if the magick that created them was cut off—if the mage had died, for example—they would have also perished, and we would have ended up with a werewolf-free world. But this unknown person didn't, and so the creatures created more of themselves by . . . erm . . . natural means. So, this long-forgotten wizard created a new race of beings, and perhaps never noticed, but we cannot know for certain as we don't know who to credit."

"The same with vampires?" Liara eagerly added, sure now that she was getting the hang of it. This was the most she could remember Nagarath ever talking with her about the Laws of Creatio.

"No," he countered glibly. "That's a curse. And they aren't alive."

Liara let out an exasperated sigh. "You know, for someone who says they have little interest in this area of study, you do seem to know a lot about it. Explain."

"Er . . ." Nagarath tugged his nose, thinking for a moment before answering. "Well, they're a bit tougher, you see. Basically, they're animated corpses. But they're also cursed. Doubly cursed, really, in that they are stuck in their terrible nonexistence until beheaded and are endlessly driven to inflict the same curse on others via their thirst for blood."

"So . . . they desire to make more of them?"

"No, no." Nagarath tried another way. "The spirit inside—trapped in the undead but un-living body—desires life. And life is one's life blood, more or less. So the vampire craves blood, inadvertently—or purposely—spreading their curse to the living when they infect their victim's bloodstream, which kills the victim and spreads the problem further when that frustrated spirit walks the earth seeking life. It really is quite an interesting spell."

"Interesting? Sounds eerie and repulsive to me."

"Well, really," Nagarath pressed, brushing past Liara in his scholarly excitement, "vampires are animated corpses of men. Granted, they are enhanced men, but compared to your werewolves, they're pretty unaltered. Then this undead creature, this bespelled-to-seeming-life is again allowed to live twenty-plus years—whether by accident or design, we do not know. And *then* their spirits' insatiable need for life provides a convenient vehicle for passing on their bespelled fate. The wizard who caused that was either a genius or an idiot!"

Liara nodded. "So far, it seems the only concessions you're willing to make on the existence of magickal beings are ones that closely resemble humans and came about through evil intent—"

"Now, don't do that, Liara. These are documented facts. Go check that library of yours."

Liara opened her mouth to retort, noticing at long last that her wrist no longer hurt. Nor did her bruises or skinned hands and knees. She looked down to where her small hand lay entwined in the mage's own pale, thin fingers. Jerking her hand free lest he notice the sudden quickening of her pulse, she stammered her thanks. Yes, she was certainly very much alive.

Per the wizard's suggestion, she retreated to the safety of the library.

Chapter Thirteen

A hand on hers. Warm smile, warm sigh. Krešimir. Liara looked up into his eyes. Black hair. Long. Black hood. Nagarath!

Liara awoke to find Nagarath in the doorway to her room, his hand on the knob and a guilty expression on his face. "Sorry. Did I wake you?"

"What on earth are you doing in my room?" The mage's guilty look redoubled as Liara pointedly tugged her bedclothes up under her chin. Surprise came first to her, fear second. "Did something—?"

"Oh, no. Sorry. I just . . ." Nagarath ran a rueful hand through his unkempt hair. "I was just worried. That's all."

He looked terrible. Two dark smudges under his eyes marked the gray pallor that had become been so prominent on his face following her tumble down the stairs the previous week. His clothes hung limp and loose about him like—Liara hated herself for the comparison—one of his much-abused spell books.

"Please tell me you've slept. Or that you've at least eaten something," Liara scolded, still holding the quilts high around her.

Nagarath waved off her concern. "There is far too much that needs doing. And I sort of fell asleep without meaning to. I really must return to my workroom—provided, of course, that you're all right."

The sympathetic look he shot her was too much, and

The Bookminder

she scowled. "I'm fine." She wasn't. "But I think you're acting like an idiot. And if you return to your workroom without so much as one—"

Nagarath blinked in surprise at her outburst, then brightened. "How about you bring me something. To my workroom. And I will eat it, right there in front of you. So that you know I'm all right."

"Fine. Deal. Now go so I can get dressed."

Liara pulled on trousers with a violent yank, her scowl darkening. Invading her room, disturbing her sleep. Weren't even her private thoughts safe from him? Her dreams apparently were not.

Warm smile. Hand on hers.

"Krešimir." The whisper came fierce. Defiant. How dare the wizard creep in where he was not wanted. Her dreams were hers.

Dreams . . . Liara splashed the ice cold water of her room's basin on her face with unnecessary vehemence. She was as bad as the mage, jumping at every little thing. From whence had this fear of magick come? She was no idle dreamer. She was a doer. And on top of it, Nagarath had assured her that she was safe, that no spell of his would harm her.

Warm hands. Warm smile. Liara shook off the lingering fog of the dream, concentrating bright focus on the day ahead.

She was going to see the wizard's workroom!

Nagarath's workroom proved to be absolutely frigid. This, unfortunately, was the first and only thing Liara noticed for several moments upon finally gaining access to a real wizard's tower. Glancing upward, she almost dropped her tray of tea and toast. There was no ceiling.

Large flakes of snow swirled down out of the gray skies, and she instinctively reached up towards them, only for the crystals to disappear into the air above her head. Laughing at the oddness of it, she turned to see Nagarath observing her from his workbench.

"About three years ago, I had an unfortunate accident occur when developing some new spells," he explained.

Liara noted the scorched ring of stone surrounding the upper reaches of the room, along with the holes indicating where ceiling beams might once have been. Typical Nagarath.

He continued, shrugging, "And then I found the new arrangement convenient enough that I never bothered to repair it, for it solved the problem of how to access the sky directly for my nighttime experiments."

"What happens when it rains?" Liara asked, gaping up into the snow that never quite reached the ground.

"I've wards and enchantments placed on the room that—well, you can see what they do. They interfere with spellwork that needs access to the real sky, but then, I would not bother working such spells in bad weather." Nagarath waved the question aside, grabbing a large stuffed chair and shoving its pile of contents onto the floor. "Have a seat, Liara."

He turned to his still-shivering ward and slapped a hand to his forehead. "Oh, idiot me! I've again forgotten to see to it that you're properly equipped to deal with the oddities of my humble abode. If I may?"

Nagarath gently took hold of her hands and murmured under his breath. Shocking warmth seeped into her limbs until she felt as if she stood not in a drafty, open-aired room in mid-winter, but in a hall that had been heated and ventilated to her exact specifications. Nagarath nodded with satisfaction at her stunned reaction, explaining with some pride, "Those enchantments are of my own design. They work within the confines of this room to make it more livable—in a similar fashion to the enchantments I used to replace the roof, actually."

"It's amazing. Have you considered creating an enchantment that works outside of this room? It would save considerable effort . . ." Liara stopped, blushing under the stern eye of the wizard.

"Come, now. You know I don't go in for that sort of day-to-day shortcuts rubbish. I enjoy a pleasant, comfortable existence as much as the next person. But these magicks? They each have a cost. Take the spells that protect the room from the elements." He waved to the gently falling snowflakes in illustration, releasing her hands. With a jolt, Liara realized that not all of the warmth she'd felt a moment before had been the result of spellwork. She turned away quickly. Nagarath did not appear to notice, lost as he was in his lecture.

"Like our defensive spells, when first constructed, the workroom spells drew power from me—either directly or by draining power from objects created by myself. Now, this was only a temporary solution. You see, if I were to keep every spell tied back to myself, over time—" Nagarath trailed off as he turned to discover Liara's attention had wandered.

She found herself drawn to one of the room's bookshelves, a moth to the flame. Gently caressing the spine of a book bound in deepest black, she shivered and turned to the mage, questions awash in eyes bleak with fear. "Are these . . . ?"

"Yes, Liara. Those are spell books for the dark arts."

"Why would you have these?"

Nagarath approached her, face falling as she shied away. "You must understand . . . not all power ascribed to dark magick is necessarily evil. I have found that it pays to know all types of magickal Arts, even if one does not put them to use. However, I am aware that the price one pays for even the most nobly intended spells using dark powers is almost always too high."

"The price you pay is me." Liara looked from mage to books, still feeling their power pulling at her. Her voice came out a whisper. "I can feel them, Nagarath. Like the books in your library, but more so."

Nagarath nodded, his own reply soft. "Yes. I was very much aware. And I'm sorry for it. It is, in fact, the reason I would have you understand why I keep such books here, and warn you against ever attempting to utilize them in any way."

"Use them?" Liara sputtered, eyes flashing.

"Yes!" Nagarath thundered, pacing the room. "Your origin makes you susceptible to their pull. The spells in those books, the powers they command—they know you *as their own.* Your own inherited magickal signature resonates with them."

Nagarath stopped and knelt before her, his tone softened, kind, speaking as one would to coax forth a cat from the shadows. "I can see it now, right here in front of me. As we've talked, I've watched your magickal aura pulsing in cadence with the darker artifacts in this room."

The Bookminder

"Law the First of Magick Creatio: Magickal power mimics the Magickal signature of the originating or altering power," Liara dutifully recited, her voice calm and steady. "Show me."

"Now, Liara, I—"

"Show me." Tears sprang to her eyes, but did not fall. "Please."

With a sigh, Nagarath murmured a few words of magick, gently touching Liara's palms, then her temples.

Gasping, Liara watched as her skin erupted into sparkles. It was like gazing upon the snow on a sunny day. She raised her hands in front of her, amazed. She'd read about auras in her studies, had a working description of how they worked, what they looked like. One, in fact, saw something of them when testing the magickal power of an artifact. But she had never expected them to be so beautiful, so alive.

The aura—*my magickal signature*—pulsed in the air around her fingers. She glanced to the bookshelf next to her. There, the books arrayed on the shelves pulsed in cadence, emitting a dark, menacing cloud, one that seemed to suck the light out of everything it touched.

Averting her eyes, she saw that other items in the room had various auras of their own. Different colors, different consistencies—each one wrapped in its own little bank of colored fog. But none resonated with her aura quite like the books of dark magick.

Inspecting her own signature once more, she now noted the dark streaks, the anti-light that seemed to live within the brightness. With a cry, she looked away, jolting herself from Nagarath's touch and ending the spell.

"I'm . . . one of them. I mean, I knew that my father—" she stumbled over the word "—that he was evil, but I didn't know that I, too . . ."

"No . . . No, Liara. You are not evil. You are not a demon, or dark spirit." Awkwardly patting Liara on the back, Nagarath turned to logic for inspiration. "It's only your point of origin. You are fast becoming something of your own making, my little magpie."

Liara gulped back the tears still welling in her heart, wanting to believe the mage, his kind eyes and words. A thought occurred to her. "Nagarath, where is . . .?"

She trailed off, suddenly shy. It wouldn't be fair to ask him to repeat the spell. Not after she had ended it so abruptly. But it occurred to her that, wrapped up as she was in herself, she hadn't noted Nagarath's signature. No, that wasn't quite true, either. It was as if he simply hadn't had one.

Refocusing her eyes, Liara saw that the wizard had perched himself on the arm of his overstuffed chair, dutifully eating the breakfast she had made.

"See? I eat." Nagarath raised a slice of toast in a salute of sorts.

Liara nodded, a memory springing unbidden to her mind—that of a younger man sitting just so on the edge of Parentino's tumbledown wall, happily sharing a picnic Liara had packed. *Krešimir.*

Brightening, she realized that there might be more she could do for herself and Nagarath than make toast and tea. The words bubbled out before she knew what she was about. "He might not be dead."

"Who might not be?" Nagarath wiped crumbs from his fingertips, his brow darkening.

Blushing, for there was no turning back now, Liara

explained. "Krešimir. My . . . friend. He lived in the woods outside of Dvigrad."

"Now, Liara, we don't know that—"

"Listen!" Liara would not let herself be interrupted, her eyes alight. "When I did that thing with the trees—made them pink—Krešimir was there with me. He happened upon me and we talked. I asked him why he was out that far, of course. And he said he was on some sort of errand for Father Phenlick. So there's a chance that he might not have been in Dvigrad at all when . . . when—" She struggled to continue, then avoided the thought altogether. "And it means that Krešimir might have been off doing something that has to do with those soldiers you said weren't in the village."

She finished triumphantly, waiting on the mage's response.

~*~

Nagarath wanted Liara's words to make sense, wanted her to have some hope to cling to. He'd heard the catch in her voice when she'd called the boy her friend. But at the rest of her short report, he struggled to keep the worry out of his face.

There had been a witness to Liara's folly in the woods. Had Krešimir been traveling alone? He had certainly indicated as much to Liara. But her heart was in her eyes when she talked of the woodsman, so her judge of character was clouded on this instance.

And what was the errand to which Krešimir had professed? If he was on Father Phenlick's side but traveling away from Dvigrad, what did that portend? Had the soldiers moved to take over the town, wrest power from the priest? Wherein lay the danger now?

"Thank you, Liara," Nagarath sighed, and rose to his feet. The urgency of the magick he had yet to do that morning weighed heavily upon him. "I'm glad to think your friend may be safe."

He kept the sentiments kind but neutral, afraid that his growing misgivings could be read on his face. For all that Liara's words had come from a place of hope for her, to him they simply served to add to his already heightened fears.

What if he and the girl were the last survivors in a full-blown war on magick? If sending the soldiers away had been a ruse to draw closed the noose around Parentino? What if—? A tremor shot through him. What if Krešimir had run for help and returned to find Dvigrad empty? What if they blamed not Nagarath, but Liara?

Again, Liara's blind trust in Krešimir bothered him. Krešimir hadn't come forward to help the girl when she had needed him most. Nagarath had. And yet, here she was mooning over this boy. *I was right all along,* Nagarath concluded. *Liara has been so adrift her whole life that she'd trust just about anything told to her by a kind face.*

Resolving anew to keep her safe, he lost himself in his magick, never noticing Liara slipping quietly out of the room.

The library door opened with a bang, startling Liara so that she lost her page in the book she'd been reading.

The Bookminder

Annoyed at the interruption, she watched with a smirk of satisfaction as the mage looked around the room, clearly unable to find what he sought.

"I'm up here," she called from the upper balcony.

"Ah." He shielded his eyes and looked upward, the relief on his face evident even from across the library's dim space. Liara felt a momentary twinge of guilt for having worried him so. Still, it wasn't as if she was going to follow him around all day. She had work to do.

"Working or reading?" Nagarath smiled at the book in Liara's hand as she wound her way down the stairs to greet him.

"A bit of both. You know, most of your collection has proven to be quite salvageable." *Bit of a miracle, really,* she added silently. "But that, erm, special collection of yours near the door? It still hates me. Familiarity with my aura or not. I was reading to see if there was something we could do about that," she said, with a matter-of-factness stating she didn't care one whit what the crabby collection thought of her.

Nagarath threw back his head and laughed, the act animating him in such a way that Liara's smile turned genuine.

She went on in a rush, "Well, I was thinking we could employ some sort of perpetual slumber so they don't need to be chained."

Liara raised her hands, imitating the casting of a spell, "Can I, perhaps, enchant them? There are all sorts of curses that produce a near death state. I mean, it's not like we need them to be able to move around and threaten us when we try to use them," she finished lamely, wondering how close Nagarath would come to identifying the true angle of her question.

His growing frown spoke the answer. "In spite of the circumstances, and in spite of your stunning demonstration with your one warding spell, the answer is no. Magick is still forbidden you, Liara.

"Besides," he said, his words chosen carefully, his explanation delicate, "we don't hurt them, punish them, for what they are."

The gentle but kindly meant remonstrance piqued Liara's guilt for having even made such a suggestion. She could tell herself all she wanted that she'd only meant the books could be kept in a state of suspension, but they both knew her poorly worded explanation had meant something infinitely more sinister.

The mage continued, "You know that such a thing would be damaging to a book, and—"

"Damage done to a magickal book affects the workings of the magick within. I know, they'd be useless to you then," Liara snapped, not wishing to be lectured, or worse, coddled.

Nagarath adopted his academic tone regardless. "Not merely useless. Dangerous. There's no telling how a spell will behave when worked from a damaged spell book."

"All right, I get it. If you're not going to help me, though, then leave," she said, this last in response to the mage reaching over to grab a book—and it had to be the middle one—out of a stack of material Liara had put aside to sort.

"Are you asking for my help?" Nagarath's face brightened.

Liara opened her mouth to say that, no, she was just fine, but something in the wizard's tired gaze held her, and she paused. The man clearly needed a break. And right now, solitude wasn't working all that well for her, either. Her mind kept returning to Dvigrad, to the sparkling auras of Nagarath's workroom, and to the questions she had for him concerning it all. She found herself saying, "Sure. Just try not to make a mess of things, please."

Nagarath promptly sat, gesturing to the nearest stack of books. Liara nodded. "Help yourself. I'm trying to sort the practical from the historical and the purely informational, at present." With that vague instruction, she whisked herself back to the third floor to re-shelve the book she carried on magickal signatures.

So it was that she did not at first note what, exactly, the mage was doing to 'help' her.

Returning downstairs to commandeer a pile of her own to sort through, Liara's eyes widened as Nagarath tossed another book into the growing pile at his feet.

"Nagarath!" Rushing over, she smoothed crumpled pages and placed the volumes in an orderly stack. Affixing Nagarath with what he liked to call her 'librarian glare,' she shook her head in dismay. "Are you trying to make more work for me?"

Nagarath protested, "They're junk. Trash. Less than useless." He gestured to the items at his feet. "They're bad books, Liara."

"No such thing. Didn't you just say?" She gathered the books into her arms, holding them protectively close. "Just let me catalog them. There's some use for these, I'm sure."

"Yes, as doorstops," Nagarath muttered mutinously.

Liara tried to page through one of the books whilst keeping hold of her armful, and failed miserably. As a whole, these rejects of Nagarath's appeared to be in miraculously good shape—hence her having left them until now.

"Bah." Nagarath waved his hand in dismissal, his nose buried in another book. Shrugging, Liara turned to place the offending volumes on her table so she could better see what had so disgusted him. The thump of another book hitting the floor sounded behind her.

Whirling around, hands on her hips, she frowned at the man and the book at his feet. He gestured to the item in question. "Be my guest. Don't expect me to use them, though. Fairy stories, all of them."

Great, this again. Liara rolled her eyes. "Did you ever stop to think there may be something to them?"

"There's not," he retorted flatly. "They damage the reputation of magick. They promise overmuch magick's capabilities, either scaring people needlessly or raising too high their expectations of what it can do."

Liara looked at the growing pile of rejects, wondering why—for someone uninterested in such books—there were so many in his collection. But then, Nagarath's library was much like his spellwork: a hodge-podge. He'd once told her he'd purchased an entire lot of old junk because of a rumor that it might contain one magicked book. She wondered where he got the resources for it.

However, he had explained one of the best things about collections gathered through lots rather than individually: such bulk methods of transfer often kept extraordinarily rare items safe from thieves and vandals. If Nagarath did not want his incidental fairy story collections, who was she to argue? She set them onto a crate to deal with later.

The Bookminder

Liara went to work on a pile of books dealing with necromancy, only for another ungainly crash of bound volumes to assault her ears a moment later. Looking up at the mess, she caught Nagarath in mid-step, a pile of books scattered over the floor.

"If you aren't going to help, at least refrain from working at cross-purposes," she scolded, noting that the tumbled stack was of medium-rare materials she'd admittedly been putting off working with, due to their relatively boring contents. No damage done there.

"Sorry. I couldn't reach." Sheepishly, Nagarath grabbed the codex off the shelf he'd been reaching for, raising it by way of explanation. He thumbed through the book, eyes alight. "I had no idea I even *had* this!"

"And if you'd just let me work, you'd know about *all* the books in this mess," Liara sighed.

"You asked for my help, little magpie," Nagarath muttered from behind his book.

Liara looked over the crumpled piles in despair. "A request I'm beginning to regret."

Nagarath left Liara alone in the library at long last, walking out with an armful of books and a faraway look. She hated seeing him go—the light banter had felt like a return to simpler times, back before she'd seen that even Nagarath had a dark side.

You're one to talk. Liara stared off into the distance, through the bookcase and heavy stone walls to the mage's tower, to a shelf lined with books bound in shades of midnight. Slowly, she raised her hands before her eyes, trying to envision the dancing sparkle of her aura. But it was as beyond imagination as it was out of her reach. The menacing glitter of the forbidden volumes she could picture, however.

"*Sh'lemull.*" Uttering the word, Liara almost dropped the stack of scrolls she was collating. That was where she'd seen such magick before. In the wholeness spell. Granted, Nagarath's spell was far more advanced. But she was in a library. With the Catalogue. And she knew a key word by which to search. She could find out her own answers to questions she dared not ask the mage.

Unfortunately, her scattered and ill-educated attempts at learning more about magickal signatures ended all too quickly when Nagarath reappeared, calling her to supper. He teased from the doorway, "And you say I get too wrapped up in my work to eat." Liara's reluctance in following him did not go unnoted. "Another secret project, my dear?"

Her nose wrinkled. She hated when he called her that. "No. Nothing like that."

The warm smells of vegetable soup wafted through the open door of the kitchen. Liara flushed with guilt. Here she'd spent the afternoon reading, and Nagarath had cooked up a lovely supper, all the while keeping Parentino's spells working. Misunderstanding Liara's expression, he quickly explained, "Without chicken, the best I could try for was vegetable. They say it's good when you're feeling run down, you know."

"What happened to the chickens?" Liara's pulse quickened in alarm.

Nagarath looked embarrassed. "They're fine. I had to venture out to the well earlier and discovered that my

The Bookminder

spells weren't perfect yet. By the time I got it right, though, it was too late to add any chicken to the soup if we were to eat today."

"So we can go outside?" Liara perked up. *Finally. Freedom.*

"I can. But you have to stay in here. The spells are connected to me only, right now. And while they'll protect you in here . . ." He let the sentence trail off.

"Oh," said Liara, disappointed. "With the cooking and all the . . . helping . . . in the library, I thought that things were all right now, that you weren't actively maintaining the spells yourself."

"If you mean I am looking better, thank you." Nagarath winked. "But the solution to extricating my personal power from the defenses has proved elusive. I'll keep working on it, of course. I can't keep up like this forever."

"Could I help?"

"Out of the question."

She was tired of being blocked at every turn. At this rate, spring would come—*and with it, Krešimir*—before she had gotten half a glance at winter. She buried her annoyance in a bowl of the steaming vegetable soup. It might well have been the first time she wished that Nagarath had decided to read at the dinner table.

"Is it because of my father?"

"Is it—? Pardon me?"

"It's my aura, isn't it? All those terrible little dark bits."

"Liara, that's preposterous and you know it."

"Then why can't I help you?"

"Because it's dangerous and you are untutored in the

Art."

Liara let her spoon clatter into her bowl. Gauntlet thrown. "I was just offering to help. There's no need to get all twitchy at me."

"Me, all twitchy?" Liara had the satisfaction of watching Nagarath's eyebrows reach for his hairline.

"Yes. Every time I mention my magick or my father, you—"

"Stop saying that."

"No. I will not."

"I mean it."

Liara jumped in surprise as Nagarath half-rose from his chair. He looked positively forbidding. But the motion proved to be in the service of him reaching for the books he'd left on the far end of the table. She watched, cowed, as his sensitive fingers sorted through the four volumes in quick succession, the tension in his frame calling for silence.

Falling back into his chair, he sighed and pressed his fingers to his temples.

"I'm sorry." She meant it. She truly did—even as much as she'd meant to antagonize him.

"No." The word came drawn, almost a sigh. "No, I'm sorry, Liara."

Nagarath darted his eyes to the scattered books, laying the blame elsewhere. "I thought that I had the volume here at hand. Well, I'd"—he blanched—"I thought I'd removed from the library all books on the topic of *aurenaurae*. Lest you come across one by mistake. Apparently I have since misplaced them."

"Aurenaurae?"

"That is the technical term for rape by magick."

A loud buzzing descended upon Liara, filling her ears. The room brightened and darkened momentarily. She blinked it away, ever so glad she was seated. "Go on."

Nagarath seemed as surprised as she to hear her speak. This time, his warning glance was one of concern. He continued, "Aurenaurae is both the term for the act and the product. The wizard responsible, the creator of the aurenaurae, is known as the *progenaurae*. Never as the father. The mage responsible for your creation gave you nothing of the stuff of life, only his magick."

The blackness that had tried to overwhelm her threatened to return. "You said I was human. A real person."

"That, Liara, is what an aurenaurae is. It is a cheating of Mother Nature through magickal means. An exceptionally rare occurrence."

"Why tell me this now?"

The question appeared to fall upon deaf ears, Nagarath giving no clue to his having heard her. Long moments passed and she opened her mouth to ask again, when the mage shook his head, as if coming to a decision after deep consideration. "Because it hurt me to hear you say 'father' each and every time you referred to the man."

Liara took this new revelation. Added it to the rest. *Aurenaurae.*

"Aurenaurae and pro—?"

"Progenaurae."

"That." Liara smiled weakly. It seemed . . . right. Like she'd somehow known this all her life and Nagarath was just reminding her. That, or—

"I read about this. When I was sorting through a particularly dusty chest of volumes." She sat upright in her chair, excited, a new hope rising in her chest. "I think it was a book discussing some of the ways the process might be achieved through means other than through black magick. Could that perhaps—?"

"Hold clues as to your origin? Mayhap." Nagarath took her news in stride. "On second thought, I think I recall which one you are referring to." He rose, distractedly mumbling about a crème leather cover with hazel-tooled accents, tugging his nose in thought.

With a heavy sigh, Liara reached across the table. She hadn't meant for him to leave without finishing his soup. Shaking her head at her book-bespelled mage, she picked up his bowl and followed him into the library.

It turned out that he did not know where the volume was after all. Liara gave him no less than six false starts before she forced the bowl of soup into his hands and held a spoon in front of his eyes.

"Eat," she commanded.

Nagarath obeyed. If was funny how mothering Liara had become. It was as if the peril in which they'd found themselves had forced her to sound unfathomed depths in herself. Bustling about the library and putting his messes to rights—and occasionally returning to make sure he was eating—Liara looked downright mature.

And then there was her magick. While Nagarath might have been known for his careless, slipshod attitude towards magick itself, if there was one thing he knew, it was his books. And the volume from which Liara cast her warding spell last month was far too advanced for one such as her. She should not have been able to manage it . . . unless she was extraordinarily lucky or exceptionally talented.

Demon's luck. That's what the mages called it. Nagarath hated the term, especially considering their current conversation. He again trained his eye on the girl, watching her glide about the room. *Aurenaurae. Made by magick.*

She really did have a fey quality about her. Sometimes Nagarath feared her to be merely a very vivid dream; a bit of magick that, if you turned so you could only see her from the corner of your eye, might very well disappear.

All of this was nonsense, of course, fears conjured by Liara's own questions. If only she'd leave well enough alone. He'd promised the priest, and that was that. *I have enough trouble as it is protecting us from goodness-knows-what, and to have her questioning me each step of the way—it's exhausting keeping track of what I can and cannot say. And perhaps, today, I have finally said too much.*

He could feel the pull of Parentino's spells. Something—likely a rabbit or a bird—had just crossed over their boundaries. Realizing now how much it had taken out of him to cook dinner, and even just to laugh and converse with Liara, he rose with the intent of taking a quick rest in the great room before continuing his work at making the defensive spells autonomous.

Unfortunately, this was as far as his plans were allowed to go. For upon rising to his feet, Nagarath had the uncomfortable sensation that he was falling. And then all was blackness.

~*~

"Nagarath!"

From across the library, Liara saw the mage sway momentarily before going down in a crumpled heap. Running over to his side, she called his name again.

No answer.

Panicking, she knelt, hesitating for the briefest of moments before turning him onto his back and holding her hand near his lips.

The faintest tickle of Nagarath's breath on the back of her knuckles roused a shudder of relief. She whispered his name again, unsure of what to do, of what had befallen her wizard. "Nagarath."

His dark eyelashes fluttered once, twice, parting to reveal his startled gray eyes looking up into her face. He seemed puzzled. "Are you well? Liara, you're shaking."

He moved to get up and paused, appearing to think better of it.

"I'm fine," Liara rushed to reassure him. "You—you fainted. I think." She couldn't stop shaking. A thought occurred to her. "Your staff—"

"Don't touch it! Please." Nagarath laid his head back down, his eyes still locked on hers. "It's all right. I'm fine. See? I'm fine."

Sometime during the short exchange, his hand had found hers. Her fingers locked fiercely within his steadying embrace, Liara felt her trembling subside. "And your magick?"

Nagarath smiled weakly. "Also fine."

"Don't you ever scare me like that again," Liara scolded, her answering smile coming out watery.

The mage endeavored to sit. "Not something I'd care to repeat, no."

"What happened?"

His answer confirmed her suspicions. "The spells on Parentino. I think something crossed one of them."

Alarm returned to Liara's face.

"No, nothing terrible. It was small. I could feel it. A bird maybe." Nagarath waved it off. That he did so demonstrated how near he was feeling to his usual self. This reassured Liara more than his sitting up and speaking with her.

"What if it happens again?" She looked him up and down. The man was in no shape to maintain his infuriating network of spells. Not in this condition.

"I think I have a solution. How much to do trust me, Liara?"

What kind of a question was that? She opened her mouth to say as much, but paused, realizing that Nagarath wore his emotions very close to the surface just now.

He did not wait for her response, his quick search of her face apparently finding an answer that satisfied. "Liara, you were right to be mad at me earlier. Your Art is very strong. And I think it possible for you to lend your strength in supporting our defenses. Until I get my own strength back and can find a solution, of course," Nagarath added hurriedly. "But would you still be willing to lend your magick?"

"But your promise to Phenlick . . ." The words were out of her mouth before she realized. She scolded herself. *What a dumb time to find a conscience, Liara.*

"Technically, I'm not teaching you anything. We're just using what you already happen to know." Nagarath shrugged, winking.

That he knew her that well brought a genuine smile to Liara's face. Nodding, she agreed to the experiment. It was, after all, the least she could do.

Chapter Fourteen

Well, the mage didn't die and nobody's stormed the castle, so I'm guessing I've done passably well. It was easier for Liara to be glib now. Three days of tender ministrations had passed and the wizard was driving her mad once more. Demanding and impulsive, Nagarath was not one readily confined to his bed. He simply didn't know how to sit still.

Liara paused outside his door, making sure to rattle the cups in their saucers as she used her elbow to gently push open the door. She'd come to realize it was better if she gave the mage warning before entering. Twice she'd caught him gingerly pacing his room and found, given the heated words exchanged as a result, that it was far easier if they both believed the lie that he was sitting meekly in bed, awaiting his caregiver's return.

"Good morning, Nagarath."

"Good morning, Liara."

A quick glance about the room told her that perhaps he hadn't been stalking about that morning. He certainly didn't look as though he'd left his bed. Rather, his bed looked as though it had left him. Pillows and blankets lay strewn about the sides and foot.

"I take it we had a rough night?" she teased, swiping pillows from the floor and tossing them at Nagarath.

"Bad dreams." He frowned as if clearing out the memory. "And you?"

"Fair enough." Liara finished her triage of the bedding situation and gestured that he come sit with her by the window where she had laid out a light breakfast. Nagarath rose to join her, waving off her offers of assistance.

"No need for that," he said, sitting heavily. "I'm better than halfway recovered. Nearly there. Tomorrow maybe?"

Liara pursed her lips, suppressing a sigh. He'd said much the same thing the past three mornings. Always a promise of 'tomorrow' and then he'd retire to his bed, requesting all sorts of odd volumes from the library. The man would subsist wholly on books—illness or not—if she didn't keep pestering him with food. Frankly, it was getting ridiculous.

She suspected he liked being coddled. But, enjoying the gentle ebb and flow of her power as the castle's spells drew at her Art, she was content to play housekeeper until the mage felt sufficiently strong again. It felt good to feel useful. Liara found it a welcome distraction from other things.

Nagarath's voice recalled her attention. "We could switch chairs if you'd like."

Being a corner room, Nagarath's windows had command of two different vantage points. The casement the pair sat next to faced a different direction from that of Liara's own room. The other offered the same view as Liara's: a glimpse of Dvigrad's dark stones in the far off distance.

Liara hadn't realized she'd been staring past Nagarath and out at the battlements. Color rising to her cheeks, she ignored the gallant offer and instead focused on her plate, trying to keep the tears from welling up once more and choking her.

Nagarath pressed, in spite of her clear desire that he leave the issue alone. "You are allowed to grieve, Liara."

"I'd rather be strong," she hissed.

She waited in silence to see if he would let the matter drop.

He did.

It was his turn to look longingly in a direction opposite the table. "Liara, would it be possible for you to fetch me some more books this morning? I think I may have come upon the solution we've been seeking with regard to the defense spells."

"Which ones?" she grumbled.

At least he had the sense to not read at the table. Even so, she glanced over to the growing pile at his bedside. What had started out as her generous gesture—a few books to help pass the time, nothing more—had become a full-blown, multi-day research session.

She still felt him too weak, too tired to do anything overly strenuous—and to her, reading was always strenuous. But as Nagarath hadn't actually tried to cast anything, she was willing to go along with his increasingly detailed requests.

One breakfast and ten title requests later, Liara found herself in the hallway with a tray of crumbs and spent books, shaking her head. At least the man had gone back to bed.

Liara returned with the fresh reading material only to

discover the gentle sound of uneven snoring drifting through Nagarath's partly open door. With a fond smile, she pushed it open further, sticking her head inside. Yes, the mage slept.

Tiptoeing through the room, lest she wake the fitful sleeper, Liara carefully placed the books within Nagarath's long-armed reach.

Straightening, she watched the soft rise and fall of the comforter as his quiet but heavy breaths filled the room. Turning to leave, she noted the careful placement of the mage's staff against the headboard of the bed—another promise of protection, even in his grave hour. Once upon a time, he wouldn't have dreamed of leaving such a valuable article unguarded in her presence. Nor would she then have ever dreamed of leaving it untouched, so deep was the call within her. But, as she'd discovered, some things were deeper, more important, than magick.

Memories of Nagarath stirred in Liara's chest; of him falling in the library, of his still form lying crumpled on the stone floor. She crept back towards the door, eager to escape risk of discovery. Her recent realization that she held such affection for the mage was still a surprise to her, and one she was eager to conceal from him, though she wasn't sure why.

A faint murmur arrested her movement. She almost answered, thinking he had awoken and was addressing her. But no. A quick glance confirmed that Nagarath was talking in his sleep.

"Dvigrad . . ."

The hair on the back of her neck prickled and she turned, waiting, straining to hear the rest. A long moment passed, shaking her from her rooted position. What was she waiting for anyway? She'd only just banished thoughts of the town, buried the lump rising in her throat whenever they emerged. The troubled sleeper shifted and she eyed the door, feeling guilty should her presence wake him. More incomprehensible mumbling gave way to a cry.

"I felt the magick. What have you done with the soldiers?" Tossing and turning, Nagarath moaned and grabbed at his covers blindly. "Don't listen to him, Liara. He didn't come for you. I did."

Those words chilled Liara more than the first. She had found Nagarath's behavior unsettling since his return from the shattered town. Normally immune to his paranoia, she'd found his fears insidious, seeping into her thoughts ever since his dramatic reentrance into Parentino following the town's destruction. Sleep-addled thoughts or not, there was something concrete in his words. *Magick? Whose magick? I thought you said you'd used your power to burn the bodies, honor the dead.*

Conveniently forgetting that her own dreams often spouted incredible nonsense, Liara crept back to the mage's side, her anger building. Who was she not supposed to listen to? Krešimir?

You don't even know him, Nagarath, Liara argued in her head. *Krešimir might not have come back for me. But neither would he skulk about some old castle. He'd sooner be dead than invisible and ineffective.* Krešimir would act. Liara would act!

But she hadn't. Instead, she'd played caregiver and ran the wizard's spells for him.

A new tone colored her growing anger. Was it her

magick he felt? Mayhap his words weren't about Dvigrad at all, but regarding her. Her fingers fairly itched at the thought. Nagarath knew her power and was keeping her here. Trapped by promises to a dead man, Liara would waste away in the castle until Nagarath's fears proved unfounded. And how long would that take?

But the soldiers . . . *'What have you done with the soldiers?'*

Liara wished that Nagarath had touched more on this point. Especially as he'd been frustratingly vague about what exactly he'd found in Dvigrad, other than the aftermath of apparent plague. Who was he addressing? Her? Someone in Dvigrad? This last question chilled her beyond the rest. Here were not merely the confused murmurings of a man facing a nightmare. This was grounded in truth. Nagarath was convinced that Parentino was a target for some horrid crusade against wizards. The mage's fears infected Liara's heart.

The thought that she could be hated so much for just being who she was had become increasingly repugnant, of late. She'd lived on both sides now; had found Nagarath to be a decent, honest man. The idea that regiments of soldiers—people she had lived alongside for most of her life—could be creeping through the woods at that very moment to smoke out the 'evil magick users' made Liara want to crawl away and hide in the pages of Nagarath's books.

Fear gripped her, like her terror the day she'd been hauled out to the woods and accused of witchcraft. Smoke from a burning tree, the suffocating heat of her worldly treasures set ablaze. . . . The memories overtook her senses, reigniting her anger.

'I felt the magick.' So had she. Time in the mage's company had afforded Liara the opportunity to realize just what she'd lost when her tree had burned. A personal assault.

What had the mage really found in Dvigrad? *And why won't he tell me? Is it because he thinks I am too useless to be of help?* Well, she could easily prove him wrong on that account. Already his words had sparked a number of ideas. Magick could be traced. If, in fact, there was any to track.

Nagarath had ceased his thrashing. Pillows lay scattered about the floor. Again. But if she was going to help, it would be via books, not bolsters. She retreated to the library once more.

Nagarath woke to a selection of thoughtfully stacked books. A glance to the window informed him that it was just past midday.

I slept the morning away, Nagarath reproached himself. He did feel much better, though. *Even if the sleep was neither necessarily sound nor restorative.*

He noticed that the pillows and blankets had been scattered from the bed again, like some strange bed-linen form of autumn. Liara would be annoyed. Nagarath smiled at the thought of her good-natured scolding, clicking her tongue and putting his topsy-turvy ways to rights. It was good for her to be busy just now, for all that he fiercely envied her for it.

Being confined to his bed was no good for him. He was used to overdoing it. He liked it that way. And in fact, it was more important than ever that he—*That I what? Work so hard that I fall and leave Liara unguarded?* Half-forgotten images from his unsteady sleep assailed him. Danger flashed, vague but pressing. He must act. Before—*Before what, mage? Before you destroy what is left of your mind, your sanity? She could be right, you know.*

Remembering Liara's white face peering into his own, the world slowly coming back to him after his fainting spell, Nagarath forcefully subdued his peevishness. *But I can at least read.* He reached over and picked up the topmost book, wincing as the stack gave a perilous sway.

He was still reading when Liara returned with a midday meal. However, he had moved to the tableside window, dragging his temporary library with him.

"Nagarath." Liara's warning came as a near-growl.

"What? I'm sitting. You let me sit at breakfast." Nagarath's reply came out more irritable than intended, and he scrambled to take a lighter tone as Liara's frown grew dark. "Besides, I slept. I'm feeling better. And I think I might have just hit upon a solution to our problem with the defensive spells."

As he predicted, the word 'our' returned him to Liara's good graces. The girl lit up and sat down at the table.

"Liara." Nagarath looked very seriously, very intently at his ward. "I need you to do me a huge favor."

"Anything."

"I need a bucket of dirt from the garden."

She raised a skeptical eyebrow at him. He nodded sagely, good humor tickling the corners of his mouth.

"I'll wait here, of course."

"Of course." Liara left the room, a quick but cool smile flitting across her features.

Now, what was that about? His only aim had been to joke with Liara as they always had.

Dismissing the thought with a shrug, Nagarath closed his eyes, running over the words of the spell in his mind. The idea was to draw the earth's own power and channel it to feed the spells defending Parentino. It had a simple elegance to it, even if it was not the sort of tactic he would normally employ. The earth did not belong to him. But the castle had been built of earth and stone, occupied its own space within the wood. Could he not use the native magicks to aid him in his defense of the area?

Liara returned with a bucket of dirt, her face carefully closed to him.

"Thank you." Nagarath gestured that she place the bucket on the table. That Liara first moved aside his spell book made him chuckle. "Now, don't be alarmed, but you're going to notice a freeing sensation on your power, if this should work."

"And if it doesn't?" Liara's question was lost in the sound of Nagarath calling the spell to life.

"*Atsmi'i chazar lekh adamah ma' atsmm laq' mimekh. If'sher na'ash lil'oth shl zanav. If'sher maa'gal mal.*"

Opening his eyes, Nagarath lifted high the bucket of dirt. Turning to the window, he flung the contents out into the garden.

"Did it work?"

"I forgot there was snow on the ground," Nagarath muttered out the window, ignoring her question once again. Fingering his jaw thoughtfully and sensing Liara's increased annoyance, he turned and asked, "How do you feel?"

Liara thought a moment. Nagarath was aware of the same tension, the stiffness she'd brought with her into the room. "I feel . . . lighter. Like I'm not getting tugged at by some invisible force."

"Me too." Nagarath's grin went unanswered. "I feel—well, I still don't feel fantastic. But I do feel less drained."

He could tell at a glance that Liara didn't feel 'fantastic' either. He wondered why.

Chapter Fifteen

Liara only barely held her temper in check as she shifted aside the books on the library shelves, searching fruitlessly for the one book she wanted to look into. That it wasn't where she thought she'd shelved it put her out of sorts. But then, everything was out of sorts.

Grieving is a process, she reminded herself, but wished fervently that her thoughts of Dvigrad could just come at her all at once and be done with it. Memories of that blasted town had a disconcerting way of sneaking up on her and catching her unawares. Unreasonable anger. Unfathomable sadness. Would not those people leave her alone, even now?

And Nagarath. He couldn't leave her be, either. *Liara, do this. Liara, fetch that.* And then he'd roll up his sleeves, close his eyes, and grandly mutter his castings, clearly desirous of some expression of awe from her. Well, he could turn full gray waiting for her to ask how he'd performed his tricks. She knew how magick worked. She'd read nearly every book in his library!

Liara stomped up the spiral stairs, taking out her ire on the very stones. She was mostly angry at herself, for her littleness of heart. By rights she should be glad that Nagarath's spell had worked. It meant he was out of danger now. *But for a few days, I felt special. Magickal. Like I'd always wanted. Like everyone in Dvigrad accused me of being.*

And there it was again—Dvigrad, rising sharply in the back of her mind.

Jerking on the cover of an unmarked book, Liara's temper got the best of her and she carelessly knocked a half-dozen other volumes to the ground. One landed with a sickening crunch, and the girl froze. Stooping to pick up the victims of her bad mood, she noted that a binding had come loose.

Unexpectedly, the sight of the sagging binding set her to tears. Liara dropped beside it and cried and cried, cradling the book and feeling nothing but sorry for herself and everything she'd ever touched.

"Liara. Oh, Liara, what is it?"

Through her haze of tears, Liara saw the wizard looking down at her, concern lining his features. Immediately, she felt stupid for her display. Scrambling to her feet, she sniffled and tried wiping her face dry. "You're up."

He nodded, the cloud of concern remaining.

"I dropped a book." Liara guiltily lifted the broken book. It wasn't a difficult repair. She didn't even quite know why it had caused such a flood of emotion.

Nagarath gently grasped the cover and took it from her with an appraising eye. "I've done worse."

"Of course you have. And it doesn't seem to bother you at all." She slapped her hands to her mouth in horror at the angry outburst. Like the sight of the fallen book setting her to tears, Liara was stunned at herself for speaking so to the mage. Why in the world were such things coming out of her today?

Nagarath stood quietly by, waiting to see if she had more in her. His passivity stirred her illogical wrath hotter still, and she lashed out again, finally catching hold of the one complaint she could identify.

"You sit and play with your power as if it's a game. 'Perhaps today I'll let Liara see one magick word,' or 'Suppose I have her help with some spellwork—but only for today,' and then you take it all away with the snap of your fingers. I'm more trapped here than I ever was in Dvigrad." This last was infinitely not true, but nothing was stopping her now. She could feel days of stress and worry loosening with the outburst. Fire, bright and warm, consumed her. She could feel it blazing in her cheeks and eyes as Nagarath took the bait.

"Liara!"

She ignored the wizard's bark. "Maybe they were right about wizards. Maybe you're all—"

"Liara. You were kept at arm's length in Dvigrad—trapped, as you say—because they feared you. They feared what you might bring down on their heads. Whereas I do what I do out of fear for your safety and do not wish any harm to come to you."

"With the way things are right now, you're doing a splendid job. Nothing's going to happen to me, ever. Magick or otherwise."

Liara's storm of words wound down. Emptied of her rancor, she now felt empty, confused as when she'd begun to speak. Abashed, she scuffed the wood floor fitfully, not daring to meet his eyes. "I can't even be your librarian right."

Nagarath bent his tall frame and sat on the floor, leaning against the nearby shelf and patting the space beside him. "Liara, things get broken. And for some reason, that seems to be the case more when wizardry is involved. That or I'm just a magnet for clumsiness—"

Liara shook her head, feeling returning tears threaten, rain to clear away the fog in her heart.

He was trying to make it better with words. Like he always did. What she needed was to get outside, to know the world was right again. Or, in the absence of that, action.

For the world will never be right again. Dvigrad's annihilation had left her without the means to fix what had been broken, to say the words that she'd denied Father Phenlick. Lectures did not fill an irreparable hole in one's heart. All the magick in the world could not heal the hurt and fear she carried inside.

And yet Liara found that she still wanted what she'd always wanted: answers, vengeance, magick—power. And it looked like none of those things would ever be hers since Nagarath was nothing save talk and spectacle. At last understanding her agitation, she opened her mouth to explain, prompting a raised hand from the mage. Nagarath said, "Hear me out. I have had very good reasons for everything I have done with regards to your magickal education . . . or lack thereof."

"The reasons being what?"

"Please, Liara. You're only sixteen."

"Seventeen since June," she corrected petulantly. Feeling stupid talking down at him, she lowered herself to the floor beside him. "You began at eight."

"Yes, and I was wretched at it," Nagarath teased, reaching out to tweak Liara's nose. She recoiled, still angry.

He continued, "My circumstances were different from yours. You are made from witchcraft, my girl. You have three years until you reach autonomy. That makes you an exceedingly quick study. And with your keen desire to learn any and all magicks . . . I don't know how most anyone could stop you once you set down that path."

Liara smiled hungrily. Didn't he know that was what she wanted?

He did. That much was obvious from the heavy sigh and fingers to his temples. "I am not the right one to teach you. I am just keeping you safe and giving you the foundation, just like Father Phenlick tried."

"Then why are you making me learn your books and help you and everything?"

"Because you're smart. And capable. And have learned things without my meaning you to. I did not ever mean to hurt you, you know that."

Liara nodded, tired. Wanting wasn't the same as needing. And she now realized that she did not need magick so much as reconciliation. But the futility of the latter had long been her excuse for focusing so single-mindedly on the former. She had desired that acceptance so deeply that the mere invocation of Father Phenlick's name stabbed her very spirit, and for a moment she was Dvigrad's orphan again. Back then, the line between necessity and desire had blurred. The two were much the same to a lonely girl riddled with doubts that haunted her relentlessly: those of herself. "Do you know what it's like to be surrounded by all of this sorcery, not knowing whether I know something or if it's just my brain playing at being a wizard like when I was a child? It's like my tree in the woods all over again."

She hadn't meant the words to come out small. It

The Bookminder

was a confession—to herself as much as the mage. Already she wanted to back down from the admission, play it off as words prompted by exhaustion, not weakness.

Her reward was a blank look from Nagarath. At least he didn't have a ready response. But neither did he understand. The ghost of her anger returned and she leaned her head back against the bookcase.

Minutes passed. *And still no glib response, no easy lecture.* Liara reveled in the small victory: Nagarath, confounded.

"How about . . ." he began at last. "Would it help you to know what you know? A sort of cataloging of the knowledge you already possess?"

Resentment came crawling back under her skin. Another lecture. She did not wish to be talked down to, just now. She did not want to be managed. She wanted to be left alone, here among the books, to see if she could fix things for herself without Nagarath telling her where she was wrong.

"Come. A tour, then." Nagarath rose to standing, offering her his hand.

She grudgingly let herself be helped to her feet. Whether or not her foul mood wanted to hover around, she was ready to move on. Action she'd wanted; action she'd get. Besides, in spite of herself, she was mildly curious over what he had to show her. She followed him, walking not down to the main floor, but towards the side door of the second balcony. Back in his element, Nagarath lectured away.

"Well, there are the books, of course. Not just the reading and the working, but the repair. Like I'd said, those clever light fingers of yours were practically made for this sort of work. Then there's also that warding spell. That was impressive craft for someone less than a novice." He turned and winked. She made a face in response.

He swept into the hall, stopping at the first window they passed. "There are, of course, the famed pink trees of Limska Draga."

Liara's scowl deepened and she stopped short, arms folded. If this was his attempt at making her feel better. . .

"No, really." Nagarath turned to defend his thoughtless comment. "You took words of magick and made a spell of them. One that—" The corners of his mouth puckered with his effort not to laugh.

". . . turned the oak leaves pink." She had the grace to laugh at herself. In spite of everything, Liara felt her good humor beginning to return. How ridiculous she'd been; how grand she'd thought herself. "It was a terrible spell."

"But it worked. And I'm betting nobody before in history had done that."

She'd never thought of it that way before.

They continued their walk, Liara following with less annoyance and more curiosity, pausing at the stairs as Nagarath looked upwards into the dark recesses of the third floor. He spoke almost to himself, "At one point, you managed to make it all the way to the second step from the top."

Liara felt her hair stand on end. Guilt, her old friend, returned to heat her cheeks, "You knew about that?"

"Of course. I know most of what happens in Parentino—provided one of my spells is involved. Making it that far was rather impressive, you understand."

"It wasn't my first attempt," Liara confessed, noting

that he seemed unsurprised by the admission. A thought struck her. "What if I had made it all the way upstairs?"

"I'd have turned you into a toad for your cheek." Nagarath turned, calling over his shoulder, "Come along, little magpie."

They descended to the main floor, entering Parentino's kitchen.

"Oh, I know all about your spells in the kitchen." Liara preened, eager to turn the tables on the mage. Enough was enough. He'd wanted a demonstration of what she knew, hadn't he?

"Do you?"

"All your shortcuts: the fireplace, the bucket for the well . . ."

". . . all of the components for the potions sitting in the cupboard," Nagarath continued for her, eyes sparkling.

Liara jumped in surprise. All posturing abandoned, she ran over to the cabinet and pulled wide the door. Nagarath's tea-making supplies. The mage was teasing her, clearly. Indignation clouded the horizon of her levity, threatening as she said, "There's nothing but herbs and cups for tea in here."

"Precisely." Nagarath joined her, gesticulating here and there. "Tea has its origins in spellwork, Liara. I thought you were aware of that." He glanced sideways at her, a sly smile playing about his lips. "Well, I suppose I've let the cat out of the bag on that one. There's no harm in telling you more."

Liara smiled at the mage's wink—genuinely this time—and sat down, the picture of an attentive student.

Nagarath tugged thoughtfully at the bridge of his

nose. "Tea drinking has its beginnings in the art of potions, back in ancient times when magickal study was in its infancy and even the most complex of spells were mere herbal lore. It's not like anyone just went out into the woods and said, 'Here now, I think I'll take a few things home, ferment them, dry them, and then boil them in water and drink whatever I get.' "

Liara challenged his explanation. "But *everyone* drinks tea, Nagarath. Even Father Phenlick liked it."

"And this is a problem because?" Nagarath sat back, clearly enjoying himself.

"Father Phenlick would never have purposefully drank tea if he'd known what he was doing. By your account, everyone drinks potions and spells without even knowing it." She paused, eyes lighting up as a delightfully wicked thought occurred. "Or do they?"

The wizard laughed. "Well, some of the old wives may know a bit more, but to most folk, tea is tea." He hurried to clarify, "And this Art is so long forgotten—we're talking of a time before the invention of the wand, for goodness sakes!—that it really is more of a history lesson than practical application."

"Oh." Liara let the matter drop, her disappointment aired as she glared at the teacups. Yet again, the promise of real magecraft had been taken away from her.

Nagarath saw the look. "There will be more on that later. You're not about to stop mixing our herbs for us. Shall we continue, then?"

Liara followed the mage as he swept back out of the room and down the hall.

He moved aside the hall tapestry that hid the entrance to the library. "Technically, you're using your Art every time you open this door . . ."

"Oh?"

"Indeed." He grinned, entering the library once more and holding the door open for Liara. "As I had said, that door was always there. Just hidden. Once I allowed it, your sight could see through my spells."

Liara wasn't sure that it all added up, but if the wizard said it was so, who was she to argue? She watched, thrilling as Nagarath walked straight up to the Catalogue and laid his hand on its cover.

"I don't think I have to point out what spells you had to have mastered for this to be possible." His voice was quiet, almost reverent. "It is a thing of exceptional beauty, this book of yours. And while I know you claim that the most mundane, practical techniques were used to make it, you have to agree that it is quite, *quite* magickal."

Liara nodded, stunned at the compliment.

"So you see, I haven't kept all from you. And I have, in fact, silently indulged in a lot of wayward learning on your part. But you'll note that my promise to Father Phenlick has stayed firm. I have not apprenticed you, little magpie."

Liara smiled. "Technically, you said you wouldn't teach me."

"Did I?"

"Outside of Dvigrad. On the path here. You said, 'I will not teach you magick.' "

Nagarath nodded. "Well, my promise to the priest was that of apprenticeship. If you want to lay claim to other words as our standard . . ."

"Gah!" Liara threw her hands in the air. "You're so

frustrating." Nagarath's smile mirrored her own. For all the secrets she feared he was keeping from her, it felt good that they might now have one of their own.

"Come, Liara. I think we have done enough mucking about with books today." Nagarath made as if to leave the library. "I, for one, am still very tired and very much need a cozy evening by the fire. Perhaps sorting through some of our tea-making supplies."

"You mean . . . spell components?" Liara teased, following the wizard as he doused the library lights with a snap.

Nagarath grinned. "Semantics."

Chapter Sixteen

Vegetable soup might have heralded the mage's collapse, but a quiet night in front of a roaring fire was just what the apothecary ordered. Another parade of flurries had blown in and snowdrifts piled high 'round Parentino's narrow windows, catching even in the ledges of the upper-story casements and shrouding the entire castle in eerie gray light. Nagarath was right. It wasn't a night for reading, not with the fitful, dim light in which they soon found themselves.

The evening darkness coming on as fast as it did, Liara guessed it to be just about the end of the year. Which was fine with her. Short days and long nights suited her darker soul. It could be winter forever, as far as she was concerned.

They had dinner in the great room, a simple affair of foodstuffs gathered from the cellar. And true to his word, Nagarath soon raided the cabinets of herbs and tea-making supplies, lecturing on what this or that was supposed to do for a person.

It not being a formal lesson, Liara curled up into a ball in front of the fire, listening to the mage drone on, occasionally asking a question here or there. She'd had no idea, for example, that a headache could be cured so many different ways.

"No wonder you were so disappointed in me the day I turned the trees pink." Liara sat upright, remembering the basket of wilted mint with which she'd returned, and realizing now why Nagarath had been so picky with everything that went into and came out of his garden.

He chuckled at the near-apology. "Yes, as with my books, the condition of an item affects its performance."

"Law the Second of Magicked Artif— But I thought you said we don't enchant the herbs, Nagarath."

He grinned in response. "The laws can still apply to the innate magick of an item. And before you ask, yes. Yes to mint and sage, lemon balm and elderflowers . . . the list goes on. All have inborn magickal properties. I mean, you're not going to become some famous warlock drinking tea, but the power is there, and its effects can be enhanced with a skillful hand and Artful eye."

"Can I?" Liara was afraid to ask, her hands fairly itching to touch the arrayed herbs, the cluster of little glass bottles sparkling in the firelight, waiting to be filled with new concoctions.

"You haven't steered us wrong thus far, Liara. Be my guest." Nagarath smiled and rose from his chair, disappearing into the shadows of the room. "You do know that, for one with your gift, it makes very little difference simply knowing that it's magick."

To me it does. Liara gently picked up a bundle of lavender, the sweet smell bringing back thoughts of summer. He was right. It felt as though an instinct guided her, something that whispered what the plant did, what it paired with, something that went beyond experience in the kitchen. To her surprise, she realized it had always felt that way.

Satisfied, she lost herself in the exploration, until Nagarath's return to his chair caught at the corner of her eye. Something in his hands drew her attention.

"You play the cindra?" Liara was skeptical. Yet, there it was, lute-like and delicate, its burnished wood gleaming in the light of the fire. It was odd how it had never occurred to her that Nagarath might have any musical inclination. Krešimir had. He'd even played for her, now and again. The memory brought tears to her eyes, and she looked to the fire, trying to draw back the sudden emotion.

"A little." Nagarath's voice seemed to come from far away. "It reminds me of home."

His words reclaimed Liara's attention. He'd never mentioned a home before. Not a real one, anyway. She pressed, gently so as not to ruin the moment. "Home?"

She needn't have worried. Nagarath seemed to be in a talkative mood. "Naples. Though, technically, I was born in England. The cindra, you see, is much like our mandolino . . . but with fewer strings, making it perfect for me."

"You're from England?"

"And Naples and France and just about everywhere else."

"How did you—?"

"End up here?" Nagarath sighed, his eyes staring into the fire.

For a moment, Liara figured that she'd killed the conversation.

"I came to Limska Draga about ten years ago. The circumstances are . . . complicated. But the place suited me, and I was able to ensure that the valley stayed safe from further invasion." Nagarath's words were slow and measured, though whether because he was thinking hard or just lost in the past, Liara couldn't tell. He snapped back into the present with a smile. "As you can see, the area grew on me. Piotr wasn't just Dvigrad's apothecary—"

"—he was your friend."

"I wouldn't go that far," Nagarath hedged. "But he was a social sort. More so than Father Phenlick, though he, too, was quite pleasant. No, Piotr simply went out of his way to make sure that I found the valley to my liking. I think he just liked having someone to drink with. Now, are you going to let me play or not?"

Liara smiled, turning back to her own quiet work as Nagarath plucked out a few notes and then began to play in earnest. He wasn't a skilled musician, but he played tolerably well. Soon the soft notes of the cindra added to the warmth of the crackling fire, and Liara found herself wanting more such nights.

Lost in her own thoughts, trying to determine which of five dried flowers would best accompany the rosehip tea with which she experimented, Liara was startled to hear Nagarath's voice join his instrument, beginning a familiar tune.

She looked up from her work, enchanted. Arms wrapped around her knees again, she sat back, listening.

Not much different in tone than his speaking or incanting, Nagarath's singing style was simple and warm with the slightest hint of a rasp. Liara found the sound quite pleasant. The rounded rise and fall of the notes, the artful interplay of soft and loud—she could tell this man believed in what he sang, and that lent a whole new timbre to his voice.

For the first time since coming to live at Parentino,

she realized how little she knew about Nagarath . . . and how little she'd really bothered to ask, having generally fixated on issues helpful to her and her pursuit of magick. In listening, it now occurred to her how deeply painful it must have been for him to come upon Dvigrad and find everyone gone.

No. Not just gone. The emptiness Liara carried within her could certainly not match the bleak reality of Nagarath's discovery. Instead of warm greetings, the mage would have found bodies. Instead of cook fires, the stench of death, of rotting, wasted flesh that had belonged to men he'd come to know—Piotr, Phenlick—and value for their friendship. People he was likely closer to than she'd ever been.

Or was that also a fallacy? She had loved them, too. Hated them, certainly, but loved them, their familiarity. And that comforting familiarity was gone, leaving in its place Nagarath. *Whom I almost lost as well.*

The moment returned to her then, the image of Nagarath lying prone on the floor of the library, seemingly lifeless, her own heart stuck high in her throat, scarcely beating with fear for him. What would it be like to find an entire settlement like that?

Liara could imagine Nagarath helplessly pacing in front of Dvigrad's gates, eventually entering and finding devastation in answer to his hails. Friends, dead and purpled with disease. And to be alone, knowing he had to use his Art, his life's love, to burn the bodies, to scour away the pestilence and honor the deceased.

Lost in black thoughts, Liara's imaginings nearly tore her from the present until Nagarath's voice, solid and reassuring, bled into her consciousness, calling her back to him. Rescue. She no longer merely listened, but clung to the mage's words, the sweet, haunting melody. Solace in the form of song—comfort she had again failed to give her wizard, lost as she'd been in her own fears and self-doubts. Hugging knees to chest, Liara lifted her face to Nagarath's and let his rich tones wash over her.

> I would pick you, my flower,
> I would pick you, my flower,
> I have no dear one whom should have you.
>
> Should my brother have you?
> Should my brother have you?
> I am his brother even without flowers.
>
> I should give you away to a young sailor,
> I should give you away to a young sailor,
> Sailing over the blue Adriatic Sea.

Liara considered his choice of song. It was one familiar to her. To her mind, the lyrics had always spoken to her of love and longing, beautiful and playful in its cadence. Had he learned it in memory of someone? His family, or a woman, perhaps? Someone he'd had to leave behind, somewhere in his homeland beyond the Adriatic Sea? What else had magick forged for this mage of hers? What had it taken from him that made him sing so?

Such questions seeming too personal to ask aloud, Liara sat silent, caught on the sweet brokenness of notes that lay just beyond Nagarath's natural range. The sliding melody carried with it a deep wistfulness that the wizard rarely, if ever, expressed.

By the end, the song's comforting familiarity was such that Liara found herself humming along under her breath, desiring to step into the flickering firelight warmth of the song, but too shy to join. She hoped that, by not joining in, she wasn't somehow insulting him. For listening provided enough participation for her, and she did not trust her high, thin voice alongside Nagarath's rich tones.

He had been nothing but kind to her. But it was only now, in the midst of the music, that Liara truly saw the tenderness in him. And something in the way the firelight flickered across his face while he sang suddenly and unexpectedly made Liara wish the song were meant for her.

Nagarath felt something ease inside his mind as the final notes of the song faded into the soft crackle of the dying fire. Sitting back, he enjoyed the moment, letting the sense of peace slide in, ousting the sorrow that had lived in his breast these last few days.

It still hurt, of course. Losing Dvigrad was one of the great horrors of his life—and that was saying something, considering the life he'd led. But the familiar melody, the meditative act of playing, had done far more for his shattered psyche than had the vast burning of magicks employed in honoring the fallen.

But the fire on the hearth isn't going to tend itself. Nagarath considered asking Liara to stoke it, but instead roused himself. The girl was still staring off into space, her own contemplative mood not something he wished to disturb just yet. It was a perfect evening, not to be spoilt by words.

Kneeling before the grate, his lanky form casting

dark shadows across Liara, Nagarath found himself hyperaware of the close and comforting intimacy of the night. Under his skillful hands, the fire blazed back to life, driving back the chill that had begun to creep in from the corners of the room, and illuminating Liara's features more clearly.

Her expression was enough to make him turn back to the blaze, where the warmth of the new flames helped cover the heat creeping into his cheeks. It was a look he'd never seen—never expected to see—on his ward's face. Empathy. Compassion. Wistfulness. A mixture of all three, completely disarming in its intensity.

"I think I'm going to head up to sleep," she said, her tone betraying that she, too, sensed the sudden tension in the room. "Good night, Nagarath."

"Good night, Liara," he spoke without turning around.

And she was gone, carrying with her the strange, bewildering quietude full of a loudness he'd been hard-pressed to ignore. *Too close. You're letting her get too close.*

The warning pounded in his ears, the sensation eerily familiar. It felt like Dvigrad. It felt like when the library had gone dark around him and he'd woken flat on his back, undone by his own spellcasting. It felt like Archmage Cromen's tutoring all over again.

He was losing control of the situation.

The thought accompanied Nagarath back to his seat, temporary peace broken and fear creeping its way back in. He wasn't just losing control of the situation, he was losing control of his magick. He stared at his fingers, his hands and wrists. This had all happened before. Spells escaping his control; consciousness slipping from him when most urgent. And then, consequences.

He looked up at the dark ceiling, towards Liara's quarters—Liara with her strange mood and unspoken questions. Though he hadn't quite figured what had come over her while they sat together by the fire, he could tell when she was holding back. She clearly had questions that went beyond magick, beyond tea-making and the like.

But so had he.

Nagarath turned his eyes back to the fire, as if staring into its searing light might burn away the fog that had settled into his mind. What he'd found in Dvigrad made no sense. He hadn't counted the bodies, but he was certain that some, if not all, of the guard had been missing. Or had they? Perhaps it was only Father Phenlick's letter making him think so. He couldn't remember.

He could remember pain. And fear. He remembered quite clearly the pull of Parentino's spells, drawing him back in an instant, away from the plague-ridden air of Dvigrad. Or had he first finished his work in the annihilated town? Again, the memories felt dulled, masked by that same mental fog, the fog that felt like wayward wizardry.

Mine or hers? The fog, its aura, foreign and yet familiar. Nagarath's pulse quickened, his breath coming in hitching gasps of building rage. Why couldn't he see it? It was confounding, as though he was looking at two overlapping realities. Or perhaps he truly was imagining the menace out there in Limska Draga. Liara could well be right about Dvigrad's devastation coming via natural, if unfortunate, means. *But the power in the air. Familiar yet*

veiled beyond the reaches of his mind—
The thought wouldn't leave him alone.

"Settle your mind, mage," he murmured angrily. Of course it wasn't Liara's power he sensed, even with her successful casting of a high-level ward. That he'd even considered her as the source of that power demonstrated his frazzled state.

"What you need are answers." What he needed was to stop blaming others.

Jumping to his feet, Nagarath left the fire's warmth, ascending to his workroom, still strangely agitated. A word of power opened the door and he reached for his cloak, another word laying bare the ceiling, stripping it of its protective network of spells. Thick, bitter snow swirled down through the open roof and he laughed aloud, challenging the winter skies with his upturned face.

Snow like white ash. The imagery brought to mind more memories of Dvigrad, jumbled as they were, arousing Nagarath's fierce anger anew.

How dare they treat his Liara so. How dare they deny magick. And how dare they parade their soldiers about the woods—his woods—keeping this quiet, peaceful region in a constant state of fear, always on the verge of panic.

Drawing a shaky breath, Nagarath closed his eyes, shutting out the completion of the thought. No, they did not deserve what had befallen them.

There. Reaching out with his Art, Nagarath could sense the fog like a blanket over the valley, like smoke on the wind. Elusive, but proof enough that the source of his terror wasn't only of his imagining. Something was out there in the wood, some menace that he could feel with his heart and nothing more. He had to know what it was.

He pushed further. Scrying outward, reaching, stretching as far as he could in all directions, Nagarath swept past the darkened shadow that had once been Dvigrad, past the empty woodsman's hut, and even back along the Pazinčica River towards the sea. His sight darted around pockets of darkness amongst the rocks and trees, a taint he could sense yet not see.

The shadow stretched to the coast, to the very limits of his power, the formless shade a match to what he felt there, right outside of Parentino. But what was it? He could not tell, his Art stretched far too thin in the search. Only that same hint of darkness and a resulting ache in his heart confirmed his fears.

Nagarath withdrew back into himself. He had half hoped that his worries would have been dispelled by the sight of the winking campfires of the Venetian soldiers or perhaps nothing at all.

But the shadow of a threat was worse than a fully visible one. One couldn't defend against a shadow. They fell where they would. So his answers were worse than the questions, serving only as proof of his inadequacy. Again.

Do I tell her? The temptation was almost more than he could bear. To be less alone in his fears. . . . But then again, most of his fears were for Liara—for the consequences of her finally holding the power to learn the truth. If she gained true knowledge of the Art, she might well bend everything in the world toward making herself whole. Which would mean finding her progenaurae. *And that would be disaster for everyone—especially you, little magpie.*

No, he more urgently feared that his power alone might not be able to protect her from what was coming. If Father Phenlick had appealed to Rome for help, the secret of Liara's past was out, and her life forfeit if they were discovered.

And then it hit him, the reason for his anxiety, his anger at himself.

What if his stubborn-heartedness had denied Liara something she might need in the days to come? What if, when that dark cloud on the horizon lay fully overhead, his little magpie was standing alone and defenseless?

Nagarath stood on the other side of the kitchen door observing, as best he could, Liara as she hummed under her breath and flitted about, readying breakfast. He wondered if she was even aware that she was doing it.

She might not have joined in last night, but she certainly knew the melodies, Nagarath noted with surprise. For some reason, he had long assumed that Liara's refusal to acknowledge Dvigrad as her home also meant that she would have rejected its culture. But then, in his long wanderings, he had encountered very few people who could resist the charm of a simple song. He entered the kitchen, eager to start the day and further remove himself from the memories of a sleepless night.

"Good morning, Liara."

"Good morning, Nagarath."

She was up to something. Nagarath noted the carefully laid implements for tea, the eager greeting, the self-absorbed smirk on her face. "And what are we making?"

"Tea." Liara glided over, cup at the ready. "I managed to create three new kinds. Would you like to know what they do?"

Nagarath could feel a repeat of yesterday afternoon looming. Already, he felt cornered—certain that any response he made would be the wrong one. He would inadvertently hurt Liara's feelings with some ill-timed, if educational, observation about how rudimentary tea-making was. Then she'd cry and claim that he wasn't giving her anything to do, that he was trapping her in the castle unfairly . . . which, in a way, was true.

But it's safer inside. Nagarath sat, head in his hands, having the argument for both of them. *Only because you won't teach her, mage.* He spoke through his fingers, "I have a headache, Liara. Which one helps with that?"

"Oh." Liara's monosyllabic response fell upon Nagarath like judgment.

I'm not mad at you, Liara. I'm angry at myself. He was so terribly awkward at times. But even self-accusing, he couldn't find the words with which to answer her. Not unless he wanted to delve into what he was so uneasy about. *The girl is so . . . persistent.*

Nagarath made his excuses. The evening by the fire had been wonderful, but the dead of night had been hard on him. Over and over again, he'd found himself weighing Liara's words against his conscience. Could he not just let her learn the Art? A promise to a dead man and a lot of fears—all of it holding him back.

But the danger. Both that magick poses to herself, and that of . . . whatever is out there.

Nagarath nodded his thanks as Liara placed a steaming mug in front of him, touched by how respectful she was being of his claim of a headache. He took a sip of tea. It was delicious.

As if this alone settled it, he cut through the girl's quiet readying of breakfast. "Liara. After long consideration, I think it would be prudent for me to teach you some spellwork that could aid in your defense, and in the defense of our position here, should the need arise."

She nearly dropped the teapot. "Excuse me?"

"You heard me." Nagarath lifted his tired eyes, managing a smile. "I'm teaching you magick, girl."

~*~

Liara didn't want to eat. She didn't want to move. The wizard was teaching her magecraft. Could not they begin that instant?

Nagarath raised his mug. "After we break our fast, of course."

"Of course." As if this conversation were the most natural thing in the world, as if the past eight months—nay, seventeen years—of wishing and hoping had merely been a bad dream.

Liara had never eaten so quickly in all her life. This fact was not lost on Nagarath, giving in more fully to good humor at last. "I'll wash up, little magpie. You're all aflutter anyhow, and would likely shatter the plates in your haste. If you could bring me . . ."

He paused, thinking.

Liara wished he'd think faster.

Finally, he rattled off no less than a dozen lengthy and archaic-sounding titles. "Bring them up to my workroom. We'll meet there."

"Thank you, Nagarath!" Liara flounced from the room, eager to begin her new life, and afraid that if she tarried too long, she'd forget half the titles Nagarath had bid her to fetch.

She could have been borne upon the wings of magick itself, so quickly she flew about the library. She'd half expected that her mind would have been too unsettled for the Catalogue to point the way to the books she needed. But then, Liara's heart was steady on the matter of sorcery.

It was therefore no surprise that she made it to Nagarath's workroom first, and so of course decided to use the extra time exploring the room's wonders. Doing a slow turn about the center of the floor, she once more wished that she had discovered Nagarath's trick of revealing the auras of things. The glowing mists of each individual signature had somehow impressed her more than any massive illusions might. The auras had given her a sense of belonging, that she was but one of a whole host of magicked items, rather than a solitary outcast in a town of nonbelievers. Reliving the memory, Liara recalled that she still had a question to put to the mage, that of his own aura . . . or seeming lack thereof.

Liara nearly shrieked as her slow rotation brought her gaze directly upon that of another face. A skull. Horrified but curious, she crept closer. The skull had friends.

Back in the dark recesses of a shelf, half hidden behind a few bottles and a dusty sheaf of scrolls, sat no less than a half-dozen human skulls. She nudged aside the rest of the shelf's contents that she might better view the macabre oddity. "Nagarath, what on earth?"

The skulls made no answer and, gaining a bit more courage, she reached out to one gingerly. It shifted against its fellows at her touch, and Liara leapt back as if burned. Strange. The skulls felt . . . not evil. Unlike the spell books for dark sorcery that still pulsed at her from across the room—Liara had made a wide arc of these upon entering—the skulls seemed almost friendly.

"Perhaps because they're always grinning," Liara joked to herself, then sobered. Unbidden, the spectre of Dvigrad rose in her mind. While she knew that Nagarath had used magefire to burn away the last of the plague from the village, effectively turning the remains to dust, a wild part of Liara's brain still pictured the town littered with bones. Skulls leered up at her out of the soil, accusing her of witchcraft and worse.

For hadn't their deaths been, in many ways, the cause of her learning magick today? What a price for them to have paid for Liara to finally fulfill her heart's desire. *When I said I wanted power so I could show you all what a mistake it had been to treat me thus, I hadn't meant it to turn out like this.*

The words in her heart were sincere, and she further vowed that she would use her gift to avenge them. She would. *I'm sorry.*

Shaken, she moved on to the next shelf. Eager to find anything that would distract from the turmoil of her heart, her eyes lit on a small glass bauble that seemed to shine with an inner light all its own. Half the size of her hand, the round ball sat safely on a silver ring. Liara couldn't resist.

Upon picking it up, she found that the light inside seemed to dance and swirl. She peered closer, only to jump as Nagarath's voice sounded from the doorway.

"I presume you've not been so foolish as to go around touching things without knowing what they are, Liara." He frowned at her, scolding but gentle.

Sheepishly, she reached to put the bauble back on its silver base. "What does it do?"

Nagarath opened his mouth, then shut it, looking for all the world like he didn't quite know how to answer. His sheepishness soon matched hers. "I . . . I don't remember."

"Nagarath!" Liara laughed and gestured to the books she'd brought up. "I hope you remember what you'd planned to do with these."

"Ah, yes." Nagarath hastened over and ran his index finger down the spines, carefully selecting one and handing it to her. "This will give you an excellent working foundation of what we are about to attempt. I'll be over at my workbench should you have questions."

Reading. As usual. How lovely.

Liara snatched the book from his hand, and after eyeing the nearest armchair, petulantly opted for the peace and quiet of her own room.

LIMSKA DRAGA

The silent predator winged through the barren trees of Limska Draga, searching. Beneath him on the forest floor, the eagle owl saw the telltale flash of brown that indicated a mouse fleeing for its life.

Go ahead and run, little mouse. I have other, more pressing things to do than chase after you.

While he hated letting an easy catch get away, the owl was on a mission: find the castle, the twin of the empty one across the wide valley.

Pulling up to land, the owl gave a long blink, turning his head to look about. He'd been that way before. The old tumbledown castle had been there. He was almost certain of it.

It was the 'almost' that frustrated him. In the last few days, the owl had crisscrossed the area more times than he could count. He'd have to report back to the mage soon. But if the castle refused to give up its game of hide and seek, there was little he could do.

I wonder if that mouse is still back there. The owl gave one more long look around before taking wing into the evening gloom.

Chapter Seventeen

"Finished." Liara made sure to load the word with as much frustration and annoyance as possible. She entered Nagarath's workroom, flinging herself into an armchair, not caring if she disturbed him. Nagarath, she found, never really did any delicate work that she ought to tiptoe around.

He spoke without turning. "Sick of reading, little magpie?"

Liara snorted. She felt as though she'd been tricked. She was his librarian; she could read about hexes and jinxes all she wanted, thank you very much. "I had thought we were in for a more practical demonstration."

"Granted." Nagarath turned and, leaning casually against his worktable, finally gave his ward his undivided attention. "But then you wouldn't know much of anything. You'd be copying my motions and words without knowing why. What, Liara, is the main difference between spells you incant and those you enact with a gesture?"

Liara blinked in surprise. She hadn't known there was going to be a test. "Well, you've sort of just explained the difference. One charm is done using the power of words, and the other through gesture, the motion often derived from the tracing of runes—"

Nagarath waved his hands for her to stop. "Sorry. My mistake. I was unclear. I meant the main difference as given by Archmage Loothemere in his *Chronicles of an Accidental War Mage, Tales from the Battlefield*. I did have you read that one, right?"

The fear of being caught shirking her duties—few and far between, these days—caused a tremor that shook her from head to toe. She'd read it, yes. Admittedly, she'd skimmed some parts. A lot of parts. With a title like that, Liara would have thought the book contained more fireworks and flash, and fewer meanderings of morality. She'd liked it well enough, but it hadn't made much of an impression.

Nagarath smiled. "Now you see why I wanted you to read up on some things before we simply started waving wands around."

Liara brightened. "I'm going to get a wand?"

"No. Erm . . ." Nagarath reddened. "It would actually serve you best to learn with only your hands, at present. Wands are a bit of a cheat for beginners. Makes one rely upon something other than yourself to do the work for you."

Liara let a wheedling plea creep into her voice. "But that's like making me learn calligraphy without a pen."

"No, Liara. That is not going to work on me today." Nagarath craned his neck, looking up at the sky which had only just turned sunny. "You don't suppose it's too cold to go try a few spells in the courtyard, do you?"

The look Liara shot the mage told him that she couldn't care less how cold it was, so long as they were going to do real magick.

~*~

But of course Nagararth cared. Cared enough to make Liara return to her rooms for coat and hat—gloves, he explained, would only get in the way of casting.

Spellcasting! I'm going to do real magick. Liara practically skipped down the stairs and into the kitchen, tripping over the long tail of the scarf she'd bundled into her arms. And even though she'd hurried, Nagarath stood waiting for her by the door to the courtyard. Eyeing the tangle of mismatched wool in her arms, he gave a cry of recognition. "Ah. I wondered where that had walked off to."

Reddening under his gaze, Liara was quick to explain, "You let me borrow it the night we watched the moon together. I—I forgot I had it, since you haven't let me go outside." Her flush deepened as soon as the words were out. She hadn't meant that to sound like criticism. Shutting her mouth, lest anything else creep out carelessly, she held Nagarath's scarf out to him.

Why was he looking at her so? Head cocked to the side, a curious, considering sort of smile playing about the lips. She concentrated her gaze on the open sky behind him, scarf still held outward. Anything to avoid the intent look he gave her.

"I'd rather you kept it, Liara."

The softly spoken words provoked shockwaves in her insides. The moon, luminous and enchanting, filled her vision for one brief moment. Clutching the scarf to her, she nodded her thanks, rather than trusting herself to another stammering sentence. No accusations of thievery. No chiding for her gentle—if accidental—questioning of his better judgment with regards to being castle-bound. And magick. Things truly had changed for her and her mage.

Nagarath turned, ushering her out of the kitchen and turning his frightfully forceful gaze from her. With a sigh of relief, she followed, feeling as though in those short moments she'd forgotten half of what she'd just read on the topic of defensive warding.

Walking out into the bright late-morning sunshine, Liara bade Nagarath pause a moment while she shielded her eyes, waiting for them to adjust from the castle's dim interior. It was brisk, to be sure, but it felt good to be outside.

Especially for something like this. Her heart leapt in anticipation as Nagarath stooped to set aside his staff, turning from it to face her. The wizard adopted an *en garde* position, his wand at the ready. She watched the preparation with interest, her hands tingling nervously. *So, we're in for some exacting and precise casting, after all.*

"Loothemere's first lesson," Nagarath called out, grinning. He held his wand lightly in his fingers, loose but alert.

Liara thought fast. She recalled that the story in the book had been most colorful—the *language* that mage had used!—and contained a highly detailed description of how he had worked his first shielding spell.

First call the power. Rubbing her hands together, Liara concentrated on the heat she generated. Palm swirling against palm, she felt the change—a snapping of the air around her—and she hurriedly switched the motion to counterclockwise.

Come on, come on . . . She frowned in concentration, only vaguely aware of the funny faces she made with her efforts. A spark and a burst of cold along her fingertips, and Liara fanned her hands out abruptly, hissing a quiet acknowledgement of her success. She glanced up just in time to see the telltale flash of Nagarath's spell come up against her own. A crackle of orange flame danced along the invisible rounded shield she'd made, indicating the collision of power.

Lowering his wand, Nagarath grinned at her. "Well done."

Clapping her hands in giddy delight, Liara practically flew to Nagarath, who received her impulsive embrace with no small amount of surprise.

"I did it. I really did it. First try!" She looked up to find the mage blushing, an odd look in his eyes. Embarrassed by her overzealous display, Liara extracted herself from the hug with a start. She stood breathlessly, staring at her hands in wonder. "And it was just like the spell said. First hot, then the spark, then cold. And, boom, it *worked.*"

Liara did a gleeful little dance. The experience had been more amazing than she could have dreamed. The collision of their two spells had felt positively physical. Perhaps that was why she had rushed headlong into her spontaneous embrace of the wizard.

Nodding, Nagarath challenged her to replicate the spell. Again, Liara performed the motions. Swirl of palm on palm; reverse the direction. The resulting spark fizzled as quickly as it came. No cold burst of magefire danced across her fingertips. No shield.

Liara's face fell.

"Again." Nagarath's urging was gentle.

Determined, Liara rubbed her hands together, furrowing her brow as if she could draw the magick out with an angry pull. This attempt was worse than the last. Liara was left furiously rubbing her fingers together as though they were cold.

"If I may?" Nagarath stood at her side. Liara jumped. She hadn't even felt him approach, lost as she'd been in her spellwork.

"I'm not sure what I'm doing wrong." Her fingers tingled, but not from magick. "The first time, it just came naturally. Just like the book said. First clockwise, then reverse, drawing the power into your palms . . ."

"Ha." Nagarath's booming laugh echoed off the stones. At Liara's hurt look, he hurried to explain. "I'm sorry, Liara. But you reminded me of myself, just then. Following the belief that books have all the answers, and not just feeling your gift."

Liara cast a sly glance his way. "Then why did you have me read so much before trying anything practical?"

Nagarath opened his mouth to protest, but no words came out.

"I win." Liara flounced away, screwing up her face in renewed concentration. Maybe she should press her hands together harder? Softer? She tried to remember how she'd managed it so well the first time. Frustrated, she closed her eyes and looked inside herself, certain that the magick had to be there. Where was it hiding? Why did it refuse her call?

If I could just feel it like Nagarath said, I wouldn't have to bother with learning it at all. I could just think of a thing and make it so. She scowled, sensing within herself the sparkling vein of power that she could see but not control. The wizard made no sense. To Liara, magick only felt natural when she followed exacting instructions, her conviction making it work.

Conviction. Liara's eyes snapped open. She looked at Nagarath, who smiled and raised his wand. Almost on instinct, Liara drew forth the power, the icy-hot spark of her magick dancing along her fingertips at a mere thought. She raised her hands again, catching his blow with a wolfish grin.

Nagarath lowered his wand. "Good. What changed?"

"I—" Liara didn't want to say she'd merely felt it. That was too close to his advice. She chewed her lip, thinking of a better way to express it. Loothemere's words came to her, and she quoted the ancient mage. " 'It was as if I called unto myself the deep vein of power within me, bidding it rise upward into my very fingertips. A shield made of my own Art, summoned by my heart.' "

"And that is why we begin as we do." Nagarath, thankfully, was matter-of-fact in his answer, not giving in to the petty smugness he had earned. "As I said, no book can truly tell how to use your power thusly. At least, not in any practical sense. It can show you the way, open the door, but it is you who must think and feel the path. This is especially important in the case of defensive spells, where a split second's delay for a complicated gesture or word can mean defeat or worse. Loothemere is there to show you that it can be done and only outline how."

"Again." Liara raised her hands and lowered her gaze, challenging. "*En garde*, Nagarath."

Nagarath raised his wand and attacked in one smooth motion. Liara barely got her shield up in time, catching a glancing blow that spun her sideways. She complained, "Your aim was off."

"Was it?" Nagarath cocked an eyebrow, teasing. "I presume that if you were to be attacked, you'd first ask that they pretty please aim towards your shield."

Liara pouted. It seemed to her that he was asking a bit much of her, as she'd only just figured out how to call on the spell a few moments ago. But the last thing she wanted was to ask Nagarath to slow down. If the wizard thought she could do it, she wasn't going to disappoint.

Raising her hands, Liara called her Art into her fingers to form her shield again. This time she concentrated on how it felt, where the process wavered and where it felt strong. There was a thickness to it, and a current. Liara realized that if she bore down with her mind, she could mold the shield from its basic shape, stretching and bending it. In a way, it was like working with clay or mud. But unlike either, she did not have the option of adding more along the edges, unless she took some from the middle.

Or unless I call more magick into my shield, Liara concluded. This time her shield rebuffed Nagarath's glancing blow, earning her yet another smile and nod from her teacher.

Eager to see what happened if she put more into it, Liara took a deep breath and called the shield into being, reaching deep and calling once she was sure she had it right. "Hit me."

"Good work." Nagarath glanced at her shield casually. He bent to inspect something, a small bit of foliage from the garden, clinging to the hem of his robes. In waiting, Liara realized that putting more power into her shield meant it was harder to keep up. She wavered just as Nagarath turned from her, the mage flicking his wand over his shoulder.

The mage's spell shattered the last of her overextended defenses. The dull thump of colliding enchantments reverberated through the garden and off the walls, shaking snow from the nearby eaves. Caught as she was between the two powers, Liara had the sensation that a winter squall had begun—snow, wind, and the bright sparkle of magick whipping around her then dying, quick as it had come. Scowling, she reached up to wipe her cheek, finding that her glove came away wet with snow and dark with soot.

"No fair. You cheated," Liara accused, too angry to puzzle over what spell the mage had used to hit her, angrily scrubbing black ash from her glowering face.

"And how did I cheat?" Nagarath leaned comfortably against the sun-warmed stones of the garden wall, watching Liara's futile attempt to rid herself of the after-effects of his spell.

"You waited until I put my shield down."

"I had my back turned. How would I have known?"

"I don't know. You just did."

"Yes, it was like *magick*," the wizard teased, grinning. At Liara's pout, he adopted a more serious tone. "You'll find this helps." He tossed a clean cloth to her. "It was a lesson."

"In what?"

"Keeping your guard up. Remember, that shielding spell is designed to be defensive. Learn to be ready."

"Even against you?"

Nagarath's smile was enigmatic. Secreting his wand back into the folds of his robe, he reclaimed his staff and motioned for her to approach. "Here, I'll show you a shortcut for cleaning up that mess."

Liara approached, lifting her face expectantly to the mage, both of them leaping back as a sparrow came darting between them. It landed on the wall, twittering away as the two magick-users stared, unmoving.

"Liara. Go inside." Nagarath flattened his voice and leveled his staff, adopting an approximation of first position, such as the Dvigrad guards might have used when skirmishing. The motion seemed out of place on her lanky friend, and Liara startled at the sight, glad now that their own good-natured sparring but moments before had involved the wizard's wand instead of staff.

"But—"

"Now."

Though Liara could tell that he hadn't meant to bark at her, she had to work hard to bite back the hurt retort that sprang to her lips, and the protest that followed. *But I could help! Couldn't I?*

Something in Nagarath's voice brooked no argument, tension springing into his shoulders and darkening his eyes. Liara fled inside, wondering what he intended to do with the intruder, small and innocent as it seemed.

How did it get past the wall? An icy prickle of fear blossomed in her chest. The castle wards were compromised, perhaps ineffective. Visions filled her head of soldiers storming the ramparts, a dark wizard at their back shouting sharp words of magick. She again pictured Nagarath's tense face, eyes that had seen Dvigrad fall and feared the same for Parentino. Liara was tempted to march straight into the library and rifle through spell books, but stopped short, remembering the sooty state of her face and hands.

"Scared of a sparrow."

The fear dismissed, she turned with a sigh toward her room. It would have been nice if Nagarath had gotten around to telling her what shortcut he had in mind before sending her off into the castle. Instead, she was going to have to scrub herself clean the hard way.

~*~

"*Ata her'ah.*" Nagarath kept his voice low as he gave his command to the sparrow.

Hopping along the uneven stones of the garden wall, the little bird pecked at a shriveled vine, trying to pry off one of the long-dried berries that clung there. It paid little mind as Nagarath closed the distance between them.

He repeated his command. "*Ata her'ah.* Show yourself."

Startled, the bird took flight, perching in the lower branches of a tree along the inside wall, chirping angrily for having been disturbed. Having spoken its mind, the sparrow took off, darting over the boundaries of the castle grounds and disappearing out into the woods.

Nagarath stared at the silent forest for one long moment, then turned and retreated into the dark interior of the castle. His robes swirled around him, black as his mood. Taking the stairs two at a time, he tried to grasp at the varied threads of the spells working through Parentino. That sparrow wasn't one of his. It shouldn't have been able to gain access to the castle grounds. Something was wrong with their defenses. The very thought made his breath hitch in his chest, the dread like a physical blow.

Searching, fighting the frantic impulse that threatened to mar his concentration, Nagarath gasped as his mind caught on a snag in the spells. Mentally retracing his steps, he threw his power at the web, illuminating the dark corners, chasing away doubt until he could better see the problem.

The workroom? Nagarath frowned, unable to grasp why a problem would stem from there, the inner sanctum and heart of Parentino. The thought chilled him, for it meant that their fortification was truly vulnerable. *I wonder what changed.* Memories of a shadow on the horizon rose up once more, urging him to a greater pace.

Nagarath abruptly turned around, making for the second floor hallway. Almost without trying, he could feel with his Art that the girl was in her room. It was strange, this newfound ability to sense Liara.

She's gotten too close. He blanched at the memory of her impulsive courtyard embrace. Twice she'd been in his arms since the castle had come under attack—this from a girl who'd barely let anyone so much as brush her in passing.

She trusts you, mage. Don't let her down. He rapidly thrust such thoughts from him, making a small gesture with his wrist as he passed her room. He murmured under his breath, "Forgive me."

Telling himself it was for her own good, Nagarath went to his tower to work his next bit of sorcery. Barely through the door, he pointed skyward, throwing magefire into the spells that kept his enchanted roof aloft. A web of lightning crackled in response.

"Well, that's still working properly." He frowned. "And it's nearly identical to what I have protecting our perimeter . . ." He strode to the window, peering out into the barren woods. "So how did that little bird sneak in?"

There was a chink in the armor. And it was somewhere in this room. But where?

Liara is trusting you, mage. And you're losing your touch. He closed his eyes, shutting out the voice, checking through his network of spells once more.

There! Something was off. But only just. Nagarath's eyes snapped open, darting to one of the shelves that lined the walls. He reached out with his aura to the artifacts nestled in the darkened recesses.

"Aha!" Triumphant but puzzled, Nagarath eyed the pile of grinning skulls that he'd all but forgotten about. After all, that had been the point in assigning them custody of the spells. Borrowing the magick of the earth to run Parentino's defenses only did so much. A human hand—or in this case, head—had to be involved.

But Nagarath hadn't counted on curious hands rearranging things when his back was turned.

With a snap of his fingers, Nagarath removed the castle defenses—all save for the quick warding spell he'd placed upon Liara's room. Thinking fast, he debated whether he should return the skulls to their previous position, trying to remember if he'd ordered them any particular way when he'd first enacted the spells. *Knowing me? Likely not.*

He made a sign in the air, and felt the power bleed out of him at the effort. A breath later, the defenses returned in full, this time allowing for the skulls' new configuration. Nagarath sank into a nearby chair, spent. With a smile, he recalled Liara's youthful excitement upon enacting her first shielding spell, comparing it to his own exhaustion with a chuckle. *Ah, the energy of youth.*

Allowing himself an indulgent sigh of relief, Nagarath closed his eyes once more, feeling out the defenses with his aura. Yes, all was right. He and Liara were secure from . . . from whatever was out there.

The peace of the moment broke as he bolted upright in his chair. Jumping to his feet, Nagarath raced downstairs. He'd almost forgotten about Liara.

Undoing the spell was but the work of a moment. Pausing outside her room, Nagarath debated going in. But then, he wasn't even sure if the girl had noticed the charm he'd placed upon her door. All was quiet within. Shrugging, he decided to return to his workroom, his conscience clear.

Liara's eyes were daggers upon the mage as she entered the workroom.

"Sorry about the abrupt ending to our lesson. I presume the residue of our encounter in the courtyard wasn't all that difficult to clean up?" Nagarath pulled his book down from in front of his face long enough to flinch at the look Liara threw at him.

"Well enough . . . until you *locked me in!*"

"Ah, that . . ."

"Yes. That. Was I bothering you? Did you think I was going to get in your way, and so you locked me in my room?"

"No, no, nothing like that. I had to . . . erm, make a few small tweaks to the defenses." Nagarath appeared completely nonplussed at her words, rubbing his hands through his already tousled hair. Liara noted the slight pallor about his cheeks, the bags beneath his eyes. She wondered if he even realized what he'd done, what he'd taken from her with his thoughtless act. *Knowing him? Unlikely.* Well, it was high time he knew.

"And where does making me prisoner fit in?"

"It was only for a few minutes—"

"Minutes. Hours. Days. It shouldn't have happened at all!"

Nagarath drew himself up in his chair. "I didn't want to be disturbed. It was a delicate operation. And I wasn't even sure what I'd find. That bird getting in past the wall . . . I had to take all of our defenses down. I wanted to ensure that you were safe if . . ."

"If what?" Liara scowled, interrupting the mage and steadfastly ignoring his darkening frown. "If the imaginary boogiemen you've dreamed up stormed the castle and laid all to waste, I'd be safe and locked away in my room? No way for them to get in, and no way for me to get out. If your little experiment was so dangerous, what would have happened to me if something had happened to you?"

"The spell would have ended," Nagarath snapped back at her. "But there would have been a bit of a delay; hopefully keeping you *safe*."

"From a bird?"

"From whatever is out there—"

"We should be facing whatever it is together. You and me."

She paused, debating whether she should say what was really in her heart, concluding she must. For his own sake, she must. She forced her voice to stay even, quiet, like one speaking to a frightened child. "I don't even think there is anything out there. I think—"

"They are after me, Liara. Magick to magick—that's how these things work."

"But who—"

"An enemy. Venice. Habsburgs. Uskoks. A regiment of soldiers. A rival mage sent to rid Limska Draga of the one wizard who dares practice within the ban imposed by the Republic. I don't rightly know. And that I don't know—that I can't find out—is the greatest concern of all."

Nagarath's voice pitched higher, cracked. He rose to his feet, his black cloak swirling around him as he hurled his words at her. "There's something out there, Liara. Something—maybe magick. Something just beyond my senses. But I can feel it. Blanketing the valley and frustrating my efforts to even see it directly."

It was a sparrow, Nagarath. You were frightened out of your wits by a little bird. Anger became disdain. "If you can't see it, how do you know—?"

"Because I'm the wizard and you're not, Liara. And if you're not going to trust me to keep you safe . . ." Nagarath let the angry sentence die to silence. He turned away, throwing his hands in the air.

"I'm only 'not a wizard' because you won't let me."

He whirled around. "I'll be damned if that's ever stopped you. You defy me at every turn. Nothing else matters—no one else matters—nothing but you and your magick."

Stunned, Liara opened her mouth and found she hadn't a thing to say. Crushed, she blinked once, twice, then turned on her heel and ran from the room. She was done here. Done with magick, and done with him.

Liara had spent the remainder of the evening in her bedchamber, a petulant punishment for the mage. He wanted her locked in her room? Now he had it.

However, skipping dinner left her hungry, and infinitely restless after the tumult of the day. To think that it had begun with magick, only to end in bitter words and accusations. It still galled her, Nagarath's bespelling her room with her inside. How dare he? How dare he earn her trust, demand it of her over all these months and then run thoughtlessly over it with the flick of a wrist. He knew how hard it was for her to trust people. He knew how hard it had been on her staying inside these long weeks.

But your mage is stupid like that, Liara. You know that. And to yell at him for it? Righteous or not, she oughtn't to have done that. Tomorrow she'd have to apologize. It still stung that he hadn't come by to do so—it was very unlike him.

Which is fine by me. The passing of hours had done little to abate her anger.

Liara went to the window and threw open the casing, letting the biting wind snap at her nose and ears. The moon looked haunting, a far cry from its gentle warmth the night she and Nagarath had gazed upon it through his marvelous telescope. With a grimace, Liara acknowledged that much had changed since then.

"I'm the wizard and you're not," she repeated the words thrown at her but hours before.

But that's your fault. Not mine.

She was almost a mage. But almost didn't count. Nothing—not bolstering the defenses, or restoring the library, or nursing him in his illness—nothing had counted. She was always put back in her place at the end of the day. Nagarath took pains to do so, even in the face of all her assistance.

Did he not understand what it meant to trust someone? No, clearly he wanted to fall down exhausted from spell-casting again, tired from chasing sparrows all day. *And don't expect me to help you when you do.* She stormed away from the window, leaving it open behind her. Black and formless, her shadow loomed out over the floor of her bedchambers. She imagined that it looked just like a wizard's robes, and suppressed a shudder. If he did not trust her, how could she trust him? But then, according to him, nobody else mattered to her anyway. A rogue tear shivered down her cheek and she brushed it away angrily.

Learn to be ready . . . keep your guard up . . .

Even against you? Liara had teased. Though he'd smiled in answer, Liara felt uneasy that the words had even come to her lips. It felt too much like a premonition.

Somewhere out in the silvery, moonlit forest, an owl called out on its nightly patrol, the eerie sound prickling the hair on the back of her neck. Liara remembered the open window. Leaning forward to shut it, her gaze raked over the black skeletons of the trees.

It all seemed so peaceful. Limska Draga. Valley of her birth.

She let her eyes wander the dark hills, rising to the horizon where Dvigrad's hulking form lay stark against the blanket of stars. It looked so far away. Soon the spring would come, bringing to completion her first year outside of the city's walls. She wondered how it looked now, bereft of all inhabitants. Did snow settle onto chimneys previously glowing with warmth? Had the wind and ice carved its way through windows and doors, blotting out the memories of cozy cheer?

Not that Liara had many memories of cozy cheer. But on that dark night, she could lie to herself. With no one to correct her brash presumption, she could imagine that Dvigrad had once felt like home. For, just then, Parentino certainly did not.

The restlessness that had plagued her all evening returned full force. She had to see Dvigrad. Had to see with her own eyes what had become of her people. For though they had not trusted her, at least they had said so to her face.

Nagarath was always telling her to grieve. Hadn't she done just that? Or did he feel that he had to control that, too? This wasn't just a place she'd lived. With Dvigrad had died the last hopes she had for finding out the truth of her origins. Someone still had to have known. She had planned, one day, to go back and ask—no, demand—such information.

A thought sidled into her brain: Phenlick and Nagarath had been friends.

Hope surged and died, the anger of the afternoon's fight returning full force. *If Nagarath has kept such truths from me, so help me. . .* Another realization dawned. The mage wouldn't be privy to that sort of thing. He never concerned himself with anything outside Parentino. He didn't know anything remotely useful. All he knew was how to tug his nose and launch into a lecture about how she was wrong about everything....

Well, she'd show him.

Whispering beneath her breath the half-remembered words of hexes and enchantments that she'd worked on through the evening, Liara crossed to the wardrobe. There she tugged on coat and hat, boots and gloves, with a determined yank. Then she crept to the door—quietly, lest the wizard be up and about. Turning, she warded the room, thrilling at the shiver of her Art as it coursed through her veins.

And with that, Liara, dressed in her warmest, left Parentino by the light of the winter moon. If the wizard refused to tell her the truth of things, she would find it out herself.

Chapter Eighteen

The crust of undisturbed snow crunched under Liara's boots as she stepped at last beyond the boundary of Parentino's outer wall. Holding her breath, she waited, unmoving for one long moment, half expecting unknown horrors to assail her. The forest was still as a graveyard. Even the wind seemed to be long abed.

Stepping forward, thrilled at her daring, Liara cast a glance over her shoulder, jumping as Parentino winked out of existence behind her. Terror gripped her as she whipped around, suddenly sure that her impulsive exodus had been a terrible mistake. But there Parentino stood, solid and reassuring.

"How very odd," she murmured aloud, wondering if the castle's disappearance had been but the trick of an overwrought mind. She turned to look out over the still, silent wood. Parentino promptly wavered and disappeared.

With a shiver, Liara resisted the temptation to again turn round and stare. It was something in the mage's spells. She was sure of it. Slowly, she let her eyes slide to the side, looking at Parentino out of the corner of her eye.

Wavering, the old fortress swam back into view. So the castle was still there. For her, at least. Liara stepped over the boundary, her hands coming into contact with the cold stone of the wall as she passed. It seemed real enough.

For some reason, it bothered her. The illusion of the disappearing fortification called into sharp focus the memory of Nagarath glibly winking his cozy cottage out of existence.

"More tricks and half-truths." Liara scowled, her heart squeezing as Parentino blinked out of sight once more. It would serve the wizard right if she decided to simply camp at Krešimir's home and await his return. At least Krešimir had set off to do something; hadn't locked his doors and hidden himself away.

Cheered by the idea, and wondering if that wasn't the better option no matter what welcome she found when she returned to Parentino, Liara set out along the familiar path towards Dvigrad.

Because I'm the wizard and you're not.

Nagarath's thoughtless outburst echoed round and round in her head, stirring her anger once again. With each repetition, she felt her ire build, assigning to the words new hurts and slights. A part of her knew they were not necessarily true—the part with, admittedly, the smallest voice, at present. Said voice of reason spent much of the walk to Dvigrad trying to alert Liara to the folly of her actions.

But, up in her bedroom, hours before, she had craved action. In the absence of anything save dread over what she was likely to find in the abandoned town, it felt satisfying to be fiercely angry.

And so she embraced the riot of emotions, her mood black as the stones of the empty village now looming through the trees ahead of her, driving back the deep emptiness that threatened to overcome her. She ran the last few steps, reveling in the rise of her pulse and the quickening of her breath. It was as if her anger had summoned invisible demons to chase her through the woods, though that same small voice of reason whispered that she really ran from herself.

Fully clear of the woods at last, Liara stood on the moonlit path, catching her breath and eying the town entrance with trepidation. Inching forward, she noted that the snow had thinned and grown uneven. In many places there was more path than snow cover, as if the elements, too, had their misgivings about disturbing the empty town. Even her shadow, short and stunted by the high moonlight, stretched out feebly, appearing reluctant to reach Dvigrad's gate. She was banished, forbidden from entering. And though they who had pronounced the edict were dead, it seemed to Liara that the very walls frowned down upon her.

"Well, you can't have come all this way just to turn around." Liara reached forward, brushing the rough wood of the gate with her fingertips. She frowned at the action's timidity. *I've spent too much time around wizards.* She had forgotten what it felt like to act while unobserved. Her life without a web of spells about her was but a distant memory.

With a gentle creak, the door yielded to her push, its slight inward swing revealing more of the hollow town to its solitary invader. Although she knew better than to expect an answer, she couldn't enter without first calling out, "Anyone there?"

Sliding sideways through the gate, Liara peered about her at the cold, silent buildings. Somewhere down one of the winding streets, she thought she heard the echoing rustle of a small creature diving for cover.

Not entirely abandoned, then, she concluded, wondering what animal had claimed the village as its own. The tracks throughout the patchy snow were small and varied. Mainly those of birds. She felt a pang of guilt for having been so tardy in coming to revisit this place. *Though it really isn't my fault, since Nagarath wouldn't let me leave.*

If it weren't for the stillness that rang in her ears, Liara could almost imagine the normal hustle and bustle of the town. Nothing was missing except for the people. Not a house had been touched.

She wasn't sure what she had expected. Rows of headstones? Some sort of signpost to mark what had happened? It was Dvigrad. Familiar and more real than Parentino had ever been. But empty.

Clutching her coat to her, Liara hurried to the church, the hurt in her heart growing to a yearning to see her old residence in particular. St. Sophia's stood open to the wind and snow. Ducking her head through the door, she laughed grimly at her misjudgment. It was black as pitch inside, save for the few darts of moonlight that managed to creep in through the narrow windows. She had forgotten that the candles would be long extinguished, their flickering welcome but another memory.

False bravado snuffed out, Liara found the dead quiet all too palpable. Something deep inside her began to quake, all pretense of unreality swept away in the sobering black on black of the empty sanctuary. People had died here. She quickly exited the church, fearful now, for the silence seemed to scream at her, a nightmare become real. Phenlick . . . died here. Stumbling blind through her tears, she fought her way back to the town square.

Dvigrad's town square: site of the priest's cold pronouncement nearly one year ago, the beginning of her banishment. For some reason, she found she could not recall the words Father had used. Instead, her mind's eye remembered only a kind smile on his wrinkled face.

"He's dust, Liara," she reminded herself, the words carefully hardened. "Dust like the rest of them." She knelt and scraped her fingers along the frozen ground. It yielded reluctantly under her industrious pawing, and she soon had a handful of dirt for her efforts. She closed her eyes, waited for her mind to center. But she couldn't block out what wasn't there—no stone markers to honor those who had passed, no burial mounds or memorials to mark the fallen.

Opening her eyes, Liara peered at the gravel and dirt in her hand. It was so ordinary. More memories came, unbidden and jostling for her attention. How many times had she threatened to leave, to wipe this very dust from her feet at the gates of the town? When was the last time she had fallen face down in this dirt, tripped by another girl intent on showing the fey child her place? Wasn't it here that Father Phenlick had wiped her tears, gently lifting her and tending to her hurts and slights—a skinned knee, her bruised pride?

Recalled to the present, Liara screamed her pain, her hurt, her anger, flinging the contents of her hand, scattering the dirt over the ground. Dust among dust.

It wasn't just the town that was empty. It was Liara herself. She raged at the desolate village, screaming at the stones. "You've left me. All of you. Why? Why does everyone leave me? Why is everything I want denied me?"

Two pinpricks of light winked at her from the dark

interior of a nearby house. Her bitter words cut short, Liara scrambled backwards in alarm. Floating, the two small orbs swayed side to side, then bounced in place before winking out.

"Who's there?" Her voice came out shaky and cracked. She cleared her throat, hand reaching for the knife in her belt. The hair at the nape of her neck prickled to attention. She felt the distinct, indescribable sensation of being watched. And though it was winter, the air seemed filled with the pent-up electricity of a summer's storm.

There was magick in the air.

"Nagarath?" Liara breathed the name. Perhaps—as with everything else she ever did—the mage had known of her sneaking out. She waited long moments for an answer, growing uneasy as the white silhouette of the moon slid down past the upper edge of Dvigrad's battlements, leaving Liara in a darker blackness than before.

Dawn was coming; was, perhaps, an hour or two away. If she was to return to Parentino with any hope of sneaking back in before Nagarath awoke, she'd have to leave Dvigrad at once.

The sense of being watched fled as quickly as it came. No more tension in the air; no more glowing balls of light within the vacant houses. Rising, Liara dusted herself off, shaking off snow and paranoia in one determined movement.

You're as bad as the wizard, she scolded, feeling a fool. And though it felt terrible to think so in her current surroundings, Liara was momentarily grateful that there had been nobody around to witness her ungainly scramble.

The futility of sadness rose anew in Liara's heart, replacing her shame and fear. Alone in the gathering darkness, she turned slowly in place, soaking in memories and distantly wondering to what end she'd been saved from the ghastly fate she gazed upon.

She was nothing. A little girl frightened of the dark. A young woman who dreamed of magick, only to be frustrated at every turn. What had a useless thing like her returned to Dvigrad for? To gloat? To mourn? She could do neither properly.

Father Phenlick's voice rose in Liara's mind. *We live to love. It is in loving that we find our way, though the night may be long and the path dark.* That's what she'd come for. Not to find answers or to disprove Nagarath's silly fears, but to remember the people she'd known, and to not shrink from the touch of those memories.

"The mage cannot fault that." Setting her jaw, Liara made for the nearest house. A quick search provided both lantern and match. Shielding her eyes as the lantern flared to life, Liara gazed around the empty home, eyes raking over the smudge of gray ash here and there, the last remnants of lives cut tragically short.

She returned to the church, reentering St. Sophia's with quiet solemnity, her lantern raised. Making her way to the side altar, she slowed, feeling again that she was being watched.

Though if anyone saw you now, they'd likely laugh. The fey girl lighting candles for the dead. Liara thought of the irony but knelt to light the topmost devotional candle in the metal rack. She didn't stop there. Though some had burned longer than others, with a little determination, she was able to light each of the prayer votives.

Basking in the comforting glow of the flickering flames, Liara felt she had done well in driving back the darkness. It was the least she could do. She knelt in simple reflection, finding that Father Phenlick's guiding voice in her mind had so far stayed silent on the topic of prayer. But then, he'd always understood her better than anyone.

Rising, Liara made to leave, pausing as she wondered if she might espy where her friend and one-time protector had met his end. Sliding out the side door of the church, she headed for the priest's offices, slowing as her lantern light fell upon a strange, dark stain on the wall.

Bending closer, Liara saw that the mark was but one of six similar smudges, as if a fire had been set in the hallway at half a dozen places. Looking down to the floor, she noted the telltale gray shadow of ash, the thin layer laying in a swirled pattern—no doubt the product of the winter winds howling through the building's chinks and fissures, and her own disturbance with the door moments ago.

She looked back to the black smudges blasted into the stone wall, puzzled. Whatever would have made such marks? Liara peered closer, lifting the lantern and grateful that the morning had not yet come. Daylight, she feared, would only serve to obscure, not illuminate. She reached out a trembling hand, touching the masonry, testing it.

Cold unlike she had ever experienced shot through her fingers. She jerked her hand back from the wall with a hiss, nearly dropping the lantern. It was like being burned. Dizzily, Liara realized that merely touching the mark had drawn upon her power. There was sorcery in these stones? How?

Invasive, probing and pulling all at once; merely brushing her fingers against them had stirred the core of her Art. But there'd been none of the excitement, the spark of warming fire she'd come to know from calling her magick. Even the sensation of Nagarath's library, books whispering dangerous promises to fingers that fairly itched to open the covers, was pleasant by comparison. Sour, hateful, grasping—that's how these blackened scars felt, even to her who still knew so little about the Art. She recoiled further, her eyes darting back to the gray ash, the black blast marks telling a new story. Father Phenlick had been fleeing pursuit. Magickal pursuit.

Terrified, Liara backed away, her hand blindly seeking the door. Had Nagarath known of this? Of who had done it? Had he, perhaps, covered it up?

Was he somehow involved? He'd specifically told her that there was no other mage. But then, he'd also turned right around and locked her in Parentino, spouting fears over other magicks in the valley. Power he couldn't see. Answers he could not give when pressed. *He's protecting someone.*

Choking on the sick feeling that rose in her chest, Liara stumbled out of St. Sophia's on legs numb with fear. Nagarath had lied to her. He'd called it a plague. But what she had discovered was murder. Murder by magick.

The sky had turned from inky black to charcoal. Morning approached. And Liara had nowhere to go. If only she had magick. If only she could whisk herself away on a word of power. Or, better yet, confront the mage who'd taken everything from her.

Revenge. That's what her heart cried for. Bent on

vengeance her whole life—revenge for slights and knocks, for name-calling and exile, for a demon that had left her mother broken and bespelled—Liara's past paled in comparison to the bleak present in which she found herself.

She stood amidst the wreckage of Nagarath's promises. Safety for Limska Draga; isn't that what he'd assured the priest? The wizard's protection, something they'd all relied upon. And where had it gotten her? Where had that gotten them?

She cried out, the sound echoing off the walls of the dead village. "I trusted you," she shrieked. "I trusted you, you impotent, cowardly mage."

"Tsk, tsk. Shouting at a stone wall. And to think this one had promise." The voice, craggy and singsong, lilted at Liara from somewhere behind her.

She spun around, heart in her throat and hand at her knife. "Who's there?"

"Oh, and she goes for the knife instead of a wand. Dear me, we have such work to do," the voice teased again, closer this time.

"I'm warning you. Show yourself, or I'll—" Liara's eyes widened as two gleaming orbs winked at her from high up in the shadows next to the church.

"Or you'll what? Surely you don't wish to strike me." A dark form floated out of the gloom, winging its way to a nearby tree. Just an owl. The creature blinked, its two bright eyes glittering as it cackled, clicking its beak raucously. "I'm merely trying to help."

Bird and girl stared at each other.

I'm dreaming. It's all a bad dream. I never left Parentino. I never came to Dvigrad in the middle of the night, and there is no bird talking to me. Nagarath is the same nice, eccentric, frustrating wizard that I've believed him to be, and I'm going to wake up in my bed, and all will be well. Though Liara wouldn't classify her thoughts as a prayer, it was as close as she ever got.

"Are you going to speak to me, or aren't you?" The owl ruffled his plumage and shifted his weight, idly pulling at the bark beneath his claws.

Liara found her voice. "You said something about a wand."

"Oh, so you are listening, after all." With another cackle, the bird hopped to a lower branch as Liara lowered her knife. "Well, it's a good idea, isn't it? It'd get you what you want. Weren't you just now contemplating revenge?"

What she craved—what she'd always craved—were answers. What was done was done. But to be adrift, alone in the world, not knowing whether the home you lived in was mere illusion, if you could ever trust the words of a friend again . . . Revenge, though desirable, couldn't give her that.

"If you met the wizard who'd done this—met him on the path, right this moment—would you not want the power to justly punish him for his crime?"

Liara jutted her chin. "Magick is forbidden here."

The owl cackled again, derisively. "That's a-*dor*-able. I suppose I should be leaving, then."

"Leaving?" The wistfulness in Liara's voice surprised her.

The owl cocked its head to the side, looking at Liara almost sideways. "If magick is forbidden here, then I must be gone. Think, girl. How else would a bird speak to a non-magick-user—"

"I'm not a non-magick-user."

"Is that so? You know how to shoot fireballs, immobilize your enemy as if he were encased in ice, send his mind to another dimension entirely? I had no idea I was in the presence of a much-accomplished mage."

"No . . . nothing like that." Liara waved him off, feeling stupid but not certain why.

"Then what sorcery do you know, pray tell?" the bird challenged gleefully.

"Practical magicks," she shot back in annoyance, wishing she had never engaged the owl. "Defensive spells, warding . . ."

"Oh, so you'll *defend* your enemy to death?" The bird winked at her with his bright eyes. "No wonder you're mad at your 'impotent cowardly mage.' "

Thrown back at her in mocking tones, the words she'd screamed seemed to hold extra menace. Fearful, she stepped back, wondering how enchanted the owl really was. How much had he heard? How much did he know?

Trembling, half-afraid of the answer, Liara asked, "Do you know what happened here?"

The owl preened himself, beak buried in chest plumage and wings fluttering with his efforts. Sharp claws scratched audibly at the branch on which he sat. Ignoring her question entirely, he continued, "There is a famous war mage who lives just west of here. In Vrsar, where the river meets the sea. Goes by the name of Anisthe. He could teach you something useful, I daresay."

Liara blinked in surprise. Another mage? Living that close?

Krešimir went to Vrsar. The thought soothed her.

Perhaps she could get more out of this owl if she played it right. "And what does that matter to me?" Her flippant nonchalance returned with the ease of a well-worn slipper.

"I can see your aura, girl. I know you have questions." The owl gave his best imitation of a shrug. "My friend, the war mage of Vrsar, may have answers that your wizard refuses to give."

"My aura? My magickal signature?"

"Is strong. And my master seeks an apprentice. And as he himself has an interest in knowing what went on here in Limska Draga, an area under the protection of his old schoolmate—oops, now I have said too much. For that story, you'd have to speak to my master."

The owl flapped his wings, making as if to rise. A gray feather floated down, landing on the white snow. "A gift, girl. Should you wish to do something with your life other than waste it in the company of a mage who clearly wishes nothing more than to hide you away from the world."

Eyes still on the owl, Liara bent to pick up the offering. Just an ordinary gray feather. She tried anyway. "*Sh'lemull.*"

"Ah-ha. She does know something useful," the bird cried from above, dancing on his branch, even as the feather in Liara's hand glowed brightly for one brief moment. "Grasp it and say '*tra'shuk.*' And for the gods' sake, girl, don't let go of it until you're there."

With that, the owl took flight, his ungainly form swooping low past her on his way out of Dvigrad. The early morning darkness swallowed him in a matter of moments.

Holding the feather, Liara wondered what, exactly, *'tra'shuk'* meant. It was a word of magick, that she could guess. She would have liked to look it up in Parentino's library. But that would mean confronting Nagarath, asking him what had really happened in Dvigrad.

Admittedly, the thought no longer disgusted her. He always had a mundane explanation for every alarming thing. Dvigrad was likely no different. Remembering Nagarath's kind smile, his patient manner and his clear regard for her, Liara felt guilty for her rash accusations. Grief did funny things to a person. Perhaps she'd read the entire situation wrong.

And that owl had given her the chills with his flippant manner and eyes that glowed like embers. Liara made to drop the feather, but paused. A war mage by the coast. A former school chum of Nagarath's, and he'd never said a word. Maybe he didn't know.

Maybe Anisthe was the ally they needed. Or at least a voice of reason against Nagarath's growing paranoia.

And Vrsar is where Krešimir went.

Satisfied, she grasped the feather tightly, the word that the owl had taught her clear in her mind. "*Tra—*"

A searing cold wind tore the rest of the word from her lips, plunging her into a darkness unimaginable. Screaming aloud in the dark, only to find that the scream made no sound, Liara felt as though she'd been snuffed out of existence.

Something had gone horribly wrong.

Chapter Nineteen

It's true that the girl defies me at every opportunity. Caught up in her own machinations, not once has she checked her actions at my behest. Nagarath defended his thoughtless outburst countless times during the afternoon and evening that had followed their fight. And just as many times, he'd risen to go make amends for the hasty accusations. But he was right! Even if the words were harsh.

And then it was morning, his high temper exhausting him so much that he'd once again dozed off in his workroom, precariously perched on his stool. In the watery morning sunlight, the words still ringing terribly in his mind, he decided it was high time to apologize. *I'm the wizard and you're not.* What a fool thing to say.

"How about: I'm scared, Liara. Please help me." Nagarath scoffed as he returned to his rooms to ready himself for the day—for the apology that must come. A bracing splash of water on his face. A fresh, hastily tugged-on shirt. His hand hesitated as he reached for his black wizard's robes. Without it, he felt exposed, and yet Nagarath found it hard to don a robe of power when he felt powerless. The situation in the valley had spiraled out of his control; in many ways, long before he'd ventured into Dvigrad weeks ago; before he'd broken his promise to the priest and given Liara over to magick.

Of course, it had occurred to him that he could sit the

girl down and tell her the truth. Could tell Liara everything that he knew about her, her parentage, his awareness of her lackluster upbringing in Dvigrad amongst folk who'd hated and feared and persecuted her . . .

"And then have to explain why I sat back and did nothing. Even now." Then she'd hate him, even more than she had after last night.

He couldn't risk losing her, even over something like the truth. No mage could. Aurenaurae—such rare magicks, such pure power. In the darkest corners of his heart, he could feel pride in having had a hand in it. *And that is why she would hate you. You magick users are all alike—magick first.* His own words came back to haunt him once more.

No, the truth would not hurt her. Not anymore. He found Liara's resilience frightening. Her fearlessness was, to him, one of her more worrisome qualities. That, and her cynical, plotting, thieving nature. But then, perhaps this was their middle ground. Perhaps, in her penchant for dishonesty, Liara would understand where he was coming from.

She'd shut herself in her room. He couldn't well dissemble any longer. She didn't believe his lies, anyway.

"But can I trust her with the truth?" Around and around the argument ran.

Nagarath sat, head in his hands. The fact of the matter was that he did believe Liara was strong. Strong-willed and strong-hearted. She could deal with the reality of her origins. And she was smart. She could likely accept the argument that she oughtn't learn magick just yet.

But Nagarath did not trust himself. Nearly two decades later, and he was still haunted by the nightmares: a spell gone horribly wrong, three young mages scattering to the wind in fear and shame. He carried the burden of that awful night with him every day of his life, and still he wondered at his worth as a wizard, even now.

If he couldn't trust himself, how could he possibly ask it of Liara?

Perhaps she could accept the hard truth, as she had done so many times in her life. But he couldn't live with the thought of her hating him.

Reaching over to the wooden peg and grasping his cloak, Nagarath swallowed the lies once more. Clothing himself in his mage's robe of power—*my disguise,* he thought bitterly—he pasted on his customary smile and left to collect Liara.

She'd had a nice long sulk. Nagarath was sure he could lure his ward out with the promise of more magick. Like him, the girl was predictable in how drawn she was to the Art. Though to him it had become as commonplace, as necessary for his existence as breathing, he'd seen that magick was what made her smile, what drew her out of her scheming, sullen isolation.

Knocking on the door to her room, Nagarath rehearsed his apology. Locking her in had truly been a mistake. But he'd been in such a hurry that he hadn't thought, merely acted, counting on the girl's generosity of understanding.

No answer.

Nagarath knocked again. "Liara? Liara, if you're still angry with me from yesterday, I really would like to apologize."

He paused, already backing out of his conviction that she—a child, really—could handle the truth. But what could he offer in its place without prompting further questions? She simply didn't know how to let a matter drop.

Waiting anxiously in the hallway, Nagarath ran his mind back over the well-trod paths of the last twelve hours. Liara knew about Father Phenlick's letter. That hadn't contained anything that he couldn't tell the girl. The townsfolk had feared her, worried that leaving her in the hands of the wizard was a threat to their safety, and had acted accordingly. And as she unequivocally discounted his other fears, he really had nothing to lose, no chance of a misstep, so long as he stuck to the facts she was willing to entertain. He should keep to the present disaster in Dvigrad and steer clear of the past. Might he still have a hope of keeping his own implication in the disaster of eighteen years ago safely secreted? He could, so long as he refrained from more careless speech.

The only real fallout would be hurt feelings on Liara's part, guilt that her mere existence had put Father Phenlick in danger of losing his authority over the soldiers—nothing that a bit of soothing couldn't fix. Perhaps then she would understand some of the fears that haunted Nagarath, the threats that she clearly didn't see as real.

A whisper of magick on the wind and the fear of persecution. Nagarath's other worries rioted for attention once more. *Not telling her won't make the problem go away,* his conscience whispered at him. *She'll always look to those dark battlements across the valley and the questions will start anew.*

But that only mattered if they stayed in Parentino.

That's it. I'll take her away. We can leave today. Dvigrad was gone, the last of Liara's real ties to the valley destroyed with the death of its people. He had Liara, his books, his family seat abroad. . . . They could leave this wreck of a castle, this valley with its broken promises, and live free and clear at last. *I won't have to tell her anything just yet.*

"And I can teach her magick." The staff in his hand felt suddenly heavy, an added reminder of how troublesome a home—any home—could be. Even so, he raised his voice. This had gone on long enough. "Liara, please open the door. We need to talk about something. It's important."

The nonresponse had grown beyond petulant. Though he didn't want to disturb her privacy, a sliver of fear entered his heart. It was too quiet, even for Liara. While she liked a good sulk, there was nothing she loved more than rash words and confrontation.

Nagarath tried the knob, recoiling as a warding spell rebuffed him.

Fool girl. You learn one warding spell . . . Promises of apprenticeship and trust temporarily forgotten, Nagarath muttered a word of power under his breath. The castle, the very stone and wood of it, was his. No spell would keep him from his own.

The door unlocked, meekly squeaking as Nagarath opened it with the full force of his fear and anger.

No protest rushed to greet his unbidden entrance. The room was empty. No Liara. Annoyed at having been fooled—*she must have been up and about for hours*—Nagarath turned on his heel and strode downstairs, intent on the library.

No Liara.

Nor was she in the kitchen, the garden, the workroom, the cellar, or any of the rooms in Parentino. Returning to her bedchamber, Nagarath looked around with eyes newly opened by desperation.

Her cloak was missing. As were her warmest pairs of boots and gloves. The peg that held her hat stood empty.

Liara was gone.

She also took the scarf. With a sharp pang in his chest, he sat on the edge of Liara's sleep-tossed bed. Raising his hands, he brought the words of a spell to his lips. Faltering, he let them drop.

The spells protecting their perimeter were intact. There was no need to test them again. The girl was gone, and of her own volition. Again, he looked bleakly around the room, feeling as if the sun had failed to rise.

In the back of his mind, a voice screamed at him, goading him to action. Liara was out somewhere in the woods of Limska Draga. Perhaps in grave danger. But sitting in the quiet of her room, staring blindly out at the fitful snowfall, he found he just couldn't move.

Desolate. That's how he felt. From the soles of his feet, to the tips of his fingers, to the nape of his neck, he felt hollowed out. Empty. Like her room. It robbed him of his will, of his belief in himself.

'I'll be damned if that's ever stopped you.' No taking those words back. Hanging his head, he bowed to the shame of having lost his temper—and at a moment where she had so clearly needed him to be strong, logical. He ought to have apologized straight off. But what would that have won him? She'd have left anyhow. And it was her right. He needed no reminder that Liara was her own person. Damned. Yes, he would be.

I should have kept well out of it. The old priest would

have seen to it that the girl wasn't hanged. Consequences be damned, he was the last person on earth that ought to have been caring for a headstrong, impertinent young woman. He wasn't cut out for it. When, along the way, had he forgotten that? *Admit it, mage, you never could leave well enough alone.* And each time, he'd botched things. She'd have been better off not knowing him. Him with his hateful, thoughtless words. Protector. Bah.

'*We should be facing whatever it is together. You and me.*' Hope rose with the recollection. '*Together.*' Did that mean she cared? But then again, she'd said as much believing there to be no danger.

He stared out the window as the quiet, soft flakes of winter drifted by. *Look at it. Mayhap she was right all along. The forest is safe, and I've been a fool.* The disconnect between feeling and seeing was as profound as his sense of emptiness. It was like being ensorcelled. Or like being in love.

Shaking his head, he reached absently for his staff. No, he did not love Liara. He regarded her, most certainly. He had a fondness for her that eclipsed all things save magick. But fondness wasn't love.

Crossing over to the window, he stared out over the trees, the snow thick enough that it obscured his vision of Dvigrad up on the hill across the valley. Liara had gone there. He was sure of it.

The thought eased his heart, crowding out the rising panic, though it let his guilt lie. Surely she was still angry with him—her warded door was proof enough of that. If he followed her to Dvigrad, he'd likely be yelled at for his efforts.

Worth the risk. '*Together.*'

He was down the stairs and out the door without a second thought.

Head bent against the fitful wind, he shrugged his half-donned coat up onto his shoulders so that it wouldn't drag in the snow the whole journey to Dvigrad. One white-knuckled hand clutching his staff, the other thrust deep in his pocket, he found that he'd inadvertently brought with him a small codex and forgotten his wand. No matter. His staff would suffice, should he be called upon to use it. The book contained easy defensive spells—ones he'd intended Liara try—that did not require the precision of a wand. Liara might believe the woods empty, but there was no reason for him to abandon all caution. Even if ne'er-do-wells stalked the forest, they wouldn't likely be out in such weather. He pressed forward, steadfastly ignoring his brain's reminder that not all threats were cowed by the elements.

He sniffed and pulled his collar closer about his chin, his eyes tearing up—from the cold alone, surely. Again, he grouched at having been made to come out in such foul weather. It felt better to be angry than saddened . . . or guilty.

Even with the snow swirling about, obliterating the path and frustrating his progress, vexation paved the way. Almost there. And no footsteps, save his own. But she'd have sheltered in the town once she noted the mounting snowstorm. Or perhaps she'd meant to stay, all along. *She did run away from you, after all.* He quickened his steps. Raising his face to the falling snow, he breathed, trying to ascertain whether cook fires burned within the town.

The wind offered no clue, giving back nothing save the crisp wetness of a gathering blizzard. Memories of his last visit savaged him. Bodies. More questions than answers—or, perhaps more accurately, answers he dared not seek. He shoved away the memory of a dark cloud hanging on the edge of thought.

The gate stood open, snow blowing in and out on the whims of each fitful gust of wind, the door to the village looking for all the world like a mouth breathing. Heart squeezing with misgiving, he raised his staff, wishing again that he had his wand.

But gaining entrance to the city proved his fears unfounded. Hunched against the snow, the silent homes and businesses of Dvigrad paid no heed to their visitor. No soldiers marched the streets, no chimneys emitted the comforting gray smoke that marked civilization.

Dvigrad was just as he had left it. Cold. Desolate.

He ran to the church, sure that Liara would have gone there first, though the fallen snow made it impossible to be certain. His heart leapt as he nearly tripped over a lantern, left on the front walk of the church and half-covered in the snow. A small ring of ice lay at its base, evidence that the lantern had been allowed to burn itself out mere hours before.

Liara!

She had been here. Slipping on the snow, he scrambled up the church steps. Another door ajar, menacing as Dvigrad's front gate—add to it Liara's abandoned lantern, and the evidence boded ill. Breath stolen by crippling anxiety, he stumbled forward into St. Sophia's, glad for the brightness outside that somewhat illuminated the dark interior of the church. He refused to use his magelight here. Hallowed ground was hallowed ground. He blinked, thinking that perhaps the red-orange glow he saw up ahead in the side apse was merely an illusion, brought on by eyes dealing with the sudden transition from blinding white to near black.

But no, there were candles lit in the darkness.

"Liara," he whispered. Relieved, he crept forward, head swiveling from side to side in search of the girl. The devotional candles flickered as he approached. Burning fitfully, some were on the edge of going out—indeed, one sputtered and died as he stood watching.

Turning, for he sought answers, not clues, Nagarath strode past the side door, his heart constricting as he remembered where he had last seen the priest. Liara would have gone looking for Father Phenlick. Long legs making short work of the distance, he threw open the door to the inner hallway. "Liara?" He called her name once more. The girl had left her lantern outside. Had left it burning. But there were no signs of a struggle. What did it mean? The pressing fog of panic reentered his mind.

How will I find her? And could he do so in time? *In time for what? There is no menace here but the fault of your own distraught mind. The girl was right.* Despairing, he leaned heavily on the wall, sure that through his foolishness, he'd lost her forever.

An odd thought struck. Stumbling as one who had lost all wit, all sense of direction and hope, he reentered the church, falling to his knees as he neared the glinting rack of candles. He didn't pray, at least not with words. He just reached out, pleading with the universe that he might know Liara to be safe. No magick. No tricks. Just hope.

In the quiet comfort of St. Sophia's, he felt his heart ease, the fog recede. He was smarter than this. He had eyes and ears all over the valley. *It's time to see and be seen, Nagarath. And Liara . . . well, she'll just have to listen to reason.*

Rising to his feet, he took his leave of the dark interior of the church, realizing that it had, in some ways, been Liara who had comforted him just now. After all, she had lit the candles.

Chapter Twenty

"–shuk."

Liara fell to her knees, shaking. Gasping like one who had narrowly escaped drowning, she noted the crumpled gray feather in her clenched hand.

The world burst in upon her senses all at once. Her knees informed her that the ground beneath was rough, hard stone—she'd likely have bruises. Sweating, she realized that her winter wools were now a mite too heavy for the warm, salt-laden air around her. Blinking, she glanced around and noted that, in spite of the din of voices assailing her ears, she'd apparently landed in an alley, out of sight.

Thank the gods for small miracles. Liara wondered absently what would have happened if she'd appeared in the presence of regular folk. Wincing, she rose to her feet, reeling as if she'd been spun around in circles. Within moments, she had yet another reason to be glad that nobody saw the end to her unfortunate spell, as she promptly emptied the contents of her stomach into the nearby gutter.

Somewhere off in the woods, an owl was laughing at her. She was sure of it. Muttering black curses against owls and mages, Liara thrust the gray feather into a pocket and shielded her eyes from the bright sunshine as she surveyed the spot of her ungainly landing.

Miserable and bedraggled as she was, Liara could

not help the grin that spread over her face as realization dawned. The winding narrow alley before her ended in a low wall. And beyond that, she glimpsed a great blue-green something filling the horizon. With a squeal of delight, Liara ran to the end of the tiny street, eager to have a better view of the sea.

Here was real magick. Liara breathed in a deep lungful of the salted air and leaned forward, drinking in the sight. Those who had built the city had made sure to take full advantage of the natural geography of the coastline. This foresight served Liara well as her eyes danced over the tiled rooftops, skipped over the spires of churches, and basked in the beauty that was Vrsar.

For a moment, she almost despaired. "How will I ever find the wizard in a place like this?"

Even if she found him, what was she to do? March up to his doorstep and demand apprenticeship? It was overwhelming.

"And I must look a fright." Her hair felt damp and windblown. Her clothes were inappropriate for the balmy seaside temperatures. For a moment, she wondered if the owl's feather worked both ways. But return to Nagarath, shamefaced and defeated?

Nagarath would understand. Nagarath always understands. Liara's eyes smarted with tears at the thought of her mage. It wasn't that she hadn't meant to run away. She just hadn't meant to run this far.

Hand to her throat, Liara realized that somewhere along the way, she'd lost her scarf. Lopsided and cobbled together from any number of colors, it wasn't anything special. But Nagarath had made it.

The tears that had welled up moments before now

gathered momentum and fell.

"Hsst. . . . Wha're we a-cryin' for? Such a pretty lady needn't be a-cryin'."

Liara jumped in alarm as a voice sounded behind her in the alley. Hunched and limping, a wiry old man leered at her from under a hat as battered and dusty as the rest of him. Liara backed away, wondering how out-of-the-way this particular alleyway really was.

"Are we lost?" The old man cracked a smile, revealing more gum than teeth.

Repulsed, Liara shook her head. "No. I just—I was admiring the view and found I had misplaced something I thought I had with me."

"Was it valuable?" The man stumped forward even as Liara drew back. "I could help you look for it. We could search everywhere together."

The look in the beggar's glittering eye sent her heart racing in fear. Again she retreated, head swiveling left and right in an attempt to find someone, anyone, who might step between her and this—this—*person's* unwanted attentions.

Whipping into her vision, a cane struck the beggar hard on the shoulder. The impact knocked him back against a doorframe. Liara shrieked.

"Be gone, beggar." A voice accompanied the striking rod—a strong and musically handsome voice.

With an equally handsome visage, Liara noted. She blushed, hating herself for having screamed.

The beggar shuffled off down the alley, cursing the tall stranger. A dark, handsome stranger and a mysterious beggar. It was nearly a scene out of those fairy stories Nagarath despised so much. In the midst of the bright, confusing chaos, Liara stifled an almost manic giggle, only to swoon.

An iron grip caught her arm. Liara gulped in air and watched as the world did a dizzy turn about her.

Idiot! Hysterics will not do. She took a moment to really look at her rescuer—if, in fact, he could be called that. *Don't look a fool,* she chided herself, and closed her country-girl gaping mouth.

The man gazed at her intently. He was tall. Liara felt small in his shadow, but she set her chin with determination. She couldn't tell if he was checking on her welfare, or sizing her up. Whichever it was, what he saw clearly pleased him, for he relaxed his grip and smiled.

Oh, how the world lit up with that smile. The stress and fear of the day melted from her, and she felt as if she'd do anything to merit such a smile again.

Shyly, she smiled back.

"And where are we headed?"

Liara took her rescuer's proffered arm, noting that this charming stranger had not actually asked if she were harmed. It seemed to her that he simply knew it to be true and did not wish to embarrass her with the inquiry.

Encouraged by his manner—*and that smile*—Liara said with some pride, "I've come to find a wizard."

"You seek Anisthe?" There was no surprise or fear in his question. Perhaps wizards were better respected in cities than in backwater towns. Liara nodded her response.

"And why would a slip of a girl do such a thing?"

"Oh, the usual. Make my way in the world. Power, glory, and fame."

The man stopped and looked her up and down as if

really seeing her for the first time. "You'll do."

Liara looked into the man's warm brown eyes, and slyly asked, "You'll take me to him?"

"Hah!" the stranger laughed. "I am him. But then, you had figured that out, I daresay."

Liara grinned. Yes, she liked this tall, dark, handsome man very much.

A quick turn out of the alleyway brought Liara and her escort into a broad and bustling road. She cringed in spite of herself, the involuntary tremor earning her a gentle pat on the hand from her stately guide. It was so crowded. There were people everywhere, rushing to and fro. Carts trundled past, heavily laden and clearly assuming right-of-way.

Yet none interfered with Liara and Anisthe's leisurely progress. In fact, heads nodded as they passed, the mage's path cleared as if by magick. Liara couldn't help but gape as a richly dressed merchant called out a greeting to the wizard. It seemed that magick was held in much higher regard here along the coast.

Taking in the sights around her, Liara let herself be curious. Vrsar was certainly grand enough, its winding streets and tall buildings making her increasingly grateful for the escort. Craning her neck as another gap in the buildings afforded her a glimpse of the sea, she saw that instead of going down into town, their path seemed to be taking them along the side of the hill. The houses were richer in the lively port and, though they already far eclipsed what one found in Dvigrad, it seemed the mage was leading her to a still more impressive district.

Anisthe murmured something and Liara turned sharply, thinking he addressed her. But no, in her gawking, she had ceased to note the greetings and pleasantries from passersby. She turned to see that a middle-aged woman had actually gone so far as to give a slight curtsy to the mage as they walked past. Blushing, Liara noted also the flutter of dark eyelashes and infatuated smile turn sour as the woman regarded Anisthe's companion with what could only be described as jealousy. Feeling the stranger's eyes raking up and down, sizing up the competition, Liara stiffened and looked away, feeling a fool.

She tried to picture anyone looking at Nagarath in such an amorous way. The idea as absurd as it was unlikely, Liara laughed in spite of herself, then glanced at Anisthe, who walked at her side with single-minded purpose, his face closed but not unfriendly.

It was hard to look at the man and not immediately compare him to Nagarath. Both were tall. But where Nagarath appeared skinny, Anisthe looked aristocratically angular. Even Anisthe's black robes of power—rich and embroidered with sparkling runes—seemed to swirl about him with an air of mystery. Nagarath's cloak always seemed to flap about his ankles, threadbare, with a flyaway look about it. And where Nagarath wore his hair long and tied back, black and shot through with streaks of silvery gray—a match to his icy eyes—Anisthe kept his own mane trimmed and short, its rich brown catching the light and revealing golden notes.

The mage was certainly handsome. But his features lacked the warmth that Nagarath projected, even in his most distracted moments. If only Anisthe would smile again. He looked far less intimidating that way. *Perhaps he's embarrassed to be seen with me.* Liara recalled her tumultuous journey to Vrsar, and raised her free hand to her frazzled hair.

"And here we are, my dear." This time, Anisthe's words were for her.

Looking up from her critique of her attire, Liara sucked in a breath. "You live there?"

To her untraveled eyes, the immense house appeared a palace. With white walls and a red-tiled roof, Anisthe's home sported balconies and delicate arched doorways. Greenery abounded, expertly maintained. A liveried servant stood before them, ready to open the door. It was grander than Liara would have ever imagined, and yet it seemed appropriate for the equally impressive gentleman upon whose arm she leaned.

At her incredulity, a smile twitched about the corners of Anisthe's mouth but did not take hold. He let go her arm, gesturing that she lead on. "Come. There are prying eyes about, and I'm sure that you crave refreshment."

Overwhelmed, Liara nodded, numbly returning the servant's greeting as she crossed the threshold into the pleasantly cool interior. His touch but a whisper at the small of her back, Anisthe indicated that they proceed directly into the wide and airy front room. Sunlight sparkled over polished floors and rich trim. Liara felt increasingly shabby.

Crossing in front of her, Anisthe flung himself into a chair. He raised a hand, an order that Liara stop where she was. She froze, obedient but puzzled as the mage commanded, "Turn around."

She looked over her shoulder, unsure of what to do.

"Turn around and let me get a look at you, girl." Anisthe indicated the movement with an impatient wave of his hand.

Liara spun slowly, feeling the burn of embarrassment rising in her cheeks.

"Stop."

Liara froze, facing Anisthe once more. He was the very picture of inattention, one leg thrown carelessly over the arm of his chair. Upon the opposite, he rested his head in his hand, two fingers pressed into his forehead. Self-conscious and put off by the pose's casual familiarity, she clasped her hands in front of her.

"Well? What can you do, then?"

"What can I—?"

"The bird sent you here. Yes or no?"

"Yes. The owl did." Liara gulped, taken aback by Anisthe's curtness. What on earth had she done to offend him? Where had his glorious smile gone? Though she stood in a patch of sunlight, to Liara it seemed that the day had grown cloudy.

"So what can you do?" Anisthe huffed. "What spells can you work?"

"Oh!" Flushing, Liara hurried to explain herself. "A few wards, a defensive shield, a—"

"I'm looking for a demonstration." He spoke over her through his long and well-formed fingers.

He flicked one such delicate finger at Liara. A powerful but brief gust of wind whirled around her, catching her by surprise. It died as quickly as it came, and she found her hair neatly arrayed as if brushed and washed, her skirts and stockings aired and pressed to morning-crispness. She felt . . . almost pretty.

And exposed. Impressive or not, his spell presumed an intimacy that set Liara's cheeks afire once more.

Anisthe hadn't spoken a word, had hardly made a gesture. And yet there was more magick than she'd seen from Nagarath in nearly a year.

"Warding spells." His eyes half-closed, his words derisive, Anisthe seemed almost bored. "Nothing wrong with them, of course. They're essential, if basic."

"And that's why I wish to learn." Liara clutched her hands together, pleading.

"Don't." Anisthe sat up now, alert. His eyes narrowed as he looked her over. "Don't ever beg. A mage commands and it is done."

Then make me your apprentice. Teach me magick, real magick. Liara opened her mouth to speak, pausing as she considered her words. In her mind, she could see Father Phenlick's sad shake of the head, Nagarath's gently chiding raise of an eyebrow. Speaking boldly—indeed, acting entitled in spite of her upbringing—had been second nature to Liara but a year ago. Even some of her last words to Parentino's wizard had rung with impetuous tones. But to be so demanding, plain and presumptuous, seemed wrong, thoughtless and self-serving. It might have been who she was at one time, but no longer.

She set her jaw and lifted her head to look the war mage in the eye. "It may be that a mage may not plead, but I am no mage. Not yet. And so I respectfully request apprenticeship of you, Anisthe of Vrsar."

Liara found herself rewarded for her careful words as Anisthe's smile once again lit the room. He rose, chuckling. "You're a smart little thing, aren't you? And not half bad looking, when you're all cleaned up."

Indignant over the assessment, Liara was tempted to mutter an explanation about how the wizardry that had gotten her to Vrsar had been rough on her. But she swallowed the impulse, still aware of the mage's intense scrutiny as he approached. He seemed to yet seek something of her, though she couldn't for the life of her figure out what it was. "I can still make a demonstration, if you'd like."

Anisthe waved it aside, circling her. "No. I can see from your aura that you're as green as they come. But there's something. . . . Why are you really here?"

Liara blinked, surprised. "I came for the Art. To seek you out. When I heard there was a mage this close by, when the owl said—"

"The bird has turned your heart. That I can see. But from what? You say you have magick, having learnt but a few basic spells. But from where? Who would dare teach you so little when clearly you have so much talent?"

"My heart is steady. It wants power, has always wanted it. Ever since I was little. I am Liara of Dvigrad in the Limska Draga valley, and my talent comes from an unknown progenaurae. Our village was attacked—" Liara felt her eyes prick with tears and skirted the story. "I was orphaned very young, and only recently became the ward of the wizard Nagarath, where I have learned some magick so as to become librarian for his spell books. He refuses to teach me more."

"And so you came here." Anisthe finished, still pacing. "Did he send you?"

Liara shook her head. "I—I ran off. There has been some sort of trouble in the valley. Nagarath wouldn't tell me what. But he was using my power to defend our position—as you said, he's well aware of my potential, even if he won't apprentice me. The town was destroyed by plague, but there's something else. Something wrong going on. At first I didn't believe him, but—"

She paused, her mind's eye on the blast marks along the wall of St. Sophia's, things Nagarath hadn't told her. Her mage: fierce protector, or threat? She rushed past the memory. "But then I could feel it, too. The owl said that you and Nagarath once knew each other. I don't even think he knows you're here. He's all alone, and so I thought that . . ."

Anisthe seemed to have left the conversation, now staring through her rather than at her. She wondered if he even heard her speak.

"Come," he abruptly changed tack. "Let me show you Vrsar. I've some business in town, and if you're going to stay on here, you might as well have an idea of your surroundings."

With his familiar sparkle, the war mage was on his feet in an instant and halfway to the door a moment later. Liara thrilled at the sudden offer. A tour. He meant to keep her after all.

Chapter Twenty-one

Vrsar was Dvigrad, but ten times over. Like a basket overrun with colorful flowers, the buildings seemed to hang down the steep coastline, spilling towards the sparkling sea. Loud, bright, and crowded, the city threatened to swallow Liara whole again as she put herself into its clutches. But for Anisthe, she might have been swept away on the tide of people.

The deference that had earlier preserved Liara and Anisthe's path from interruption failed to aid them now. Or had it been magick? And if so, why didn't he use it again? At her first jostling, from a woman endowed with a large hamper and even larger bosom, Liara shrank into Anisthe's arm. A quick glance at her companion's smirk, however, had her extricating herself in a hurry. He was enjoying this. Too familiar, indeed. She averted her eyes, trying to distract herself from the unwelcome thought with a glimpse of the sea.

Even the pull of the blue-green expanse was hardly tempting enough to overcome Liara's instinctive avoidance of the general populace. Darting through the throng of mid-morning traffic with Anisthe, she observed churlishly, *People are people. And more of them aren't necessarily more interesting.*

But ships. Ships were a surprise. A common stopping point for trade coming out of Venice, the dock and shipyards were some of the busiest on the Adriatic, the ships rivaling the largest. The concept of a boat was, of course, not foreign to Liara. But the sheer size of the merchant ships staggered her imagination. Tall, spindly masts reaching up, up, up. . . . The heavy cargo being loaded and unloaded. . . . Liara found that she simply couldn't get used to them, and kept swiveling her head to take it all in.

"Would you like to see one close up?" Anisthe bent down to ask her quietly, kindly making no mention of her gape-mouthed awe.

Liara nodded, all curiosity.

Skillfully parting the never-ending crowd, the wizard guided her to one of the towering vessels. Named *Emberlynn*, the ship sported a typical figurehead: a mermaid, her hair carved in worn wooden ringlets, hands raised above her head, exposing a perfectly formed torso that segued into a powerful-looking fish's tail.

The carving—stripped even barer by salt water and time—had been rendered so as to leave little to the imagination. Anisthe noted Liara's blushing stare. "The ship, I've been told, is named for her. They say that she once safely guided it out of a storm and, upon reaching port, the captain kissed the ground, and rechristened the vessel at his first chance."

Liara laughed, a smile upon her face at the tall tale.

"Don't let them catch you laughing like that," Anisthe warned sternly. "The crew may have changed twice over since that day, but they take their history—fantastic as it may seem—very seriously."

Liara buttoned up her mouth, eyebrows still arched.

They continued on, Anisthe still eying the figurehead. "I have not met her, but I have seen her kin." He smiled, his eyes staring into a faraway memory.

"Mermaids? But . . . they're mythical. Just stories. I should think that a wizard like yourself—"

"While not a seaman, I've spent my fair share of time on the water. The first time I ever went to sea, I spotted merfolk. It's what earned me future voyages, for a time."

Liara remained incredulous. Was he mocking her? Used to Nagarath's tendency towards humor, she searched Anisthe's face for signs of a ruse. Found none.

Instead, he roused himself from his memories to startle her with a question. "And why do you not believe in merfolk? They're creatures of magick. Their whole race is gifted, not just a select few, as in the case of man."

"Well. Nagarath said . . ." She stopped, trying to puzzle through why, once upon a time, she'd abandoned her own beliefs so easily in favor of Nagarath's.

"Never you mind what 'Nagarath said,' " said Anisthe, his face dark. "Ah. Here we are."

They had approached *Emberlynn*'s aft gangplank where a man lounged at his guard duty. Casting a lazy eye over the docks, the sailor indulged in a hearty spit over the side of the ship, pushing himself into a more upright position as they approached. Liara craned her neck to look up at him, even as his eyes raked over her. She scowled. Was everyone going to assess her today?

"Master Anisthe." The man sauntered towards them and leaned over the deck rail. For all his slovenly appearance, the sailor had an obvious respect for the wizard. He grinned at Liara and waved a calloused palm. "Come to take a look at 'er then? Well, come aboard and mind your step."

Liara eyed the steep and swaying gangplank. Just like running the battlements atop Dvigrad's fortifications, in times gone by. Only moving. And uphill. *And without Krešimir.*

Brow set in a determined frown, she preceded Anisthe up the board, pausing as the gentle rock of the ship played havoc with her sense of balance. Again, she marveled at how these building-sized objects stayed afloat. *Is it magick?*

She quickly bent to peer at where the heaving bulk of the hull met the water's surface. Though she neither saw nor sensed the Art, she felt certain she was onto something. Crouched on the swaying gangplank as she was, the ungainly glimpse downward nearly toppled her. She quickly scrambled up onto the deck.

"What is it, Liara?" Anisthe looked around for the source of her excitement.

Flushed with discovery, she repeated her hypothesis to the wizard.

Throwing his head back, he laughed heartily and long. Liara blushed furiously. He wiped tears from his eyes, managing the words, "Simple science . . . I'm sorry. Did Nagarath not see to the practical side of your education at all?"

Liara shook her head, her cheeks burning.

"Well, then. After we see more of Vrsar, we'll make sure to remedy that oversight."

Anisthe moved off toward the ship's captain and took him aside, speaking in hushed angry tones, leaving Liara to fill time by exploring the foredeck. As she wandered, her mortification turned to ire. How was she supposed to know how boats floated? Again, she congratulated herself on leaving Parentino behind. *Parentino and its ineffective, sad excuse for a mage.*

The judgment was harsh, but Liara fixed her eyes on the heaving water, the endless expanse of the Adriatic, and tasted freedom. She found a perverted delight in torturing the memory of the man who'd ill-prepared her for life outside of his isolated castle. Curse Nagarath. Him and that tiny, aimless life she'd led in his company. She would find magick. And as the war mage seemed to have a ready answer for everything—more answers than even she wanted, it seemed—perhaps he could conjure up a way for her to find news of the progenaurae who had sired her. When Anisthe came to collect her at last, Liara matched his wolfish grin with one of her own.

Turning their backs on the glittering sea, Liara allowed Anisthe to escort her up and down the narrow, winding streets of the city, his own business apparently having been attended to and the hustle and bustle of the morning waning to a comfortable trickle of people in cafes and storefronts. It was after several blocks of such meandering that Anisthe returned to their previous topic.

"And so within Nagarath's unending collection of books, you found not one reference to merfolk, Liara?"

She shook her head. "Oh, Nagarath has gobs of books on all things mythical. But he doesn't like them one bit. You should see him on the topic of fairy stories. Says they 'damage the reputation of our Art.' "

Anisthe muttered something in reply, low enough that Liara didn't quite catch it. To her, it sounded something along the lines of Nagarath being the reason magick's reputation was so damaged. Liara scowled her agreement, even as her heart leapt instinctively to defend her wizard. Her scowl deepened, prompting Anisthe to continue.

"Did he . . . discard said books about myth and fairytales?"

Liara snorted. "Nagarath doesn't throw any book away, even if he has no desire to use it. Though he will, of course, damage nearly every book he can get his hands on, so they're not exactly unharmed once in his possession."

"Oh, thank you. Thank you, gods."

The relief in Anisthe's voice, on his face, was startling, tangible. Liara felt her own face go white; the words—the emotion—a near copy of Nagarath's own when he'd returned from the tragedy at Dvigrad, fearful that something had befallen her. Jolted back into the memory, she again relived the mage's hasty and heartfelt embrace, the warm whisper of his breath marking her as treasured, cherished—the first time she'd ever remembered feeling so. That Anisthe would care as deeply for a bunch of books was odd, to say the least.

"As his . . . as his librarian, you read them, yes?"

"I didn't read everything cover to cover. But I am familiar with the contents of nearly everything Nagarath has. I even made a catalogue book for the finding of materials," Liara was quick to add, seeing the glimmer of feverish excitement in Anisthe's eyes. *See? I'm not as spoilt for magick as you'd have me believe.*

"Then it's possible. Quite possible . . ."

"What's possible?"

"If I could but . . . but no, I could never—he would never—" Anisthe's jaw worked as he struggled with whether to continue or not. Liara's skin prickled with anticipation, with guilt, over seeing him thus. He shook his head, clearing his face and abandoning the thought. "Dinner, Liara?"

She nodded eagerly. Anything to get past the mage's anxiety. It was catching. *What in the world was that about?*

Liara was given guest's quarters upon their return to the house. Sumptuous as the rest of the manor, the rooms came complete with the non-magickal means to wash and refresh herself. She splashed the sea-salt air from her skin, feeling a whisper of sadness as she returned to herself, a girl bereft of ship decks and mermaids once more. Lost in her musings, she nearly missed the bell ringing her down to the dining room. *A bell? It's a bit like being a sheep. Or a noblewoman.*

Dinner proved a formal affair. A number of the mage's liveried servants stood on hand to fill plates and pour wine. The variety and amount of food was in itself a shocking indulgence—it was no wonder dinner required an entire assembly to serve. In the back of her mind, Liara wondered if Anisthe ate this way all the time, or if this was something he merely did for guests. She felt like royalty, but it was altogether unnerving to have a host of people watching her eat.

At length, she broke the silence. "So you are interested in fairy stories?"

"Passionately." Anisthe smiled, a warm and handsome enigma once more.

Though they'd touched on it earlier, she found his response refreshing. She had been shut down so often on this topic by Nagarath. Still, it was somewhat curious that an area of study so seemingly frivolous should be that which Anisthe dabbled in. He seemed too talented a mage for it.

She smiled back, feeling as though they now shared a secret. It was a start. "May I ask why?"

"Why the interest?" Her question seemed to tickle his fancy. "I don't think anyone has ever asked me that."

She shrugged, prompting him out of his surprise.

"I should think it obvious. They're about power. Each and every one."

"Power?"

"But of course. These are instruction manuals for the greatest magickal feats of ages gone by. Thousand-year curses, powerful beings from realms beyond. They tell of what has been, of what can be . . ."

"That's what spell books are for."

"Ah, your mage has you prejudiced against my magicks from the start. Tricky, tricky, Nagarath. He'd have you looking to yourself when most of the power in this world is held elsewhere. Think, girl. Where do mages keep most of their Art? In themselves? Perish the thought. We'd all be burning with magefire, if that were the case. Fairies—they fairly glitter with power. Dragons breathe it. And the wizards?"

"Yes?" Liara leaned forward eagerly, drawn out of her disbelieving banter.

"We harvest it. We collect it, store it, harness it. We beg, borrow, and steal. We seal it into books and wands and staves. Mages bind the power into mirrors and slippers, wild geese and corpses. We make magick useful. Fairy stories can be history to the discerning eye."

Enchanted, Liara inched forward to the edge of her chair, propped her elbows up onto the table.

"And your black-hearted charlatan of a wizard bought up nearly every book on the topic, stealing the rest. You know that the heart of his library are items from Cromen's collection? Items that went missing shortly after the Archmage's death. The tricky bastard. And him not even interested in the topic! I think he did it just to spite me."

Anisthe's harsh words had Liara sitting bolt upright. That did not sound like her Nagarath. And yet. . . . Had he not been careful to keep magick from her?

"He's not my wizard."

Anisthe rose to his feet. "You make that claim, but there's . . . something. Something of him in you. How long have you been in his power, girl?"

"In his power?" This confused her. Whatever enmity these two men had between them, it was not her problem. It was not her fight.

"Did he not keep you under lock and key in that rotting castle of his?"

"Not particularly. I mean, yes, he—"

"And in what way is that not having you under his power? How do I know you're free of him, even now? Poor child, you are blind. Blind to who he is. . . . What kind of mage he is . . ."

Visions of blast marks on the wall of St. Sophia's flashed through her brain. Memories of Nagarath, jealous and fearful of foreign magicks, rose bitter in her throat. Anisthe knew Nagarath better than anyone. Perhaps it was no coincidence that the two of them lived in such near proximity. Perhaps the war mage's careful concealment from Parentino's wizard was no strange happenstance of fate.

She shook off the tumult of dark thoughts. Is this what she'd been doing to others when she'd made off with personal mementos? Treasures. And he treated Anisthe's books like trash. "You said he had all the books—"

"Nearly," Anisthe amended. "Nearly. I was able to keep a few from my days as apprentice. Even then, I lost many books of notes, as well as any number of items that would have gone far in aiding my studies here."

At their return to the topic of books, his agitation was back. Curious. Liara let replay in her mind the moment from earlier in the day, Anisthe's unexpected show of emotion. She prodded carefully, an idea forming in her mind. "Which ones?"

"Which—? Well, for example, there is a very early telling of a fairy story—quite possibly the first—that Nagarath once had in his possession. I have wanted that book since . . ." He shook his head as if clearing a thought. "Its contents would help immensely in a project I've been working on."

"Would seeing it help?" Her mind alight, she wondered if what she planned was truly possible. She had made the catalogue, after all. Perhaps she and Anisthe could come up with a way to access Nagarath's library from Vrsar.

"Immensely." Anisthe turned his excited gaze fully upon Liara. She warmed with pleasure. Dinner lay long forgotten and cooling as she told the war mage of the massive catalog volume and her ideas regarding its use as a spying mechanism.

"Ah, Liara. Poor, untutored, idealistic, Liara. You are a mage after my own heart with your ambitions. The Laws, girl."

Liara flushed, thoroughly embarrassed. Of course. In her rush to impress, she'd forgotten one of the main tenets of magickal Law. The Laws of Magick Transferre were adamant—accessing a spell book remotely would never work. The enchantments would warp the power within. Feeling stupid, she ducked her head, readdressing the now cold contents of her plate.

"Still—you might be able to do something for me."

She brightened. *Anything. Just teach me in return.*

"I said before that his power still lies thick upon you. Enchantments that allow you access to his innermost secrets—" At this Liara scoffed. *Unlikely.* "—safe passage into places I could otherwise not go. Like his library."

Stunned, Liara felt the food turn to ashes in her mouth.

She'd left Nagarath, putting everything behind her, and now Anisthe wanted her to go back. She wasn't sure she had the strength. Her mage would look at her with his big, sad eyes and she'd crumble. After all, he needed her. He had no one else.

But he lied to you. He's lied to everyone.

Liara felt ill.

"Take all the time that you feel you need to decide, of course." Anisthe's tone was amiable as he toasted her with his glass. "But do remember you've no future with a man like him, a man who'd use your own power against you, to imprison you in his castle and keep you from greater things."

It was true. Nagarath *had* used her own power against her. At the time, Liara had been fool enough not to even realize it. Instead, she'd served him breakfast in bed, all the while using her own Art to maintain the spells that kept her trapped in Parentino. She'd been a simpleton, a hopeless dreamer, and altogether too trusting.

The rest of dinner passed in near silence, too many thoughts swirling about in Liara's head to do little more than wait out the time until she could retire to her rooms. From across the long dining room table, she watched Anisthe measuring her, even as she assessed him. The meal passed in agonizing slowness, populated by the shrill scrape of knife on plate, small talk of ships and seas. It seemed to her that neither wanted to give any more of themselves tonight, preferring the quiet of their own thoughts.

She could positively feel Anisthe thinking hope at her. His big brown eyes, his handsome, wistful smile was almost more than she could withstand, and she nearly agreed to go liberate the book that instant. But her heart, her stubborn heart, needed more. So much he had said added up. And yet, that curious reluctance still plagued her. Nagarath's own enmity towards his past, the sense that he'd wanted, all along, to tell her the other side of Anisthe's tale.

Anisthe could not be trusted, could he? But Nagarath? Liara scoffed to herself on the way to bed. *She trusted neither.*

~*~

A restless mind catches no sleep.

Long after deciding that she'd simply have to let her heart sort through what her brain could not, Liara tossed and turned in the too-soft bed, the too-thick quilt tucked up under her chin. The rich surroundings had settled about her like a heavy cloud, intimidating and guilt-inducing.

Nagarath's place had been, well, quaint . . . rustic even. Living apart from other people, he'd gotten good at doing everything himself. And the fact that Parentino had been an abandoned wreck of a castle before he took residency there didn't help much. His home was simple, as were his tastes.

Anisthe, on the other hand, lived like a king—or, like Liara expected a king would live. Perhaps even better than a king, for he had his power, too.

It brought to mind yet another major difference between Nagarath and his one-time-friend: Anisthe surrounded himself, rather generously, with the benefits of his Art. Solid illumination marked the hallways rather than flickering torchlight. Fireplaces were self-replenishing to save the servants that arduous task and free them for more important work. And the food! Anisthe had already made it no secret that he sold any number of castings and sendings in exchange for exotic spices and fine spirits to augment the fruits of his own greenhouse—magickally maintained, of course.

Liara wondered about the true extent of the mage's enchantments. Did he, for example, have warding spells upon the library and workroom, as Nagarath did? For all his witchery, Anisthe actually seemed an open sort of mage, not once suggesting that anything lay out of bounds for her.

As she lay, the irrepressible need to explore, to poke her nose into places it most definitely did not belong, swelled like the dark underbelly of a storm cloud. Fingers fairly itching with energy, Liara threw back the covers and donned robe and slippers.

Approaching the door to her chambers on cat's feet, Liara paused at the keyhole and steadied the door with one hand whilst trying the latch with the other. She let loose a soft sigh as the lock turned smoothly and she opened the door with nary a rattle nor a squeak. Leaving it to rest slightly ajar, she padded over to the fireplace, pleased to note the coals still glowing within.

"*Ruwachkan'a*," she whispered, coaxing the tiniest of flames to life. Pulling loose a strand of hair, she balled the fiber in her left palm and whispered a few more words of magick before grasping it between forefinger and thumb, passing it swiftly through the dying flame. Quickly palming the bright sparkle of fire as the hair ignited, Liara finished the spell and opened her hand, palm up. A dancing tongue of flame hovered above her index finger.

"First try," she congratulated herself under her breath. Far better than the faltering glow of regular magelight, it really was a pretty little spell. *One that ought to be written down in Nagarath's library.* At the thought, her conscience gave a pang. Not from having devised such an enchantment—much as she'd done with the pink trees, albeit more successfully. Or even that she hadn't yet written it down. But rather: Nagarath. Frowning in her flickering magick light, Liara pushed the sentiment away to feed her little flame more magick. She wondered, not for the first time, how short-haired wizards like Anisthe might perform such a spell.

And now the dilemma. The blandness of the place had nearly quelled her curiosity when Anisthe had given her a quick tour shortly before retiring. Unlike Parentino with its ill-lit hallways, locked rooms, and arcane clutter, Anisthe's manor carried an air of respectability and modernity. In Parentino, every hallway was an adventure. In a house such as Anisthe's—normal in appearance and lacking in readily apparent dark corners and nooks—where did one start?

The library, of course. Perhaps it is not near as empty as Anisthe claims.

Shaking her head over having not thought of it straight away, Liara rose to her feet and again approached the door, her mind full and heart leaping in anticipation. She watched as a mild draft in the corridor played with the puff-flame dancing in her hand. *This way's as good as any,* she philosophized, following the draft.

Reaching out with her mind to see the spells at work around her—she'd only recently found espying auras an easy enough trick once mastered, so long as there were no protections to pierce—Liara was delighted and surprised to see the world light up. She'd come looking for magecraft and mystery, wonder and power, and here it was.

The walls shimmered with spells, the floor positively dazzled. Turning in a giddy circle, Liara nearly forgot the need for silence as she gazed in open awe at the power flowing through every wood molding, each doorknob and wall hanging. With a frown, she approached the window, noting the oppressive darkness outside.

The enchantment was localized to the house, not some general phenomenon. Of course, there were bits and sparkles of light amongst the trees and rocks—the stars were their usual dazzling selves—but the concentration of power there was of the normal, dull sort she'd seen time and again through her tutelage under Nagarath. No, the magick working through the house was of specific and magely design.

Anisthe's power impressed Liara anew, and in a fleeting moment of intimidation, she nearly turned 'round to flee to her rooms. Here was a man who really could and *would* turn her into a mouse if he so chose. And yet . . . . Eyes caught by a glimmer of light under a door propelled her forward.

As Liara approached silently, she smiled at the will-o'-the-wisp light dancing in the keyhole. *Something worth protecting!* she crowed inwardly, heart pounding with excitement.

She bent to peer through the locked door, then nearly screamed as something soft and very much alive bumped her leg unexpectedly. Two glowing eyes looked up at her, the slit pupils dancing as they darted to follow the flickering flame of witchlight that still hovered in Liara's palm.

"Meow?" The cat rubbed her legs again, raising little bits of fur along its midnight black back.

"Shh . . ." Liara hushed it gently, prompting another rubbing pass and a purr. Bending down to the lock, she was again buffeted by the affectionate creature. "Oh, come on." She rolled her eyes as the feline now flopped to the floor and indulged in a luxurious stretch, its bright eyes still on her.

The quick glance she'd managed to get through the keyhole had revealed nothing more than an apprentice workspace, so she shrugged and left the cat rolling and purring on the floor. Quick to its feet, the cat padded along to greet her at the end of the hallway, prompting another exasperated sigh.

Stepping around the persistent kitty, Liara decided to descend to the main floor and see what the great room held. She was still enthralled by the amazing, sparkling extent of the spells woven through the place, and was curious how Anisthe had chosen to permeate the main living area with his spellwork.

Noting with satisfaction that the cat had left, Liara descended the stairs, instinctively avoiding the two squeaky steps she'd noted on her way up earlier in the evening.

As with the spaces she'd explored thus far, the great room fairly glittered. Strangely enough, some of the more arcane and fascinating objects—a shield and crossed swords over the fireplace, a book and dagger on a shelf—emitted little to no aura. Snorting at Anisthe's sense of humor over what impressed the Art-less versus what he truly valued, Liara bent to examine an oddity in the room.

A small ceramic cup, such as was used at the mage's dining table, sat by Anisthe's armchair on a small table. Empty and abandoned by its owner after he retired to bed, the cup's aura was one of the strongest in the room. Gently picking it up, she peered at it in the dying light of the witchfire, trying to ascertain why such an object would be so heavily bespelled. Did the war mage make a habit of drinking potions, transferring residual magicks to the cup over time?

The clearing of a throat behind her made Liara jump. She nearly juggled the delicate ceramic vessel out of her hands in her startlement, extinguishing her puff-flame spell in the process. Anisthe himself stood frowning in the doorway, surprisingly well-kempt given the lateness of the hour. A small black cat sat at his feet, washing a paw, a smug expression on its face.

Traitor, Liara glowered at the arrival. Realizing that the wizard was waiting on her to speak, Liara placed the cup back on its saucer and self-consciously picked at her bird's-nest hair. "I couldn't sleep."

"Apparently." Anisthe glided into the room, pointing to the fireplace as he did so. A few small pieces of kindling rose and neatened themselves on the grate above the coals. Newly born flames stirred the room to life. In the increased light, Liara noted with relief that the mage didn't appear angry, just stern.

"Were you wishing for a cup of tea to ease you to sleep?" He gestured to the chair behind Liara, but she declined the invitation.

"I—" She swallowed and decided to come clean. "I checked its aura. You see, I discovered there was magick *everywhere* and so I went to look. I only went into places—"

"Where you're allowed, yes, I know." Anisthe impatiently waved her explanation away. "And the cup?" His voice lifted and Liara caught the note of genuine warmth that had entered his tone. For the first time, she could see a slight resemblance between the war mage and Nagarath in how they approached teachable moments, and she unconsciously blushed.

"Well, it was brighter than most anything else in the room." She sat at last, feeling as if she'd passed a test when Anisthe nodded.

He turned abruptly. "Come. Let me show you something."

He crossed to the door and Liara followed. Without her little guide light, she found herself stumbling slightly in the dark. For all their subtle brightness, the myriad of auras inhabiting the world around her were not an adequate replacement for real illumination. Stopping suddenly as she sensed Anisthe halt in the semi-darkness, she heard him fiddle with a latch.

"Still reading those auras, girl?" he called over his shoulder. At her affirmation, he responded, "Good," and then threw open the door to the kitchens.

For a moment, Liara thought that someone had left candles burning or that the morning had chosen to dawn early. Breath catching in her throat, she realized that it was the dishes themselves that bathed the room in light.

"But why?" She thought back to the small cup in the sitting room and blanched, recognizing the enchanted flatware and cutlery from dinner.

"Well, for one, my cook isn't particularly talented, so I help where I can," Anisthe snorted, running his finger along the edge of a pot that glowed copper. "For another, let's just say I am not everyone's favorite fellow, and I've learned the value of taking the proper precautions."

"It's . . . beautiful." Liara couldn't believe how enchanted she was by, of all things, dishes. It suddenly dawned on her what Anisthe had said, and she felt a thrill run down her spine. "People have tried to . . . poison you?"

Nodding, Anisthe let out a sigh and permitted a small frown to flit over his countenance. "Poison, stab, bespell—I've lived a dangerous life."

"Oh, but you're amazing. Who would want to kill you?"

Smiling sadly, Anisthe ruffled Liara's already sleep-tousled hair. "Ah, my innocent little apprentice, you would be surprised." His piercing eyes took on a fierce look as he glanced meaningfully at her.

He means Nagarath, she thought, trying to shut out the idea. She knew Nagarath and Anisthe did not get along, were rivals of a sort. She knew now that Nagarath had gone so far as to try to limit Anisthe's practice of magick, but such enemies that each would seek to harm the other? No, Nagarath wasn't like that.

"I . . . I should get to sleep," she stammered, disquieted by this new possibility. "Thank you. For showing me the—" She gestured to the various kitchen implements and made as if to leave.

"My pleasure, Liara," Anisthe answered softly. "Sometimes one can sleep more soundly knowing they're safe."

With a quivery sort of smile, Liara took her leave and swiftly returned to her room, her seeing spell extinguished. Somehow the sparkling auras all around had lost their glimmer to her eyes.

Chapter Twenty-two

Returned to her bed's rich blankets and pillows, Liara told herself that Anisthe's statement had been one of comfort. And yet. . . . She found her eyes fixed on the dying coals of the fireplace, the shifting red glow like the gaping maw of hell, Anisthe's words seeming more a veiled threat.

When at last she slipped into slumber, she slept soundly and devoid of dreams. The morning came quickly, bringing with it a refreshed outlook. Liara had her answer.

Yawning, she turned to the window, blinking in the filtered morning rays, her mind on the day ahead, her heart surprisingly light. What Anisthe proposed was not altogether impossible. Stealing a book that Nagarath clearly didn't want would be far from the worst thing she'd done. And with luck, through cutting all ties with Dvigrad—with Limska Draga—she might finally be able to see the mystery of her origins from a new perspective. One that might provide answers which had thus far proved elusive. *It's not as if Nagarath has shown himself to know anything. And besides, I'll be apprenticed. Even if Master Anisthe cannot help me, I shall soon be able to help myself.*

A knock on the door startled Liara from her reverie, cutting short her growing excitement. A female voice called through the door, "Breakfast will be served in the main dining hall in half an hour, miss."

Liara swallowed her 'thank you,' having learned the previous day that one only commanded servants. Instead, she leapt from the bed, wondering how to make herself sufficiently presentable in the time allotted. A quick glance in the mirror told her that a splash of water and hairbrush would only go so far. And she had only the one dress, still crumpled and travel-worn in spite of Anisthe's neatening trick yesterday.

If only I knew how to do that one, Liara lamented, recalling the shocking rush of Anisthe's spell. It occurred to her that the mage had used no words, only flicking a finger at her—and casually, at that. Perhaps it was as simple as a shielding spell, requiring only thoughts and direction.

Frowning, Liara turned to her dress, searching deeply for the thread of her power.

Approaching the dining room, Liara caught a glimpse of Anisthe as he gazed out the window. Another of his servants stood at his elbow, apparently deep in conversation with the wizard. The sound of his voice sharpened as Liara drew closer, escalating until Anisthe drew his hand up quickly, as if intending to backhand the servant across the face. His face was purple with rage and Liara drew back in shock. Though she knew a master was allowed to hit his servants, it was nonetheless disconcerting to witness.

Standing unseen in the hall, she heard no telltale slap following the threat. But the mage's appearance—and the memory of what it had been—alarmed her. Careworn and haggard, he looked a good fifteen years older than he had the day before. The handsome young mage was gone. In his place, a man approaching middle-age and looking none too happy about it. Taking a deep breath, Liara endeavored to erase all signs of concern from her face and rounded the corner, hiding her surprise at finding Anisthe alone in the dining room, his back to her as he stared out over the sea. He turned, drawing a gasp from Liara.

The haggard look was gone. Anisthe's hair again showed the sheen of youth, the lines on his face smoothed and replaced by a healthy glow. Liara paused, wondering if what she thought she'd seen had been merely a trick of the light, or perhaps an ugly side effect of his rage. But whatever had so bothered him had passed, his smile as bright as ever.

He gave her a quick once-over. "You are a fast learner, Liara. Not to say that you weren't pretty enough, but your Art has done wonders for that dress."

Liara hid her flush of pride by turning to admire the spread on the table. While Nagarath dined on rustic bread, cheese, and herbal tea, Anisthe had laid out another feast fit for royalty. Eyes dazzled by the sparkling utensils, Liara hungrily gazed upon the platters of crusty breads, hard– and soft-cooked eggs, and cold cuts. Last night's fresh fish had become a fitting accompaniment to pungent cheeses, and more fresh fruit graced the table.

At Anisthe's invitation, she sat and allowed her plate to be filled by the two servers who had emerged from a shadowed corner alcove. Her toilette enhanced by her witching, Liara felt worthy of the service and strove to maintain the appropriate decorum, though she wanted to beam from ear to ear. A mage's apprentice at last.

"I presume you slept well?" Anisthe inquired in his rich, musical voice, his smile adding more light to the room than the early morning sunshine.

"Yes. Thank you."

The bed was too soft, she added silently, laughing at herself. If that was her only complaint . . .

"And so you think you'll be staying on here?"

Liara politely swallowed her mouthful before responding. She was certain he could hear the pounding of her heart from across the table. "Of course. Well, that is . . . if your offer of apprenticeship still stands. And I would need some sort of assistance in procuring the book."

Anisthe frowned slightly, raising a hand. A servant sprang forward, awaiting his master's orders. The mage addressed Liara, "You did not ward your rooms?"

She looked up in surprise followed by suspicion. "No, I—"

"Lesson One," Anisthe snapped, his smile fleeing. "A mage never leaves his rooms unwarded."

He inclined his head towards the servant who still stood at attention at his elbow. "Go to the lady's rooms and move her belongings to . . ." He paused to think. ". . . to the Onyx Room."

Bowing, the servant left.

"Of the three wizard's suites available here, your new quarters have the best lighting in the attached mage-room. But it is the smallest of them, unfortunately. I hope you don't mind sacrificing some comfort for the Art."

Liara nodded mutely, surprised once again by Anisthe's affluence. It appeared that he, too, desired her to stay. And yet he'd avoided answering her question about the book. Surely he didn't intend for her to walk all the way to Parentino. Once again, she found herself wondering if the owl's feather worked both ways.

She tried again. "Master Anisthe, if I am to retrieve that book from Nagarath, the one you mentioned when we were talking about mermaids—"

"Merfolk," he corrected. "The creatures may have a female-dominated population, but they greatly dislike having it pointed out more than necessary." He furrowed his brow in thought for a moment, and then, some conclusion apparently reached, called another servant over and whispered instructions into his ear.

"What, my dear, is it about merfolk that so intrigues you?" he inquired afterward, again seeming to take pleasure at redirecting the conversation.

"Well, mermai—merfolk. Are they, for instance, similar to werewolves?"

"What do werewolves have to do with merfolk?"

"For one thing, they're both human-like, so . . ." Liara shrugged. "How else could they exist except through a mage's mistake?"

"Hah!" Anisthe's mirthless laugh startled her. "Lesson Two. Is Magick borne of Men or Nature?"

She opened her mouth to answer and paused, trying to tease out any known instances of magick not involving a wizard's influence. None came to mind. It seemed that there was always someone pulling the strings, intentionally or incidentally. Magick might be a worldly force but, as Anisthe had said but yesterday, it was men who'd harnessed and used it.

"Wrong." Anisthe didn't wait for Liara's slow brain

to arrive at an answer. "Trick question. It's neither."

"Neither? But where else could it have come from?"

"That, my dear, is a point of great debate amongst our more scholarly brethren. For the purposes of our discussion, it is sufficient to note the distinction. Werewolves, merfolk, and elves: what makes us think of them as magickal creatures versus, say, bears, robins, and cats?"

"Magickal creatures are different . . ."

"Different. But I am a man and also a wizard. Your village only knew you as 'different' based on their knowledge of your background. Neither of us carry an outward sign of the force within us. Our ability to manipulate magick, our reliance on it, marks us as outside of nature. Just like merfolk, werewolves, and the like."

"But . . . maybe mermaids are just . . . normal," Liara reasoned. "Werewolves came about via a mage's interference. Maybe merfolk are just very rare creatures."

"Creatures that shouldn't exist, Liara. Man is Man. Separate from Animal in his ability to reason and communicate. Merfolk cross that divide by being half-human, half-fish. And what makes you think werewolves were a mistake?"

The wicked grin on the war mage's face sent a shiver down Liara's spine. *Black magicks.* Her breath hitched in her chest as Nagarath's warning sounded in her memory. Angrily, she pushed it away. She'd learn it all. If only to spite him and his squeamish desire to stop all magicks save his own.

Anisthe shook his head in mock sadness. "You are a funny one. Quick to ascribe wizardry to simple things like the floating of a ship, but reluctant to acknowledge the existence of magickal beings like merfolk. You could use a great deal of instruction indeed. And so we come back to the question of my book."

"Yes, I—I haven't the power to go back the way I came. The owl's feather . . ."

Anisthe waved the concern aside. "I was not about to let you enter the dragon's den unarmed, my dear. I am used to putting my power into lesser vessels. But we will have to be careful, so as not to disturb the spells already at work on you. The ones that mark you as his apprentice."

"I'm not his apprentice," Liara corrected automatically. She really wished he'd stop saying that.

"Oh, but you are. I see his influence when I look at you. You work in his style, think with his logic. I would know; I once knew him intimately. Your very aura speaks of Nagarath."

This last caught Liara's ears, and she looked up sharply. Nagarath's aura? In fleeing Limska Draga, she'd put the question of auras behind her. After all, Anisthe too seemed keen on keeping his hidden. She had seen nary a glimmer on the war mage during the previous night's revelations, and had assumed that hiding one's signature was just something accomplished mages did. Did Anisthe know more about Parentino's wizard than he had so far let on? He and Nagarath had known each other, once upon a time. What had happened between them, exactly? Liara's curiosity grew and she leaned in, eyes alight.

"Liara, you've no idea how delighted I am to hear that you are willing—eager, even—to do what must be done. None least because I want—nay, must have—that collection of stories. You must understand that, when I knew the man, he was a puling weakling. Couldn't cast a spell without a book in his hand and hours of debate leading up to it. He ruined our education. I would not have him ruining yours.

"Did he tell you our apprenticeship was cut short? How he got in the way of a delicate and powerful bit of sorcery, the spell subsequently backfiring and causing the death of our mentor? His petty jealousy of my magickal power robbed me of the future I had planned. We had been friends. Friends, Liara. How wrong I had been about that miserable excuse for a mage."

Liara cringed involuntarily as Anisthe heaped more and more accusations upon Nagarath, his voice pitching higher as he spoke. Nagarath, of course, hadn't told her any such thing. But then, he'd always been reticent in matters of his past and was, at times, painfully shy of magecraft that he hadn't thoroughly examined. Slipshod methods wrapped in timidity. No wonder he needed so many books—and was forever damaging them. To hear Anisthe speak so freely answered many questions.

"So you see, Liara, I understand. I know what it is like to trust him, befriend him, and then learn the hard way of my mistake. You and I are very much alike."

Liara looked at Anisthe with new eyes, seeing now the mage who had built a home, a reputation, from nothing. Trusting in a friend only to have jealousy interfere. He did understand her. More than ever, she desired apprenticeship of this man. She felt it altogether too fitting.

Anisthe rose and walked over to her end of the table, reaching for the chain of a necklace that peeked through his collar. Pulling the amber pendant from the folds of his robe, he presented the object for Liara to see.

"A token. The symbol of an apprenticeship left unfinished."

Gently reaching out towards the pendant, she eyed the golden resin, inside of which was trapped a silver spider.

"All that you see around you, all of my magick save the barest thread, lives within the stone." He snatched it away before she could touch it, secreting the pendant beneath his robes once more. He stood back, eyes dark and brooding. Liara felt her breath return to her in a rush. She hadn't realized how close the mage had leaned in to show her his token.

"All you see here at work comes from that little lump of hardened sap. For years, I have channeled and stored my powers there. Building, saving, constructing the world as I want. With the archmage's death, I learned. I will not readily suffer a similar accident. I have more power than Nagarath has ever dreamed of. I would that you have the same."

"All of your power? In such a fragile bauble?" She focused her gaze on the chain at Anisthe's neck, anything to not look him directly in the eye while she questioned his judgment. Amber was well known for its natural compatibility with sorcery, but . . . "I knocked an amber cross against one of the shelves inside of my tree, and it cracked. Such a material is—"

"Beautiful? Delicate? Rare?" He gently lifted her chin to face him. "Yes, Liara, but I am not careless with my things. The very properties you decry are those that make my choice all the more rewarding. And now, though I have served kings and consorts, princes and empires, I am committed to—my loyalties are to—myself alone. Serve me and that changes. Share my power—nay, unlock your own—and I will see to it that magick bows to us."

Liara smiled up into his warm brown eyes, glimmering with illusions that made him seem younger, charming, more than a mere man, and felt her heart ease. No wonder Nagarath had been jealous of Anisthe. The golden sunshine itself seemed to bend to the war mage's command.

Next to him she felt . . . insignificant, yes. But special. This is what she'd been looking for her whole life. Not Nagarath and his dusty collection of books, his homespun living arrangements. Remembering the way he had collapsed when his own spells had pulled too much out of him, Liara realized there was simply no comparison.

She opened her mouth to respond, but stopped short as Anisthe's doorman entered the room, beckoning the mage to the side for a hushed conversation. Anisthe looked alternately pleased and annoyed. He finally dismissed the man, adding, "Do I need to do everything myself around here?"

As if remembering Liara, he turned to her, his beaming smile turning wolfish. "Ready for another lesson, girl?"

Anisthe's lesson apparently involved shopping for spell components, though why he thought Liara needed to accompany him was beyond her. Stepping out the door into the salt-bedewed sunshine, she crinkled her face against the brightness. Again, she leaned into his offered arm, deciding that Vrsar would always be too sunny and too crowded for her to ever feel at home. But then, with unlimited power, she could change things to her liking, could she not?

Luckily, the shop Anisthe needed to visit was set along the hill, far from the docks they visited the previous day, affording Liara all the view but half the winding steps downward. *One more thing that could take getting used to,* she observed, as they rounded another turn on the path. *This feeling of constantly moving up or down, this brash exposure to the elements—and to think that rumors name the seaside as healthful. No wonder Anisthe spends so much of his Art improving upon his looks.*

This last thought set her wondering again. How old was Anisthe? With the glimmers he cast about himself, it was hard to tell. He currently appeared several years younger than Nagarath to Liara's unpracticed eye. And though she hadn't gotten all that good a view of him that morning, she knew Anisthe was certainly downplaying some of his more weathered aspects. It occurred to her that, as the two mages had been schoolmates at one point—with Nagarath claiming the honor of youngest pupil—perhaps she had long been wrong in her assessment of Nagarath's age. He'd never alluded to it, and it had never occurred to her to ask. She'd simply classified him as 'older.' Not Phenlick-old, of course, but old enough to put a comfortable, respectful distance between mage and ward.

However, having seen Anisthe's tricks that morning, Liara wondered if perhaps spellwork was hard on the body and Nagarath's pepperings of gray were merely a sign of the wizard's disinclination towards making himself up. It would certainly be in keeping with his attitudes towards magecraft. *Though not exactly consistent with his other attitudes regarding honesty and candor.*

Left to her own devices as Anisthe greeted the shopkeeper warmly, Liara endeavored to hide herself behind a tall rack of spices, away from prying eyes. The memory of the previous day's cold curtsy from the woman in the street rose fresh in her mind as two gentlemen just outside the doorway put their heads together, whispering. She could feel their eyes on her as she moved about the small shop.

In fact, surreptitious glances had followed them the whole way there. Memories of Dvigrad resurfaced, the slights and knocks of years past still stinging. Back then, she'd fled, but now she was apprentice to a powerful war mage. Or soon would be. Impatience struck her—a restless urge to wait outside. But then she'd be fully visible to any number of gawkers.

Glancing back sourly, she saw that the men's gaze had turned elsewhere, though their hushed conversation continued. She followed their line of sight, only to note with some surprise that they had turned their attention to another young woman.

Could it be that they had been *admiring* Liara?

Curious to test her theory, she sidled towards the front window, keeping only half an eye to the store as Anisthe's conversation with the shopkeep turned heated. Then she stiffened, her aura tingling. Preoccupation with the flirtations of strangers forgotten in a flash, she tightened her focus on the enchantments at work in the room.

The war mage was using magick. Strange how near his power felt to her own. She settled back to watch and learn.

While she could not tell what exactly Anisthe was casting—for he used no words, no gestures—she could see the effect it had on the store's owner, giving her a good idea of the spell's intent. She watched in astonishment as the man's face went from naked anger to abject adoration. Liara had never seen someone so eager to please, so willing to make a bargain. She stifled a giggle when the man actually bowed to Anisthe, thanking him profusely for his business, even as the mage continued to verbally thrash the oblivious merchant.

But it wasn't funny. Liara berated herself for finding amusement in this clear abuse of power. What Anisthe was doing was unkind. Unfair. *Is that what all power is?* Advantage; disadvantage. Was there a way to wield it so as not to cross that line? *And where is said line?* Disturbed, she decided to wait outside after all while the wizard turned to give instructions to the delivery boy for his copious purchases.

Anisthe soon exited the shop, looking rather pleased with himself. He waved Liara over, offering his arm.

Liara did not accept, walking stolidly beside him instead. "You ensorcelled him."

"It helped, did it not?" Anisthe countered, clearly at ease with his manipulation. "Don't look at me like that, Liara. I am entitled to use my abilities as I see fit. Lesson Three."

Liara gawked in disbelief. She had assumed there'd be some admission of guilt or remorse. He was acting as though he'd done nothing wrong.

"Would you ask a wolf to refrain from using his teeth during a hunt because his intended kill was a defenseless rabbit?" Anisthe challenged. "Would he be allowed to only use his cunning, depending on the size or speed of the game?"

"That's a bad comparison—"

"Is it? How are our abilities different from physical prowess, speed, intellect?"

"It just doesn't seem fair. I mean, it's not like people—regular people—can defend against magick."

"So, you're implying that it would be forgivable, would be fair, if I were to bespell you?"

Angry now, Liara accused, "How do I know you haven't?"

"Now that," Anisthe's voice was low and firm, "goes against my honor."

Liara stopped short and threw her hands in the air with exasperation, not quite caring who witnessed her row with the obstinate mage. "That makes even less sense."

"No, Liara. A mage respects his own. I would find it exceedingly rude if a fellow mage were to attempt to ensorcell me unless I were his enemy or he mine."

Liara searched Anisthe's face, measuring him in this new light. "So . . . you haven't tried to bespell me?"

"You insult me to ask that. And honestly, I could not, even if I wanted to. As I have said before, you are too closely aligned with Nagarath—who, despite his shortcomings is, at times, a very accomplished wizard when he sets out to be. Had he been able to keep you with him, far from me, I have no doubt he would have."

Even in the warm coastal sunlight, Liara felt a chill

pass through her. *No doubt.* She closed her face, her mind, to the words, earning Anisthe's misinterpretation.

"Oh, you think I lie? Liara, he—" Anisthe bit off the words, running a hand through his golden-brown hair, regret carving lines into his face. "No, I cannot say it . . ."

"Say what?" Liara felt her own face go white. Fear prickled down her back, her arms. Something in her screamed for him to stop, begged her not to ask. Observations, half-forgotten phrases reassembled themselves in her mind. A dread beyond her animosity towards Nagarath, his misdeeds and misdirections, gripped her.

Anisthe shook his head, still clearly struggling. The pause was agony. When at last the dam burst, flooding emotion into his face, his voice came out a hiss. "Have you seen his aura, girl?"

"What do you mean?"

Anisthe looked taken aback, anguish lining his handsome features. He whispered, "My dear, I thought that's why you left Dvigrad."

"I told you the trouble in Dvigrad—"

"—had no witnesses left but Nagarath," Anisthe completed. "And it brought you closer to him, did it not?"

The image of blackened patches on a gray stone wall flashed into Liara's head. Murder by magick. Her mind had taken up the issue over and again. She'd rejected it as preposterous, finding other ways to hate Nagarath. But here Anisthe echoed her own fears, and him unknowing of the truth of what she'd seen. Again, the warning sounded in her heart, begging for a way out of what had to come next.

Scared, she shook her head, mentally backing away from Anisthe's words and physically shrinking from the war mage. "Stop it."

"Has he hidden his aura from you, Liara?"

Her voice came out small. "Yes."

"But he allowed you glimpses of your own?"

"Only because I pressed him." The warning became a buzz, became a roar.

"Because they're the same."

The world was crashing down on her under the weight of Anisthe's declaration. The mage was stealing the air from her, killing her with that one sentence. It wasn't possible. It simply couldn't be. And still Anisthe continued, his verbal assault hammering Liara as she fought the growing blackness in her vision, her hands blindly seeking for a place for her to crumple over, to get off of her wobbly legs. What she found was a low stone wall. She gasped, "No."

"Yes, Liara. Your aura. Same as his. Magickal Law The First, Number One."

"Magickal power mimics the Magickal signature. . ." Liara recited, habit having made the response rote.

". . . of the originating power. He had to hide it from you, Liara, else you'd see the truth. Why else would he be in Limska Draga all those years? Take you in? Then refuse to disclose certain truths?"

Why else indeed? Liara slumped against Anisthe's steadying arm, sick with the knowledge that Nagarath—her mentor, her friend, and protector—could actually be the father-in-magick she'd sought all these years. Deep within, the same voice that had shouted a warning now crowed victory. She was right—Anisthe would lead her to all of her answers. And it made so much sense. She really, truly, had been blind.

'There's something. Something of him in you.' Anisthe had been trying to tell her all along. Hot tears streaked down her cheeks, a grief greater than anything she'd ever felt choking her so that she could hardly voice a protest. "It's not true."

"Your presence here begs to differ. . ."

As Anisthe gently pulled the sobbing girl into his arms, she let herself cry in earnest. While she'd never been under the illusion that the attack on her mother had been anything but terrible, finding her father had become a point of pride with Liara. Some part of her imagined a happy homecoming, a partnering of interests—her and her progenaurae against the world.

Meeting Nagarath had buried that dream, magecraft becoming yet another practicality—and a dangerous one at that. Under his roof, she'd learned to love those she'd left rather than seek revenge. Within the walls of Parentino, Liara had found trust and empathy.

And all of it, lies. All save one. She really did have magick.

She recalled her shock at encountering Nagarath's spell books for the dark arts. Her aura had resonated with them. Did they contain the enchantments used in conjuring the creatures that had burned the town and raped her mother? Was she to see the volumes as brothers, sisters?

Is that what I am to him? Another book for his library? Some magicked item he felt entitled to claim?

It was over. She'd left. And she could stop searching, her questions finally answered. But what would she do now? How would she fill the howling emptiness inside of her?

Liara's voice came low and brittle. "I hate magick."

"No, you don't." Anisthe leaned back, freeing Liara's tearstained face from his robes.

"All right, I don't hate it. But right now I hate *something*," she sniffled, indecorously wiping her nose with her sleeve. She shook her head at the offered handkerchief. She was in a mood to go it alone.

"You came to me wanting to prove yourself—to him, to the world. If that is something you still want, I can give you that kind of power. Perhaps we—"

"I hate him. I want him dead. I want to kill him," Liara wailed, hysterical. Her face in her hands, she turned from the mage and curled herself into a miserable ball.

Anisthe's answer seemed to come at her from a distance. "Why don't you?"

The question danced down her spine like icy fingers. Liara looked up, startled. "I couldn't. Even if I could, I couldn't. Destroying him destroys me."

Shaking her head, she added, "Maybe it would be a good idea. I'm just a mistake anyway."

"It can be done," Anisthe promised, reaching out to lift Liara's face to his. "And with no peril to your existence. I can make it possible."

Chapter Twenty-three

Stepping from the darkness that lives between one place and another, Nagarath fingered the scarf at his neck. Wobbly stitches. Mismatched colors. It was hers. It had once been his, until a full-moon night not even three months prior.

Every limb of his body shook. The magickal strain of repeatedly traveling in this manner could very well tear him apart. Nagarath was willing to take that risk. It didn't matter what happened to him if Liara was lost. He had nothing left.

Two days, and this was the closest he'd come. It was worth burning up all the power in the world on this, his latest, and potentially only, chance. Scrying spells. Finding spells. Linking spells. All had failed. Wherever Liara had betaken herself, it was somewhere beyond the reach of his Art—until just now.

"*I'shor.*" He whispered the spell a second time. Reverent. Hopeful. Almost immediately, a responding glimmer kindled in the scarf at his neck. Following the pull of the magickal thread against the well of his power, he strode forward, seeking the other end.

"Liara?" Cracking but functional, his voice returned to him, only to echo futilely in the snow-swept wood. And then the tendril wrenched away again, fast as thought.

With a grimace, Nagarath made the sign that would transport him once more, not caring that the pattern of movement made little sense. It was a chance. He had to follow it. Even if . . .

Materializing in a new section of the wood, Nagarath pitched forward, leaning heavily on his staff. A rustle in the branches of the tree above him started him into action, instinct taking over.

"*Her'ah.*" He gasped as the command of revelation pulled on his Art, emptying him further. "*Atsmi'i, yal'ad ata.*"

A scream sounded in his ear. For a moment, his heart squeezed, then stilled as a power—familiar, haunting, yet evasive—buffeted against his own.

"Liara!" A glimpse of gray and brown flashed in his vision and he ducked, shouting the word that would send him after his only lead through the forest. He swayed as the trees wavered, then straightened, his magick warping the world around him for one brief and terrifying moment.

"All worth it, so long as she's safe," he wheezed, stomping forward as the spell released its hold. Here were unfamiliar woods. How far had he traveled? No matter. He reached again for the scarf at his neck, finding it unwound and trailing on the forest floor. Stooping to catch the free end, he froze as a movement of gray and brown caught his eye once more.

A wolf.

The realization calmed him. The wolf was one of his own. Far-ranging and better than some at telling one human from another, he'd employed a number of them soon after discovering Liara's flight to—and subsequent disappearance from—Dvigrad.

Again leaning heavily on his staff, Nagarath coaxed the wolf the last several feet towards him. With slow, steady movements, he gently placed his hands on the creature's muzzle. He laughed mirthlessly at himself. *Wizard or no, this is not something anyone ought to be doing with a wolf.* Even so, he had to know if there was any more news of Liara. Forest knew, he was out of options.

Gazing into the wolf's eyes, Nagarath linked minds and provided any information he could, explaining the scarf and the connections to its owner, his own wild tear through the woods. It was a wonder the creature tolerated his presence, smelling of magick as he did.

Certainly, he could have merely rooted around the wolf's memory for any reference to the girl, but this was an invasive process to begin with, and Nagarath preferred to ask. He gently prodded for information—sight, sound, rumor. . . . Sitting back, he waited. Impatience, he'd learned, never sat well with wolves. The seconds ticked by, maddening moments in which he strove to keep his mind from racing. It helped to focus instead on steadying the tormented waters of his magick. He might well need it again, after all.

And then the wolf blinked, remembering. There was something. A female. Long-haired—tall, skinny, pale, smelling of berries and sparkly fire, like the wizard. The wolf had stayed far off when he spotted her. After all, this rare instance excepted, he generally avoided those who smelled of magick.

The wolf whined anxiously, eager to be off. His linked mind gave Nagarath pictures of the woods—trees were of no help to the man, but the approximation of the sun and river in the wolf's memories helped him to make a good guess as to where Liara might now be. It appeared she'd stuck to the main road, at least. How had he missed her up until now? Was she, perhaps, returning to him, her little sulk over?

Relieved beyond measure, Nagarath thanked the wolf and broke the link.

Rising, he dusted off his knees and peered north, the direction Liara had last been seen. Then he spoke the word of power that would bring him to her.

Oh gods, let nothing have happened to her, he pleaded, fearing the most disastrous of outcomes. Bandits, soldiers, and worse haunted him as he materialized on the edge of her shabby little camp. There, at last: Liara, his joy and delight, sleeping in a cold cave in the middle of winter. His heart went out to her.

"Ah, little magpie, have you so little regard for your own safety?" he murmured, turning to build the fire, glad beyond measure that he'd be there for her upon her waking.

The sleeping form shifted, then settled again, her breath rising and falling at regular intervals. Nagarath froze, waiting. The breathing stopped for a moment, and then the girl sat up to look at the newcomer.

"Now, Liara, I—"

Nagarath stopped. Something was wrong. He felt a chill as the girl moved not a muscle—all semblance of humanity temporarily suspended.

Then the marble-like visage smiled. "Hello, Nagarath."

Not smiled. Grinned. And in such a way as to mock

any real expression of mirth.

"You're not her. Who—what—are you?" Nagarath barely managed the words, his hand grasping for his staff. The Liara-like puppet shrugged, giving him nothing. Recoiling, the wizard reached out with his aura . . . and shuddered. The magickal signature was tangibly Liara's, and yet seemed diminished—more so than would make the maintenance of such an illusion feasible. Anger and fear on the rise, Nagarath stripped away the masking aura of the puppet, revealing a subtle shift in spectrum and a much stronger force. An aura Nagarath had hoped never to see again.

"Hello, Nagarath," the puppet said again, this time in a voice nothing like the girl's. A warm, soft, male voice that, for all its soothing pleasantness, made Nagarath's blood run cold.

"Anisthe!" Nagarath lashed out in a rage, lifting his staff and blasting the Liara-puppet backwards into a tree. "You snake! You fiend! You—BRING HER BACK!" Nagarath throttled the creature in his helpless rage, tears streaming down his cheeks.

Dissolving into the morning fog, the puppet chuckled, final words hanging in the air like mist: "Tut, tut, Nagarath. Share and share alike. For your sake, I'll ask which of us she'd prefer, but do remember, I offer more than you ever could with your magick of twigs and rocks. And you know Liara . . ."

The sound of his own screams woke him. How long had he lain there? Struggling to hands and knees, Nagarath shut his eyes against the slow turn of the earth, gingerly shaking the snow from him. Memories of another such blackout returned to haunt him.

Only this time, I have no Liara to see me well again. Too much magick. He'd used too much when he'd—when he'd what? *Where am I? Do I still have the Art? Oh, gods!* Nagarath scrambled for his staff. Burning hot, it lay on a sodden section of forest floor, the spent power having melted through the thin layer of snow.

Solid and steady, the sight of the familiar object still proved insufficient at driving the nightmare from him. Anisthe. The very thought of his old adversary brought Nagarath's strength blazing back.

Memories, fractured and incomplete, slid into place as his fingers dove into the soft wool of the scarf bundled beneath his chin: A frantic search. A thread of magick, leading out into the darkness. The glimpse of an owl winging its way through the wood.

"*I'shor.*" No trace of breathlessness now. At his neck, the uneven stitches of Liara's scarf glowed faintly, that which tied the article to its last owner thin but steady. His chase through the woods, at least, had been real, then; had been what had caused his fall. *I hope.*

And the wolf? Nagarath looked to the ground around him, trying to gauge whether this patch of woods was at all familiar. Which was real? Which was dream? *And which is foolish hope?*

No animal tracks marred the snow. Again, his eyes fell upon his staff. Next to it? A single gray feather.

Reaching out, he again felt the rebuff against his magick. *Not one of mine, then.* Anisthe sprang anew into his thoughts, menacing, mocking. Was this his only hint, then? A feather? Was he to burn out the rest of his magicks chasing ghosts?

A tremor rippled through his magick, one unconnected with the burning of so much of his power.

Someone had gained access to Parentino. That was what had woken him. Rising to his feet, Nagarath grasped his staff, praying he had enough strength to see him home.

It was either her or it wasn't . . . *If it's her, it's worth burning all the magick in the world.*

And if it isn't?

Then it didn't matter whether or not he had the power to stop them.

The sunlight streaming onto the tapestry that concealed Parentino's library door wavered and then dimmed, a shadow coalescing across its faded embroidered surface.

Stumbling as the spell let her loose from its power, Liara leaned forward, her hand falling atop Saint Jerome's own, the man forever arrested in the act of aiding the lion. Having observed the scene hundreds of times in her months at Parentino, Liara let her eyes follow the familiar threads, a wave of homesickness rising in her. She shoved the feeling down with a frown, pulling her hand from the wall-covering as if it were a snake.

Panic lodged in her throat as she realized she'd not felt the entrance to the library through the cloth. But no, the thick tapestry had but masked the contours of the door hidden at its back. The way was still available to her. As she wrested the heavy cloth aside and tumbled into the library, she held her breath lest she be discovered by the wizard.

The room lay in darkness, its master absent. With a sigh of relief, Liara whispered her magelight into existence, blinking as Nagarath's library was thrown into sharp relief. Deep shadows played over the contours of the tall bookshelves and squat, comfortable chairs preferred by Parentino's mage. From their corner, the chained books snarled their warning.

"Hush," Liara shushed them, striding to the catalogue book that still lay in state upon its heavy wooden lectern in the room's center. Distracted, she flicked her magelight upwards, leaving it to hover by her shoulder. *Yet another thing Anisthe taught me that you refused to, Nagarath.*

Liara hoisted open the cover of the massive book, noting the fine coating of dust across its surface. *Has Nagarath not been using his library? Strange.* With yet another pang of regret, Liara struggled to calm her churning mind. She had to work fast. Anisthe had warned her that the magick he'd employed to get her to Parentino would reverse its course quickly, calling her back to Vrsar as swiftly as she'd come. If she should return empty-handed . . . Shivering, Liara tried not to think about it.

Taking a deep breath and closing her eyes, Liara placed her trembling fingers on the open page and tried to recall Anisthe's description of the book. The war mage had gone into great detail. More original than the commonplace, the stories in this book had their birth in real accounts. Recent and popular tellings of the stories called them fairy tales. There was more history than happily-ever-after. Anisthe's face had grown dreamy as he'd recounted the contents. Having seen Nagarath fall into equal rapture over a rare magickal tome, Liara could finally see how the two men might once have been friends.

The catalogue's tingling under Liara's fingers recalled her thoughts to the present. She gazed intently as a location and shelf number bled into existence, the black ink spidering onto the parchment. It seemed an odd thing now for her to view her own handwriting. Since Anisthe's pronouncement to her that morning, Parentino had seemed but a bad dream.

Liara rushed from the wooden pedestal, intent on finding the book and fleeing before she was tested further. What if she encountered Nagarath after all? Words of spells hastily learned sprang to mind, defenses drilled into her by an anxious Anisthe in the hours before she left Vrsar, whisked east on his borrowed power. Could she use them on her progenaurae, on Nagarath who had been kind in spite of his lies?

She didn't want to find out. In the time since her tears had dried, Liara had found that her heart was empty. As barren as it was of love, so did it also lack the desire for revenge, now that the shock had worn off. She had her answers—answers she had sought as far back as she could remember. The missing pieces of herself had come together, and while the discovery hadn't been as pleasing to her as she'd long hoped, Liara found that she simply didn't care anymore about the past. *It is the future that I now desire.*

She found what she sought, high on a darkened corner shelf. The book was old and careworn, but not broken as most other volumes in Nagarath's possession. Liara flipped to the frontispiece, noting the woodcut exactly as Anisthe had described it, the title and dedication painstakingly hand-lettered.

Setting her jaw, Liara turned to leave, some instinct in her yelling to run, to flee before the master of the castle returned to find her there. She had the book. That would simply have to be enough.

Liara padded across the library, her swift steps drawing little whispers from the gray stones. Intent on the door, she clutched Anisthe's book, wondering what else Nagarath would have taken from the war mage.

'I, too, have been where you now stand.'
'You were caught stealing?'
'Goodness, no.'

With a shake of her head, Liara cleared the memory. *Another lie, Nagarath?*

Recalling Nagarath's books of notes, scrawls and jottings from his time as apprentice, Liara felt her curiosity swell again. Answers. Confirmation of Anisthe's claims. For though it all added up now, her heart kept whispering its doubts, pleading for there to be some mistake in Anisthe's understanding of events. She knelt by the low bookshelf kept near the door for Nagarath's personal use, pawing through the thin notebooks, hoping and dreading.

Nagarath's pointed longhand danced across the pages as Liara skimmed first one, then another of the booklets. Throwing them down and selecting another handful, she flipped through, finding nothing but evidence of Nagarath's studies.

And then disaster—confirmation!—as Liara's eyes snagged on writing in a different hand. Rounder, blacker, the strings of letters marched upon her brain as coldly as Anisthe's words had in the streets of Vrsar that morning. A signature, one she hadn't really understood back when she'd catalogued the material, glared accusingly from the yellowing page.

Anisthe, magus, 1660.

She let the book drop from her hand, emitting a strangled sob. It was true. Everything Anisthe had said was true. Nagarath, a liar and a thief. *Much like his daughter-in-magick.* It was a jarring revelation, how similar they were to one another. Rising to her feet, Liara whispered, "Nagarath, how could you?"

Even in the midst of the ground falling out from beneath her—again—there was something comforting, righting her swiftly tilting world. An ugly truth was much better than endless lies.

She looked to the fairy stories in her hand. Was there such thing as righteous thievery? She'd grown up believing so. Now . . . she wasn't quite as sure. Even her fresh start would be tainted—begun with a dishonest act, the creeping of a criminal.

Standing rooted amongst the archival autumn of scattered books and scrolls, her brain screamed at her to run. Run like Anisthe, a powerful mage who still felt the need to hide from the likes of his enemy. Scatterbrained or not, Nagarath was a formidable opponent. Far worse than silly old Babić. Far more dangerous to steal from . . .

What if he followed her? Terror raced to outpace guilt. Nagarath would know what she'd done. Would know that she'd come back, stolen the book. And with the catalogue, he'd even know which book she'd stolen, where she'd run off to.

'Had he been able to keep you with him, far from me, I have no doubt he would have.'

Anisthe's enchantment would reverse at any moment . . .

No. She would not lead him to Vrsar.

He will not use my magick against me again.

Rage gripped her, unstoppable and fierce. She crossed the room to the podium in three short strides, eyes on the catalogue book lying open. Seizing a corner of the topmost page, she tore down, first feeling a resistance, then satisfying give. The library echoed with the sound of one long ripping noise, the paper coming loose from its binding. Setting down Anisthe's book, she crumpled the torn page, tossing it angrily into a dark corner of the room.

"Let him try to use the catalogue now," Liara cursed, picking up Anisthe's book and turning to the door. It opened, even as Nagarath froze, his hand on the knob, his lanky frame silhouetted in the doorway.

"Liara."

Her heart stopped at the hoarse and broken sound. Her witchlight flickered as Nagarath stumbled into the room, his eyes bright in a gaunt and haggard face. He looked hopeful, fearful, seemingly as worried that Liara might be a dream as she'd hoped Parentino had been. The two of them stood unmoving, each at a loss for words, regarding the other in shock.

Now or never. Wincing—for in spite of her reluctance, she had to know—Liara lifted her free hand and dove deep within herself for her Art, the words of Anisthe's spell cutting cleanly through her turbulent mind.

"*Atsmi'i, yal'ad ata me-ata. Her'ah sh'lemull hikir nif'tach.*" Magick ripped out of her, gouging her heart, searing her eyes, pouring as liquid lightning from her outstretched hand. Liara gasped, doubling over, even as she saw what she had feared.

Nagarath's magickal signature glowed under the application of the spell, a twin to her own.

Chapter Twenty-four

"Liara." Nagarath only just managed her name, the girl's magelight casting bright flickers over the sight dearest in the world to him. Liara's dark hair, her pale white moon of a face . . . She'd come back. His little magpie had returned.

He watched, the scene somehow distant, dreamlike, as Liara raised a hand toward him.

Nagarath had once seen a tree get struck by lightning. As Liara's spell hit him, he thought that perhaps the sensation was similar. Arching his back, lips parted in a silent scream, Nagarath felt his protégé's magick—powerful, terrifying—sear through to his soul. If his well of power could feel pain, it would have cried out in agony from the impact. Gasping, Nagarath could tell in an instant that his defenses had been taken down, protections that—

She's seen my aura.

The thought grounded him, stopping the room from taking another dizzy turn as he leaned heavily upon his staff. He'd been so careful. *But that doesn't matter now. She's seen why you hid it away.* But why such a spell? And how? He could explain. He had to.

"Liara, please. Wait. Talk to me."

When did she become so powerful? Liara, where have you been?

Without a word, she brushed past him, her eyes burning but cold. Nagarath staggered to follow, unable to summon the words, the howling hole made by his overuse of power—torn wider still by Liara's attack—robbing him of speech. But he had to stop her; had to make her see the truth she'd decided to so violently expose.

He reached out, plucking at the girl's sleeve, cringing as she shook him off. Even in the twilight of the hallway, her flickering witchlight still hovering nearby, he could see that she was shaking, and not from any expenditure of power. Blackness threatened and receded.

"How could you?" She whirled upon him, shouting. "How could you lie to me?"

"I have not lied to you. Not once."

Nagarath passed a shaky hand over his eyes. He'd burnt through so much magick in his searching; in his return to Parentino. He couldn't think. Couldn't breathe. His tongue felt thick. Her aura—he couldn't think over the sound of its brilliance. She was back. But not. "You don't understand. Everything I did, everything I said—and didn't say—was all for you, to protect you."

Go to her. She's hurting. Focusing on her, he could think again. His eyes darted to the item clutched in her hands, the white of her knuckles stark against the burgundy binding of the small book. Was she stealing from him? *Liara, back to her old tricks. But what for?* Heart full, he couldn't squeeze any more words past it.

Liara was frightened. She needed him.

He stumbled forward, letting go of his staff of power. He'd protect her. Brain disorderly, body failing, power dying . . . he needed her to understand. He needed her.

~*~

She had done it—stripped him of his power. Or near enough. And it was awful. And intoxicating—this heady swoon of overextension. The pull on her Art, far greater than any ever she'd felt, was still but a shadow of what Nagarath was experiencing, if his pallor and unsteadiness was any indication. The limit; a reminder to be cautious. Anisthe hadn't warned her to have any such care.

The sensation served to heighten her physical reaction to the revelation, the evidence that her—Anisthe's—spell had uncovered. Her hands trembled from rage, not weakness. She could only watch, mesmerized—horrified—as Nagarath stumbled forward, his aura gleaming, then fading in turns. *'Your aura. Same as his.'* Anisthe's voice, strong in her mind, pulled her out of her daze.

'Kill him. I'll give you the power. I'll teach you the words.' She lifted her hand, fingers itching, eager, her eyes glinting. *Yes.* No.

No. Incantate, but no further. Then he cannot follow. That would be worse. Far, far worse. She'd leave Nagarath to live with the knowledge that he'd failed. Her eyes darted to the damaged catalogue. He couldn't follow her anyway. She'd mask her aura. With Anisthe's help, she could disappear.

She backed away, suddenly feeling sick both from the drain on her power and the haunted look in Nagarath's face as his eyes met hers. Panic set in. *What if, in blasting apart Nagarath's defenses, I used too much of my magick for Anisthe to bring me back to Vrsar?*

The thought angered her anew, the idea that she'd question the war mage's dependability simply because

Nagarath was a lying, weak-willed coward. Straightening, Liara noted with some surprise that she was now looking down on the mage; Nagarath seemingly brought low by her display of power. The old wooden staff was the only thing keeping the wizard on his feet.

Did I do that? Resisting the impulse to look at her hands—*hands that have cast such spells*—Liara held her head high and addressed her progenaurae. She let the words pour out of her, bleeding out the poisons the last few days had left with her.

"I told you. I told you on that very first day what I wanted. I have needed magick since I was a little girl. While other children played in the streets, my veins burned with fire, keeping me from friendship, family, denying me respect. I wanted to know who my father was, to understand why they hated me, feared me. And then you came along. You with your promises and secrets, keeping everything from me. All while pretending that you cared."

"I do care, Liara," Nagarath cut in, his unnerving gaze steady upon her. "I care that you ran away. Do you not think I have been all over these woods the past two days, searching for you and fearing the worst? Not knowing what had happened to you?"

"My town gets murdered, and I have only your word for what happened. I want to avenge Dvigrad—my friends, my people—and you lock me in a tower. You, with your hiding, sulking, spying." Liara threw her condemnations like daggers, satisfied to see the mage flinch.

"Murdered? I—"

"I want magick. I want power. I want apprenticeship. I want to control and master my Art. I want something bigger than you can possibly give me. After everything I've done for you, after all I've learned on my own, I have earned it at long last." Liara swelled with triumph, reveled in the new questions that flashed in Nagarath's eyes.

"Oh, yes, you thought you could keep him from me. Someone who appreciates my talent and asks very little in return. I am your librarian no longer, Nagarath. I am an apprentice to the Art of magecraft. You can't keep me here anymore. My Art is not yours to claim."

She turned to leave, the cracks in her temporary armor of bravado starting to undermine her courage. Already she could feel her power rebounding, surging in her breast, but that was nothing if she couldn't return to Vrsar. The war mage hadn't given her that knowledge, instead promising her that his power would pluck her from the valley once her task was complete. Surely Anisthe would have reversed his spell before now. What if, after all she said, he had abandoned her in Parentino, a stolen book in her arms and unforgivable words on her lips?

Then I'd find a way out. She had power, true power. That was what Nagarath feared. Feared and envied.

Nagarath's fingers brushed her arm, the mage still sputtering ineffectively, more excuses and lies. "Liara, stay. Don't leave. You must tell me what has happened. Where you went, who you spoke to."

How dare he touch her.

Liara whipped around, reacting before she thought. Her spell lashed out, a pulse of power and light that neither expected. It separated mage from staff, sending both to the ground quick as cut wheat. But it was costly, her impassioned mistake. This time, the bleed of magick left her dizzy.

"Don't you understand? I owe you nothing—just as for seventeen years you gave me nothing. If anything, you owe me for what you've done. All my life I've wanted to meet my father, but I don't want to know you."

She fled, still clutching Anisthe's book, sure now that she'd been forsaken by her rescuer, having nowhere else to go but away from Parentino, and not enough of her own magick to do anything save run.

Liara's attack—different this time, not a warning, not an exploration—sent shockwaves through Nagarath's aura, sending him sprawling across the floor of the library. Eyes and ears awash in the disorienting sparkles that heralded collapse, he groped about blindly for his staff. His fingers brushed the well-worn wood, closing instinctively and willing the joining of its power with his. A brief flash, then a whimper. Spent as it was, the artifact failed to do anything more than clear his head. The girl was gone.

Liara! Thinking nothing save his desperate need to stop her, he flung out his arms, flashing his aura into the defensive spells of Parentino. Rippling outward, they arced, warped, then snapped as his power rallied, then foundered. Dried up. Empty. *Time. I need time.* He cursed his empty hands, his weakened well of power. *Time I do not have if I wish to go after her.*

Her father. She blames me for it! Knocked back as he had been, he'd only half heard Liara's tirade. Her anger—her power—still echoing in his ears, Nagarath struggled to his feet in the darkness of the library, trying to make sense of what had just happened.

Maa'o—He let the spell of illumination die unspoken. No need to spend power on such things; not drained as he was. He didn't need light to think. Nor did he need magick, though he could yet feel a shard of his aura glowing deep inside. *Not incantate, then, by the girl's ruthless actions, thank the gods.* Gone for not quite two days, and Liara seemed a different person. He had to follow her. He'd find a way. *But how?*

Something crumpled under his foot. He looked down. A notebook. One of his own.

Nagarath bent, curious as to why Liara would have ransacked those. Now he truly did need illumination. Torn between urgency and better judgment, he again considered his magelight, faltering as it must be in his current state. But no, gods knew, it would take him frighteningly long to recover. Instead, he held the page close before his eyes, peering in the dark at the sole clue Liara had left behind.

Anisthe, magus, 1660. His heart clenched as he saw the inscription on the page. A condemnation.

'You thought you could keep him from me; someone who appreciates my talent and asks very little in return.' Him. And her words had been those of knowledge, of familiarity. She'd somehow met Anisthe—Nagarath's own worst dreams become real.

"But that's impossible." Even as he spoke, the much-abused notebook falling from shaking hands, Nagarath knew it to be quite possible, just unlikely. *And if it is possible, then Liara is in danger of far more than frostbite and draining her magick on a wild tear through the woods.*

"Liara." He stumbled through the doorway, frantically trying to think. Power. He needed power if he was to find her, save her. Gripping his mage's staff, he whispered the words of a spell. It was a gross violation of one of his own personal Laws of Magick, and he shuddered to think of the cost. To use the staff was one thing, but the cinnabar stone buried in the haft—that was borrowed power, energy vouchsafed him to protect.

But the task would not have fallen to me were I not strong enough to resist its call. Fire flooded back into his veins, the dying flicker of his magick revived by the half-hidden gemstone atop his staff. Nagarath wrenched himself free of the connection and pushed the staff away. It clattered to the ground, the magick sealed safely within its stone once more.

Out in the deepening gloom of the hallway, Nagarath hesitated. Anisthe or not, how was he to find Liara? She could have gone most anywhere with the war mage's assistance. *And she'd come here first?*

Books. Always books with her. Caught up in Liara's outburst, her spells, he'd almost forgotten.

He was smarter than that. Smarter than large demonstrations, burning massive amounts of power. He could follow her. Could follow her even to Anisthe, to the ends of this world and others. *Work smarter, not harder. A lesson Anisthe never learned.*

Turning abruptly, he strode back through the library door, his eyes on the catalogue lying open on its pedestal. Of course Liara would have had to use it to find whatever she had stolen for Anisthe.

Shuddering, trying to calm himself, Nagarath concentrated on the catalogue itself, forming his query, asking it to repeat its last request . . .

~*~

Sniffling, Liara blindly followed the path leading out of Parentino and north to Dvigrad. If Anisthe had forsaken her, she'd move on to another mage, just as she had with Nagarath. *Aurenaurae: made from magick.* She had power enough to go it alone—especially now that she had the book the war mage so desperately desired, enough that he'd lent her some of his own Art to collect it. She'd simply have to wait out her temporary weakness in magick at Krešimir's hut.

Turning, she checked that Nagarath wasn't following, her hands itching with the anticipation that she'd have to use yet more of her Art today. She told herself over and over that she hadn't meant to hurt him—that it was fair, considering his lies to her all those months.

"You were supposed to fight me. Tell me I was wrong. Make me see." Even now, some small part of her still hoped it was all a mistake. Not even a lie, but a mistake.

But no, the path was empty save for Parentino at its end. Noting that it hadn't wavered and disappeared at her back, Liara wondered if her stripping of Nagarath's defenses had also disrupted those at work on the castle. Hardening her heart, she decided, *Let him deal with it. He likes tinkering with his precious wards and barricades. He—*

A massive explosion from somewhere deep within

the castle rocked the landscape, tearing the fortress apart. Liara lifted her hands to her mouth as Parentino heaved and roared, the stones offering no more resistance than a child's toy, tumbling and burning, the tall tower collapsing into itself and the walls crumbling to the ruins Nagarath had long pretended they were.

"Nagara—" The name stuck in Liara's throat as Anisthe's spell reclaimed her at long last, whisking her off into the flicker of pressing, whirling darkness that heralded her return to Vrsar.

Chapter Twenty-five

Liara pitched forward, falling hard on her knees as Anisthe's spell loosed its hold, depositing her in the war mage's foyer. Willing herself not to faint—or throw up—she gulped in air, eyes watering as she huddled miserably on the intricate mosaic that graced Anisthe's entryway. *I killed him. I killed Nagarath.* Her throat closed tight, and for a moment, she was sure she would faint.

"I'm not dead," she said shakily.

One of Anisthe's servants was at her side in an instant, pressing a cool beverage into her shaking hands and helping Liara to her feet. As she stood, she realized that the moisture in her eyes wasn't due her violent journey, but rather from tears she couldn't seem to stem.

Her throat closed tight, and for a moment, she was sure she would faint. A handkerchief was waved in front of her face, and she snatched at it gratefully, marveling that she still had hands, fingers . . . that she existed at all.

Removing the handkerchief from her streaming eyes and nose, she saw that Anisthe stood by, a look of patient concern glowing in his warm eyes. "Nagarath's de— gone. And I'm still here."

The war mage nodded, gently guiding Liara into his front parlor where she sat numbly on one of his richly cushioned couches. A fire crackled in the massive stone fireplace, warming the room. Liara stared into the flames, feeling none of the heat, none of the comfort it promised.

Anisthe leaned forward. "And how did he die?"

Lightning shot through Liara's veins, causing her to quake. How could he ask such a question? The words unbidden, her voice dull and strange to her ears, she answered, "I—I don't know. I left him incantate, Anisthe. But there was an explosion. It leveled the castle."

"You shrink from the truth, even now. Did I not tell you that you'd be safe in the event of the mage's death? Think. Exactly what did you do?"

Liara wilted under the war mage's probing, her mind slow to accept the grisly reality. "I damaged the catalogue. I was angry and I didn't want him to know what I took. But I didn't—"

"A mere book destroyed an entire castle?"

"I don't know. Could it? It was tied to the entire collection via spells and enchantments. One could locate any book in the library with a mere thought."

"Impressive." Liara flushed under the war mage's incredulity, remembering Nagarath's praise for the artifact. "What an effective trap you laid."

"It wasn't—I hadn't thought—"

"Come now. You lived with the man for nearly a year and you didn't think that the first thing he'd do? Discover what you took, perhaps trace its signature to learn where you went. You said yourself the book was magickly bound to all others in the collection. It only follows that there would be a spectacular misfiring of its power the moment it was put to use. These are acts we must own to when we wield with such powers. Spare me your surprise. You killed him. Just as we planned."

"Law The Second of Magicked Artifacts. Damage to

either the physical or magickal condition of a Magicked Artifact . . ." He was right. Anisthe, immensely adept at probing—at knowing—her dark corners, had seen the lies in Liara's heart. She'd known. Had not Liara even said such words? *Nagarath. I hate him. I want him dead.*

She held up the book Anisthe had asked for, the cover now seeming more blood red than burgundy to her shock-ridden eyes. Her fingers itched with the memory of their savaging the catalogue. Her heart pounded confirmation of the war mage's words: *'Just as we'd planned . . . an effective trap'. Killer. Murderer. Is that who I am? Is that all that my magick is good for?*

Hungrily, Anisthe snatched the book from Liara's nerveless fingers, his bright smile returning. He paged through, increasingly excited, exclaiming softly to himself and ignoring Liara completely.

Trembling, Liara relived the horrors of the afternoon, trying to find comfort in the war mage's clear satisfaction and finding none for herself. They'd won. She'd gained her freedom, her revenge.

But the pain. . . . This was not how she had imagined her apprenticeship would begin. No triumph, no sunny day. With her terrible act, the howling hole inside herself had grown, needing magick to fill the space, now more than ever. Anything to look forward and not back at her treachery. *'You killed him. Just as we planned.'* The sting of Anisthe's charge—her betrayal of Nagarath's trust—would haunt her forever. *But then, I never imagined betrayal on such a scale as I found with Nagarath.*

Anisthe's voice cut through her thoughts, sharp and powerful. "So he saw you?"

"I got the book first—"

"And he saw you? You spoke with him?"

Startled at the intensity with which Anisthe searched her face, Liara broke down, telling him all that had transpired—what she'd said, the magicks she'd burned in her attempts to get away, even her fears that Anisthe had abandoned her.

Anisthe waited until Liara finished her story, even as she broke down into more tears. He turned to the uniformed servant that stood waiting, his command practically a growl. "Leave us." The servant sprang to attention, bowing lightly, the silver tray he held flashing in the firelight as he left the room.

Anisthe turned back to his new apprentice. "You are to be congratulated, Liara. For now you are mine."

The death of her one-time friend was not something for which Liara wished congratulations. If anything, she wanted only to escape to her rooms, to hide from the world and what she'd done.

"How am I alive if Nagarath is dead?" she breathed. "The Laws of Magick Creatio . . ." The thought cut short, Liara suddenly conscious of Anisthe's hand on her cheek. She shied away from his unexpected closeness.

"I told you that you would be safe, did I not? I can promise you the world and deliver it to you on a silver salver," he murmured, leaning in again. He stroked her hair, tucking an errant strand behind her ear. His voice was soft, enthralling. "You are special, Liara. There are things you and I could do together. . . . We could rewrite the laws of magick, you know."

Again Liara jerked away, shrinking from his touch. She averted her face, sure now of his intent and wishing to gently dissuade his misguided affections. "I . . . I can only be your apprentice. I'm sorry."

"I honestly could not care less about what you think." Anisthe grabbed her wrist, pulling her to him. Knotting her hair painfully in his fingers, he whispered into her ear, surprise dotting his tone. "I can smell the burnt power on you, the dross of magick gone wrong. . . . Tell me, sweet, how did the castle look as it crumbled? Did it burn?"

Liara's stomach churned. *Oh, God! Help! Somebody!* She writhed, seeking escape. Her wrist wrenched within his iron grasp. Trapped. His breath, hot upon her forehead, stirred wispy, clinging tendrils of hair. Her strength, never much, was no match for his. With a strangled sob, she tried to avert her face, remove herself as far as possible from the dark gleam in his eye, itself a violation.

"Oh, no you don't." Anisthe's bulk leaned into her, pinning knees and shoulders. He murmured, almost to himself, "You won't keep me from mine."

A tremor—unbridled terror—shook Liara as Anisthe's eyes turned cold, scientific. Pinioned, she could only squirm helplessly as the war mage continued his cold and horribly familiar examination. Extracting his free hand from her hair, he studied a solitary dark strand before letting his hand crawl up along her collarbone. His fingers danced through the hollows, pausing as he reached the point where her blood raced beneath the thin, pale surface of her shivering skin.

Even as he felt for her pulse, examining her with his detached sort of intimacy, Liara realized how much Nagarath truly taught her. From him, she learned to know her aura, and as she reached within herself, she had to give him the credit.

"You will yield to me, my dear. You can become mine willingly, or unwillingly, but I'll have you either way, magick of my magick."

Body rigid, heart pounding, Liara summoned every spark of her power. *'It was as if I called unto myself the deep vein of power within me, bidding it rise upward into my very fingertips. A shield made of my own Art, summoned by my heart.'* Loothemere's Lesson.

The blast of her resulting shield threw Anisthe from her and sent the couch upon which she sat to skittering backward across the tiled floor. Anisthe toppled backward into the fire, screaming as the flames caught his robes, set his golden-brown hair alight.

Liara's scream clashed with Anisthe's in a horrible cacophony. She watched as he tumbled into the flames, tangled in his robes of magely power. Unlike the catalogue, this—this she'd meant to do. Or would have, if she understood what she'd done.

What had she done? She'd only meant to rebuff him, shield herself from his assault and buy herself time. She hadn't expected the mage would be thrown across the room, into the fire. And yet there was something familiar in it. But what? A memory sprang to mind, that of the lodestones Nagarath kept in his study, each attracted to and yet repelled by the other. Liara shook off the odd thought, stumbling as she backed towards the door, towards freedom, her spinning head a testament to how much of her magick she had expended.

Anisthe scrambled to his feet, desperate to escape the flames. Liara screamed again as his eyes met hers, his face a fury of burning wrath and crisscrossed with the red pucker of blistering skin. He looked like the very devil

Father Phenlick had long shouted about from his pulpit. The sight of his gaze galvanized Liara into action.

She turned and ran, running straight into the arms of one of the household staff. Even as Liara kicked and wriggled in his grasp, the man pinned her arms, securing her for his master. Anisthe advanced upon her, burning embers scattering from his cloak as he crossed the room.

"Thank you." His words came out ragged, thin as smoke.

The servant holding Liara captive shoved her towards the mage. Anisthe caught her wrist with his unburnt hand.

"I'm . . . I'm sorry," Liara managed, terror robbing her of strength. She sagged in his grasp, staring wide-eyed at the angry red of the wizard's arm. Again, the memory of Nagarath's lodestones flashed in her head. Anisthe's power and hers . . . Some instinct of Liara's caught on something she had seen.

"Look at me," Anisthe commanded, the words hot as red coals. "Look at me!"

His mage's robes hung about him, scorched blacker than black. What was left of his hair had plastered itself to his temples and forehead, black on skin white with rage and pain. Anisthe's left arm was charred and withered, having taken the brunt of the fire when he had fallen into the hearth.

He raised his hand, enjoying Liara's look of sick horror for a moment before plunging his fingers into the tattered remains of his cloak to bare his amber pendant. It glittered wickedly in the remnant of the flames.

"I didn't mean to . . . I don't know what happened–" Liara pulled ineffectually against the mage's iron restraint.

A word of power, and Anisthe shivered violently as the cloudy mist of his signature sparkled into being. The hazy luminescence swirled about the mage, his hair regrowing and laying itself neatly back into place, skin returning to a healthy pink shade. He let go the amber token, the golden droplet falling hidden once more amongst his robes, his hand whole and youthful once more. Only his cloak remained burnt and blackened, its silver runes tarnished gray with ash.

"It seems you need a lesson in what real power is."

"You—your magick—" His aura. *Her* aura.

Anisthe smiled. "You were mine to claim from the beginning. Not his. Mine. You hear me? And to think I did not know of your existence until your town started falling apart, coughing out refugees . . . some of whom carried with them the most delicious gossip."

"It was you," she accused. "You killed them. The town."

Anisthe thundered on, shaking Liara. "Yes, I killed your sorry little town. I killed its messenger. And it was you that helped me finish off Limska Draga's ineffective protector. . . . Do you even understand what I've lost not having you, a product of my magick, kin of my own creations? The magicks I could do with a strand of your hair entwined with mine, the blood in your veins, the tears that you shed—mine. Mine!"

Krešimir. He killed Krešimir. Sagging in Anisthe's grasp, Liara felt her last sliver of hope die within her.

Anisthe paused to take a shuddering breath, collecting himself. When he spoke again, his voice carried an alarming, husky softness. "And you are older now, a woman grown. Oh, the possibilities that have opened up with that, my dear . . . I wasn't lying when I said that you and I could well change the very laws of magick." He reached out a hand, stroking her cheek.

Liara jerked backward, eyes locked in horror on the wizard's newly healed fingers. The only thing that kept her from swooning was fear for what would happen to her if she did. What a fool she'd been, listening to the lies of this viper, letting her own fears and habitual mistrust cloud her judgment, drowning out what her heart had wanted to tell her all along. Krešimir, her first love. Phenlick, who'd believed in her in spite of all. Nagarath, her protector, her champion. And how had she repaid them? How had she repaid *him*?

Eyes widening, she realized the full import of her own role in this, and how utterly alone it made her. Alone save for whatever of her wits she could still gather. *'Liara, you're smart. And capable. And have learned things without my meaning you to . . . The Laws of Magick Transferre. Recite.'*

Nagarath's words. And with them, a plan. But she was worse than dead if Anisthe figured out what she was contemplating. She first had to draw him close, make him feel the victor, loathsome as the idea was. Nagarath was gone, Liara's own magick was near drained—it would not be hard to make the war mage believe he had won.

But Anisthe's words sickened her. She could not fail, could not let him win. Not in this way. She owed Nagarath, Father Phenlick, Krešimir, Dvigrad that much.

Liara squirmed, earning the transfer of his vice-like grip from her arm to the back of her neck. Tears of pain stung her eyes, hiding their sparkle, and she whimpered,

The Bookminder

"You're my—you're . . ."

She let the words die in the air between them.

"So you do see." Anisthe's eyes searched her own, reading her heartache. "Perhaps I have misjudged you, girl. You're not just an empty-headed bookworm like that fool Naragath. But then, as my aurenaurae, I should have expected more."

Swaying as Anisthe shoved her into one of the decorative tables lining the wall, Liara saw the hint of a chance, the glint of amber winking from amongst the mage's robes. Playing to Anisthe's arrogance, she pushed back weakly as his hands again roughly grasped her hair, lifting her pale and frightened face to meet his leer. His robes, charred from the fire, chafed her fingers as she clawed at her attacker.

He chuckled darkly, crooning, "You'll see my side of things soon enough."

"STOP."

The booming command came with an equally deafening explosion. Anisthe's grip slackened, manic laughter bubbling up in his throat as he turned to regard the thick smoke choking the front hall, obscuring the entryway to the parlor.

Weak and confused, Liara slumped back against the table and peered into the darkened hallway, catching a glimpse of a splintered door and the black night beyond.

Then she saw him.

Limping, bandaged, but alive, Nagarath stepped over the wreckage of the door, his face a thundercloud.

~*~

Bursting through the doors, Nagarath's sharp eyes took note of his surroundings in an instant, his mind following somewhat belatedly, as if watching a dream unfold: Liara, white-faced with shock and terror, sagged against a narrow decorative table. Anisthe, a snarl masking his own surprise, backed towards the center of the room, positioning himself for attack. Soot, ash, and half-burnt firewood spilled from the hearth at the end of the room—signs of a recent struggle.

Nagarath allowed himself a small smile at this last observation. *Good job, Liara.*

"Did he harm you?" His voice was low and dangerous as he maneuvered to Liara's side, flicking an appraising glance to her before settling his steel gray eyes back on the war mage.

"No, not rea—"

"Good." Nagarath advanced, Anisthe retreating to the other end of the room with his arms spread wide, laughing as if it were all a joke.

Wand held at the ready, Nagarath crossed the room rapidly, willing himself not to limp and making sure his trajectory took him away from Liara as Anisthe leveled his own wand towards him. The war mage looked much as Nagarath remembered him—hale and hardy, graced with the face and manners that young women swooned over.

In contrast, Nagarath's hand trembled in the firelight. His hasty bandage served only to hide the damage caused by the backfiring catalogue. A tickle at the nape of his neck—more likely a trickle of blood than sweat—recalled more of his injuries. Nagarath pushed such thoughts away. His utmost concern: which spells could he safely employ against his opponent?

He could not win this fight—not if he wanted Liara to live. Killing Anisthe would kill the girl, product of the war mage's magick. But Nagarath could buy her time.

In Nagarath's hesitation, Anisthe struck. Purple-blue lightning slashed through the long room. He barely got his shield up in time. Nagarath murmuring counter-incantations as quickly as he could, his aura flashed and crackled under the deafening boom of the enemy wizard's onslaught.

The room seemed to shake even as Anisthe's preliminary attack subsided. Nagarath blinked the stars out of his eyes and tried to clear the ringing from his ears. He could barely hear Anisthe's mocking laughter.

"A wizard's duel, then? To the death?" Anisthe let his wand arm drop, an invitation.

"You know I can't do that."

"Come now, you can't tell me you came here just to let me hurl bolts of lightning at you. Not looking like that. My, my, dear Nagarath, can it be that your charmed life has left you by the wayside? What hard times it would seem we have fallen upon. I suppose I should give you a moment to gather yourself before I finish the job our mutual acquaintance began." As he spoke, Anisthe maneuvered to the far end of the room, the light from the dying fire dancing upon his face.

Nagarath leveled his wand at the war mage once more. "And you, old friend, are looking rather well. Were the years so unkind to you that you must improve upon yourself so heavily with magick?" He darted his eyes to the side, a warning glance to Liara to flee at the first opportunity. So far, she hadn't moved. Didn't she know how this must end?

Of course not. The poor thing didn't know that Anisthe was her progenaurae. She thought it was Nagarath himself.

How long had it been? Seventeen, eighteen years? And Anisthe was up to his old tricks again, laying waste and then casting the consequences on others. How many lies had the war mage fed Nagarath's little magpie? Doubtless many.

Enraged but keeping his voice calm, Nagarath continued, goading Anisthe so that he'd forget Liara, still standing wide-eyed to the side. "By the by, were you aware that your defenses appear to be down, at present? Seems you might have had a little trouble with the fire?"

At that, Anisthe jabbed again with his wand, a fencer with a sword. Blue-green flames wrapped in wind shot from the tip, engulfing Nagarath even as he skipped sideways, defensive spells taking the brunt of the attack. The long curtains nearby caught fire, stirring to bright life and throwing the room into violent fragments of shadow and light. A scream ripped from Nagarath's throat as Anisthe's fire snatched at the edges of his spell, eating at his increasingly weakened defenses.

Again, Nagarath tried to lock eyes with Liara, shouting through the war mage's attack, "Run!"

He raised his wand, seeing his opening as Anisthe let the spell die out and worked to change his incantation. While he desperately wished to do more than defend himself with his failing magick, Nagarath checked his anger, deftly deflecting Anisthe's next blow and dropping to one knee. Pain shot through his back, a reminder of the injuries he'd sustained in Parentino.

Through the pale shimmer of his own defensive spells, Nagarath shouted another warning. But Liara only stood stiff by the wall, a look of intense contrition on her face as she gazed back at him, unmoving. Fool girl. Didn't she know the time for talk was over? Hadn't she seen that he'd come here to save her?

Realization dawned. *She's waiting for me. She doesn't know that I cannot flee with her, that I cannot harm Anisthe without risking her.*

Nagarath lowered his wand, weariness coming over him as Anisthe's relentless attacks found purchase at last, sparking through his weak resistance. For a moment, it seemed to Nagarath that he was back in his quiet library, his hand on Liara's catalogue—her gift to him—and feeling the magecraft backfire, the world collapsing inward, the power burning from the inside out, swallowing him whole.

He closed his eyes, praying Liara would at last see that it was done. She'd run out on him before, could not she run now? Could he not at last save her from herself and from the awful truth of her origins? She always thought him a coward. Let her see that now and flee.

Run, Liara. Parentino's wizard raised his hands once more, summoning what magick remained in his already overtaxed body. Anisthe was a blur, his laughing face distorted by the warring powers between them. The war mage's parlor, edged in flame, looked like the portal to the Other World. Nagarath had but a moment left before his shields would shatter. Lowering his eyes, he braced himself for the impact.

And then, nothing. The magefire around him vanished, the room grown silent save for the crackle of the dying flames along the nearby window and Anisthe's heavy breathing. Out of the darkness, something had thrown itself at him.

Liara.

~*~

Please don't be dead. Please don't be dead. Please—
Kneeling by Nagarath, shielding his body with hers, Liara cupped the mage's cheek in her hand.

Her decision to act had been made for her when she saw Nagarath fall at long last. Running in front of Anisthe's attack, throwing herself at the wizard of Parentino, Liara let instinct overrule her fear.

Instantly, Anisthe had pulled back his power as she'd known he must.

Nagarath stirred beneath her touch. "Liara? I—"

'Run,' her mage had told her.

And leave you? she'd silently asked.

Not for a second time. Rather, it had been her turn to protect him.

Leaning close, Liara clutched at Nagarath's black robes of power. Homespun and rough on her questing fingers, she felt her heart ease as she poured out her confession. "I'm so sorry, Nagarath. I thought it was you. You that killed Dvigrad, hurt my mother . . . I should have trusted you, even when you told me nothing. I should have realized what you were saving me from. It's all my fault."

Nagarath's face was as unreadable as it was tired. For a moment, Liara wondered if her apology had fallen upon deaf ears. And then . . . his face crumpled in despair. "I was going to save you."

Whether Nagarath's broken words were an apology for his last actions or his explanation for his presence, Liara never found out.

Anisthe's laugh sounded again. "Oh, yes, Nagarath. She already knows. Little minx rebuffed me with an aura strike before you got here. Late to the party, even to the very end." He strutted triumphantly before the fireplace, enjoying his moment. "Liara, feel free to run along as you're told. I'll find you as soon as I've killed off your ineffective rescuer. You can't hurt me with your— correction—*my* magick, and Nagarath is about to run out of his own. I am actually quite at my leisure to wait for any pathetic apologies and puling expressions of endearment that you feel you need to blather through."

"It will be all right, Nagarath. I am . . . so sorry. For what I did. For what I thought."

Liara leaned close, tears stinging her eyes as she pressed her hand into his. Hidden within her grasp, a way to defeat Anisthe. But she needed him. She whispered, "Attack him. For all he's worth. Do this for me, because I cannot. Make him use his power to defend himself. Please. It will be all right. Trust me."

"Liara. Get behind me," Nagarath's words came measured, the eyes that gazed into her own bright with emotion. Parentino's mage summoned the last of his strength, rising to his feet, his hand still clasping Liara's own.

She faltered, sensing the wizard's struggle.

Trust me. Even though she'd proven untrustworthy.

It will be all right. And yet there were no such assurances.

I'm sorry. The echo of this last thought broke her heart, even as Nagarath gently moved her aside, placing himself between her and Anisthe. She had no way of knowing whether she had gotten through to him, whether her secret communication had been understood . . . whether either of them would survive this after all.

Chapter Twenty-Six

Reaching deep, Nagarath sounded what remained of his Art. It was not much, but there was power enough for whatever plan Liara had in mind.

Attack him. For all he's worth. Her urging echoed in his mind.

Memories of the girl, headstrong and willful, came thick and fast to Nagarath's mind as he stood to face Anisthe. He'd heard of such things happening when you died, a brief reliving in your final moments. Odd that his memories should be so full of Liara: Liara laughing in the sunlit garden; Liara, petulant and pouting, as she demanded magecraft of him; Liara, his little magpie, dutifully reciting the laws of magick . . .

Setting his jaw, Nagarath raised his wand one last time, the act as galvanizing as the realization that he'd been wrong about the girl all along. Liara knew her Art, even if he had been so misguided as to keep it from her. She knew magick because, in many ways, she was magick, more so than any mere mage might lay claim to.

Nagarath risked a look to Liara as she stood her ground behind him. She looked calm but terrified, even as she opened her mouth to address their enemy.

"Anisthe of Vrsar," she began, "I give you a choice. Let me go. Release any and all claim upon me and mine. And I will not destroy you."

Anisthe raised his hands in mock surrender. "Stupid girl, you should know that you cannot hurt me—"

The room brightened as Liara lifted one hand, forcing her power outward, a wavering shield of light that caught the war mage a glancing blow.

"I warned you." Liara advanced, her hand held up, palm out.

Stumbling as his own aura flashed, rebuffing Liara's challenge, Anisthe growled. "As my own creation, you cannot hope to destroy me without destroying yourself. You see what happens when your aura hits mine. You cannot hurt me with my magick."

"No. But I can!" With Anisthe distracted, Nagarath saw his chance. Lightning, bright and deadly, flashed from his wand towards the war mage, forcing Anisthe to draw deep—Art for Art, spell for spell, a true wizard's duel at last.

Out of the corner of his eye, Nagarath saw Liara leap into action. Her face was set like stone, resolute and fearless, as she dashed her free hand against the hard tile floor, the object hidden in her grasp yielding with a resounding crack.

Oh, my clever magpie. With a twist of his wrist, Nagarath called back his attack, even as he felt the shift in the war mage's aura, the dangerous undertow of a receding wave. Power bled into the air, white-hot and terrible. And at the center of this magickal maelstrom crouched Liara, unmoving on the parlor floor, her eyes reflecting the dazzling brilliance that leaked out from under her hands.

~*~

Liara watched, mesmerized as magick, pearl white and blinding, bled out from beneath her prone hand, illuminating the tile floor and turning the tips of her fingers a translucent pink. Distracted by the sight, she felt more than saw Nagarath pull back on his attack, the energy in the room shifting. With a shiver, she sat back onto her heels, blinking color and form back into her sight and wondering at the sudden silence.

It was like a raincloud had opened up in Anisthe's parlor. The air felt cleansed, fresh, as the war mage's freed sorcery darted about the corners of the room, seeking release. Drawing a shaky breath, Liara winced as sound returned: Anisthe's anguished howls of despair raked at her ears, his words of magick devolved into babbled gibberish.

Her plan had worked.

Liara found her voice. "Laws of Magick Transferre. First Law: a Magicked Artifact must be sound both physically and magickally in order to function as intended. Second Law: damage to either the physical or magickal condition of a Magicked Artifact will affect the outcome of Magicks performed through said Artifact."

She raised her hand, revealing Anisthe's pendant, lifted from the wizard moments before Nagarath had burst into the room. The amulet of power twisted on its chain, the large crack in its side catching the firelight, the silver spider within looking warped through the fractured amber.

Nagarath knelt by the war mage who lay on his side, moaning as the power fled his body. "You were always one to rely on tricks and outside trinkets. Tell me, how much of your Art had you passed to that pendant?"

The Bookminder

Anisthe lay limply on the tile floor, his eyes feverish, his words so faint that one could hardly hear his whisper.

"Could you cast *anything* without it anymore?" Nagarath was beyond incredulous. Anisthe shook his head weakly.

Liara rose shakily to her feet, more stars dancing in her vision with the movement. Her knees turned to jelly and she stumbled, her eyes still on the war mage.

Nagarath rushed to her side, worry etched into his every feature. Liara waved him off. "I'm all right. Just. . . weak."

Nagarath nodded, his eyes darting to fix on a point somewhere past her shoulder. Liara turned to see a handful of Anisthe's servants standing white-faced in the doorway.

"Your master is incantate." Nagarath raised his wand, a gentle threat. "I suggest you seek employment elsewhere and not detain us."

Liara sank back into the couch, relieved as the servants looked to their master, whispering amongst themselves before fleeing into the night.

Incantate. Liara looked back to the broken pendant in her hands. It wasn't that she had expected anything else when she'd formulated her wild plan for freedom. Where other spells of the war mage might have ended, as a living, breathing human being, she would likely never feel any other effects of the magickal tie between herself and the wizard who had lost his gift—so long as he stayed alive. She would reach the age of autonomy with her twentieth year, not but three years hence. Surely she and Nagarath could keep the man out of trouble until then.

~*~

In spite of all, Liara's words to Nagarath were a gentle remonstrance. "Why didn't you just tell me? Trust me?"

He swallowed tightly. "I feared—I feared that somehow you knowing who your progenaurae was might lead him to you or you to him. Anisthe is—has always been—charming, and I worried what influence he might be able to gain over you. I promised this to Father Phenlick long years ago, when I moved to Limska Draga. Barely fifteen, my education incomplete—to this day, I see it as a small miracle that he didn't simply have me run out of the valley. You were six at the time. And Anisthe was long gone, scattered to the winds. I had no idea, little magpie, that he was this close by. I did not realize it was he who had destroyed Dvigrad. Had I known . . ."

He shook his head, choking on his words. Had he known, he wouldn't have done a thing different, caught up as he'd been in his own immediate fears and the stubborn belief that he was the only one who could keep them safe. And that was his mistake. The image of Liara, confident in the face of her own potential destruction, rose to his mind.

Nagarath's voice sank to a whisper. "The truth is, in the beginning I wanted to protect you. I wanted to save you from all of this. I thought that if I kept magick from you, kept knowledge of him from you, you would be safe. You were my penance for past actions, Liara. I let Anisthe loose upon the world, and his misdeeds were my own. Then, last spring, you suddenly became my full-time responsibility, and I soon realized I didn't just want to keep you safe out of duty, but because I'd grown to care for you."

"And then I betrayed you—tried to kill you." Liara's voice hitched, a sob cutting through.

Memories of the catalogue's spells pulling him in, the parchment boiling as the finding spell cracked and unraveled underneath his outstretched hand, echoed through Nagarath's mind. Anisthe's amber-encased spider winked in Liara's hand. *His clever magpie. Aurenaurae—made from magick and just as dangerous.* He shivered, once more grateful that most of his injuries were physical.

Nagarath considered hiding the truth from Liara once again, downplaying the danger to protect her from her guilt. But then, they'd seen where that got them. Smiling weakly, he continued, "You know me. All I knew was that you'd stripped me of the careful wards I'd placed about my aura . . . wards that, yes, I had placed for the sole purpose of hiding how close our signatures were. I knew full well there'd be questions."

"And if you'd answered them, you'd have had to tell me about Anisthe and how you knew him."

"Yes, for we are—were—brothers-in-magick through our apprenticeship to Archmage Cromen, our signatures patterned after his own and therefore nearly identical, save for what we've managed to make of ourselves in the years since," Nagarath finished. He flicked his eyes to where the huddled Anisthe had managed to sit up, if delicately.

"We *are* brothers-in-magick, Nagarath," he protested, his voice weak. "And Liara is mine, whether I have the Art to claim her or not. I will find a way to get my power back. And when I do—"

"Do be so kind as to let us know." Nagarath rose to his feet, looking down on his former friend. "I can only spend so much energy keeping an eye on what you do.

"Come." His voice now betraying a slight rasp, his gait a slight limp, Nagarath offered his arm to Liara, turning his back on Anisthe. Together, the pair walked out the shattered door, neither looking back at the broken man they left behind. Anisthe of Vrsar was a war mage no longer.

"Why did you come back after . . .?" Liara choked on the words as she truly looked at Nagarath's haggard face and battered body for the first time. In Anisthe's house, Nagarath had seemed invincible, his wounds superficial.

"Oh, my Liara, must you ask?" He stopped and cupped his good hand around her cheek. "How could I not?"

The sweet, familiar gesture reduced Liara to tears. Sobbing, she flung herself against Nagarath, her voice muffled in the folds of his cloak. "But I'm awful. I'm bad. . . and evil . . . and awful, and yet you came for me."

"Liara, my dear little magpie, I—"

He paused, his face contorting with pain as he grasped his side. Liara hastily extricated herself from the embrace, remembering that she was likely worsening her mage's injuries. He continued, weak, though his gaze blazed with an intensity she'd never seen before. "Liara, I would never have left you to Anisthe's designs."

"I should give up magick." The words were out of

her mouth before she thought about them. She owed Nagarath something, some sacrifice of herself. And as she had nothing but her Art to give . . .

"No, Liara. That I won't allow. You will not be less of yourself. I have lived my life that way for years, and so thought it the right path for you. But no, you proved today that you will make a fine magus. And, I suppose, you'll always be a passable good thief."

Liara allowed herself to smile with him.

"I think, in fact, that you'll be getting all of your heart's wishes in one day." Nagarath's eyes held the sparkle of mischief. "Your apprenticeship will begin with a spell to get us home, provided you've the strength. I, unfortunately, used most of what power I had left in getting me to Vrsar."

Liara felt a new stab of sorrow. In the terror and tumult following Nagarath's entrance, she hadn't noticed that there was something different about him other than injury and exhaustion. "Your staff . . ."

Nagarath looked about himself, confused. "My—? Oh." He rushed to ease her conscience. "I left it in Limska Draga for this one-way journey. I was not eager that Anisthe discover its secrets."

Liara blushed with the heat of his intended sacrifice. Tears stung her eyes. "Nagarath. If you didn't know where I had gone, how did you find me?"

The mage chuckled and tweaked her nose. "Don't you remember my telling you that I am quite hard to steal from, little magpie?"

Liara blinked in surprise at his sudden humor. For a moment, she wondered if Nagarath had done more injury to his head than was visible. But then, he'd always been this way. Glib. Endearing. She liked it.

She ventured, "So . . . back to Parentino? For that is where Anisthe—*my* spell—took me before."

Nagarath's mouth twitched, rueful, as he gingerly ran his fingers through his hair. "You'll find that Parentino is not exactly fit for habitation, at present. And, as I hesitate to linger here . . . Dvigrad? Yes, before you ask, my dear: I trust you. Let us away."

Breathlessly, Liara felt the world stretch out before her, a future unrealized and uncertain, but full of possibilities. She had lost so much that day, yet what she'd gained was far beyond what she'd let herself dream. It was, in a way, its own sort of magick.

Liara's gaze caught at Nagarath's gray eyes as the mage held out his hand to her. With only the smallest of hesitation, Liara took it, whispering the words of magick that would take them home.

END

Appendices:

The Laws of Magick:

Laws of Magick Creatio

Law The First: Magickal power mimics the Magickal signature of the originating or altering power.

Law The Second: Once the age of twenty has been reached, a subservient power gains autonomy and its signature is fixed.

Law The Third: The destruction of an originating power subsequently destroys the magickal properties of its surrogate. In the case of Magicked Artifacts, the Second Law of Transferre applies.

Laws of Magick Transferre

Law The First of Magicked Artifacts: A Magicked Artifact must be sound both physically and magickally in order to function as intended.

Law The Second of Magicked Artifacts: Damage to either the physical or magickal condition of a Magicked Artifact will affect the outcome of Magicks performed through said Artifact.

Addendum: It has been found that these atypical results are often of an unpredictable, uncontrollable, and highly undesirable nature. Purposeful damage to a Magicked Artifact for experimental purposes is not recommended.

Dictionary of magick words:

Terminology

aurenaurae /ˈɔ reɪ ˌnɑ reɪ/
The act of copulation between a human and a magickal creature; also the product of such a union when life is conceived. As most such unions are nonviable, a human aurenaurae is exceptionally rare and would be directly subject to the Laws of Magick Creatio.

incantate /ˈɪn kæn ˌteɪt/
A mage who has permanently lost his or her magick. While there are some that say that a magick user may regain their Art, these tales are generally dismissed as rumor.

progenaurae /ˈproʊ dʒɛ ˌnɑ reɪ/
An indirect participant in the act of aurenaurae via their Art; the mage responsible for the creation and control of the magickal being involved. When said copulation results in offspring, the power signatures of both aurenaurae and progenaurae are identical per the Laws of Magick Creatio.

Green Language

*Please forgive the lack of pronunciation for these terms. Magick in the wrong hands can be highly dangerous and so by not aiding in proper pronunciation, the author has erred on the side of caution.

ata	you (from the Hebrew)
atsmi'i	I, magus (from the Hebrew)
gidel	grow command, as applied to the unliving (from the Hebrew for "cultivate") (see tzamach)
he'eniq	give / grant (from the Hebrew)
her'ah	show (from the Hebrew)
h'ayim	life (from the Hebrew)
i'shor	follow (from the Hebrew)
maa'ome	flame, light (from the Hebrew for "light")
nif'tach	open command (from the Hebrew)
ruwachkan'a	radiate (Heart of the puff flame spell used by Liara. It is of her own design.)
shinah	change, to be used as a command (from the Hebrew)
sh'lemull	to be complete (from the Hebrew for "wholeness, perfection"). Commonly used to check the soundness of magickal artifacts.
tzamach	grow command, as applied to the living (From the Hebrew) (see gidel)
tra'shuk	heart of the travel spell (from the Hebrew for "return")
yal'ad	bring forth, bear (From the Hebrew)

Pronunciation Guide

Ana /ˈɔ nɔ/
Liara's mother. Deceased.
Anisthe /ˈæn ɪsθ/
War mage, former apprentice to Archmage Cromen and therefore school-mate of Nagarath. Liara's progenaurae.
Đerkan Babić /ˈdʒɛər kɔn ˈbɔ bɪtʃ/
Son on Zarije Babić.
Zarije Babić /zɔr i ˌyeɪ ˈbɔ bɪtʃ/
Personal enemy of Liara, gossip of Dvigrad. Mother of Đerkan Babić.
Briscola /ˈbri skoʊ lɑ/
A card game for two to six players where the goal is to take tricks. The game utilizes a 40-card Italian deck. Popular along the Mediterranean.
cindra /ˈsin drʌ/
A stringed instrument similar to a mandolin.
Archmage Cromen /ˈkroʊ ˌmɛn/
Former Master for both Nagarath and Anisthe. The Archmage lived in south central France and took on students of magick until his untimely death.
domaći /ˈdoʊ ˌmɑ tʃi/
Protective house spirits
Dvigrad /ˈdvi ˌgrɑd/
Translated as "twin-town," this fortification can be found in the Draga Valley in the central portion of what is modern day Istria, Croatia.
Krešimir /ˈkrɛʃ i mir/
Liara's friend in Dvigrad. A woodsman.
Liara /ˈli ɑ rɑ/

An aurenaurae, the result of an attack on her town. Anisthe is her progenaurae.

Limska Draga /ˈlim skɑ ˈdrɑ gɑ/
Translated, the "Lim Valley". This 35km valley runs past Dvigrad out to Lim Bay, near Vrsar.

magick /ˈmæ dʒɪk/
Archaic pronunciation and spelling of the modern "magic."

Nagarath /ˈnæ gʌ ræθ/
Local wizard who adopts Liara upon her exile from Dvigrad. Former school-mate of Anisthe under Archmage Cromen.

Parentino /ˈpɛər ɛnˌti noʊ/
Dvigrad's twin fortification across Limska Draga. Abandoned.

Pazinčica River /ˈpɑ zinˌtʃi sɑ/
The river that flows along the Lim valley.

George Phenlick /ˈfɛnˌlɪk/
Priest elected by Rome to serve the Venetian Republic. Placed in Dvigrad by the doge of Venice.

Uskok /ˈusˌkoʊk/
Raiders, guerrilla soldiers fighting on behalf of the Habsburg side of the Habsburg-Venetian conflict in the area that is now modern day Istria, Croatia.

Vrsar /vərˈsɑr/
Coastal town along the Adriatic Sea.

Zvončari /ˈzvoʊnˌtʃɑ ri/
Translated "the bellmen." Per local pagan tradition, men travel from village to village in the springtime, scaring away the spirits of winter with bells.

About the author:

M. K. Wiseman was born in Wisconsin but lived in New Mexico for a time, falling in love with the Southwest. She later returned to Milwaukee, immersing herself in her Croatian culture. With degrees from the University of Wisconsin-Madison in animation/video and library science, she lives for stories. Books are her life and she sincerely hopes that you enjoy this, her first.

Other works by M. K. Wiseman:

"Clockwork Ballet" in Mechanized Masterpieces: A Steampunk Anthology (2013)

"Downward Mobility" in Legends and Lore: An Anthology of Mythical Proportions (2014)

"Silver Scams" in Mechanized Masterpieces 2: An American Anthology (2015)

Website: www.mkwiseman.com

Facebook: http://www.facebook.com/faublesfables

Twitter: http://twitter.com/FaublesFables

Pinterest: https://www.pinterest.com/faublesfables

Amazon: http://www.amazon.com/M.-K.-Wiseman/e/B00CMJK19W

Goodreads: http://goodreads.com/MKWiseman

Acknowledgments:

A librarian and animator by training, M. K. Wiseman decided to merge her two passions, putting pen to paper at long last. This novel, her first, is the product of many hours of labor, countless edits, and one very vibrant dream that occurred in early 2004.

She would like to thank the team at Xchyler Publishing for believing that this story should be shared, especially Penny, Danielle, and Jessica—for putting up with her ceaseless devotion to certain turns of phrase and pulling better prose out of her. And for Terri, who worked with her to get the early incarnation into something readable.

And, of course, thank you to all the friends and family who've put up with M. K.'s living in a dream world, scribbling into notebooks at odd hours, and staring dreamily into the distance while muttering about the merits of one word over another.

ABOUT XCHYLER PUBLISHING

Xchyler Publishing strives to bring intelligent, engaging speculative fiction from emerging authors to discriminating readers. While we specialize in fantasy, Steampunk, and paranormal genres, we are also expanding into more general fiction categories, including several manuscripts in the developmental phase. We believe that "family friendly" books don't have to be boring or inane. We exert our best creative efforts to expand the horizons of our readers with imaginative worlds and thought-provoking content.

Watch for these titles in 2016:

KINGDOM CITY: REVOLT by Ben Ireland (January 2016)

Paul Stevens has survived a terrorist attack, vivisection, and an attempt by the government to "neutralize" their rogue medical experiments. However, his escape cost him his wife, and he battles to overthrow Brian Shuman, the dictator responsible for her death.

With the kidnapping of his daughter and the disappearance of his son, he must choose between saving what may remain of his family or the fledgling rebellion on the verge of collapse.

BINDINGS AND SPINES by R.M. Ridley

The second full novel in the WHITE DRAGON BLACK universe of Jonathan Alvey, a hardboiled detective in the best tradition of film noir, with a slight twist:

Alvey is a "practitioner" of the magic arts, his clients usually victims of the supernatural. Other titles include TOMORROW WENDELL, and BLONDES, BOOKS & BOURBON, a short story anthology.

Other High Fantasy and Urban Fantasy titles you may enjoy:

Vivatera by Candace J. Thomas http://bit.ly/CJThomasAMZ

Conjectrix Book 2 of the Vivatera series

Everstar Book 3 of the Vivatera series coming in 2016

The Accidental Apprentice by Anika Arrington http://bit.ly/AAringtonAMZ

The Vanguard Legacy series by Joanne Kershaw http://bit.ly/JKershawAMZ

    Foretold (Book 1)
    Reflected (Book 2)
    Fated (Book 3)

Sigil of the Wyrm by A. J. Campbell http://bit.ly/AJCampbellAMZ

Forte by JD Spero http://bit.ly/JDSpero

Made in the USA
Lexington, KY
11 March 2017